Criminal Chokehold

Criminal Chokehold

A Carrie Shatner Mystery

—◆—

Randee Green

coffeetownpress

Kenmore, WA

Coffeetown Press
6524 NE 81st St.
Suite 2
Kenmore WA

For more information go to: www.coffeetownpress.com
www.randeegreen.com

This is a work of nonfiction. Real names have been used with permission; others have been changed.

Cover design by Dawn Anderson

Produced in the United States of America

For Snookums
The cat formerly known as Manny
You're the king of my heart

CHAPTER ONE

"ALL RIGHT, NAOMI, what is so important that you needed me to come over here? Don't you know I have things to do tonight? Places I should already be at? People who are…Hold on, why are you wearing lingerie?" I asked my younger cousin as it finally hit me that she'd answered the door wearing a set of lacy black and pink lingerie. And, if the lingerie wasn't off-putting enough, the two-handed death-grip that she had on a hot pink handgun was downright alarming. "What is going on? What's the gun for? Are you okay?"

"I'm fine, Carrie," Naomi said as she retreated backwards into her foyer and urgently gestured for me to follow. "But this scumbag I shot isn't. I really need your help."

"Please tell me you're joking," I said as I took a step backwards and almost fell off Naomi's front porch. "Is he dead?"

A couple minutes earlier, when Naomi called and sweet-talked me into coming over to her house, she hadn't mentioned that she'd shot anyone and needed my help in disposing of a body. All she'd told me was that she needed a little help with something around her house. Ever since Naomi moved into the house across the street from me about two years ago, she'd developed the bad habit of calling me every time she needed help with something – from hanging a picture on the wall to fixing the hot water heater. Even though I had been in the middle of getting ready to head out for the night, I jogged across the street to her house to see if there was anything I could do to help with her latest problem.

"He's not dead yet," Naomi said

"Well, that's a plus." Crap! Crap! Crap! I stepped into Naomi's foyer and kicked the front door shut behind me. "Where is this shot-up scumbag?"

"My bedroom," Naomi said as she spun on her bare heel and then scampered back the hallway towards her bedroom. The hot pink handgun was still clenched in her hand.

"Then let's get to it." I said.

I stomped back the hallway to Naomi's master bedroom. Shoving the door aside, I stepped into the bedroom and encountered a whimpering, half-naked man lying spread eagle on the bed. Short pieces of rope bound him to the four posts of the canopy bed, and he had a ball gag in his mouth. The only clothing, he had on were his boxers, a plaid dress shirt, and a pair of beat-up cowboy boots. One of the buttons on the dress shirt had come undone and revealed, much to my disgust, a patch of thick brown hair and a lint filled belly button. Stepping closer to the bed, I noticed that there was blood oozing out of a hole in the man's right boot.

"Is this some sort of sex thing gone wrong? Did you shoot him by accident? Or did you mean to do this?" I asked.

"I was shooting to kill," Naomi said. Her blue eyes, which were almost the same shade as mine, were wide and rolling. She also had that crazed look in her eye that we Shatner women tended to get when we really were thinking about killing someone. "Then I thought, this is going to be messy. I don't want blood and guts all over my bedroom. That would totally mess up everything. So, fortunately, I only winged him. Then I called you to come help me clean up."

"You do know that killing people is illegal right? So is shooting them," I said as I gathered up my long, brown curls into a sloppy ponytail. "You could wind up going to jail for this, Naomi. And this guy doesn't look like he's worth going to jail over."

I knelt on the floor next to the bed and I untied the man's right leg from the bedpost so that I could examine the damage inflicted by Naomi. The bullet had hit the outside edge of the man's worn-out cowboy boot, and, through the hole, I could make out a bloody section of sock.

"What do you mean I could go to jail?" Naomi asked as she stuck out her lower lip in a pout. "I'm too pretty to go to jail."

"It doesn't matter how pretty you are." Standing up, I held out my hand towards Naomi. She was amped up, and I was concerned that, while in her current state, she might shoot the man a second time. "Give me the gun. Now! And then you better get to explaining what is going on here. And what exactly you want my help with."

"I want your help with…you know," Naomi said as flipped on the safety and then handed me her gun. "Cleaning up my situation."

"Do you mean getting this guy out of here and cleaning up the blood? Or do you mean you want my help in finishing this guy off? And then getting rid of the body?" I asked as I removed the clip from the gun and stuck it in my back pocket. After confirming that there weren't any bullets in the gun, I tucked the gun into the waistband of my shorts.

"Umm…whichever one you think is best, I guess. I mean, ain't it kinda your job?" Naomi asked.

"Killing people and disposing of dead bodies is not part of my job description," I said.

I'm not going to lie…I'm related to a bunch of criminals. At least half of the extended Shatner family was currently active in breaking the law. But their crimes mainly involved brewing and selling moonshine, as well as growing and selling marijuana. They also laundered money and scammed insurance companies. And I'm sure there were a whole lot of other crimes they were committing that I didn't know about. That I didn't want to know about. But it's a family tradition. The Shatners have been frequently breaking the law for as far back as the family can be traced. And they've mostly been able to get away with it, too.

When I was younger, I was proud of my lineage of outlaws and miscreants. Now that I'm in my early thirties, I've gotten over the novelty of being descended from criminals and that proud feeling has faded away. The other reason that I was no longer proud of my family's tradition of being able to break the law and get away with it was because it was my job to uphold the law. For almost four years now I've been employed as the detective and crime scene specialist for the Wyatt County Sheriff's Department in Eastern Texas. I had grown up in Wyatt County, and it was where nearly all of the Shatners called home. Wyatt County was southeast of Tyler and northwest of Nacogdoches, and the county was so small it usually got left out on state maps.

Being related to the local criminals made my job a bit more difficult for me to uphold law and order. Especially when my family members expected me to either look the other way or help them get away with their crimes. My unofficial job at the sheriff's department was to help keep my family out of jail. Note that I didn't say that my job was to keep them out of trouble. That was an impossible task. For the most part, I ignored the moonshine distilling, marijuana growing, and other general lawlessness my family members took part in on a daily basis. Until one or more of them got caught, I liked to pretend that it wasn't happening. Then, not only did I have to acknowledge it, I also had to swoop in and cover it up. That happened about once a week. At least I had job security.

I believed in law and order – I really did – but I also loved my family. And, most of the time, family loyalty won out. No, I didn't really want the Shatners to be committing all those crimes, but I also didn't want them to go to jail for them either. And that's the main reason why I stayed at my job and stuck around in Wyatt County – to keep an eye on my law-breaking family members.

Other than her bad habit of sunbathing topless in her backyard, Naomi had never really caused much of a problem for me. For the most part, she stayed out of trouble and had never committed a crime – a rarity among my relatives.

"Can't you make an exception for your favorite cousin?" Naomi gave me a cheeky but pleading smile. "I'm still your favorite, right?"

Naomi was actually a distant cousin. Our grandfathers were brothers. But, with the Shatners, family was family no matter how distant. Naomi, who was five years younger than me, idolized me when she was a child. She would follow me around and mimic everything I did. Regrettably, I was not the best of role models back then. To be honest, I was still not the best of role models. For two of the six years that I had lived in Nashville, Tennessee, and worked for the Nashville Crime Scene Investigation Section, Naomi had lived with me. While there, Naomi had gone to cosmetology school for makeup and hair. She then moved home to Wyatt County and got a job beautifying corpses at the End of the Line Funeral Home. The two years we'd lived together had been a wild ride, and Naomi insisted that we keep on hanging out after I had moved home four years ago. Unfortunately for us, Wyatt County didn't offer anywhere near the same number or forms of entertainment and activities that Nashville had.

"Yes, you're still my favorite female cousin," I said. "And no, I'm not making an exception. What is wrong with you?"

"As far as I can tell, nothing's wrong with me," Naomi said, flipping her long blonde hair over her shoulders.

"Are you kidding me?" I asked, snapping at Naomi because I was upset with her. I finished untying the man's left arm. I then yanked the ball gag out of his mouth. "I could write a book on all of the things that are wrong with you."

"What's wrong with her is that she's a fricking lunatic! She practically shot my foot off!" the man yelled as he wrapped his chubby hands around his foot.

"Excuse me, but I wasn't talking to you. Besides, that's barely a flesh wound," I said to the irate man.

"Yeah, well, it still hurts. Who are you, anyway?" the man asked.

"Detective Carrie Shatner. I'm with the Wyatt County Sheriff's Department." I held up my badge for the man to see. My badge was the only thing I had grabbed before rushing across the street to Naomi's house. And the only reason I had grabbed it was because I had a rule to never leave home without it. I never know when I might need it. "I'm also Naomi's cousin. And who are you?"

"Dustin Thompson. I'm Naomi's boyfriend."

"Seriously, Naomi? Why are you dating this guy?" I asked as I glanced back and forth between them and tried to figure out the attraction. I could understand him being attracted to her. Naomi looked like a Barbie doll come to life. She was all about big hair, high heels, and rhinestones. And almost everything she owned was pink – including her car. Naomi, who was a serial dater, preferred men roughly the size of a refrigerator, and not much smarter. Dustin appeared to fit that mold, but it was the receding hairline and beer belly that I couldn't wrap my head around. "You know what…I don't want to know. All I want to know is what just happened."

"Like I said, Naomi shot me," Dustin said.

"Would you shut up? She isn't talking to you," Naomi snapped at Dustin. "I told you, Carrie, I was fixing to kill him."

"And I'm pretty sure I made it clear that I won't be part of that," I said.

"Thank God. At least one of you isn't a total psycho," Dustin said.

"Hey, I can be so crazy that I make Naomi look sane." Pointing at the whimpering, bleeding man, I turned to Naomi and asked, "Now, what did he do to get you so worked up that you felt that it was a good idea to tie him to the bed, stick a ball gag in his mouth, and then shoot him in the foot?"

"He cheated on me!"

"What? He cheated on you?" I leaned over towards Dustin and asked, "You cheated on her? Are you kidding me? Look at her. What is wrong with you?"

"The jerk is married," Naomi said.

"Hold on a minute…you have a wife?" I asked. When Dustin nodded, I addressed Naomi. "Then, technically, he's cheating on his wife with you."

"Whatever. Point is, he's still a cheater! Now do you understand why I wanted to kill him?" Naomi asked, stamping her bare foot on the floor.

"Oh, I understand. I'm almost tempted to let you kill him and then call it an accident," I said. This was just another example of the morally and ethically questionable things that my family members had compelled me to consider over the past four years that I'd worked for the sheriff's department. But if I let Naomi kill him, I would get in a lot of trouble. I would also have to fill out a stack of paperwork. There would be a trial. Naomi would go to jail. I would probably go to jail, too. Fortunately, my moral compass pointed in the general direction of northwest, and being part of a murder or an assault was not something I would ever willingly do. "But I have to ask…did you give Dustin a chance to explain?"

"What is there to explain?" Naomi screamed as she lunged at Dustin. "He's married!"

"Naomi! You need to calm down!" I grabbed Naomi around the waist and tried to hold her back. It was not the easiest thing to do considering she was five inches taller and outweighed me by at least twenty pounds. She was also the next thing to naked, and that seriously hindered my grappling ability. Wrestling Naomi to the ground, I had a seat on the small of her back.

"Here, use these." Dustin tossed me a pair of fur-lined, plastic handcuffs. "Or you two can keep wrestling. I really wouldn't mind."

I looked up and found Dustin standing next to me, reeking of cigarette smoke and body odor. Letting go of Naomi, I scrambled to my feet as I grabbed Dustin by the arm. Ducking around behind him, I twisted his arm around so that the back of his hand was pressed against the small of his back. I then pulled his arm up behind him in a move that pro wrestlers call a hammerlock. The farther I pulled his arm upwards, the more pain it caused to his shoulder joints. And I pulled his arm up as far up as I could.

"You need to learn when to stop running your mouth," I said.

"What should we do with him?" Naomi asked as she jumped around the room in excitement. "Wait, I know. Let's strip him naked, tie him up, and dump him on his front lawn for his wife to find."

"Tempting. But out of the question," I said. Actually, I liked the idea. But it seemed like a lot of work and I didn't think Naomi and I were strong enough to physically haul Dustin's weight around. We could call some of our family members to help, but the less people who knew that Naomi shot someone, the better.

"Then what are we going to do?" Naomi asked.

"You are going to put some clothes on while Dustin and I go in the other room and have a chat about what to do about his foot. Right, Dustin?" I gave him a shove towards the doorway and then marched him down the hallway into the living room. After letting go of Dustin's arm, I gestured for him to have a seat on Naomi's pink couch. Dustin was dribbling blood on the hardwood floor, and I was worried that Naomi had done more than graze his foot. I should have called for an ambulance and had Dustin taken to the hospital, but I had to talk to Dustin and get some answers before I did that. It wasn't like he was going to bleed to death in the next few minutes.

"I'm going to file a complaint against you and press charges against Naomi," Dustin said, cradling his injured foot in his hands

"No, you're not. Because, if you do, you're going to have to explain to everyone that you were cheating on your wife. Do you want to do that?"

"Not really...But it might be worth upsetting my wife. The general public should not be subjected to you or Naomi. Both of you are nuts." Dustin pointed at the badge clipped to the waistband of my pants. "How did you get a job at the sheriff's department?"

"My uncle is the sheriff," I said. "Clearly you don't know how things work in Wyatt County, so let me fill you in. The Shatners get away with everything… including murder. I would keep my mouth shut if I were you."

"Is that a threat? Are you threatening to kill me?"

"Oh no, I'm not threatening you." Okay, maybe I was threatening him a little. But not because I would actually kill him. That would be illegal. "I'm warning you. Keep your mouth shut about tonight and you'll get to maintain the quality of life that you're used to. Now…what kind of lying, low-down scumbag, piece of trash are you? What's your side of this story? Why are you cheating on your wife and making my cousin the other woman?"

"It's not like I planned to cheat on my wife. It just happened." Dustin ran his hands over his face, rubbing at the uneven brown stubble and leaving streaks of blood on his face. "Look, Naomi and I met earlier this month at the bar. I was playing pool with some of the guys when Naomi walked in. Pretty much every man in the place wanted to take her home. I just happened to be the lucky one…I'll admit I screwed up. But I took one look at Naomi and I couldn't help myself. I'm weak."

"Does your wife know you've been cheating on her?"

"No! And I don't want her to find out."

"Good, then there is no need for the three of us to ever speak of this again, is there?"

"No." Dustin buried his face in his hands and whimpered. "I won't say a word."

"Fantastic. Now, I'm going to give you ten seconds to get out of here. One…two…" I pulled back the hammer on Naomi's hot pink handgun. I'd already pulled out the clip and made sure there weren't any bullets in the gun. Otherwise I never would have pointed the gun at Dustin. I knew better than to point a loaded gun at someone unless I planned to use it.

"You're right, lady, you're about five beers short of a six pack." Dustin hopped towards the front door. "Has anyone ever told you that you ain't right?"

"Just about every day," I said.

"What am I supposed to do about my foot?" Dustin asked.

"Go to the hospital and get it patched up. Or put a Band-Aid on it. Just don't tell anyone about what happened. Or you might wind up shot somewhere far more painful than your foot. You think Naomi and I are crazy…wait till you meet the rest of the Shatners."

I yanked open the front door and gave Dustin a shove out onto the porch. I kept an eye on him while he hobbled over to his truck that was parked in the driveway. Once Dustin had disappeared down the street, I slammed the door shut and went in search of Naomi. I found her curled up on her bed, crying while clutching both of her Persian cats to her chest. Cinderella and Snow White looked less than thrilled.

"What were you thinking? Do you have any idea how much trouble we would both get in if someone found out you shot Dustin? By all rights, I should arrest you!" I shouted.

"I know. And I'm sorry. I didn't know he was married."

"Regardless, did you look at him?"

"He is pretty ugly, isn't he?"

"Naomi, I need you to repeat after me…I will never again shoot someone."

"But what if they deserve it?" Naomi asked as she abruptly stopped crying. She continued to clutch the two cats. "Like I'm being attacked, and it's a kill or be killed type of thing? Or I'm saving someone else from being attacked? Should I not shoot someone then?"

Sighing, I said, "Let me rephrase. 'I will not shoot someone for upsetting me. Regardless of what they've done or how upset I am.' Is that acceptable to you?"

"I can agree to that," Naomi said. "But I'm still mad at Dustin. What a scumbag. I hope his foot gets infected and falls off."

"You better hope it heals up just fine. If something bad happens to Dustin's foot, it'll come out that you shot him. Then we'll both get in trouble."

"Oh…Then I hope it heals. But that the scab is really itchy!"

"That's the spirit!" I gave Naomi a high-five. "I also want you to promise me that you'll use a little more discretion next time you decide to bring some strange man home with you. Actually, I just want you to stop bringing strange men home."

" You want me to go home with them?" Naomi asked.

"No! I want you to stop wasting your time on scuzzy guys who aren't good enough for you. Maybe that way you can find a nice man and have a meaningful relationship. I had a bad relationship, too. But I don't play musical beds with strange men I pick up in bars."

Before she became a serial dater, Naomi was engaged to her high school sweetheart. They had set the date, reserved the church, and sent out the invitations. All they had to do was walk down the aisle when the fiancé got cold feet and called off the wedding two days before the event. A week later, Naomi moved to Nashville, taking over my apartment in the process. But since her fiancé had dumped her, Naomi hadn't had a relationship that lasted more than two or three months.

"No, but how many relationships have you been in since you ended things with what's-his-name and moved back from Nashville? And that was, what? Four years ago? As far as I know, you've only seriously dated one man since then." Naomi jabbed me in the side with her finger and mockingly asked,

"And, tell me, Miss I-Am-An-Expert-On-Relationships, how well did things go with that sexy Texas Ranger?"

"We broke up a month ago. As you know."

"No, I don't know. You never told me why you guys broke up."

"That's because it's none of your business. Or anyone else's."

"Oh, come on, Carrie. You need to talk to someone about it. Why not me?"

"Maybe another time. You know, when I'm not still furious at you for shooting someone."

"You'll get over it. I mean, you can't stay mad at me forever, right?" Naomi asked before giving me a mischievous grin. "Hey, you want to hang out tonight?"

"Can't. I'm valeting at the pro wrestling event tonight. And, thanks to you, I'm running late. If it wasn't for you getting trigger happy, I would be there already."

"Oooh. I'm coming with you. I want to valet for someone," Naomi said as she rolled off her bed and grabbed a pair of shorts off the floor. "And I could use some hot, sweaty men in Speedos in my life right about now."

"Right now, the only things you need are a cold shower and a chastity belt."

~*~*~

There were few things in this world that my family members take more seriously than professional wrestling – possibly only the Dallas Cowboys, family loyalty, NASCAR, and breaking the law. My uncle Sterling Mount, who was the oldest son of my grandfather's only sister, loved pro wrestling so much that he started his own independent wrestling organization called SWAT – the Shatner Wrestling Association of Texas. As far as I knew, SWAT was the only thing that Uncle Sterling was involved in that fell on the right side of the law. Everything else he did was either illegal, immoral, or ill-advised. Not that SWAT wasn't ill-advised most of the time.

The first SWAT show was held eleven years ago in a poorly constructed wrestling ring set up in an empty field on Sterling's property. He let anyone who knew how to take a bump, swing a steel chair, and make a pinfall compete. I was one of those people. In my first of many SWAT appearances, I competed in a two-minute match against a man in drag. I was supposed to wrestle another woman, but that fell through at the last minute when we realized that the only wrestling matches, she had competed in took place in blow-up pools full of Jell-O.

The beginnings of SWAT may have been a borderline disaster, but Uncle Sterling persisted until he had built up one of the biggest independent wrestling promotions in Texas. He started out by building a better ring, hiring some better trained talent, and holding shows in whatever building he could find – from the VFW ballroom to high school gyms, and firehouses to the occasional abandoned warehouse. It was about two years ago that Uncle Sterling built the SWAT Zone in the empty field where the first show was held.

Pulling into an empty parking space behind the SWAT Zone, I almost ran over a hyperventilating Uncle Sterling as he jumped in front of my Jeep. Uncle Sterling, who was about five pounds away from being considered obese, had on bright purple cotton shorts that were riding up in the crotch. It was an image I could have done without.

"I'm glad you're here!" Sterling screeched as he swung open the driver's side door and pulled me out of the car. "You're the only one who can talk any sense into that idiot."

"Which Shatner is it this time?" I asked, frustrated that I might have to deal with a second misbehaving Shatner.

"It ain't a Shatner for once. But, oh, Lord, I'm having a conniption."

Sterling snatched the questionable looking toupee off his head and then used a handkerchief to dab at the sweat cascading down his shaved head. The reason Sterling had the atrocious toupee on his head was because he burnt off all his hair while attempting to deep fry a turkey for Thanksgiving a few years ago. Most of Sterling's hair grew back after the fiery incident, but he enjoyed his wigs and toupees too much to give them up.

"Then who is it?" Naomi and I both asked.

"It's Red," Sterling said.

Red Devereux, also known as the Ravishing Redneck, was the most popular baby face, or good guy, in SWAT. He was also very popular at a number of other wrestling promotions throughout Texas, Louisiana, Arkansas, and Oklahoma. I'd been valeting for Red off-and-on since he made his debut as a gangly nineteen-year-old. Since I was only seventeen at the time, we had to lie about my age so that the promotor would allow me to take part in the show. It was neither the first nor the last time that Red and I would lie about our ages.

In my role as Red's valet, I basically just escorted him down to the ring and then hung around ringside during the match to cheer for him. I would also occasionally interfere in the match to help Red or prevent his opponent from cheating. In the past, I had also served as a diversion – distracting either Red, his opponent, the referee, or the fans. I'd also competed in the occasional mixed tag team match as Red's partner.

"I've been trying to talk some sense into Red since we were teenagers, and I have yet to succeed," I said to Uncle Sterling. "But I'll give it a try. What did he do?"

"Red's ruining everything! He's gonna bring about the end of SWAT! I need you to stop him! And you're running out of time. The doors open in ten minutes, and then it's an hour until I have to announce the changes to the main event! And, look at me, I'm nowhere near ready for any of this!" Sterling placed the sopping handkerchief on his head, and then smacked me on the arm with the toupee. "Oh, Lord, where's my wife? I need a handful of her happy pills if I'm going to survive tonight."

Uncle Sterling took off, huffing and puffing his way around to the front of the building where Aunt Priscilla was probably selling tickets to the fans who were lining up at the front door. I had no doubt that he would avail himself of her extensive collection of anxiety medications.

"Come on, Naomi, let's go find out what Red did to upset Uncle Sterling," I said.

I had brought Naomi along with me to the show because I figured she would wind up there anyway. She had also begged me to convince Uncle Sterling to let her be part of the show. With Uncle Sterling in his current state, he hadn't even noticed that Naomi was with me. Chances where he wouldn't notice her later when she appeared at ringside next to one of the wrestlers. Naomi had never valeted before, but she desperately wanted to. I figured she could handle standing ringside and looking pretty. It was just a matter of finding a wrestler who I trusted with Naomi.

Ushering Naomi through the back door of the SWAT Zone, we stepped into the small backstage area and allowed our eyes to adjust to the dim light. A good portion of the backstage area was taken up by the audio and lighting equipment, as well as the steps to the entrance stage. On either side of us were the locker rooms – a large one for the men, and a smaller one for the occasional female talents. After tossing our bags into the women's locker room, I led Naomi up the steps to the back of the entrance stage. We then stepped through the black velvet curtains and out onto the stage. Naomi and I then paused at the top of the short ramp and looked out over the SWAT Zone. On either side of the large room were retractable bleachers that Sterling had installed last year. Across from us, on the other side of the ring, were twelve to fifteen rows of chairs. Beyond them were the concession stands and merchandise tables.

Directly in front of us, at the bottom of the ramp, was the eighteen-by-eighteen-foot ring. And leaning against the ring ropes as he stared up at the ceiling was the Ravishing Redneck. His ratty t-shirt and jeans could have been mistaken for street clothes, but the clothes were actually his ring gear. The only thing he had to do to finish getting ready for his match was set his shoulder-length, light blonde hair free of its hair tie.

Red climbed up on one of the corners of the ring and flexed his overdeveloped muscles. He had a scantily clad pinup girl tattooed on his upper right arm, and, when he flexed, her large breasts expanded. The pinup looked a little too much like a cartoonish version of me for comfort.

"Hey, if it isn't the two hottest women in Wyatt County. But it's about time you got here, Carrie. I was starting to think you were gonna stand me up," Red said.

"It's my fault she's late," Naomi said. "I shot a guy. Carrie was busy covering it up."

"Naomi!" Jabbing her in the ribs with my elbow, I said, "I told you not to tell anyone about that."

"But Red's not just anyone. He's family," Naomi said.

Naomi made a good point. Red was practically family. His father, Leslie "Catfish" Devereux, was best friends with Naomi's grandfather, Samuel Houston. Since before they could walk, Catfish and Houston had been partners in crime. And I mean that literally. I didn't even want to know what kind of laws they'd broken together. Or how many. Over the years, when he wasn't running wild with Houston, Catfish produced eleven children with six women – all of whom he named Leslie in honor of himself. Five of those children had married into the extensive Shatner family, and one of Catfish's grandchildren was about to.

Red and I had been friends pretty much since the day I was born, but it wasn't until we were teenagers that we really started running around together. We earned a bad reputation around town and were given the nicknames of Bonnie and Clyde by those who suspected we were going to come to a bad end.

"Now, Red, what did you do to get Uncle Sterling's panties in a wad?" I asked.

"I told him that tonight is going to be my last match. I'm retiring," Red said.

"Oh my God! No!" Naomi said.

"Why? What happened? What's wrong?" I asked, knowing Red wouldn't just up and retire unless he was being forced to.

"You know how I hurt my back the other week?" Red asked as he guided me and Naomi towards the card table on which he had set up all of his merchandise.

"How could I forget? I spent the night in the ER with you," I said.

A few weeks earlier, Red had dragged me along to valet for him at an event in Austin. It wasn't until we arrived at the arena that Red found out that he was going to be competing in a tables match. To win the match a wrestler had to put his opponent through a table. Red wasn't a big fan of gimmick matches, such as a tables match, simply because the chances of getting injured were higher. But, with no way to get out of the match, Red went out and competed.

The match had been scripted to end with the other wrestler shoving Red off the top rope so that Red then crashed through a table. Unfortunately, Red's foot slipped on the rope as he started to fall and it prevented him from pushing himself out far enough to land squarely on the table. Instead, he slammed the small of his back on the edge of the table. Immediately after the match, I collected Red's payment and then drove him to the hospital for x-rays.

"Yeah, well, my back is more messed up than my doctor originally thought. You know I crushed a vertebra that night. But it turns out that I also have a couple herniated discs. I might need to have surgery." Red drew in a deep breath and then shakily exhaled. "The doctor doesn't want me to wrestle tonight. Or ever again. Between this and all the other injuries I've had over the past fifteen years, I figure it's time I hang up my boots. But I need this last match. To know it's my last match. And I can't just hand over the SWAT title belt. I want to lose it so that I can help set up a new storyline."

Uncle Sterling might have desperately wanted me to talk Red out of retiring, but I did the exact opposite. I backed up Red's reasons for hanging up his wrestling boots. Hearing me tell him it was a good idea to retire was what Red needed to hear. Otherwise, he would have talked himself out of it.

I didn't have much time to talk to Red before the doors opened and his merchandise table was swamped with fans. Red, Naomi, and I spent the next hour signing autographs and taking pictures with the fans.

About five minutes before the show was scheduled to start, Sterling popped his head through a hole in the curtain that hung along the side wall of the SWAT Zone to hide the cramped walkway behind the retractable bleachers.

"Hey, Carrie, please tell me you've talked some sense into Red," Sterling said.

"No, and I won't," I said. "But I did try to talk him out of the match's stipulation."

"And…" Sterling asked, his plump face lighting up with hope.

I shook my head. "It's what Red wants."

"Dang it!" Sterling disappeared behind the curtain, but I could still hear him swearing. "That's it, SWAT is over!"

Five minutes later, the houselights dimmed and Uncle Sterling lumbered out onto the stage to the "Dueling Banjos" song that he used as his entrance music. Sterling, now playing the role of CEO Sterling Shatner, had traded in the purple cotton shorts for ragged overalls and a plaid suit jacket. Replacing the toupee was a disheveled mullet wig that resembled roadkill. Sterling used his mother's maiden name for his character because he thought Sterling Shatner sounded better than Sterling Mount.

"Ladies and gentlemen, boys and girls, and wrestling fans of all ages, welcome to the SWAT Zone for the one hundred and twenty-fifth Shatner

Wrestling Association of Texas event!" Sterling said. He then went over a list of rules – mainly no throwing anything at the wrestlers or getting involved in the action – before he gave a rundown of some of the night's matches. "And in tonight's main event, The Ravishing Redneck will put the SWAT Heavyweight Championship on the line against the Beast from East Texas in a No Disqualification, Falls Count Anywhere match."

In a No Disqualification Match – also known as a No Holds Barred Match – the competitors could do just about anything without getting disqualified. They could use weapons such as steel chairs, and other people could interfere. Falls Count Anywhere meant that the pinfall could take place anywhere in the arena. In a traditional match, the pinfall had to take place within the confines of the ring.

Heralded by his boy band-sounding entrance music, the Beast from East Texas strutted out on stage in his tiny, blue speedo.

"What a diva…" Red pretended to throw up. "That's the only downfall for my last match. Sure, I trained the guy. Or, at least, I tried to. But, if I got to pick, he ain't someone I'd ever consider for my final opponent. But, oh well, this match was made last month."

The Beast from East Texas, whose real name was Travis Yeager, was from Wyatt County. He had the muscular look of a professional wrestler, but not the skill set. Over the past few years, Travis had learned how to adequately hit five or six moves, and those were basically the only moves he used in every one of his matches. I once saw a guy wrestle a blow-up doll that had more in-ring ability than Travis did. Despite his lack of talent, Travis had become one of the top heels, or bad guys, in SWAT over the past year or so. What he lacked in wrestling ability, he made up for in skills on the microphone. Travis was arrogant and he had a smug face that most people wanted to punch. The majority of the fans despised him – as did most of the wrestlers.

Alongside Travis was his gorgeous Latina valet. He referred to her at the Beauty of East Texas. Marisol Santiago's sparkly skirt was so short that, when she bent over to step between the bottom and middle ring ropes, she awarded part of the crowd with a glimpse of her purple thong.

Snatching the microphone out of Uncle Sterling's hand, Travis said, "I think we need to add one more stipulation to tonight's main event. I think it also needs to be a Loser Leaves Town match. What do you say, Red? Are you man enough to put your career on the line?"

Red climbed up onto his merchandise table and then grabbed the microphone that I held up to him.

"No one will ever call me a chicken. And it will be an honor to send you packing from SWAT. I know I'm sick of you, and I bet these fans are too!" Red said.

"You heard it everyone. The main event is now a No Disqualification, Falls Count Anywhere, Loser Leaves Town match for the SWAT Heavyweight Championship," Uncle Sterling announced. "Whoever loses will be forced to leave SWAT...Forever."

CHAPTER TWO

"MAKING HIS WAY to the ring, accompanied by the Dixie Divas, Carrie and Naomi Shatner…He is your SWAT Heavyweight Champion…The Ravishing Redneck…Red Devereux!"

"I can't believe this is my last match," Red said as followed me and Naomi through the black velvet curtains and out onto the stage. "This is not how I want it to end."

"Me either. I'm going to miss this." I said.

When Red told me that tonight was going to be his last match, I realized that it was also going to be my final time valeting. I could easily find another wrestler to escort to the ring, but it wouldn't be the same. I'd only ever valeted for Red, and, let's face it, I wouldn't be doing it if it wasn't for him. It was over our shared love of professional wrestling that Red and I bonded years ago. For a short time, we dreamed of one day becoming the next Macho Man Randy Savage and Miss Elizabeth. Macho Man was one of the most popular and charismatic wrestlers on television when we were growing up. And Miss Elizabeth was his gorgeous manager and real-life wife.

Pausing on the stage, Naomi and I waved and blew kisses to the crowd while Red danced along to his honky-tonk entrance music. A handful of the other wrestlers had been more than willing to have Naomi valet for them, but, in the end, Red and I had decided that it would be for the best to have Naomi join us. That way I wouldn't have to worry about her taking off with one of the other wrestlers while I was ringside with Red. Naomi and I were dressed in Daisy Duke jean shorts and Ravishing Redneck t-shirts. Naomi had hacked off the bottom half of the shirts so that our midriffs were showing.

"This hero's welcome is what I'm going to miss the most," Red said as a handful of bras and at least a dozen pairs of women's underwear – including a pair of floral granny panties – landed on the stage at his feet. The lingerie was accompanied by multi-colored streamers and rolls of toilet paper that blanketed the stage, the ramp, and the entire ringside area.

Meanwhile, The Beast from East Texas strutted around in the ring and talked trash to the crowd. Marisol pranced around after him. The fans were nearly hostile in response – none more so than the Shatners and the Devereuxs who were seated at ringside.

"I just hope Travis can remember what we've planned out for the match. All of the guys that I've talked to are getting real annoyed with his habit of forgetting the plan and then trying to improvise on the spot. I don't want anything to go wrong with this match," Red said.

"Stop worrying. It'll be fine," I said.

"I hope so," Red said.

After getting into the ring, Red jogged over to one corner and climbed onto the middle rope. I noticed that he was taking his time, savoring the cheers, streamers, and underwear that were still being flung in his direction as he posed with the SWAT title belt for the last time.

As Red headed across the ring towards the opposite corner, Travis pushed past me, stepped in front of Red, and cut him off. Red, who probably could have stopped, barreled into his opponent and knocked him back a step or two. I took a step in their direction, though I wasn't sure what I would do if they started exchanging blows.

"Get out of my way, you prick. This is my moment," Red said.

"And it's taking too long. Can we get this thing started, you overrated has-been? I'm sick of being held back because Sterling has a man crush on you. It's going to be my pleasure to retire your sorry ass," Travis said.

"My left foot has more in ring ability than you do." Red shoved Travis aside and continued on to the corner of the ring. "And so does every single talent in the locker room."

"Oh yeah, if I suck that much how come I'm gonna be top dog now that you're done?" Travis shouted after him.

"Top dog?" I asked as I took a step closer to Travis. "You seem to have a rather high opinion of yourself, Travis. You do realize you aren't half as good as you think you are, right?"

"Hey, don't talk to my man like that," Marisol screeched in my face. "You and Red just need to shut up! And accept that me and Trav are the new King and Queen of SWAT."

"Oh, please, no one will ever replace Carrie and Red," Naomi said as she shoved her way in to the conversation.

As Red continued to walk around the ring and pose at each corner, and a couple teenagers cleared the ring of the streamers and underwear, Uncle Sterling climbed between the bottom and middle ring ropes. To live up to his character's bumbling reputation, Sterling pretended to trip over the bottom rope and then executed a sloppy somersault that left him flailing around on his back in the middle of the ring. The mullet wig went flying partway through the somersault. Naomi and I rushed to help Sterling to his feet while Aunt Priscilla, who had been the SWAT ring announcer since the first show, slapped the wig back on top of her husband's head.

"Thank you, girls…" Sterling said as he adjusted the wig. "Ladies…and the guy who threw the boxers with the skid mark…what did I say about throwing stuff that ain't streamers? I'm gonna let this go for tonight since the majority of your skivvies are harmless."

"That means keep throwing them," Red said, leaning close to Sterling so that the microphone picked up his voice. "The Ravishing Redneck appreciates the love."

"Quit encouraging them, Red," Sterling said as he shook the finger of shame under Red's nose. "Anyhow, ladies and gentlemen, as the chief executive officer of the Shatner Wrestling Association of Texas, it's my honor to bring you the main event for this month's show. I don't know how we're going to top it next month on the third Saturday in June…Now, before we ring the bell, I want to remind y'all that this is a No Disqualification, Falls Count Anywhere match for the SWAT Heavyweight Championship. It is also a Loser Leaves Town match."

"Fuck him up, Red!" yelled Red's one-hundred-and-two-year-old grandma. She had both of her arthritic middle fingers aimed in Travis's direction.

The middle-aged male referee took the expensive, custom made SWAT title belt away from Red, and then walked around the ring to show it off to the crowd.

"That's our cue to leave, girls," Sterling said as he helped me, Priscilla, Naomi, and Marisol out of the ring.

"I have a bad feeling that this isn't going to end well," I said to Sterling. "The fans are going to be upset when Red loses. Especially since it's to Travis."

"There's fixin' to be a yellow jacket in the outhouse," Sterling said. "I should never have let Red talk me into making this a Loser Leaves Town match. We should have just kept it the way it was supposed to be with Red winning the match. Afterwards he could have announced his retirement and handed over the title. That way I could have had a month to decide what I want to do with the championship belt. And I could have dedicated next month's show to Red's retirement and to determining a new champion. But no…Red just had to have it his way. And you failed me at talking any sense into the boy."

"I said I would try. I didn't promise results. We might not like it, but this is how Red wants his career to end," I said.

"Ring the bell!" the referee shouted at Priscilla.

"Let's do this!" Red yelled before he took a step forward, reaching for Travis's right shoulder and his left arm to pull him in for a collar-and-elbow tie up.

A collar-and-elbow tie up is a grappling position than is generally used to start out matches so that the two combatants are in a neutral position. Typically, the wrestler who breaks the hold will start out with the upper hand in the match. Instead of moving towards Red to engage in the hold, Travis scuttled backwards and jumped out of the ring.

"What are you doing? Get back in the ring!" the referee yelled as he leaned over the ring ropes.

"Hold on!" Travis held up his hands in the universal signal for 'timeout.' "I'm not ready. I need a minute to stretch."

"Take those tube socks out of your speedo, grow some nuts, and come fight me like a man!" Red yelled, earning a laugh from the crowd.

Instead of climbing back in the ring, Travis romped around the ringside area, doing jumping jacks and stretching his quads. I tried not to laugh as Marisol scurried around after Travis to massage his shoulders. The longer it went, the more riled up the fans got. Within seconds of Travis demanding a timeout, the fans were hurling insults and chanting "The Beast is a wimp! The Beast is a wimp!" When he wasn't covering his ears to block out the insults, Travis got into the faces of some of the fans in the front row and called them unflattering names. Travis had just passed me during his second lap around the ringside area, when a boisterous young fan leaned in front of Travis and waved around a sign that read "Travis Yeager Sux!"

"You suck, Travis!" shouted Red's nephew, Dougie Devereux. Dougie's father was one of Red's many half-brothers. Rooster Devereux was married to my cousin Becky, and that made Dougie one of my distant cousins. "My uncle is going to kick your butt!"

Prior to the show, Uncle Sterling had handed Dougie the sign and instructed him to antagonize Travis from his front row seat. It was Dougie's first time being used as a plant, and he had been honored to be chosen out of all of the other Shatners at ringside. Plants are people who are chosen to sit at ringside and engage with the heel wrestlers. It was a good way to get the rest of the crowd even more riled up against the bad guy – especially if the plant was a kid.

"Punk kid." Travis grabbed the sign away from Dougie and slowly tore it in half, earning even more heat from the crowd.

"Excuse me, Travis," I said as I tapped him on the shoulder. When Travis turned to face me, Naomi scooted around behind him and got down on her hands and knees. "Dougie isn't just Red's nephew. He's also my cousin."

"No wonder he looks like a failed genetic experiment," Travis said.

"What I'm trying to tell you is that no one messes with my family!" I yelled.

Drawing my arm back, I slapped Travis across the face. There was really no way to fake a slap and still make it look authentic, so I gave it all I had. Prior to the match, we had planned all of this out. Everything from Travis avoiding the start of the match up through the final pinfall had been strategically plotted out move-by-move so that Red and Travis knew exactly what they were doing even before they set foot in the ring.

Reeling back from the slap, Travis stumbled backwards and tripped over Naomi. He went down hard, smacking the back of his head on the floor. Only a thin layer of carpet and a gym mat cushioned his head against the concrete floor.

"Ow! That freaking hurt!" Travis cried.

"Travis!" Marisol dropped to her knees and cradled Travis's head in her arms. "Oh, my sweet man! Are you all right?"

"You still have no idea how to properly take a bump, Travis. And it's not like it's hard. Red taught me how to take a bump in a of couple hours," I said.

Over the five years Red had spent working with him, Travis still hadn't mastered the art of taking a bump. A bump is when a wrestler falls flat on his back to spread out the surface area upon which he is landing. Instead, when Travis went down, he just flopped onto the ground and landed on whichever body part he felt like.

"All right, boys, time to get back in the ring," the referee said.

"Yeah, we're coming," Red said.

Picking up Travis, Red shoved him under the bottom ring rope to get him back inside the ring. Red then walked up the small set of metal ring steps and vaulted over the top rope. Red was midair when Travis clambered to his feet and executed a dropkick as he drove his feet into Red's midsection. Having earned the upper hand, Travis went on the offensive and hit a series of back-to-back moves for a thirty-second span before Red reversed a hold and made a comeback. They then went back-and-forth, exchanging a series of holds, moves, and near-pinfalls.

Clutching Red around the neck in a modified headlock, Travis pulled him towards the middle of the ring. Travis was going for a Running Bulldog, which was one of his signature moves. It was also a simple move to execute. All Travis really had to do was continue to hold on to Red's head while he basically just sat down. Red was responsible for throwing himself forward so that he landed on his stomach. Tonight, Travis let go of Red's head a step or two too early. With Travis no longer guiding him, Red didn't bother to complete his half of the move. That left Red standing in the ring while Travis flopped around on the mat.

Naomi and I tried to hide our giggles as the fans chanted "You screwed up! You screwed up!" They enjoyed Travis's blunder as much as I did.

"Seriously? You couldn't have sold it for me? You couldn't have finished the move and acted like it hurt?" Travis asked as he lay on the mat looking up at Red.

"I ain't selling anything for you!" Red shouted as he smacked Travis upside the head. "I trained you better than this."

"You're a jerk!" Travis took a swing at Red, catching him on the jaw.

"Is that the best insult you can come up with?" Red drove his fist into Travis's stomach. "You're such a jackass!"

"I think they're hitting each other for real," Naomi said to me.

"Yeah, they definitely are. They've also gone off script," I said as Red and Travis, who were pummeling each other, rolled out of the ring and landed on the floor at our feet. Just because Red and Travis had planned the entire match out in advance didn't mean they couldn't improvise should the need arise. This didn't look like they were improvising. This looked like their fake fight was about to turn real. "Hey! Get back to the plan!"

"Then get out of my way!" Travis kicked out at me and Naomi, causing us to jump backwards against the fence-style barricade that separated the ringside area from the front row.

"That's no way to treat the ladies," Red said as he punched Travis in the ribs.

"Except they ain't ladies! Naomi is a skank, and Carrie is crazy."

"You're one to talk. Your girlfriend is a drama queen," Red said.

Shoving the ring apron aside, Red yanked out a metal trashcan full of two-by-fours, a frying pan, a baseball bat covered in barbed wire, an orange traffic cone, and a set of Sterling's golf clubs that I had stolen out of the back of his truck. The weapons had been placed under the ring prior to the show so that Red and Travis could use them during the match. After dumping the weapons onto the floor, Red raised the trashcan above his head and prepared to bring it down on Travis's back. He was just about to swing it downwards when Marisol hurled herself on top of Travis.

"Stop! Please don't hit him!" Marisol screamed as she hammed up her concern.

"Carrie, get her out of the way," Red said to me.

"Get her, Carrie! Kick her butt!" said Dougie from his nearby ringside seat.

"Fuck her up, Carrie!" yelled MeMaw Devereux.

"Behind you, Marisol," I said, warning her that I was coming up behind her. Marisol had little experience as a valet and needed to be talked through her planned actions. I seized two handfuls of Marisol's long, ebony hair, and attempted to pull her off of Travis. Instead, I ripped out two sections of her clip-in hair extensions. Earlier, when the five of us sat down and planned out the match, we had all agreed that I would pull Marisol's hair. So it wasn't like she didn't know it was going to happen. She'd had ample opportunity to warn me that she had hair extensions. "That wasn't supposed to happen. Why didn't you tell me you have extensions?"

"My hair!" Marisol screamed as she spun around to face me. Wrapping her arms around my waist, Marisol dragged me down to the ground. She then grabbed a handful of my hair and gave it a good yank. "How do you like it?"

"Let go! That's my actual hair!"

"Get off of her!" Naomi shoved her way into what was supposed to be a pretend cat fight but was quickly escalating into a real one. She slapped at Marisol's hands that were still wrapped around my curls. "Let go!"

"Stay out of this, Naomi," Marisol yelled. She finally let go of my hair, but that was only so she could take a wild swing at Naomi. She missed hitting Naomi in the face, but still landed a punch on my cousin's shoulder.

"Don't hit her!" I yelled. Even though it wasn't part of the plan, I slapped Marisol. I didn't hit her nearly as hard as I had struck Travis. I didn't want to hurt her, I just wanted to get her attention. "You need to calm down. It's only supposed to look like we're fighting."

Marisol unleashed a primal scream as she swung her arm at me. Her long, acrylic nails slashed across my left cheek.

"Girls! What are you doing?" Sterling asked as he shoved his way into the cat fight. "Help me break it up, boys!"

Red dropped the trash can that he'd been bashing over Travis's back to assist Sterling in breaking up the cat fight. While Red pulled Naomi out of the fray, Sterling picked up Marisol and dragged her away from me.

"What is wrong with you?" Travis asked as he grabbed me by the throat and shoved me backwards against one of the ring posts. Pain radiated from the back of my skull all of the way down my spine to my tailbone. "You've got balls to hit Marisol!"

"Let go," I said. Travis wasn't squeezing my throat very hard, but should he decide to put some real pressure on me, my skinny neck wouldn't stand much of a chance against his unnaturally large muscles. "Now."

"Screw. You." Travis said. "And Red. And Naomi. And your Uncle Sterling. SWAT's mine now."

"Oh my God! Oh my God! Oh my God! I don't think this is supposed to be happening!" Naomi screamed. After breaking away from Red, Naomi picked up a steel chair and used it to thump Travis across the back. "Let go of her!"

"Fuck him up, Naomi!" yelled MeMaw.

"Naomi! Move!" Red yelled before he hurled a kitchen sink at Travis. The sink slammed into Travis's shoulder, prompting him to let go of my throat. Red then swung one of the golf clubs at Travis, catching him in the ribs. With Travis down, clutching his abdomen, Red gathered me up in his arms while Naomi poked around my neck.

"This match certainly isn't going as planned," I said.

"Are you okay, Carrie? I'm going to kill Travis," Red said.

"I'm okay," I said. "He wasn't really choking me that hard."

"He might not have hurt you, but Marisol did. You've got three bloody scratches on your cheek," Naomi said.

"Don't worry about it. I've been hurt worse," I said. That's not to say my cheek and scalp didn't hurt thanks to Marisol's assault. "Red, did you really just throw a sink?"

"I've always wanted to hit someone with a kitchen sink! Not that I got to enjoy it since I was trying to save you. I can't believe Travis put his hands on you. I seriously am going to kill him," Red said.

"If you don't hurry up, MeMaw is going to beat him to death with her cane," Sterling said as he knelt next to Naomi. He then gestured over his shoulder to where MeMaw Devereux was walloping Travis with her cane. "Look, I don't know what y'all have planned out for this match. But I know this wasn't it. Can we try to be professionals for the next few minutes so we can get this match wrapped up?"

"Take care of her, Naomi. I've got to rescue Travis before MeMaw cracks his head open. I keep telling MeMaw to stop trying to get involved in my matches…" Red said. Leaving me in Naomi's somewhat capable hands, Red went over to where MeMaw Devereux was beating Travis around the shoulders with her cane. Picking up Travis, Red heaved him over the fan barricade and then went over after him.

"Would one of you help me up?" I asked. "I'd like to see the end of this match."

"I'm not sure if this is even a match anymore," Sterling said as he pulled me to my feet. "I think it's an actual fight."

"Did Travis just hit Red with a prosthetic leg?" Naomi asked.

"That's what it looks like," I said.

Red and Travis fought their way through the chairs, knocking them over and scattering the fans. They then battled their way up the bleacher steps, using anything they could get their hands on as a weapon. Red and Travis had planned to take their match through the crowd as they battled throughout the arena. I don't think either of them had planned on it being this out of control. The referee and a handful of security guards followed along behind Red and

Travis, trying – but failing – to break things up.

"Seriously, Red, a tray of nachos is not an effective weapon," Naomi said.

"It is when you blind your opponent with the cheese. I need to get those two nutcases back in the ring before they destroy this place." Sterling hustled over to where Aunt Priscilla was seated and borrowed her microphone. "Bring it back, boys. Time to bring it home."

Fighting their way back through the crowd, Red dragged Travis back to the ring. Once they were inside the ring, Red picked up Travis in a fireman's carry and began to spin around in circles. The fans, who had no idea that the match had turned into a legitimate fight, went wild when Red started setting up for his finishing move with the Airplane Spin.

After ten complete rotations, Red let go of Travis and sent him flying across the ring. Red then stumbled around, playing up that he was dizzy. Red ran over to the corner of the ring that was closest to Travis and climbed to the top rope. He was about to backflip off the top rope to land his finishing move known as the Ravishing Moonsault, when Marisol scrambled up onto the ring apron and shoved him off. Red came down so that he was straddling the top rope. He remained that way, clutching the family jewels, long enough for Travis to hit him in the head with a steel chair. Red then toppled into the ring.

"One!...Two!...Three!..." called out the referee as he counted the pinfall. "Ring the bell!"

"The winner of the Loser Leaves Town match...and your new SWAT Heavyweight Champion...The Beast from East Texas, Travis Yeager!" Aunt Priscilla announced.

"I'll take that, old man." Travis yanked the title belt out of Sterling's hands. He then held the title above his head as he ran in circles inside the ring. "I'm the champ! I'm the champ!"

Aside from the intermittent fans who were thrilled with the match's outcome, the majority of the crowd seemed stunned. As I looked around at the fans, I saw countless looks of shock, disgust, and panic. Some fans just stared at the ring in disbelief, while others burst into tears and turned to the people around them to confirm if Travis had really just beat the Ravishing Redneck in a Loser Leaves Town Match.

The calm faded and the storm hit when someone yelled, "What just happened?"

"Is this a joke?"

"Rematch! We need a rematch!"

Red's considerably older half-brother, Pork Chop, nonverbally voiced his displeasure when he hurled a beer can at the ring and narrowly missed hitting Travis in the arm. The beer can wound up hitting someone in the head on the other side of the ring.

"Knock it off, Pork Chop!" Red dove across the barricade to prevent his brother from throwing a chair into the ring. "You knew I was losing! I told you before the show started!"

"You throw like a girl, Pork Chop!" MeMaw Devereux popped the dentures out of her mouth, wound up her scrawny arm, and let loose. "That's how you're supposed to throw!"

The dentures struck Travis in the forehead as he knelt in the ring, clutching the title to his chest. Blood dribbled down his forehead and dripped onto his nose. I'd have to compliment MeMaw Devereux on her aim, but only after I scolded her for throwing her dentures in the first place.

"Nice throw, MeMaw!" said Dougie as more fans began to throw items at the ring.

"Naomi, watch out!" I dove at my cousin, knocking her out of the way of a men's sneaker flying in our direction. "This is turning into a riot!"

"Get under the ring!" Red shoved me and Naomi towards the ring as more fans threw items in our general direction. "Hurry!"

"You've got some real classy fans, Red," Travis said. He, along with Marisol, Priscilla, the referee, and the ringside cameraman had already taken up refuge under the ring.

"Where's Uncle Sterling?" I asked.

"He took off running for the back after Pork Chop threw the beer can," Priscilla said. "The jerk left me to fend for myself in the middle of a riot! Just wait until I get my hands on him! I'm going to wring his thick neck!"

Lifting the edge of the ring apron, Red and I peeked out at the angry crowd. From what we could see, the fans were throwing just about anything they could get their hands on into the ring. And those that weren't throwing things, were egging on those that were. MeMaw Devereux was in the middle of the melee, waving her cane around like a general about to lead a charge.

"For God's sake, there are kids and old people out there. Old people who aren't as crazy as MeMaw. Someone is going to get hurt," I said.

"This is my fault. I should never have insisted on this being a Loser Leaves Town match. I should have just done what Sterling wanted, won the match, and then handed over the title. My retirement still wouldn't have gone over well, but no one would have rioted," Red said.

"Aunt Priscilla, do you still have the microphone?" I asked. Priscilla held up the microphone for me to see in the dim light under the ring. She then rolled it across the ground towards me. Turning on the microphone, I said, "Sterling, you better be doing something to get these people calmed down. Someone better be doing – What is all that screaming for?!?"

"The sprinklers are going off," Red said.

"Oh great. Someone decided to burn down the SWAT Zone," I said.

"I don't smell smoke," Red said. "But I wouldn't put it past some of these people. Be prepared to make a run for it just in case."

"What are y'all doing? You done lost your dang minds!" Sterling's voice echoed throughout the arena, drowning out the fading protests of the crowd. Lifting the ring apron a little higher, Red and I looked up at Sterling who was standing on the stage. He huddled under a children's umbrella in an attempt to keep the microphone and his mullet wig dry. "It's a wrestling match…Yeah, that cocky sumbitch cheated to win, but that's what was supposed to happen! Y'all know its fake, don't you?"

"Ain't nothing fake about 'rassling!" yelled an irate fan.

"All right, it ain't fake. But it's scripted. The outcome of each match is predetermined. I'm the one who decides on the matches and picks which one of the wrestlers is going to win." Sterling yanked off the drenched wig, dropped it onto the stage, and then stomped on it. "Travis was supposed to win. Red was supposed to lose… I know you're not happy, but that ain't no excuse to trash my arena and behave like lunatics!"

"What happens to the Ravishing Redneck now?" shouted a fan.

"He's done with SWAT…" Sterling announced to a chorus of boos and shrieks. "Could someone please get this water turned off? We're fixin' to drown out here… Red, where did you get to? Get out here and tell your fans what's going on."

"The rest of you stay under here in case they start rioting again." Red pulled the microphone out of my hands and then rolled out from under the ring. Using a trash can lid as an umbrella, Red joined Sterling at the top of the ramp. His reappearance in the arena brought about a moment of hysteria from the fans. Red held the microphone up to his mouth and said, "Sterling's right, I was supposed to lose the match. Tonight was my last match for SWAT. My last wrestling match, period. My body just can't take the punishment anymore, so it's time for me to hang up my boots. I know you're not happy with what just happened. And I appreciate that you love me so much that you'd riot because I lost, but that was insane…I had a retirement speech planned, but now I can't remember anything I was going to say."

"Thank you, Red!" chanted the crowd. "Thank you, Red!"

"No, I should be thanking you guys. Whether you've been a fan since my first match or since last month, you guys are the ones who made this fun for me…You're the reason I put my body on the line each week…Darn it, I didn't want to cry," Red said.

"What a fruit," Travis said. "Crying like a woman."

"Screw you." I kicked out at Travis, striking him in the shoulder. "I'm going out there. Travis, I suggest you stay under the ring until the arena is empty."

"I'm coming with you," Naomi said. "Even if it means getting drenched."

Crawling out from under the ring, Naomi and I crowded under a golf umbrella that one of the security guards handed us.

"Fans, let's hear it for my valets, Carrie and Naomi Shatner!" Red stepped back, allowing me and Naomi to enjoy the cheers and applause. "Like I said, I had this whole speech planned for after my match. You know…when I officially announced my retirement. But now I can't remember half of what I wanted to say. Let's see…There are so many people I should be thanking. My family and friends who've supported my crazy dream to be a professional wrestler. And everyone else who helped make that dream a reality. Including Sterling, who basically started SWAT, just so I would have a home arena to wrestle in every month. But…well, out of everyone who I should be thanking…Carrie, you're the one I want to thank the most. Not all of you know this, but Carrie Shatner is more than just my valet. She's also one of my best friends and my biggest fan. She's the Bonnie to my Clyde. So, Carrie, I just want to thank you for all of the support and love you've given me over the years."

"Someone had to keep you in line," I said, drawing a laugh from the crowd. "But it's been an honor."

"Thank you everyone," Red said. "Thank you for everything."

"Thank you, Red!" Soon every single person in the arena was on their feet, giving the Ravishing Redneck the standing ovation he deserved. "Thank you, Red!"

~*~*~

"My arena is destroyed!" Sterling said. "Totally destroyed. I may as well just burn it down and cash in on the insurance money."

"First of all, that's a crime. Just ask your brother-in-law. How many years did Uncle Butch spend in prison after he burnt down the bowling alley?" I asked, referring to Red's older half-brother who was married to Sterling's sister Suzette.

"Too many," Sterling said. "My sister and nieces were lost without him."

"No, they weren't," I said as I looked around at the trashed arena. In the ring, and piled up around the ringside area, were chairs, food, and bottles. I spotted a little girl's doll among the debris. "Second, it's not destroyed. It's just soaked. All it needs is dried out. And the mess needs cleaned up."

"The carpet is ruined!" Sterling said.

"The carpet needed replaced anyway. It's threadbare in spots." Aunt Priscilla held up an orange prescription bottle. "Here, have some anxiety pills and calm down. It's not as bad as you want to think it is."

"No, it's worse!" Sterling snatched the bottle out of his wife's hand. "I need to get back there and pay the wrestlers. Maybe I'll withhold payment until they've helped clean this place up a bit. That'll get me a step closer to fixing this mess."

"That won't go over any better than my loss did," Red snapped. "Which, by the way, my last match sucked thanks to my crappy opponent screwing up almost everything."

"Come on, Red, let's get your money and get out of here," I said, not that Red would be getting paid more than a couple hundred dollars for his performance. It was still better than the early days when there were times when his only payment was free food at the concession stand. "How 'bout we go hang out and reminisce on all the good matches you've had over the years."

"In a few minutes. I need to…soak it in, I guess." After climbing into the ring, Red scooped up an armful of debris and then heaved it onto the floor. "God! Damn! It!"

"Give the boy a moment. Then talk him off the cliff. I'll be in the back." Sterling trudged up the ramp and disappeared through the curtain with Priscilla on his heels.

"You think he's going to be okay?" Naomi asked as she gestured towards where Red was picking up the steel chairs that had been tossed into the ring. One-by-one, Red flung the chairs into the empty bleachers. "Should we do something?"

"I'll handle it." I climbed up onto the side of the ring and yelled, "Red! RED! You better get that burr out from under your saddle real quick!"

"Are you kidding me?" Red threw one more chair into the bleachers and then stomped towards me. "That was the worst match of my career! And it was the last one, too! Do you have any idea how pissed off I am because THAT monstrosity was my final match?"

"I have a good idea how upset you are." I could commiserate with Red's anger. I wasn't exactly pleased about the match either. "And you're right, that match sucked. But we both know that tonight's match was nowhere near the worst match of your career. I can name at least ten matches that were worse than tonight's match, and that's without putting any thought into it."

"Well, yeah, I've had worse matches. I once wrestled a midget on a trampoline at a truck stop in the back woods of Arkansas!" Red shouted.

"Seriously?" Naomi asked. "That match actually happened? Oh my God, that's insane!"

"Oh, it happened," Red said. "Just ask your cousin."

"Red's opponent was drunk. The promoters were ex-convicts trying to make a quick buck. There were a bunch of people dressed up as clowns roaming around for no apparent reason. And it got raided by the police halfway through the show. It was a train wreck," I said.

"More like a cataclysmic disaster. I didn't think we'd get out of that one alive," Red said. "But that wasn't my last match. Which is why tonight's match is the worst match of my career!"

"All right, all right, it was the worst match of your career," I said. Come morning, I hoped Red would calm down enough to accept that his final match wasn't as horrible as he currently thought. "Now let's get out of here."

Red, Naomi, and I were halfway up the ramp when Priscilla ran out onto the stage. "Carrie! Oh, God, Carrie, you've got to get back there! It's Marisol! And your cousins! Something bad happened."

"Which cousins? I've got so many I can't kept track of them all."

Shoving past Priscilla, I jumped down the stage steps and raced over to the back door where Sterling attempted to calm down my cousins Kermit and Keaton. They were Sterling's younger brother's kids. Uncle Vernon hadn't been able to be in attendance to support his sons since he was still on house arrest for a DUI. Kermit and Keaton, both of whom were younger than me, were known on the wrestling circuit as the Beer Buddies. Kermit was Myller Lyte and Keaton was Buddy Lyte. Pushing through the other wrestlers who were crowding around, I found a hysterical Marisol sitting on the floor at Keaton's feet. Blood spilled down her arm.

"What the…Marisol! What's going on? What happened?" I asked

"That's what I'm trying to figure out," Sterling said. "Pris, get the other guys back in the locker room. I don't think they need to hear this."

"Marisol, can you tell me what happened." Kneeling next to Marisol, I eyed up the bloody gash on her upper left arm. It was hard to get a good look at it considering the amount of blood, but it appeared she had either been shot or stabbed.

"Travis…Help Travis," Marisol mumbled.

"Where's Travis?" I asked.

"Trav…" Marisol whispered before fainting into my arms.

"Naomi, help her. She's going into shock. See if you can wake her up. And whatever you do, don't let Aunt Pris try to medicate her," I said as I shoved Marisol towards my cousin. "Keaton, go see if the doctor in attendance is still hanging around."

"He should be. I haven't paid him yet," Sterling said.

"Run, Keaton. Now! And, you, Sterl, call for an ambulance. Marisol needs to go to the hospital. Then call the sheriff's department. Tell them there's been an assault and to send the closest deputies to the hospital. But tell them I said to hold off on sending anyone here until I've assessed the situation. Then I'll call back and let them know what I need them to do."

"Carrie! Marisol's awake. She's mumbling about Travis being dead," Naomi said.

"Kermit! What happened? What did you do?" I asked.

I grabbed my younger cousin's arms and eyed up his bloody hands. Like most of the other Shatners, Kermit and Keaton have been known to break the law. But their crimes usually involved selling marijuana and fencing stolen items. They'd never assaulted anyone. At least not that I knew of.

"I ain't done nothing except try to help Marisol. Keaton and I were sneaking out since we didn't want to stick around and help clean this mess up. We were –"

"You lazy bums!" Sterling moved his cell phone away from his mouth so the 911 operator couldn't hear him cuss out his nephew. "Wait till I tell your parents. Vernon and Georgina are going to beat your worthless butts. I'm tempted to call them right now."

"Leave it, Sterling. You've got more important calls to be making," I snapped. "Kermit, I don't care what you were doing. Tell me what happened."

"Like I said, we were leaving. We snuck out the one side door and headed around back to Keaton's car. That's when we heard Marisol screaming. She was down at the far end of the parking lot. The one light is burned out and the lot is really dark down at that end."

"I've been meaning to get that light fixed for months," Sterling said.

"Would you shut up?" I said to Sterling. "Kermit, what happened after you heard Marisol screaming?"

"We dropped our bags and ran down there to help. We found Marisol staggering our way. She was carrying on about Travis being dead. I saw the blood running down her arm and tried to stop it." Kermit held up his blood covered hands. "Keaton ran down towards where she was coming from and found Travis lying on the ground."

"I didn't get a good look, but Travis didn't react when I kicked his leg," Keaton said. He'd found the doctor in attendance and brought him back to help Marisol. "I then ran back and helped Kermit bring Marisol inside."

"Sterling, don't let anyone out into the parking lot until I get back," I said. "Kermit, your hands are now evidence. Don't touch anything, and definitely don't wash them. Keaton, you're with me. I hate to do this to you, but I need you to show me where the body is."

"I don't have to look at it again, do I?" Keaton asked.

"No, you don't have to look at it."

"I'm coming with you," Red said. "Just give me a minute to grab a flashlight."

Red bolted into the men's locker room. He returned a minute later with a flashlight in one hand, and a handgun in the other. He handed me the flashlight and then pushed open the door.

"Let's get this over with," Keaton said.

"Watch where you walk, boys. Don't step on my evidence."

Stepping outside, I realized just how dark the far end of the parking lot really was. Two of the three overhead lights were doing their job, as was the light over the back door. But the light at the far end of the lot was burned out, leaving that end in darkness. With no other buildings or parking lots nearby, there wasn't anything to help light up the area.

"See that truck with the KC lights on the roof?" Keaton asked, pointing to the far end of the parking lot.

"That's my truck," Red said.

"Yeah, well, Travis is between that and the light colored sedan next to it. Can I go back inside now?"

"Not yet. I might need you."

The parking lot behind the SWAT building was reserved for the wrestlers and the people putting on the show. The lot was made up of four rows of parking spaces. The first row was along the building, and the last row butted up against the wooded area behind the lot. Altogether, there were between forty and fifty parking spaces. Roughly two-thirds of them were taken. The truck and the sedan that Keaton pointed out were in one of the two middle rows. I led the way down to the other end of the parking lot.

When we got to within fifteen feet of where Keaton said Travis's body was, I said, "You two can stay here while I go check things out."

"I'm coming with you," Red said.

"Not me, I'm no hero," Keaton said.

"I never thought you were, Keaton. And, Red, watch where you step and don't touch anything. This is a crime scene."

Using the flashlight, I slowly panned back and forth across the ground until the beam lit up two duffle bags lying on the ground behind the sedan. I assumed that Travis and Marisol had dropped the bags when they were assaulted. Keeping away from the blood spatter, Red and I moved closer to the duffle bags. As we got closer, we could see that there was a body lying on the ground on the other side of the bags.

"What happened back here?" Red whispered.

"I don't know, but it's going to be my job to figure it out," I said

The SWAT Zone, which was towards the east side of Wyatt County was within my jurisdiction. The Wyatt County Sheriff's Department had jurisdiction everywhere in the county except for the three largest towns. Holler, Wilder, and Mooresville each had their own police departments to maintain law and order within their respective city's limits. Holler, the largest of the three towns and the county seat, was a couple miles to the west of the SWAT Zone. Just over a third of the roughly twelve thousand people who lived in Wyatt County lived within the Holler city limits. The rest of the population was scattered between Wilder, Mooresville, two unincorporated towns, and the rural areas. The Wyatt County Sheriff's Department headquarters was in the town of Holler.

"I don't envy you the job," Red said.

"Oh well, processing crimes scenes is my job. And I'm good at it." Moving the flashlight beam away from the two duffle bags, I lit up the back of the sedan. Blood had sprayed over part of the trunk and most of the back windshield. "Well, that's blood spatter. That could be from a bullet wound or some type of assault."

"What are you waiting for? Light him up," Red said.

Travis Yeager lay face-down on the pavement. Starting at the gold wrestling boots, I ran the flashlight beam up the body, revealing Travis's knee pads, muscular thighs, and then the dark blue speedo. On the back of the speedo was an image of a roaring beast that appeared to be a cross between a Sasquatch and Betty White.

"Brace yourself, Red. We don't know what happened to him."

I slowly ran the flashlight beam along Travis's body until I came to the tail end of an arrow shaft sticking out of his back.

CHAPTER THREE

"NOW THAT'S SOMETHING you don't see every day," I whispered as I stumbled a step backwards and almost dropped the flashlight.

"Holy shit! That's an arrow!" Red said. "It's been, what, fifteen minutes since he crawled out from under the ring? Twenty minutes tops?"

"This just happened in the last ten minutes," I said, shocked that Travis Yeager had been brutally killed in the short period of time since he'd emerged from his hiding spot under the ring.

Red's impromptu retirement speech had calmed the crowd down, and, with some gentle urging from the security guards, we had gotten the fans out of the building and into the parking lot. The last time I saw Travis, he'd been going through the curtains to the backstage area. He'd had the SWAT Heavyweight Championship title belt held high above his head as he loudly announced to everyone in the back that he was the new champion. Now the title belt lay on the ground in a pool of Travis's blood.

"Should we check for a pulse?" Red asked. "Just in case he's not dead."

"He's not moving, Red. And look where the arrow hit him. That's a kill shot." The arrow had struck Travis in the left side of the back, entering at an angle that left about six to eight inches of shaft sticking out of the back of his body. The very end of the shaft was tipped with three plastic vanes – two were neon orange and the third was lime green. There was drying blood on the two inches of the shaft that was closest to Travis's body. Since blood doesn't travel uphill, I assumed that, when Travis landed face-down, gravity caused his body to slide down the shaft that was sticking out of the front of his body. I would have to wait until later – once the crime scene had been processed and we were able to move the body – to get a look at the exit wound on Travis's chest. And it would be up to the medical examiner to determine the amount of damage to Travis's internal organs.

"Marisol's lucky she only got wounded. Either the killer missed or she moved just in time," Red said.

"Or she wasn't the target." Raising my voice, I asked, "Keaton, how much of the body did you see?"

"Just the legs. Like I told you, I kicked his legs a couple times. When he didn't respond, I figured he was a goner. So I went to help Kermit with Marisol. You ain't gonna make me come over there and look at him, are you?" Keaton asked.

"That won't be necessary." Taking a step closer to Red, I lowered my voice and said, "And, Red, the sheriff's department might want to keep the cause of death under wraps for the first few days of the investigation, so don't tell anyone about how he was killed."

"I can keep my mouth shut. But this is messed up."

"Yeah, it definitely is." Taking Red by the arm, I pulled him away from the crime scene. "Come on, we need to get back inside."

"Are you serious?" Red asked. "We can't leave Travis out here by himself. Even if he is dead. And don't you have to secure the crime scene? Because this is a crime scene, right?"

I continued tugging on Red's arm, dragging him towards where Keaton sat on the hood of his El Camino. Even if the overhead light had been on, I still wouldn't have felt safe lingering in the parking lot. The area behind the parking lot, and along both sides of the building, was heavily wooded. The killer could be lurking behind a tree or hiding in one of the thirty to forty cars parked behind the building.

"I can't say it's definitely a homicide, but I really don't think someone shot Travis and Marisol by accident. And, yes, under normal circumstances, I should be securing the crime scene. But these aren't normal circumstances. It's dark out here, and for all we know the killer is still hanging around, looking to shish kabob a few more people. And I don't know about you, but that's not on my agenda for tonight."

"Good point." Red put his arm around my shoulders, drawing me closer. "I may not have liked the guy, but I still feel bad for leaving him out here by himself."

"Red, there's nothing we can do for him. What I feel bad about is abandoning the crime scene. If something gets contaminated or lost, it's going to be my fault. But there's no way I'm staying out here in this dark parking lot while the killer might still be hanging around."

"If it was me, I'd be long gone by now," Red said.

"Me too," Keaton added as he slid off the El Camino and hustled towards the back door.

The three of us had almost reached the back door when Sterling shoved the door open and asked, "What is going on there? Is Travis really dead? What killed him?"

"Keep your voice down." Pushing Sterling away from the door, I left it propped open enough so that I could keep an eye on the far end of the parking lot. I couldn't see Travis's body, but I could see the truck that he was lying next to. "Where's Marisol?"

"The doctor walked her over to the other side of the building. I told the nine-one-one operator to have the ambulance come to the front doors. Figured you wouldn't want them coming around back," Sterling said.

"Good thinking," I said. "And, to answer your question, Travis is dead. All I'm going to tell you is that it is most likely a homicide. Your parking lot is now a crime scene."

"I don't need this crap. Can't you move the body somewhere else and claim he got killed there?" Sterling asked.

"I really hope that you're joking," I hissed, even though I had been somewhat expecting Sterling to ask me to relocate the body away from his arena. "Now stop whining because I need your help. You've got to put this building on lockdown. No one leaves until they've been questioned by someone with the sheriff's department. Red and Naomi, I want you on the back door with me. Aunt Pris, I want you back here, too. I might need your help with crowd control."

"No one handles a crowd better than me," Priscilla said.

"Kermit and Keaton can take one of the side doors. And, no, Kermit, you still can't wash the blood off your hands. Sterling, I want you out front, but not by yourself. I also need two people on the other side door." I grabbed Sterling's arm and shook it. "Come on, who's backstage that can help? I need people I can trust. Grab any Shatner or Devereux that you know has been backstage for the past twenty minutes and stick them on the doors. Now! I can't risk having anyone leave this building. Make that anyone else. I've already lost over six-hundred of my suspects."

The majority of the Shatners and Devereuxs may be extremely untrustworthy at the best of times, but, in this situation, they were the only people I felt I could depend on. Especially if they had been backstage since Travis went out into the parking lot, and had at least one person who could vouch for their whereabouts. As for the Shatners and Devereuxs who had been in the crowd, they were currently part of my extensive suspect list. Any one of them could have killed Travis because he or she was mad about the way the match ended, for manhandling me, or over a personal reason that I had no knowledge of. Or it could be as simple as temporary insanity – a disorder that my family members claimed to periodically suffer from. Then again, those motives could apply to every single person who had been in the SWAT Zone tonight.

"One of your cousins was running the audio tonight. And two of Red's brothers are on my security team. I'll go grab them." Sterling took off, leaving me, Naomi, Red, and Priscilla by the back door.

"Could one of y'all please tell me what's going on?" Priscilla asked.

"Yeah, Carrie, what happened to Travis?" Naomi asked.

"This is a police investigation. I can't tell you anything," I said.

Had Priscilla not been with us, I probably would have told Naomi that Travis had been shot by a bow and arrow. Aside from Red, Naomi was the only other person who I was positive was not the killer. Both of them had been in the arena with me when Travis was killed. But, as far as I knew, there wasn't anyone who could alibi Priscilla for the roughly fifteen-minute long window in which Travis was killed. No, I didn't think Priscilla was the killer, but I couldn't take any chances. She was the driving force behind many of Sterling's criminal activities, and I knew she didn't mind getting her hands dirty. I just didn't think she'd ever do something that could result in her breaking a nail.

"I need the three of you to keep an eye on the parking lot while I run in the locker room. I have to call the sheriff's department and then change into something a little more crime scene appropriate," I said. Except the only other outfit I had with me wasn't much more appropriate than the short shorts and cropped shirt, but the capri style leggings and old Pat Green tour shirt would have to do for the time being.

The water from the sprinklers had pooled in the middle of the locker room floor. Stepping over the puddle, I pulled my slightly damp bag out of one of the metal lockers. The clothes inside were thankfully dry.

"Shaniqua…Hey, it's Detective Shatner." I turned on the speaker phone, pulled my sodden curls into a ponytail, and then began to wiggle out of the tight, skimpy shorts.

"Yo, girl, Sterling called. Said you've got a situation going on over at SWAT," said Shaniqua, the overnight dispatcher for the Wyatt County Sheriff's Department. "Don't tell me…one of your bat-shit-crazy family members is up to no good."

"It's Saturday night, I'm sure at least one of them is raising hell somewhere," I said. "But my family is only indirectly involved in my current problem. I've got a dead body over here. And it looks like a homicide. I need you to send me all of the deputies that are on duty. Tell one of them to bring my big crime scene kit and all of our portable work lights. I'll take care of calling the sheriff considering he's my uncle and all. But I need you to call the Chief Deputy and send him over. And call the Department of Public Safety while you're at it. Let them know what's going on and that we've got it handled."

"All right, girl. Help is on the way. Stay safe out there," Shaniqua said.

I ended the call and was about to place another one to the sheriff when Naomi burst through the locker room door.

"Oh my God, Carrie, you need to get out there! Vlad was trying to leave, but Red wouldn't let him. So Vlad took a swing at Red. And now they're fighting!"

Shoving past Naomi, I ran out into the backstage area just in time to see some of the other wrestlers pull Red and Vladimir Khrushchev apart. One wrestler had Red around the waist. Another wrestler had Vlad, and his oversized ushanka hat, in a headlock. Aunt Priscilla was in the thick of things, yelling at everyone to calm down.

"Hey!" I screamed in an effort to be heard over all of the shouting. A few of the wrestlers who were on the outskirts of the fight heard me, and they started admonishing the others to quiet down. "What is going on out here?"

"I was trying to leave and Red told me I'm not allowed to," Vlad said.

"That's right, you're not allowed to leave. No one is." Before anyone could start protesting, I held up my sheriff's department badge that I never left home without. "There is currently a police matter going on out in the parking lot. No one will be allowed to leave until after that matter has been taken care of, and you've all been questioned."

"What happened out there?" asked one of the security guards. "I heard Marisol was shot and that Yeager is dead."

"Hey, I ain't talking to the fuzz. No matter what happened," said a scrawny Hispanic man wearing traditional lucha libre gear. His full-faced teal and lime green mask matched his pants.

"You will if you don't want to get charged with a crime," I said. "Now, I'm going to need all of you to head out into the arena and get comfortable. It's going to be a long night. Aunt Priscilla, you keep an eye on them. And, while you're at it, put together a list of names. I'm going to need to know who all is still here."

"You can keep everyone else here, but I'm going home. You know where to find me, Carrie," Vlad said.

Vladimir Khrushchev, whose real name was Frank Smith, was no more Russian than I was. But, over the twenty-five years he had wrestled on the independent circuit, he capitalized on being the scary, angry Russian bad guy. It was lazy character development – Russian and German characters were almost always bad guys because it was so easy to get the fans to hate them – but Frank made the stereotype work. It didn't hurt that he was seven-feet tall, and built like a Cold War Era tank.

Frank lived with his wife towards the western side of Wyatt County.

Oksana, who was quite possibly a Russian mail-order bride, had been valeting for Frank for almost his entire career. Even when she was pregnant with their children, she would come ringside to be in her man's corner. I looked around the small crowd for Oksana's platinum blonde hair and was surprised when I didn't see her. Oksana was typically attached to Frank's hip at wrestling events.

While Oksana worked two jobs to support them, Frank's only source of income was whatever he made from wrestling and selling his merchandise each weekend. During the week, Frank spent the mornings working out in the gym. His afternoons were spent ignoring his wife as she sporadically called him to check in. I wasn't sure if Oksana thought he was doing something she wouldn't approve of, or if she was worried about his health. Whenever Frank didn't answer – which was at least once a week – Oksana called the sheriff's department and begged us to go check on him. Normally Frank was either sleeping, drunk, or just ignoring his phone. Though there was that one time we caught him dancing around in his underwear while listening to George Strait. But we're all guilty of that.

"Vlad...Frank, you aren't going anywhere," I said. "No one is going anywhere. So y'all may as well march into the arena and have a seat. It's going to be a long night."

"Let's go, boys." Priscilla herded the wrestlers towards the stage steps.

Of the twenty-two wrestlers – plus the two other valets and the three managers – who had been a part of tonight's show, it looked like the majority of them were still hanging out in the SWAT Zone. I would have to get a list of all of the wrestlers, as well as the security crew and the production team, from Sterling. Every one of them would have to be questioned in regard to what happened to Travis and Marisol.

"You all right, Red?" I asked.

"I'm fine. Frank couldn't land a real punch if his wrestling career depended on it."

"That bruise forming on your chin says otherwise."

"It's nothing." Red poked at his chin and winced. "Oh, and Carrie, Frank had an altercation with Travis in the locker room right after intermission. I don't know what it was about, but some of the other boys broke it up before they came to blows."

"I'll be sure to look into it."

Stepping away from Red and Naomi, I called my uncle Murph. Murph, who was my great-uncle Samuel Bowie Shatner's oldest son, had been the sheriff of Wyatt County for about thirteen years now. Before him, my granddaddy had been the man in charge. If you're wondering how two men who are related to a bunch of criminals managed to get elected as sheriff, your guess is as good as mine. I suspected voter fraud and ballot tampering. Regardless of how they got there, having Granddaddy and then Murph as the sheriff proved quite beneficial to my more criminally inclined family members. Granddaddy may have covered up a fair share of the family's illegal activities, but, despite that, he had been an excellent sheriff. And he always had the county's best interests at heart. As for Murph, his main concern was keeping his family out of jail. He left just about everything else up to the Chief Deputy.

"You have any idea what time it is?" Murph asked. "Someone better be dead."

"You're in luck. It's a homicide."

"What the…you joking?"

"Wish I was. I'm over at the SWAT Zone and I've got a dead wrestler in the parking lot."

"What…Did you say the SWAT Zone? Crap on a cracker! The kiddies are having their Post-Prom Party over at the high school. They just got locked in at midnight."

"Oh, no, that is tonight." The Big Pine Senior High School was a few hundred yards away from the SWAT Zone. Only a grove of trees and a soccer field separated the school from the crime scene. "My victim was killed sometime between eleven-thirty and eleven-forty-five."

"I'm heading over to the school to check on the kids. My baby girl is at the party. Once I know that the kids are safe, I'll come by to get the details. Then I'll go notify the victim's family. If you need me, call me," Murph said before he hung up on me.

"As long as a Shatner isn't the killer, you're basically useless," I mumbled to myself. Uncle Murph wasn't the most trustworthy person considering he would cover up any crime that one of the Shatners committed. And, if a Shatner wasn't involved, his interest in the investigation waned considerably.

"Carrie, your backup has arrived," Naomi said, coming up behind me. "Red went out back to make sure they don't park near the body."

"Then I guess I better get out there. Stay by the back door until I can spare a deputy." Heading out into the parking lot, I found Red talking to two of the Wyatt County deputies. He was pointing towards the other end of the parking lot and explaining that the body was down there. "I've got it from here, Red."

"Howdy, Detective Shatner." Deputy Ryan Mathews said, greeting me as I joined the small group. Mathews was a few years younger than me and was still learning the ropes. "Red said you've got a dead body back here."

"We sure do," I said, "Did you bring my crime scene kit?"

"Someone else is bringing that and the lights. We were on patrol, so we headed directly here. The others should be here soon." said Deputy Christian Richards. The lanky deputy had worked for the sheriff's department for almost as long as Deputy Mathews had been alive, and he was attempting to teach the younger deputy everything he knew.

"That's fine. As long as you guys have some crime scene tape, we can get started on securing the scene. Let's start out by moving your car to the very bottom of the drive. Then you can rope off the entire parking lot. We might have to expand the area once we figure out where the killer was standing when he…shot the victim."

Deputies Richards and Mathews had just started hanging up the crime scene tape when two more sheriff's department cruisers parked along the drive. In the first cruiser were two deputies. They must have been hanging around the department when the call came in, because they had my crime scene kit and the work lights in the trunk. After sending them off in search of electrical outlets, I turned to greet the driver of the second cruiser.

"You got here fast. And you're looking a little disheveled," I said to Chief Deputy Juan Quaranta. He'd worked for the Wyatt County Sheriff's Department since he was twenty-one years old. He started out as deputy, and then spent the next twenty or so years working his way up the ranks until he was appointed Chief Deputy.

Quaranta and I got along most of the time, but there was always going to be some tension between us. Four years ago, Quaranta had adamantly been against the Wyatt County Sheriff's Department hiring me. Despite my degree in criminal justice and years of experience working for the Nashville Crime Scene Investigation Section while I lived in Tennessee, Quaranta didn't think I had the skills or training necessary for the detective job since I had never been a police officer. Regardless, Uncle Murph hired me – though he mainly hired me to help him clean up after the family. Things had gotten better between me and Quaranta over time.

"I tend to move fast when there's a dead body involved. And Shaniqua gave me a heads up that there had been an assault. I was already on my way here when she called me about the dead body." Quaranta stroked his Fu Manchu mustache and looked off towards the far end of the parking lot. "I heard you've got a…what was that wrestler's name who was killed by the other wrestler?"

"You talking about Bruiser Brody?" I asked as I waved at Deputies Richards and Mathews. They had just finished hanging up the crime scene tape and were headed back our way.

"That's it. You've got a Bruiser Brody situation," Quaranta said.

"It's nowhere near the same aside from a wrestler getting killed. Bruiser was stabbed in the shower. And everyone there knew who killed him. My guy got shot with a…well, you've got to see it to believe it. But it happened in the parking lot. And, at the moment, I've got no freaking clue as to who might have done it."

On July 16, 1988, Bruiser Brody was scheduled to wrestle at an event in Puerto Rico. Before the show, José Huertas González asked Brody to step into the shower area with him. González then stabbed Brody multiple times. Brody died a few hours later from his injuries. During the trial, González pled self-defense and was later acquitted.

"Show me what you've got and then we can get started on figuring it out," Quaranta said.

After putting disposable cloth booties over our shoes – or flip flops in my case because my cowboy boots had gotten soaked – I led Quaranta to the other end of the parking lot.

"The victim is one of the wrestlers. His name is Travis Yeager," I said.

"The Beast from East Texas?" Quaranta asked.

"I didn't know you were a wrestling fan," I said.

"I'm not. Yeager is my oldest son's gym teacher. My boy is going to be crushed."

"Travis is a teacher? At Big Pine? I had no idea." Admittedly, I didn't know all that much about who Travis was away from wrestling. Even though I never gave it too much thought, I never would have pictured Travis as a teacher. I couldn't imagine him working with children, much less being good at it. That could be because I'd only ever seen him act like a jerk towards the children in the audience. I wondered how many of the teenagers he'd talked trash to at events were his students.

"According to my son, Yeager is one of the most popular teachers. He's also the school's archery instructor," Quaranta said.

"Big Pine has an archery club? Since when?" I asked.

Back when I was in high school, I hadn't paid all that much attention to things that weren't directly related to me, including the various clubs and organizations. But, if there had been an archery club back then, I'm positive I would have at least heard about it. No, the only archery we had when I was in high school was during gym class. Every fall and spring, the gym classes had an archery unit. The arrows were barely sharp enough to penetrate the targets and the bows were so old and primitive that I'm fairly certain they were passed on to us directly from Robin Hood.

"I have no idea how long the club's been around." Quaranta ran his flashlight over Travis's body, stopping when he came to the arrow. As he crossed himself, Quaranta whispered, "Madre de Dios. What kind of person does this?"

"Personally, I think it took a special kind of crazy."

CHAPTER FOUR

"LET'S GET THIS PLACE lit up so we can start processing the crime scene." Gathering up an armful of extension cords, Quaranta barked at the deputies to stop standing around, and start setting up the work lights. "Carrie, do you want to make the video of the scene? Take the crime scene photos? Draw up the sketch?"

"I'll take the pictures. We both know I'm better at it," I said. "You can make the video and sketch the scene. Then we can work together to collect the evidence."

Quaranta had a talent for taking blurry pictures. And when his pictures weren't blurry, he cut half of the subject out of the frame. I was much more conscious of what I was taking pictures of and, while my crime scene photos wouldn't be considered artwork, they were at least mostly flawless.

"Good plan. I'll video the scene now, and then I'll head inside and get the deputies started on questioning everyone who's still here," Quaranta said.

"It's mainly wrestlers and other people who were backstage during the show. The majority of the fans were all out of the building by the time Travis was shot. And that makes them all suspects," I said.

"You talk to Sergeant Hardy about what's going on down here? Is he on his way down to help out?" Quaranta asked, referring to the Texas Ranger who oversaw Wyatt County as well as two other nearby counties.

Sergeant Jerrod Hardy was part of the Texas Ranger's Company B Division. He worked out of an office in Tyler, Texas – which was less than an hour up the road from Holler. The Texas Rangers were part of the Department of Public Safety and, as such, had statewide jurisdiction. As soon as I saw the arrow sticking out of Travis Yeager's back, I knew that Hardy would show up at my crime scene sooner or later. He couldn't possibly make an appearance at every crime scene that popped up in the three counties that he oversaw, and he certainly didn't take part in every single criminal investigation. But there was no doubt in my mind that he would take a special interest in my current homicide simply because of how unique the murder weapon was. And if Hardy wanted to take over the investigation, there was nothing that I could do to stop him.

"No, I didn't call him. But I'm sure someone from the Department of Public Safety has informed Hardy that we've got a homicide on our hands. I had Shaniqua call them to let them know what's going on down here," I said.

"Carrie, I've been keeping my nose out of your personal life for a long time now. Which is why I didn't say anything when you started dating Sergeant Hardy a few months ago. And it's why I didn't say anything when you two broke up the other week. But now that it's over, I'm going to say my piece," Quaranta said

"I don't need a lecture, Juan. Especially not right now."

"This isn't a lecture. It's just some advice," Quaranta said. Placing his hands on my shoulders, Quaranta forced me to look at him. "Sergeant Hardy is the Ranger for Wyatt County. You work for the Wyatt County Sheriff's Department. Unless he transfers to a different part of the state, or you quit your job or move away again, there are going to be times when the two of you will be working together. That means you're going to have to put aside your personal feelings towards the man. And you're going to have to do it now, because I can guarantee Hardy is going to show up in the very near future."

"I know, Juan. I think I can handle it," I said. "It's almost going to be déjà vu of the first time Hardy and I met. You know…standing over a dead body."

"It really wasn't the most romantic of first meetings, was it?" Quaranta chuckled as he programed the settings in one of the sheriff's department's video cameras. "I'm going to make sure these idiotas get our lights set up right. Then I'll video the scene. How about you suck it up and give Sergeant Hardy a call. Let him know what's going on."

"Why don't you just call him? I've got to go through my crime scene kit and make sure that I have everything that we're going to need. I don't want to get halfway through and realize we don't have enough evidence bags."

"Carrie…Just give the man a call. It'll be good for you," Quaranta said as he walked off. "I'll let you know when I'm done with the video."

"Fine…I'll call him. After I go through my kit." Having a seat on the ground, I flipped open the lid of my crime scene kit to reveal that it was well stocked with swabs, evidence markers, vials of fingerprint powders, and everything else we could possibly need tonight. "Well, my kit is ready to go. Which is more than I can say for myself."

Sergeant Jerrod Hardy and I met on what was beginning to look like the worst day of my life. I had just discovered a dead body, and I had a sinking suspicion that one of my criminally inclined family members was the person responsible for the victim winding up in their current lifeless state. Hardy, who had just started his job as a Texas Ranger a few weeks earlier, showed up at the crime scene to take over the investigation. Sparks flew between us – some good, some bad – and, a few days after our initial meeting, Hardy asked me out on a date. I was shocked Hardy wanted anything to do with me considering he was a Texas Ranger and I was related to a whole bunch of criminals. Looking back, it seemed pretty obvious that our relationship was doomed from the start.

Hardy and I wound up dating for about four months. Somehow, up until the last night, our relationship progressed smoothly. Hardy's job didn't always make it easy for us to get together, but we did the best that we could. We hit the first – and only – real hiccup a little over a month ago. We hadn't seen each other in over a week because Hardy had been busy working on a case. He'd just wrapped it up, so I drove up to Tyler so we could have dinner. After enjoying our steaks, we decided to skip having dessert at the restaurant and instead have a different kind of dessert at Hardy's place. We were anxiously waiting for our server to bring us the check when one of the busboys wandered over and asked if he could buy some homegrown pot off of me. I shouldn't have been surprised, not when that sort of thing happened to me on a frequent basis, but having it happen in front of the Texas Ranger I happened to be dating left me momentarily speechless. Not to mention mortified and ashamed.

Even after I made it clear that I didn't sell pot – much less carry it around on me – the busboy just wouldn't drop it. He went so far as to follow us out to the parking lot where he started making this big deal about how other Shatners sell pot and demanded to know why I didn't. Hardy finally flashed his badge and told the kid to go away, but the damage had been done. Even though I wanted to flee back to my own home where I could die of embarrassment in private, I followed Hardy over to the house that he was renting. Instead of having "dessert," we spent the rest of the night arguing. It was after midnight when we finally accepted that Hardy couldn't keep living in denial, and that the only way for us to continue in a relationship would be if I quit my job and cut off all contact with the majority of my family. I'd been hurt at first – after all, breakups are tough – but pain quickly segued into anger. I wasn't mad at Hardy for breaking up with me. No, I completely understood his reluctance to get any farther involved with me considering who I was related to. Especially considering that he was a Texas Ranger. I was mad at my family because their persistence to live outside the confines of the law had messed with my personal life. And it wasn't the first time their lawbreaking activities had ruined a relationship or friendship for me. This time just upset me more than all of the others simply because I really liked Hardy.

Closing my eyes, I leaned back against the cruiser's right rear tire and thought about Hardy. The breakup might have been mutual – and the best decision for both of us – but that didn't mean that I didn't take it hard. To be honest, I was still pretty upset about it. Being forced to see him before I was ready was going to put me back a step or two in the healing process.

But Quaranta was right, it was time to put my personal feelings aside and get on with it. I had a crime scene to process, a murder to solve, and a killer to apprehend. And if I had to work with Hardy to get the job done, then that was how it was going to be. Either way, my focus needed to be on the case and not on my heartache.

I sucked in a couple deep breaths and then I called Hardy.

"Hello?" Hardy mumbled, sounding half-asleep.

"Hi, Jerrod," I said around the large, throbbing lump that had just formed in my throat. Hearing Hardy's voice for the first time since the breakup brought a tidal wave of unwelcome emotions crashing down on me. I pressed my fingers to my neck, hoping to relieve the lump.

"Carrie? What…What's going on? It's one-thirty in the morning. Are you all right?"

"I'm fine. And I'm sorry if I woke you up, but I've got a dead body on my hands."

"Which one of your family members is responsible?" Hardy asked, sounding much more alert than he had when he'd answered the phone.

"Huh? Oh, no. I'm not trying to dispose of a body. But thanks for assuming I'm covering up a murder for one of my family members. Makes me feel real good about myself." I said.

The accusation caused me to miss Hardy a little bit less. Sure, I'd shredded some speeding tickets, talked countless people out of pressing charges, and basically just looked the other way when I knew a crime had been committed. But a murder was something I would never cover up. Just attempted murder in the case of Naomi.

Continuing, I said, "I'm at a crime scene. Give me a second and I'll send you a picture of the victim so you can understand what I'm up against."

"Sorry, darling. It's been a long, bad day. And I'm not in a good mood. I know you don't cover up murders."

"You want to talk about it? I mean, now really isn't a good time. But…well, I'll listen if you want me to," I said.

Hardy didn't have any family, he was too much of a loner to have many friends, and he didn't like sharing too much personal information with his coworkers. Not long before we broke up, Hardy told me that I was the only person he'd allowed himself to get close to in years.

"Thanks, Carrie. I know you probably don't want to talk to me. We didn't exactly part on the best of terms. But you've got some experience with what I'm going through and…Hold on, picture just came through," Hardy said. There was a moment of silence and then he said, "What the…Is that seriously an arrow?"

"That's pretty much been everyone's reaction so far," I said.

"Your victim sure pissed someone off."

"His name is Travis Yeager. You saw him at the SWAT shows you went to…Two of my cousins found him after tonight's show. His girlfriend was also struck in the arm with an arrow. She's in bad shape, so I had to send her to the hospital before I could talk to her."

"I remember Travis and Marisol. Neither of them are popular with the fans. Looks like you've got your work cut out for you on this case," Hardy said.

"Tell me about it…Quaranta and I are about to get started on processing the crime scene. I just wanted to let you know what I've got going on down here. We don't necessarily need your help, but we wouldn't mind having it."

"Right now, I'm at a truck stop in Oklahoma. I was trying to get a couple hours of sleep before I drive the rest of the way home from Kansas City. According to my GPS, if I leave now, I can be there sometime after seven… Call me if you need anything. Otherwise, I'll see you in about six hours."

"Thanks, Jerrod." Hanging up, I said, "That wasn't as awkward or as painful as I thought it would be."

"You talking to yourself, Carrie? According to the sheriff, that's a sign that your cheese has slid off your cracker."

Biting back a scream, I spun around and snapped, "You almost scared the crap out of me, Juan. Don't you know not to sneak up on people at a crime scene? Especially when the killer is still on the loose?"

"You would have heard me walking up had you not been having a conversation with yourself. Keep doing that and people will think you're crazy," Quaranta said.

"Most people already know I'm crazy."

"It's in your genes."

"And I wasn't talking to myself. I was talking to Sergeant Hardy. He'll be here in the morning."

"Good." Quaranta tucked the video camera away in his crime scene kit. "Crime scene is all yours. Before I head inside, is there anything you need help with or that I can get for you?"

"No, I think I have everything I'll need," I said.

Deputies Richards and Mathews were still hanging around the crime scene. I'd have Richards take my notes while I focused on taking photos. One of the downsides of photographing a crime scene was the extensive number of notes we had to take. The digital camera I use would record what time each picture was taken, but I still needed to take notes on the camera settings and the distance to the subject. I would also need to jot down a brief description of each image. The process was very time consuming, but it had to be done. Having Richards take the notes for me would speed things up a little bit.

Realizing that there was something Quaranta could do for me, I stopped him before he headed inside the SWAT Zone. Calling after him, I yelled, "Juan, if you see Deputy Grant inside, could you send him back here? I could use his help."

"Timmy? What could you possibly need his help with? I try to refrain from calling the boy a screw up, but that's basically what he is," Quaranta said.

Deputy Timmy Grant was one of the youngest and most inexperienced deputies in the department. He was always eager to assist with everything, though he usually messed things up more than he helped. Some days I still had trouble believing that Timmy was a deputy. So far this year, he had tasered himself twice, accidently discharged his weapon three times, broken almost seven hundred dollars' worth of equipment, and totaled the rear end of one of the department's cruisers when he backed into a light pole. I think Uncle Murph kept Timmy around because he felt bad for him.

"Despite the fact that he's a screw up, Timmy is also a huge pro wrestling fan. I saw him before the show started, so I know he was here. I'd like to hear what he has to say about Travis and Marisol, and find out if he has any theories on who our killer might be."

"I'll send him back when I find him," Quaranta said before he headed towards the back door of the SWAT Zone.

After handing out notebooks and pens to Mathews and Richards, I gave Mathews the task of taking notes on the make, model, and color of each car in the parking lot, as well as the license plate numbers and where exactly the cars were parked in relation to the body. I also instructed Mathews to look in the car windows to see if he could spot a bow or arrows. Before we could let anyone leave, someone would have to take a closer look inside all of the cars. Personally, I didn't think we'd find the murder weapon that easily – unless the killer was extremely stupid or trying to frame someone else.

"The victim has enough junk in the back of his car," Mathews said. "Two big plastic boxes and a smaller cardboard box."

"It's his merchandise. Before the show, Travis and Marisol were selling shirts, sweatshirts, and pictures. At least they were trying to. It didn't look like they were making many sales," I said.

"Not a shocker considering how hated you say they were," Mathews said.

Pacing back and forth in front of the crime scene, I formed my plan of attack. Thanks to the work lights illuminating the area, I could finally see the crime scene as a whole. The blood spatter appeared to be limited to the back of the sedan. We had confirmed that the sedan belonged to Travis, leaving me to believe that he and Marisol were about to throw their duffle bags in the trunk when the shooter fired the first arrow. The question was whether Travis was shot first, or if Marisol was. I was betting on it being Travis. Either way, once he'd been shot, Travis probably fell onto the trunk. The arrow then gouged the top of the trunk before leaving a scratch down the side as Travis collapsed to the ground next to his car.

The other arrow – the one that had struck Marisol in the arm – lay on the ground under Red's truck. I could only see the very tail end of it.

Turning my back to the sedan, I lined my body up with the blood spatter, so that I was standing in roughly the same place Travis had been when he was shot. There was only one car parked in the row behind them, but it was a few spots to the one side. Whether the killer had been standing on the edge of the parking lot or in the trees directly behind it, there wouldn't have been any obstacles in the way when it came to hitting his target.

"I don't think this was a spur of the moment killing. Not when the killer used a bow and arrow and shot the victim from a distance. I bet the killer was lying in wait for Travis and Marisol to come outside. That's if they were the intended victims. Could be our killer didn't care who he killed and was just waiting for the first person to come outside," I said to Richards.

"I hope the killer ain't that crazy. We don't need some sort of serial killer on our hands," Richards said as he adjusted his reading glasses. He had a bad habit of wearing reading glasses that were clearly meant for women. His current pair was leopard print.

"No, we definitely do not." Turning my back to the woods, I said, "All right, enough supposing. Time to get to work. I'm going to start out taking wide shots and then move in for the close-ups. Though the cars on either side of the body are going to complicate things. But if I stand in the truck bed, I can get some good overhead shots. I'll let you know what I want you to take notes on, Richards."

Standing back from the sedan, I took a few wide shots, before I began moving in for close-ups of the blood spatter.

"We have company, Detective Shatner," Richards said. "Deputy Grant is headed over."

Looking over the top of the sedan, I spotted Deputy Timmy Grant's bright red hair as he meandered through the parking lot. I'd known Timmy since he was a kid. Red and I used to see him and his mom at ringside at nearly every pro wrestling event that we went to as teenagers and that Red wrestled at as an adult. We used to have a theory that one of the wrestlers was Timmy's father.

It wasn't until Timmy joined the sheriff's department that I found out that his dad died from cancer when he was a kid.

"Howdy, Detective Shatner. The Chief Deputy said you've got a doozy back here. I can't believe someone killed the Beast from East Texas," Timmy said. After taking one look at Travis's body, Timmy smacked both hands over his mouth and quickly turned away.

"Don't you dare throw up on my crime scene," I snapped.

"I swallowed it," Timmy said. He drew in a few deep breaths and some of the color returned to his pale face. "The Chief Deputy told me what happened, but it's just horrible to see it. I'm okay now. What can I do to help?"

"It is horrible. But if you want to help, you can hold this," I said. To make him feel useful, I handed Timmy a large, handheld light and instructed him to point it where I told him. The work lights cast shadows on the crime scene, and it was crucial that we light up those shadowy areas so that they did not distort the pictures.

"I can do that," Timmy said as he snatched the light out of my hands.

"I also want you to talk to me about tonight. Give me your impression of the match and the riot," I said.

"Well, the match kinda sucked. I mean, it started out okay. Aside from Travis botching every third move he went for. It got bad when they started fighting for real. The Ravishing Redneck deserved better for his last match," Timmy said before he gave me a move-by-move review of the match. "But that riot was insane. Mama and I just ducked down and tried to stay out of it."

"Any ideas on who our killer might be? I know you're friends with a lot of the wrestlers and the fans. Is there anyone who hates Travis or Marisol enough to have done this?" I asked.

"I don't know about Marisol. She hasn't been around all that long. Not that she's won over many fans in that time. I do know there's a lot of fans who don't like Travis. Me included. But I doubt that everyone who hates him knows how to use a bow and arrow," Timmy said.

"Or has access to them," I said.

"Or just happened to have them stashed in the backseat of their car," Mathews said as he joined us. "And, by the way, I looked in all the car windows. Didn't see a bow or arrow."

"I didn't think you would. But all this leads me back to the theory that the killer had planned this in advance and was lying in wait. The killer just got lucky that no one else was in the parking lot when this happened. Or at least anyone that we know about." Moving closer to the crime scene, I began taking close ups of the SWAT Heavyweight Championship title belt that laid in a pool of Travis's blood. "Timmy, do you know of any wrestlers who were here tonight who know how to use a bow and arrow? What about fans?"

Timmy shrugged. "That's not something I'd talk to people about."

"Then talk to me about motive," I said as I moved closer to Travis's body and took pictures of his wrestling boots. "Forget about how Travis was killed and focus on who might have killed him."

"I guess it could have been a fan. Travis was an arrogant jerk to everyone. People really did hate him. And a lot of the fans were upset that he beat Red tonight," Timmy said.

"But if someone killed Travis over tonight's match, that means he or she already had the bow and arrow in the car," I said, moving up Travis's body to take pictures of the blood drops on the back of his bare, hairy thighs. "The killer would have had to get outside, grab the bow and arrow out of his car, and then get in position. It's not improbable. The killer would have had enough time. But if it was me, and I was that mad, I would have wanted a face-to-face confrontation. I would have wanted Travis to know why I was coming after him. I wouldn't have shot him in the back. And I would have finished off Marisol whether she was my target or not. Why leave a witness?"

That didn't mean the killer wasn't a fan though. Any one of the over six hundred people who were in attendance could have killed Travis for any number of reasons. Unfortunately, there was no way we would be able to determine the identity of every single person in the crowd. There would be a record of the people who bought their tickets online or paid for them with credit cards at the door. It was the people who paid with cash that there wouldn't be a record of.

"Almost all of the wrestlers don't like Travis," Timmy said as he adjusted the flashlight beam so that it was lighting up the pool of blood on Travis's right side. "From what I hear, he's got no respect for the guys who've been around longer. He's also not that talented, but he's been pushed over the better wrestlers. One of them could be mad that Travis got to win the title and retire the Ravishing Redneck."

"Except Red was supposed to win. He only decided to retire a couple hours before the match. But it's still a good theory. One of them could have been enraged over the turn of events. But why the bow and arrow? Most of the wrestlers have knives and guns that they carry with them," I said.

The wrestlers carry the guns and knives as a form of self-defense. Some fans – and other wrestlers – take the storylines too seriously and have been known to occasionally wait around in the parking lot after the show to confront one or more of the wrestlers. And it's not unheard of for someone to try to rob the wrestlers of the cash they were paid for appearing at the event along with any money they made selling t-shirts and signed pictures.

"But if it was a wrestler, using a knife or a gun – even one they took out of someone else's bag – would draw attention to them," Richards said.

"Maybe it was a wrestler who wasn't on tonight's card," Timmy suggested. "Travis wrestles for a lot of other promotions all over Texas and in other states. Those wrestlers don't like him either. Especially that guy whose neck Travis broke."

"Travis broke another wrestler's neck?" I asked. After taking one last picture of the end of the arrow shaft protruding from Travis's back, I pivoted around to face Timmy. "When did that happen? And why didn't I hear about it?"

"It happened five or six weeks ago," Timmy said. "Travis drove all the way over to the other side of the state to wrestle in Lubbock. All I know is that he attempted to do a piledriver, messed up, and wound up slamming the other guy's head into the mat."

"We're going to have to track this wrestler down," I said.

The piledriver is one of the most dangerous moves in professional wrestling, which is why it had been banned in a lot of promotions. Sterling won't allow any of his wrestlers to attempt the move due to the risk of injury. To execute a piledriver, one wrestler grabs his opponent, turns him upside-down, and then goes down to either a sitting or kneeling position as he sends his opponent head-first into the mat. When the move is properly executed, the opponent's head only brushes the mat, or doesn't touch it at all.

"Come on, I've got all the pictures I need from over here. Time to move around to the other side of the body so I can get some pictures from that angle," I said, as I walked around Red's truck to the other side. Timmy, Richards, and Mathews crowded in behind me as I knelt by Travis's head. Returning to the topic at hand, I asked, "What about Travis's personal life, Timmy? You know anything about that?"

"I went to Chastain High with Travis. He was a senior when I was a freshman," Mathews said, jumping into the conversation before Timmy could open his mouth. "Travis was an arrogant guy back then, too. I played on the freshman football team, and Travis used to haze us all the time. Always acting like the big man on campus even though he was only the kicker. Then he totally messed up and cost our team a chance at the State Championship. He went from hero to zero."

There were two school districts in Wyatt County. Big Pine School District covered roughly the northern half of the county, while Chastain School District covered the southern half. When I was a kid, Chastain and Big Pine were school rivals.

"I remember that," Richards said. "He was going for the game winning field goal and tripped over his own feet. Shanked the kick wide of the goal."

"People are still upset about it," Mathews said.

"If someone killed Travis over a football game that happened ten years ago, then that person has a serious problem. Not that our killer doesn't have a serious problem considering the murder weapon. Speaking of which, the victim is the archery instructor at Big Pine," I said.

"Are you kidding me?" Richards asked.

"Oh, no, I really hope a kid didn't do this," Timmy said.

"Me, too," I said. "Timmy, point that light under Red's truck. The arrow that hit Marisol is under here."

After Timmy did as I instructed, I snapped a few photos of the arrow. I then stuck my head under the truck to get a better look. The shaft was about two feet long, and it was almost entirely covered in dried, brownish-red blood. The shaft was topped off with a lethal looking head that was made up of three blades. It had an inch to an inch-and-a-half diameter at the base.

"Can you imagine getting hit with one of those?" I asked.

"I don't want to." Timmy said as he poked his head under the truck. "I just want to know what that pointy thing is."

"Easy way to find out." I grabbed my cell phone out of my crime scene kit, got on the Bass Pro Shop's website, and started doing research on the arrow head. I learned that it was a fixed-blade broadhead, and it was designed to plunge through an animal's hide, organs, and bones. "If anyone had any doubts about this being an accident, this should convince them that the killer did this on purpose. These broadhead things are meant to kill."

"Did you ever think this was an accident?" Richards asked.

"Nope." Backing away from the crime scene, I turned off the digital camera and announced, "That's it for now, boys. I still need pictures of the front of Travis's body. But I can't get those until we're done processing the scene and can move the body. I'll also need to get pictures of the blood Marisol dripped across the parking lot, but we'll have to save those for last since we'll need to move the work lights around. Or wait until the sun comes up."

"Then I guess I have good timing. Find anything interesting?" Quaranta asked as he rejoined us.

"Aside from the nasty looking arrow head, we didn't find anything too interesting. We did have a long chat about Travis and came up with some theories. Of course, that's if he was the intended victim and not Marisol. How's it going inside?" I asked.

"Interviews seem to be going well, and everyone is cooperating," Quaranta said. "I personally interviewed your Uncle Sterling. According to him, after Travis and Marisol crawled out from under the ring, they immediately went backstage, grabbed their stuff out of the locker rooms, demanded their money, and then bolted out the back door. Sterling says it was no more than ten minutes later when your cousins brought Marisol in through the back door."

"Small timeframe," I said.

"Might make things easier. Also, might make them harder," Quaranta said. "If you're done for the time being, I'm going to draw up the sketch of the crime scene."

Quaranta and I worked together to take measurements for the sketch. Quaranta then collected samples from the blood spatter and the pool of blood that had collected around Travis's body. While he did that, I bagged the bloody SWAT Heavyweight Championship title belt and then turned my attention to Travis's duffle bag. Inside the bag, I found Travis's street clothes and a pair of sneakers, an extra Speedo, his wallet, an almost empty bottle of baby oil, and his cell phone. Marisol's duffle bag contained similar items.

"I'm ready to move the body whenever you are," Quaranta said.

"There's something we need to do first," I said as I grabbed a container of black fingerprint powder, a brush, and a handful of lift tapes out of my crime scene kit. I then carefully dusted the shiny, red arrow shaft for prints while Quaranta held a piece of plastic over the body to protect it from the excess powder that fell from the brush. "I've got three partial prints. Two don't have much detail, but the third could be usable for making comparisons."

"You see any other evidence that we need to collect from the body?" Quaranta asked.

"Nope. Time for you boys to lift him up while I get my pictures. Just don't anyone touch the arrow shaft," I said.

Quaranta, Richards, and Mathews worked together to pick up Travis's body, turning him so that I could see the front of him. About three to four inches of the arrow shaft stuck out from Travis's torn up, bloody chest. At the end of the shaft was another of the three-blade broadheads.

"You're right, Carrie. It took a special kind of crazy to do this," Quaranta said.

"And a whole lot of rage," I added.

CHAPTER FIVE

THE SUN WAS BEGINNING to creep over the horizon when Quaranta and I decided that we were done processing the immediate crime scene. The temperatures had only gone down to the upper-seventies overnight, and I had a feeling that it was going to be an unseasonably hot day. Given seasonable in May, in my part of Texas, was in the low-eighties.

"I'll get together a group of deputies to start combing through the woods and the soccer field, then I'll head back to the department to see what the sheriff needs help with," Quaranta said.

"I'll check on how it's going inside. Maybe, if we're lucky, one of the wrestlers or security guards will have confessed to killing Yeager," I said.

"It would make our job a lot easier," Quaranta said, sounding wistful.

"Yeah…I don't know about you, but I've never been that lucky," I said.

I waved at Quaranta and then staggered across the parking lot towards the back door of the SWAT Zone. Adrenaline had gotten me through the first few hours of processing the crime scene, but physical and mental exhaustion had snuck up on me about an hour earlier. The only thing that had kept me going was the knowledge that the responsibility of processing the crime scene and collecting all of the evidence partially fell on my weary shoulders. Slacking at my job just because I was tired could ultimately result in the case not being solved. And that was a guilt I did not want to live with.

Mumbling to myself, I said, "I need a nap. But I'll settle for some food. Food should get me through another few hours before I drop."

Motivated by the thought of food – maybe there was still something left over at the concession stands – I yanked open the back door of the SWAT Zone and then collided with someone standing just inside. The Texas Ranger badge pinned to the front of the man's white shirt almost jabbed me in the eye.

"Hi Jerrod," I said as I tipped back my head to look up at him. Hardy was over six feet tall, making him about a foot taller than me. "You look like crap."

Hardy had purple bags under his bloodshot, mahogany brown eyes. His usually lightly tanned skin was pale, and the black stubble on his cheeks was at an unattractive length. Despite looking as exhausted as I felt, Hardy still had that ruggedly handsome look about him. I reached up and tried to smooth out Hardy's tousled, black hair. Chunks of hair were sticking out in all directions. Using my fingers, I brushed the hair back from his forehead and revealed a faint scar that sliced along his scalp just below the hairline. He had another faded scar on his chin. The scars were a visible reminder of a tragic car accident Hardy was in when he was eighteen. The emotional scars were far worse. Hardy's twin brother, Josh, was killed in the accident.

"And I feel like crap, too," Hardy said before giving me a lopsided grin. "But you look beautiful."

"Shut up, I do not," I said.

Hardy draped his arm over my shoulders and guided me back into the parking lot as he asked, "Want to give me the grand tour of the crime scene while you tell me about what's going on? If I'm going to be any help at all, I'll need all the details."

"Sure. Though there's not much to see, aside from a bloodstain on the pavement. We just packed up the body and sent it over to the hospital about fifteen minutes ago. Our plan is to get the body x-rayed with the arrow shaft still in it. Then we'll take the shaft out and send the body to the medical examiner's office. We can't, you know, just leave it in the body…"

"So, tell me, what did the Beast from East Texas do last night to upset someone enough to kill him? Or do you think it was Marisol?"

"Honestly, it could have been either of them. But the majority of us are betting on Travis being the intended victim," I said as I led Hardy over towards where Travis had been shot. "Last night, Travis took on Red in the main event. And won."

"I can see how Red losing the title to Travis might upset some people."

"It was in a Loser Leaves Town match. And things got ugly," I said.

"I think you better tell me about everything that happened last night."

"I'd start at the beginning, but I'm not really sure what the beginning is. So I'll just go back to around six o'clock last night. That's when Naomi and I got here, and Red told us that he was retiring," I said. I gave Hardy a quick rundown of the events leading up to when my cousins found Marisol screaming in the parking lot. I then summed up the hours spent processing the crime scene. "As you can see, there's not much left of the crime scene to look at aside from the blood. But I've got over a thousand pictures that you can look at later."

After checking out the dried blood, Hardy and I walked back across the parking lot and went inside the SWAT Zone. We found all of the wrestlers, security guards, and everyone else who had still been in the building when my cousins found Yeager's body. They were spread out over both sets of bleachers, sitting far enough apart that it would have made a private conversation impossible. The majority of the people were asleep.

"Yo, Carrie, when are you gonna let us go?" asked one of the security guards.

"Yeah, I ain't the one who killed Yeager. Why do I gotta be here?" asked a wrestler.

"Soon. Y'all should be able to get out of here soon," I announced. Scanning the scattered crowd I finally spotted Naomi sitting at one of the merchandise tables with Red, Aunt Priscilla, and a glassy-eyed Uncle Sterling. "How's it going? Any idea on who the killer might be?"

"We don't even know how Travis got killed. Well, Red does. But he won't tell us," Naomi said, sticking out her lower lip in a pout.

"I'd say take your pick," Red said as he gestured towards the people scattered across the bleachers. "I'm sure just about everyone here hated Trav. I just don't know if any of them hated him enough to kill him. Or had the, uh, means to kill him."

"What about Marisol?" I asked. So far we'd mainly focused on figuring out why someone would have wanted to kill Travis. But it was entirely possible that Marisol was the target all along. "I'll admit she's not my favorite person. And I'm still ticked off that she scratched up my face. But I wouldn't have killed her over it."

"Don't be nice, Carrie," Priscilla said. "Marisol is a vain little brat."

"And she always has been," Naomi added. "Don't yell at me – because I totally didn't tell her why I was asking – but I texted my sister and asked her about Marisol. They were in the same graduating class. Marisol used to pick on Olivia all the time in ninth grade. She was making Olivia's freshman year a living hell. I had a little 'chat' with her after school one day. Let's just say Marisol left Olivia alone after that."

"I had a few of those 'chats' with people when I was in high school," I said. Thanks to my job, I still had those 'chats' with people.

"Anyway, Olivia said that by the time they graduated, most of the girls in their class couldn't stand Marisol. Apparently, she had a real talent for getting on everyone's nerves."

"So, either of them could be the victim. Or neither of them. Or just one," Hardy said.

"Maybe Marisol saw something. Let's get things wrapped up here and head over to the hospital to talk to her." Tossing my car keys to Naomi, I said, "The four of you are free to go. Naomi, you may as well take my car. I can get a ride."

"I'm sure you can," Naomi said, gesturing to Hardy.

"Come on, Sterl, Carrie said we can go home," Priscilla said.

Yanking on Sterling's arms, Priscilla tried to get her husband to stand up. Sterling allowed his wife to pull him out of the chair, but, instead of standing up, he toppled forward and landed on his knees. Priscilla jumped to the side just before Sterling collapsed onto his face.

"What's wrong with him?" I asked, finally realizing how weird it was for Sterling to have not said a word in the past few minutes.

"He took all my Xanax," Priscilla said as she pulled an empty prescription bottle out of her purse and chucked it at her husband's head. "It's a good thing I stole that doctor's prescription pad. I'll have to write myself a prescription to get through until my next refill."

"I didn't hear that," I said.

"I heard it, but I'm going to pretend that I didn't. And that's only because I've got more important things to be concerned about at the moment," Hardy said as he slowly shook his head. "To avoid hearing anything else, I'm going to go find the person in charge."

"The Chief Deputy left Lieutenant Gregory in charge of us. He's got a bad attitude and no sense of humor," Red said as Hardy turned to walk away.

Byron Gregory was the current lieutenant of the Wyatt County Sheriff's Department. That put him third in the chain of command. He'd been with the sheriff's department almost as long as Uncle Murph, but not quite as long as Chief Deputy Quaranta. I didn't have much to do with Gregory simply because he was an unpleasant person to be around.

"Lieutenant Gregory is good at his job. Sadly, that's one of his few redeeming qualities," I said. "He also leaves me and Uncle Murph alone when we…you know."

"Cover up our family's crimes," Naomi said.

"Yeah, that. Though considering how oblivious Lieutenant Gregory is, he probably has no idea that the Shatners are breaking the law," I said.

At my feet, Sterling gagged a few times and then threw up. I took a step backwards to prevent the vomit from running into my shoes.

"That'll get some of the pills out of his system," Priscilla said.

"And all those beers that he chugged," Red said.

"That probably wasn't good for him," I said, sidestepping the vomit to nudge Sterling with my foot. "You okay, Uncle Sterling?"

"It might not have been good for him, but it finally shut him up," Naomi said. "We had to listen to him go on and on all night about all the bad publicity

SWAT is going to get because Travis got killed in the parking lot. And what kind of memorial he needs to do to honor Travis."

"And Sterling kept asking us what we think he should do at next month's show and who we think should be the next champion," Priscilla said.

"Then Sterling spent at least an hour begging me not to retire," Red added. "I told him that I'll do one more match –"

"You are not getting in that ring again. Not with your back the way it is. Do you want to wind up getting crippled?" I asked.

"It's one match, Carrie. Sterling said I can wrestle anyone I want. I'll pick someone I've worked with before. Someone who I can trust in the ring."

"I still don't like it," I said.

"I know you don't. But I need this. Last night's match sucked. And then with Trav getting killed afterwards... Just promise you'll valet for me."

"You know I will. Now get out of here. I have work to do," I said.

Before she walked off, Naomi leaned closer to me and asked, "Hey, you doing okay? Or is it weird having to see Sergeant Hardy?"

"It's totally weird. But I'm so caught up in the case that I haven't had a chance to really think about it. So far, he's been...he's been Jerrod. I don't know what to think," I said. After saying goodbye to Naomi, I walked over to where Hardy was talking to the paunchy, middle-aged Lieutenant Byron Gregory. "Please tell me someone confessed."

"No, Detective Shatner. No one has confessed to the murder. Nor has anyone admitted to having been in the parking lot at the time of the attack," Gregory said. "I read over all of the interview notes. Almost every single person here claims to have an alibi during the short time period in which the victim was killed. Your Uncle Sterling had sent all of the security guards out to the front parking lot to keep an eye on the fans as they left. He claims he was worried about the fans starting another riot out there. As for the wrestlers and refs and whoever else was part of the show, most of them were backstage."

"Did we get anything worthwhile? Like some gossip about suspects or motive. Travis Yeager was not a popular guy around here. Are you telling me that suddenly everyone loves him and they're his best friend?" I asked.

"No witnesses. But there was a lot of finger pointing. And the majority of those fingers were pointed at your buddy Frank Smith," Gregory said. "One reason is because Smith is mad that the victim stole the top bad guy spot from him. Apparently that's a big deal to him. Smith also got into an altercation with the victim following intermission. The fight was quickly broken up, but Smith allegedly threatened to kill the victim."

"Did you see the altercation, Carrie?" Hardy asked.

"No. It happened in the men's locker room after intermission. I don't hang out in there because...well, because I don't have the right equipment," I said.

"What did Smith have to say about the altercation?" Hardy asked Gregory.

"He didn't have much to say. According to the deputy who interviewed him, Mr. Smith was very uncooperative," Gregory said.

"Frank is always uncooperative…Does he have an alibi?" I asked.

"Not a good one. He claims he was on the phone with his wife," Gregory said.

"On the phone? But Oksana was here last night. I talked to her. Why would Frank need to call her if she was here?" I asked, realizing that I hadn't seen Oksana since last night after intermission. Naomi and I had been going into the women's locker room to touch up our makeup and fix our hair when Oksana almost knocked us over as she charged out of the small room. Oksana, who'd had her duffle bag slung over her shoulder, had been dressed in street clothes.

Gregory shrugged. "Mr. Smith claims he was up by the concession stands because he said it was too loud backstage to hear anything. He said the only people who might have seen him up there were you, your cousin, and the Ravishing Redneck."

"I wasn't really paying attention. Of course, I was also trying to get Red to calm down. But I remember seeing someone walking around the concession stands," I said.

"Your cousin and Mr. Redneck said the same thing," Gregory said.

"Frank doesn't exactly have a solid alibi…Let's go see what he has to say for himself," I said. I walked over to where Frank was stretched out on the bottom row of the bleachers. He was using his furry ushanka hat as a pillow, and was snoring loud enough to annoy the people around him. Kicking the bleacher next to Frank's head, I yelled, "Wakey, wakey, Frankie, baby! We've got some questions for you."

"What do you want?" Frank muttered as he opened his bloodshot blue eyes. "Can I go home now? Oksana is probably losing her mind wondering where I am."

"Oksana's whereabouts is one of the things that I want to ask you about," I said, as I kicked the bleacher a second time. "Now get up. We have some questions for you, Frank. And the sooner you talk to me and the Texas Ranger, the sooner you get to go home."

"What about the rest of us?" asked SWAT's only female referee. "I need to get home to my kids."

"The rest of you can go," Hardy announced, starting a mass exodus towards the backstage. He didn't tell them that the deputies would be searching all of their cars before they would be allowed to drive off.

"All right, go ahead and ask your questions," Frank said as sat up and then pulled the ushanka hat down over his ears.

"Where's Oksana? Did she leave early last night?" I asked.

"Our youngest daughter wasn't feeling too good last night. So, since I wrestled before intermission, I told Oksana to just take Sonya home and put her to bed," Frank said, referring to his twelve-year-old daughter. "No point in either of them sticking around after my match. Especially when I knew Oksana didn't want to see Travis win the title. She was sick to her stomach just thinking about it."

"Sick enough that she would have come back and killed Travis?" I asked.

"What the…No! I told you, Oksana took Sonya home. She didn't come back. Not when Sonya was puking her guts out," Frank said.

"How about you? Did you shoot Marisol and kill Travis?" I asked.

"No," Frank said.

"But you threatened to kill Travis," I pointed out.

"Yeah. So what? I threaten to kill a lot of people," Frank said, shrugging his massive shoulders.

"No, Vladimir Khrushchev threatens to kill people. It's practically your catch phrase. And has been for as long as I can remember." I sat down next to Frank. "What happened, Frank? Just tell me what the altercation with Travis was about, and then you can go home. And I can get on with solving this murder."

"You know how Travis is. Strutting around like he's The Shit. And his woman ain't much better." Frank sighed. "Look, I know I'm not the best wrestler on the card. And I can accept that I'm not as good as I used to be. But Travis…botches every other move, yet he acts like he's the next Shawn Michaels."

"There's never going to be another Heartbreak Kid," I said. Shawn Michaels, a Texas native, was one of the greatest professional wrestlers of all time. In my opinion, he had been the best of his generation, and no one before or after has come anywhere close to being his equal.

"You know how Sterling arranges his matches and plans his main storylines a few months in advance? Well, I was supposed to wrestle Red at next month's show. And win the SWAT Championship. Sterling wanted a heel to carry the title for the summer months. But, before the show, Sterling and Red pulled me aside to tell me there had been a change in plans. So, yeah, I was mad. But I get it. Red's a good guy, and we've had some unforgettable matches. I'm glad he's retiring before he cripples himself. He don't deserve that."

"And the altercation?" I asked, prompting Frank to move the story along.

"Travis started taunting me. Telling me I'm washed up. He knew I was supposed to win the title next month, so he decided to rub it in my face that he was going to win it tonight instead. I took a swing at him. Said some things I shouldn't have. It was nothing."

"Except now Travis is dead," I pointed out. "And a lot of people heard you threaten to kill him."

"Yeah, well, I didn't."

~*~*~

"Thanks for taking me by my house so I could change into my uniform," I said as I flipped down the passenger-side sun visor so that I could see my reflection in the little mirror and examine the three scratches that Marisol had carved into my cheek. I had tried to cover the scratches with concealer, but that only made the scabbed-over abrasions more obvious.

I lived only a couple minutes' drive north of the SWAT Zone. Unfortunately, there wasn't a road that directly connected the two. Hardy had to drive almost the whole way to Holler before he could get to a road that would take him to my neighborhood.

The neighborhood – which had a little over fifty houses, each of which sat on roughly an acre of land – was less than ten minutes away from the eastern outskirts of Holler. My morning commute to the Wyatt County Sheriff's Department in downtown Holler took fifteen minutes.

I currently resided in the same house that I had lived in up until I was almost seventeen. When I was sixteen, my dad was killed in a motorcycle accident. After that, my mom sold the house to my paternal grandparents. She then gave me the choice to move to Dallas with her or to stay in Wyatt County with my grandparents. I chose to stay. My grandparents held on to the house for me – renting it out to various Shatners over the years – and then sold it to me for next-to-nothing when I moved home from Nashville.

"Not a problem," Hardy said. "Besides it was nice getting to see Manny again. Even though he still hates me."

"The cat doesn't hate you. He just doesn't like you," I said.

Not long after Hardy moved into the house, he was renting in Tyler; a scrawny orange cat forced his way inside. Hardy's new neighbors informed him that Manny had belonged to the family who had lived in the house before him. Instead of taking their cat with them, they dumped the poor baby outside. Feeling bad for Manny, Hardy allowed him to move back into his former home. Despite everything that Hardy did for him, Manny never quite warmed up to his new owner. During my first visit to Hardy's house, Manny curled up in my lap and made it clear that was where he wanted to stay. A month later, we packed up Manny's various toys and bed, and then moved the cat to my house. My dog, Molly, was thrilled with her new feline companion. Manny enjoyed tormenting her.

"That cat is evil and you know it," Hardy said.

I rolled my eyes and then asked, "You want to tell me about what you were doing up in Kansas City?"

"I went to see my father."

"Your birth father or stepfather?" I asked.

Hardy had told me about each one. His parents were seventeen years old when he and his twin brother, Josh, were born. Their dad was already gone by then, taking off not long after he found out about the pregnancy. Hardy told me that he only saw his father a handful of times when he was a little kid. The stepfather, on the other hand, was a real piece of work. He beat up his stepsons on a regular basis for six or seven years. Then the local Child Protective Services got involved and the stepfather wound up going to prison.

"Birth father," Hardy said. He made a disgusted face as if just mentioning his father left a nasty taste in his mouth. "I have no idea what happened to my stepfather after he went to prison. And I have no plans to look him up to find out."

"I thought you didn't know about what happened to your birth father either," I said.

"I didn't until about three weeks ago," Hardy said.

Hardy pulled up to the stop sign at the end of my street and put his truck in park. He then picked up his cell phone and played around with it for a few seconds. Once he had found what he was looking for, Hardy handed me the phone so that I could look at a picture of two young boys and a man in his mid-twenties. None of them looked happy, or even comfortable, to be together. The boys, who appeared to be about six or seven years old, were looking at each other out of the corners of their eyes. They were dressed in old, faded clothes and were in need of a haircut. The man had a cigarette hanging out of his mouth, and his eyes were narrow and cold. Aside from that, he was handsome. Hardy had gotten his looks from his father.

"That picture was taken on our seventh birthday," Hardy said as he pointed at the picture on his phone. "It was the last time I saw my father until yesterday."

"What about when Josh died?" I asked.

When Jerrod and Josh were seniors in high school, their football team won the State Championship. The night after the big game, they were out partying with some of their teammates. They were driving through downtown Waco when a drunk driver blew through a red light and t-boned the passenger side of the car. Josh was killed in the accident. Jerrod, who was behind the wheel, was badly injured.

"Yeah, he showed up for Josh's funeral. And the nurses told me that my father came to see me in the hospital. But I had a head injury and was out of it for over a week. He was gone by the time I realized what was going on," Hardy said as he put the truck in drive and turned left out of my neighborhood and headed towards Holler.

"And that's it? Your father didn't write or call for the next nineteen years? Why now?"

"Dear old dad has pancreatic cancer and is dying. There's nothing like impending death to make you rethink all of the horrible things you've done in your life. He decided he wanted to make amends with me," Hardy said.

"How did that go?" I asked as I tucked Hardy's cell phone in one of the cup holders in the center console.

Leaning forward, I peered out the windshield at the empty two-lane road ahead of us. There were pine trees and cottonwoods growing thickly on either side of the road. Dark gray and deep blue storm clouds were rolling in from the west, threatening rain and a drop-in temperature.

"It didn't go good at all," Hardy said. "I mean, I'm sure you can imagine how surprised I was three weeks ago when some woman named Vanessa called my office claiming to be my stepmother. I didn't know my father had gotten married. But I guess Vanessa was the one who encouraged my father to find me. When he dragged his heels, she Googled my name, found out that I'm a Texas Ranger, and contacted me. When I got the message, I figured Vanessa was just some nut. Then she emailed me pictures my father still had of me and Josh. After that, she begged me to come up to Kansas City to see my father before it's too late. I was going to just ignore them, but then I started to feel bad and I decided to go see my father before he dies. I hate the man, but I wouldn't be here without his sperm donation. I felt like I needed to make peace with him before he died. He's currently in hospice, so I had to see him while I have the chance. Hence while I drove up to Kansas City."

"And…did you make peace with him?" I asked.

"Nope. The hospital has my father on a morphine drip and he is in pretty bad shape. But that didn't stop him from preaching God and forgiveness at me. Then he made this big speech about how he was sorry that he walked out on me and Josh. I think he was just fishing for forgiveness, but within the first minute or two, I realized that I couldn't make peace with him. Not after he abandoned me and my brother. I listened to about all I could stomach, and then I told him to go to hell. I was so angry that I just had to get out of there. But, as I was leaving, in comes Vanessa with this teenage boy who looks almost exactly like Josh and I did when we were that age. Except the boy has blue eyes and his hair has more of a curl to it than mine."

"You have a half-brother?" I asked. "I see why you wanted to talk to me. No one knows better than me what it's like to acquire half-siblings."

My dad frequently cheated on my mom, and, as a result, I have two younger half-brothers. The older of the two was adopted by one of my uncles and his wife. I didn't know he was my brother until he turned eighteen. I found out about the younger one before he was born. It had been a horrifying experience when my oldest sister's best friend showed up at Dad's memorial service sporting a four-month baby bump and loudly proclaiming that she was carrying my father's child.

Hardy shook his head. "I don't have a half-brother. Or any half-siblings. At least none provided by my father. My mother…well, I have my doubts she had any more since the last time I saw her when I was eighteen."

"Then who is the teenage boy? A cousin or something?" I asked.

"He's my nephew. His name is Jake, and he just turned eighteen," Hardy said as he decreased his speed to drive through Holler. "The kid is my nephew."

Assuming that the boy had to be Josh's son, I asked, "Did you know Josh was a father? Going to be a father?"

"Yeah, I knew," Hardy said. "The fall of our senior year of high school, Josh started dating a girl who was a grade behind us. Nice girl. Really smart. I honestly don't know what she wanted with Josh. He was…my brother was smart, but he didn't apply himself any more than he had to. He kept his grades high enough to play football. The rest of the time he just goofed around. But none of that matters now. What matters is that Josh and his girlfriend weren't as careful as they should have been. A month or so before the accident, Josh told me that he had gotten his girlfriend pregnant. He was pretty worked up and wanted me to tell him what to do. He wanted to be there for his kid, but he didn't think he and his girlfriend were ready to be parents."

"What happened? How did your father wind up with Josh's kid?" I asked.

"After the accident, Josh's girlfriend disappeared and her parents wouldn't tell me where she had gone. All they would tell me was that she'd had a miscarriage and that she'd gone somewhere to recover and mourn for Josh. It was all a pack of lies," Hardy said as he punched the steering wheel and blasted the horn. "I guess when my father came to see me at the hospital he bumped into Josh's girlfriend. He and his wife couldn't have kids so they offered to raise Josh's baby. But they didn't want me to know about it. My father was trying to explain why when I…I stormed out of the hospice place, got in my truck, and started driving home."

"You need to find out the whole story, Jerrod," I said. "You need to give your father a chance to explain. And you definitely need to get to know Josh's son."

"I know. I know. And I will. I just need some time to…to breathe," Hardy said as he turned into the drive that leads to the Wyatt County General Hospital. "But I don't want to see my father again. There's no fixing what he did to me and Josh. Vanessa can explain everything to me once he's gone."

"Then you're never going to get all of the answers, Jerrod," I said.

"I don't want to talk about it anymore, Carrie," Hardy said.

Driving past the Emergency Room entrance, Hardy had to slam on the brakes to avoid running over a man as he limped across the parking lot. On one foot the man wore a shabby cowboy boot; he had the other foot wrapped up in a large bandage. Just as the man hobbled in front of the truck, he looked in my direction and we made eye contact through the windshield. The wide-eyed, panicked look on Dustin Thompson's face communicated that he wasn't any happier to see me than I was to see him.

"You've got to be kidding me." I silently cursed myself for having forgotten about Dustin. I might be caught up in a homicide investigation but keeping Naomi out of trouble was still a priority.

"You know that guy?" Hardy asked.

"He's a friend of my cousin. I'm going to check on him real quick." I shoved the car door open and jumped out. I then ran over to Dustin. "Did you seriously come here to get that scratch looked at?"

"It's a lot more than a scratch. That crazy cousin of yours mutilated my foot." Dustin yanked the grimy, bloodstained bandage off his foot, revealing that a chunk of flesh was missing from the outside edge of his foot. A trickle of blood seeped from the gory wound.

"Oh, gross, is that bone?" Trying not to gag, I said, "Okay, it's more than a scratch."

"You're damn straight it's more than a scratch," Dustin said as he waved the bloody bandage around under my nose.

"Hey, Carrie!" Hardy stuck his head out of the driver's side window. "Is everything all right? Or is that guy giving you a problem?"

"Everything is fine, Jerrod."

"Who's he? Is that your boyfriend?" Dustin didn't wait for me to answer, he just raised his voice and started shouting at Hardy. "Hey, mister, do you have any idea what kind of psycho you're dating. She and her crazy cousin – OUCH!"

To shut Dustin up, I stomped down on his injured foot, causing him to scream. I felt horrible for doing it, but I couldn't have Dustin blurt out to Hardy that Naomi had shot him.

"Hey, buddy, there's no need to be calling Detective Shatner nasty names." Hardy parked the truck and then walked over. "Whoa, what happened to your foot?"

"Yes, Dustin, tell us what happened to your foot." I pushed my sunglasses on top of my head so that I could give Dustin a meaningful glare.

Dustin looked at me when he answered. "I was…umm…I was chopping up a tree…that fell over in my backyard. I, uh, the axe slipped out of my hands and hit me in the foot."

"You should be more careful, buddy," Hardy said. "You have any idea how many people accidently cut off a limb while chopping up trees and firewood?"

"No, I don't," Dustin said. "Do you?"

"Honestly, no. But I bet a lot of people have suffered axe related injuries," Hardy said.

"I'm sure Dustin learned his lesson and will be much more careful when he's chopping wood," I said, emphasizing the last two words.

"Don't worry, I'm done chopping wood. If I can get my chainsaw working, I'll only use that in the future," Dustin said.

Hardy looked back and forth between me and Dustin before he said, "Well, whatever you decide to do, be careful."

"Dustin…what are you doing in the middle of the parking lot? I told you to wait in the car!" yelled a woman standing outside the Emergency Room entrance. She wore an unflattering, ruffled, floor-length maroon sundress, and her mousy brown hair was pulled back in a bun.

"Is that your wife?" I asked.

"Yeah…That's Belinda." Dustin took two steps towards his wife before collapsing against a lamppost. "I'll probably be a cripple for the rest of my life thanks to…thanks to my own stupidity."

I eyed up Belinda Thompson as she scurried across the parking lot with a wheelchair. As she got closer, I noticed that there wasn't a trace of makeup on her plain, pale face. Going on looks and fashion sense alone, Belinda and Naomi appeared to be polar opposites.

"Oh, Dustin, why didn't you listen to me? You will end up doing more damage to your foot if you keep hobbling around. Now sit down," Belinda said as she shoved the wheelchair into the back of Dustin's legs, forcing him to fall over backwards into the chair. She then helped him put his injured foot into the wheelchair's footrest. Satisfied that she had her husband where she wanted him, Belinda turned to me and Hardy and asked, "Excuse me, who are you and why are you talking to my husband?"

"I'm Detective Shatner. I work for the Wyatt County Sheriff's Department." I held up my badge for Belinda to see. "And this is Sergeant Hardy. He's with the Texas Rangers."

"Is this about Travis?" Belinda asked. "I told Sheriff Shatner that we'll be in after Dustin has had his foot patched up."

"How do you know Travis?" I asked as a large raindrop pelted me on the forehead.

"Travis and Dustin are brothers," Belinda said before her husband had a chance to open his mouth.

"Stepbrothers," Dustin added. "My dad married his mom."

"Let's get you inside. Maybe we can have a quick chat before you get medical attention," Hardy said as he grabbed the wheelchair's handles and gave Dustin a shove towards the building.

I kept my eye on Hardy and Dustin as they made their way across the parking lot. Dustin had twisted around in the wheelchair and was looking up at Hardy. They were talking and Dustin was gesturing towards his foot. If Dustin told Hardy about what really happened to his foot, the shit would hit the fan. Hardy would insist on arresting and charging Naomi. And I would also have to explain why I hadn't already done that. I'd be hard pressed to come up with a reasonable sounding answer. Saying that Dustin kind of deserved it probably wouldn't fly with Hardy. He didn't believe in karma like I did. The way I saw it, Dustin getting shot in the foot was the universe's way of punishing him for cheating on his wife.

Hardy, who had been working for the Texas Department of Public Safety for the past fifteen years, saw everything as either black or white. Right or wrong. Good or bad. There was no gray area for him. As for me, I embraced the gray areas. It was where my family operated and was most comfortable. The Shatners were born and raised in the gray area. We lived our lives in the gray area and would someday die in the gray area. Then we would go to the gray area known as the afterlife.

"How do you know Dustin?" Belinda asked, as she scurried to keep up with me as I rushed after Hardy and Dustin.

"Dustin's a friend of my cousin's," I said, sticking to the truth. I could only hope Belinda didn't ask either me or Dustin for more details. "I saw him limping across the parking lot and stopped to see how he was doing. It's awful what happened to his foot."

"I'm just so thankful that he didn't injure himself worse." Belinda caught up to me and whispered, "Can you believe that he didn't want to see a doctor? I brought him here as soon as I arrived home from chaperoning the Post Prom. I walked in the house to find Dustin bleeding all over the bathroom and crying about what happened to his poor brother. I cannot believe I was only a few hundred yards away when Travis was murdered. And poor Marisol. I understand she was injured as well."

"Yeah, it's hard to believe. I was inside the SWAT Zone when it happened," I said. Stepping around a teenager crying over an injured wrist, I joined Hardy and Dustin at the check-in desk. "So, Dustin, what can you tell me about Travis?"

"I don't know. I figure you know more about him getting murdered than I do," Dustin said. "Ain't it your department investigating what happened to him?"

Rolling my eyes, I asked, "What can you tell me about Travis as a person? How close were you? Do you know who might have wanted to kill him?"

"They were very close," Belinda said at the same time Dustin muttered, "I could barely stand the bastard."

"Dustin, don't call your brother such a horrible name!" Belinda screeched in a high-pitched nasally voice. "You should know better than to speak ill of the dead."

"Why? It won't help Detective Shatner and the Ranger find the killer if we don't tell 'em the truth about Travis." Turning to me, Dustin said, "I couldn't stand Travis as a kid, though a lot of that had to do with my dad. When I was eight, my dad left my mom to hook up with Travis's mom. My dad had custody of me every other weekend, but I barely got to see him because he was always coaching Travis's sports teams or doing 'manly' stuff with Travis. I wasn't any good at sports, so my dad had no time for me except during hunting season."

"What about as adults?" Hardy asked.

Shrugging, Dustin said, "I still can't stand Travis. He's the same jerk and bully that he was when he was a kid. And my dad still prefers him over me. I think he loves Travis more than his wife and both of their daughters."

"Mr. Thompson, we can see you now," announced a nurse.

"We will come in to the sheriff's department as soon as we're done here," Belinda said as she pushed Dustin's wheelchair towards the emergency room doors. "And, if you see Marisol, please tell her how sorry we are."

After Dustin and Belinda disappeared through the double doors, Hardy turned to me and said, "Your friend Dustin is an interesting guy. He demanded to see my Rangers' badge and then he kept asking me if I know what kind of people work for the Wyatt County Sheriff's Department. Are you sure Dustin cut his foot while chopping up a tree?"

"That's what he said, Jerrod. It's not like I was there when it happened."

"I didn't say you were. Maybe I'm just imagining things, but I got the impression that something shady was going on between you two."

"Like what?"

"Like maybe you're helping him cover up some sort of crime."

"What? No. Of course not." I turned to Hardy with a smile that I hoped look genuine. "You know I only cover up crimes that my family members commit."

CHAPTER SIX

"WHEN YOU FIND the person who killed Travis, ask him why he couldn't have done me a favor and killed me, too."

It was the second complete and coherent sentence that Marisol Santiago uttered since Hardy and I walked into her hospital room half-an-hour earlier. The doctor warned us that, during the early morning, Marisol had slipped into a near-catatonic state due to the aftereffects of shock. The sedatives she had been given, along with the anesthesia she'd been put under while a plastic surgeon repaired the gash on her arm, also played a role in her unresponsiveness. The doctor almost refused to let us check Marisol out of the hospital. It was Marisol, who'd firmly but quietly stated she was leaving, that convinced the doctor to let his patient go.

"Travis is the love of my life," Marisol said. Her body suddenly went limp and she slid out of the chair, collapsing in a heap on the floor. "I can't do this… Not without Travis. Oh, God, why did you take him and not me?"

Dropping the voice recorder that I'd been setting up, I rushed around the side of my desk and knelt beside Marisol's prostrate form. She lay curled up in the fetal position, with her arms wrapped around her head. I was no good with crying females, and I didn't quite have the touch when it came to comforting bereaved loved ones. Patting Marisol on the shoulder, I said some things that I thought sounded comforting. My placating gestures only made her cry harder.

Marisol had her face pressed against the dirty carpet and was mumbling something about how she should just kill herself, when Hardy walked in my office carrying three water bottles. He stood in the doorway, surveying the scene, before he tossed the bottles onto my desk. He then gently picked up Marisol and returned her to the chair. Hardy's sharp command to 'pull yourself together' had the desired effect – Marisol ceased sobbing, but she continued to sniffle a bit.

After giving Marisol another minute to calm down, Hardy began asking her simple questions about her family, how long they'd lived in Wyatt County, and what she did for a living. Marisol started out giving us one- or two-word answers. Her detached manner made it a frustrating and time-consuming process to get any useful information out of her. It wasn't until Marisol began talking about her job at the Abbott Equestrian Center that her passion for her job overtook her uncommunicative attitude and she finally provided us with detailed answers.

"Have you recently had any problems at work?" Hardy asked.

"With who? The horses? Considering they have hooves, I doubt they could use a bow and arrow," Marisol said.

"You just said that you give horseback riding lessons. Could one of the people you're working with be upset with you? What about your coworkers? Or the people who board their horses there?" Hardy asked.

"No. I get along with everyone. I've been boarding my horse at Abbott since I was twelve. I started working there off-and-on when I was sixteen, and I've been there full-time since I graduated from college two years ago. In all those years I haven't had any problems with anyone."

"What about your personal life? Anyone you can think of who would have a reason to attack you and Travis?" I asked.

"I can't imagine anyone hating me or Travis enough to want to kill us. That's why I figure it's a fan who couldn't handle Travis winning the title and the Ravishing Redneck retiring. Are you telling me it wasn't a crazy fan?" Marisol asked.

"We're looking into all possibilities," Hardy said. "Both in your personal life and in Travis's personal life. While you give it some more thought, why don't you tell us about how you and Travis met?"

"We met almost two years ago. My baby sister, Evita, is in the Big Pine archery club. She's the one who introduced us," Marisol said.

"Your sister is in Travis's archery club? How old is she?" I asked.

I glanced over at Hardy. He quickly made eye contact with me and gave me a small nod. Marisol probably wouldn't have noticed the slight movements, but it was enough for me to know that Hardy had also made the same connection that I had. We needed to talk to Evita Santiago, and we needed to talk to her soon.

"Eighteen. I guess she's not really a baby anymore since she's about to graduate from high school. But she'll always be a baby to me," Marisol said, sounding wistful.

"Are you and Evita close?" I asked.

"We weren't until about a year ago. She was only twelve when I moved to Colorado, so she was still a kid when I went off to college," Marisol said. She then told us about the four years she spent earning her Bachelor's in Equine Science at Colorado State University. "I didn't come home much during the four years I was away at college. It wasn't until after I graduated and moved home two years ago that I finally realized Evita had grown up. I knew she had joined the archery club in ninth grade, but I never really talked to her about it or how she was doing in high school. To be honest, I really didn't talk to her at all. Mom and my other sister, Annalisa, told me what Evita was up to, but I didn't pay much attention to what they had to say."

"But you and Evita are close now?" I asked.

"Oh, yeah. Practically inseparable since I moved home. Well, practically inseparable when I'm not with…oh, Travis…Anyway, I had just moved home and Evita had this big archery tournament. So I tagged along with my parents and Annalisa to see it. I was sitting there, totally bored, when I looked over at Evita's team and I saw Travis. I was shocked when Travis asked me out right away. Things started off really fast," Marisol said before she blew her nose. Marisol then launched into a description of hers and Travis's fairy tale relationship. If Marisol was to be believed, she and Travis never fought and hardly ever argued.

"Did Travis get you hooked on archery?" Hardy asked.

"Not really. He showed me how to do it, but I just never got into it," Marisol said.

"You did get into wrestling though," I said.

Marisol laughed. "I was into pro wrestling long before I met Travis. My mamá hates wrestling. She banned it from our house. But she had book club meetings every Monday night when I was a growing up. So my papá and I would watch Monday Night Raw whenever she was gone. It was our big secret. When I started dating Travis, I asked him to train me so that I could valet for him."

"You said earlier that you think the killer is a crazy fan. Is there anyone in particular that comes to mind?" I asked.

"Most of the fans know that it's a soap opera, but there are some that get way too into it. You know what I mean, Detective Shatner," Marisol said.

"I do. Red and I have had some unpleasant run-ins with fans, and Red is a face. I can't imagine how bad it might have been for Travis considering he's a heel," I said, thinking about how there have been times when fans were waiting for Red after the show with the intention of fighting him because they were mad that he won or because he lost or because he said something that they didn't appreciate.

"Travis has gotten some really nasty letters and emails over the past couple years. He saves the letters and prints out the emails because he thinks they're funny," Marisol said.

"Do you know where he keeps them?" Hardy asked. "We will need to see them."

"He saves them in binders. They're at our house. Oh, God…Now what am I going to do? I can't afford the rent on my own. I'll have to move back in with my parents," Marisol whined.

"Take it one step at a time, Marisol," I said.

"Yes, right now we need your help in figuring out who might have wanted you and Travis dead," Hardy said. "Did you see any of this hate mail Travis received? Was there anyone you were concerned about? Or that he was concerned about?"

"Like I said, Travis thought it was funny. He never seemed worried about any of it. He just laughed it off. But I was really creeped out by it. I think that's why Travis stopped showing me the letters. I was starting to have anxiety attacks," Marisol said.

"Marisol, what exactly happened last night?" I asked.

"My boyfriend was murdered," Marisol said.

Hardy gave me an irritated look, and then said, "What Detective Shatner meant to ask is why you and Travis left the SWAT Zone almost immediately after his match."

"That was my idea," Marisol said. "Normally we stick around. I mean, I've only been valeting for him for about a year or so. But I've been to a lot of wrestling shows during the two years that Travis and I were dating. And we've hung out afterwards at almost every one. But, after what happened last night, I just wanted to get out of there."

"What exactly happened?" Hardy asked.

"The fans rioted after Travis beat the Ravishing Redneck. It was nuts. Travis thought it was funny, but it really scared me. You were scared, too, right, Detective Shatner?"

"It was frightening," I said.

"See what I mean? I didn't want to stick around after that. Especially since a lot of the people in the back were mad about it, too. It didn't exactly feel like we were welcome backstage. So I told Travis to grab his stuff because I wanted to leave," Marisol said. Tears overflowed from Marisol's eyes, dripped down her cheeks, and landed on her lap. "Oh, God, it's my fault he's dead. Travis wanted to stick around and hang out with the other wrestlers. He always does. But I wanted to leave. If I hadn't made him leave, he wouldn't be dead."

"Miss Santiago, it's not your fault," Hardy said as he leaned over and patted Marisol on the back. "Take a few deep breaths. I know this is difficult, but you're doing great."

"If I'd known what…what was about to happen, I would have…I would have told him I loved him. Instead, I wasted our last few minutes together pestering him about getting married," Marisol said before she covered her face with her hands as heart-wrenching sobs racked her body. "Oh, God, Travis, I'm so sorry."

Hardy and I sat there while Marisol wept. It was difficult listening to her and I was glad when she began to quiet down and finally stopped crying. After using up at least a fourth of a box of tissues, Marisol stated that she was ready to continue.

"Miss Santiago, we need to know about what happened right after Travis was shot. We know he was standing directly behind the car when he was struck with the arrow. But where were you? What did you do?" Hardy asked.

"Yes, Travis was standing behind the car. He'd forgotten to get his car keys out of his bag, so he was standing there, trying to find them. But he couldn't exactly see what he was doing since the overhead light was burnt out. I was standing along the passenger side of the car, talking about how I want to get married, when he asked me to come help him look for the keys. I was looking at my phone, you know, to turn the flashlight on, when Travis kind of gasped. I looked…I looked up and saw him collapse on the trunk of the car. He then…oh Jesus…Travis then fell to the ground. I could see the arrow sticking out of his back, but I couldn't tell what it was. I…I don't know. I might have screamed. Or maybe I didn't scream until I was hit. But I saw Travis on the ground with something sticking out of his back. I was…I had my hand pressed to his neck…I know it was impossible…but I was desperate to find a pulse. That's when I got hit in the arm…I know I screamed then…And I kept screaming," Marisol said.

"Did you hear anything or see anyone, Marisol?" Hardy asked.

"I think I heard someone shouting and maybe running. But, like I said, I was screaming. And…and…I don't know. As soon as I got hit, I laid down on the ground and stayed there for…I don't know, a couple minutes at least. I was too scared to get up. I was afraid that as soon as I got up, I'd get shot. After a few minutes passed, I crawled around the side of Travis's car and started walking towards the building. I really don't remember much after that. I know someone helped me inside. And I remember talking to you, Detective Shatner. But I can't really remember anything until I woke up in the hospital this morning. I'm sorry. I wish I could be more helpful."

"You're doing fine," Hardy said. "Are you sure you don't remember anything else from before the attack? Did you hear anything that might have been out of the ordinary? Or maybe see someone else in the parking lot?"

Marisol closed her eyes for a few seconds while she thought about it. She then said, "No. Travis and I were talking. I really wasn't paying attention to anything else. I wish I had. Maybe then Travis would still be alive."

"Marisol, who hates you or Travis enough to have done this? Who have you had a problem with recently?" I asked, hoping Marisol could now come up with a name.

"No one. There's no one I can come up with. Well, no one aside from the guy I dated when I was in high school. He's already attacked one of my boyfriends, so I wouldn't put it past him. Except there's no way my ex-boyfriend did it because he's been living in a group home for over a year. And he's not allowed to leave," Marisol said.

"What's your ex-boyfriend's name?" Hardy asked.

"Xavier Ortega. You should remember him, Detective Shatner. You arrested him a few years ago."

Pulling my keyboard closer, I typed 'Xavier Ortega' into the criminal database and brought up two mug shots. In the first mug shot, Xavier's long, stringy, brown hair framed his lean face. One of Xavier's eyes was swollen shut and the other stared vacantly at the camera. He also had a shallow cut on his forehead. In the second mug shot, Xavier's long hair was gone and his cheeks had filled out. He'd put on about fifty pounds in the time between his arrests.

"Fill me in," Hardy said. "What did Xavier do?"

"The first time we arrested Xavier was for assault with a deadly weapon. He tried to stab Marisol's new boyfriend with a broken bottle," I said.

Almost four years ago, mere days after I started working at the sheriff's department, on a sweltering day in mid-July, we got a frantic call from some people who were partying down at Wyatt Lake. Marisol and a group of her friends had been hanging out when Xavier attacked her new boyfriend with the broken bottle. The boyfriend only suffered superficial wounds before some of the other men at the party overpowered Xavier and tied him up.

After taking Xavier into custody, Quaranta tried talking to him. But Xavier kept screaming at him and was spouting nonsense about how Marisol was his girlfriend and that the guy he attacked was trying to hurt her. Xavier was so determined to get back to Marisol that he managed to escape the deputies and run across the manmade beach to where she was hovering over the EMTs bandaging her boyfriend's wounds. One of the other partygoers tackled Xavier, driving him headfirst into the side of the ambulance and knocking him out. Since we couldn't tell if Xavier was under the influence of anything or not, we transported him to the hospital to get checked out. The doctor was worried about Xavier's mental state and decided it would be best if we had him involuntarily committed to the hospital's psychiatric ward. The doctors there determined that Xavier is a paranoid schizophrenic. He was also suffering from delusions that he was convinced were real.

"When was the second time Xavier was arrested, Marisol? Because I don't think I was part of that," I said.

"No, it was the Holler police who arrested him that time. But I know someone from the sheriff's department was involved," Marisol said. "But it was about a year-and-a-half after his first arrest. I came home over Christmas break. Xavier broke into my parents' house when I was home alone. He had a knife and was threatening to kill himself. I had called the police as soon as I heard the window shatter, so the police got there before Xavier had a chance to do anything aside from scare me. I remember they took him to the hospital and had him involuntarily committed again. He was in the psych ward for a while, and then he moved into the group home."

"We'll check into him," Hardy said.

~*~*~

"Howdy, Sergeant Hardy," Uncle Murph said. "You ain't planning to steal our case, are you?"

I almost couldn't see my uncle over the small mountain of paperwork piled on his desk in the sheriff's office. But there he was, messing around on his computer while shoveling Fritos into his mouth by the handful.

"It's all yours. I'm just here to help," Hardy said.

"How'd it go with Miss Santiago?" Quaranta asked.

"It went. Marisol didn't see or hear anything. And she's convinced it had to be a crazy fan who couldn't handle the outcome of the main event. She's giving a statement to one of the deputies right now," I said.

Stepping over the flat tire that was lying on the floor, I moved a crash test dummy off one of the guest chairs and dropped it onto the floor. I wasn't sure where we got the dummy, but the deputies occasionally used him for target practice. We also had a collection of CPR dummies and mannequins for the same purpose.

"Wrestling fans can be pretty crazy," Murph said as he moved aside a pile of paperwork so that he could see Hardy. "And I'm talking from personal experience."

"The only other suspect that Marisol came up with is her ex-boyfriend," I said. "Juan, do you remember Xavier Ortega?"

"The schizophrenic kid? He's hard to forget," Quaranta said.

"Marisol said Xavier's been living in a group home for over a year now. And he's not allowed to leave," I said.

"I'll try to get some warrants and check into it," Murph said.

"What about the victim? Were they able to get x-rays of him?" Quaranta asked.

"Yes, and they came out beautifully," I said as I brought up one of the x-rays of Travis's chest on my tablet and then handed it to Quaranta. "The arrow passed right through the heart. And it also hit both lungs."

"The victim is now on his way to the medical examiner's office. They're going to autopsy him first thing tomorrow morning. I'm interested in seeing how much internal damage this baby caused," Hardy said, laying the evidence bag containing the murder weapon on top of the piles of paperwork on Murph's desk.

"So am I," Quaranta said. "Was the arrow shaft hard to remove?"

"Not really," I said. "We did some research and learned that at the business end of the arrow shaft is this thing called an insert. The broadhead either glues into that, or it screws in. The broadhead the killer used screwed in. All we had to do was unscrew it. Then Sergeant Hardy pulled the shaft out of the body."

"Which wasn't hard to do considering how big of a hole the broadhead left," Hardy said. He found a chair buried under a pile of overflowing dry cleaning bags. After tossing the bags into the corner of the cluttered office, he dragged the chair closer to the desk and had a seat. "How did things go at the SWAT Zone? Did you find anything while combing the woods?"

"We were able to track the shooter's path through the woods. There were a lot of scuff marks in the dirt and broken branches on the trees and bushes. But once the shooter got to the soccer field, we lost the trail. We did find two of those vane things. An orange one and a lime green one." Quaranta held up an evidence bag containing the two vanes.

"Uncle Sterling has security cameras inside the building. Are there any outside?" I asked.

"Just over the doors. We know exactly what time the victims left," Quaranta said.

"But the indoor security cameras filmed the riot. And provided your buddy Vladimir Khrushchev with an alibi. He was by the concession stand just like he claimed," Murph said.

"Good. Not that I really thought Frank was the killer. I just couldn't picture him lurking in the parking lot with a bow and arrow. But what about Post Prom? Was everything okay at the high school?" I asked Murph.

"Everything was A-Okay," Murph said. Frito crumbs spewed out of his mouth, flew across the desk, and struck me in the face. "The prom was held in the Simmonds Hotel's ballroom. It ended around ten o'clock, and Post Prom began at ten-thirty at the high school. The kids had until midnight to get inside before they locked the doors."

"Chew before you speak, Uncle Murph," I said, brushing the crumbs off the front of my shirt. "So, if they didn't have to be inside until midnight, chances are there were probably some kids still hanging out in the parking lot when Travis was shot. One of them could be the killer."

"Trust me, I've already considered that possibility. The victim was the instructor of the archery club after all," Murph said before he spit on his fingers and rubbed them over a stain on his black tie. "But the good thing is that the chaperones were checking IDs and making the kids sign in. We'll have a record of everyone who was at the Post Prom, and what time they entered the building. And once they were inside, they stayed inside until it ended at seven this morning."

"We used to sneak out of the high school all the time," I said.

"Yeah, yeah, yeah. And I know what you kids were sneaking out of school to do," Murph said, winking at me. "I thought about shutting the shindig down and sending the kids home, but I figured they were safe in there. I mean, all the doors were locked. And there were a whole bunch of teachers and parents chaperoning the event. I did leave a couple deputies on site to be safe."

"You did the right thing," I said. "The kids would have been upset if you shut it down. And so would the parents. A lot of their time, money, and hard work went into putting that Post Prom together."

"Tell me about it. I've barely seen my wife for the past two months because she was so busy with the Post Prom committee and helping Luanne get ready for the dance," Murph said just as his phone chimed. He picked it up and winced. "Speaking of my girl…She's been texting me all day to tell me that last night was the most embarrassing moment of her life. She's also accused me of trying to ruin her life."

"What did you do? Or is Luanne just upset that her daddy made an appearance?" I asked.

Knowing Murph, he probably had done something that caused his little girl all sorts of embarrassment. Of course, he wouldn't see it that way. My dad, on the other hand, would have gone out of his way to do something to humiliate me or my two older sisters. The more upset or embarrassed I got; the funnier Dad would have found it. Murph, at least, didn't get a sick joy out of embarrassing his kids.

"Well…you see, I wasn't just going to take the chaperones' word that all of the high school's exterior doors were locked," Murph said. "I had to go around and check for myself. I needed to know that the kids were safe. So I took a lap around the school building to check. I then went back inside to have a quick look around. And, let me tell you, those kids were having quite the party. They had a mechanical bull set up in the one foyer, a dodgeball tournament going on in the gym, movies in the auditorium, and there were video games and karaoke in the cafeteria. Not to mention there were all sorts of carnival games and other stuff for them to do. There was even a magic show that started at three in the morning. We didn't have that sort of thing after my prom. Instead we all got drunk and then tried to get lucky."

"So, did we," Quaranta said.

"I didn't go to my prom," Hardy said.

"I lost count of how many proms I went to," I said.

"Anyway, Luanne was in the cafeteria with a group of her friends. They were taking turns making fools out of themselves while attempting to sing karaoke. I might have caused a tiny scene when I grabbed her idiot boyfriend and hauled him away from her. The way they were dancing…it looked like they were making whoopee with their clothes on. I was tempted to shoot the little twerp right in the shorts," Murph said.

I had some doubts about how 'tiny' the scene was. But it also probably wasn't as huge as Luanne was going to make it out to be.

"I'm sure he'll be forever grateful that you kept such a cool, level head. But that's how kids dance these days. It's called bumping and grinding. And then there's the twerking," I said.

Murph snorted. "Well, it's not how we danced back in my day."

"That's because disco is dead. But don't feel bad. Luanne will get over it," I said.

"If she keeps complaining about it, I'll just remind her that other people had a worse night than she did. Travis's little brother was at the Post Prom. Zachary didn't find out until this morning that his brother had been murdered. And, sadly, he had to hear it from me," Murph said.

"Where are their parents?" Hardy asked.

"Travis's parents are divorced. Have been since Travis was five or six. Both parents remarried and had other kids. Zachary is the victim's half-brother. He and Travis share a father. I had a hard time tracking down Travis's father and stepmother last night. Turns out they were in Corpus Christi for a wedding. They had too much to drink at the reception and didn't hear their phones ringing. I only talked to them a couple hours ago. They're headed back, but I'm sure it's going to be a long six-hour drive for them. But if they left when they said they were going to; they should be getting here in the next hour or two."

"What about the rest of the family?" I asked.

"Travis has an older sister. She took a few deputies over to the house that Travis and Marisol are renting so that we can start collecting their personal stuff. So far, we've got both of their laptops. And Travis had a tablet that he used for school. We also collected Travis's archery equipment," Murph said.

"The victim had four bows, and around five dozen arrows." Quaranta picked up an arrow and laid it down next to the murder weapon. "What he didn't find were broadheads."

"Why is Travis's arrow three or four inches longer than the murder weapon?" I asked.

"That we don't know," Murph said. "Clearly we need to learn a lot more about archery."

"I'll call Uncle Leroy and Uncle Delmar. I'm sure they can educate us," I said, referring to two of my uncles who owned an outdoor store. "Did Travis's sister tell you anything interesting?"

"Not really. She was at last night's event, along with their mom, stepdad, and two younger half-sisters. They all know how mad the fans were, so, at first, they were convinced it was someone in the audience who killed Travis."

"How many people were there last night?" Hardy asked.

"Priscilla counted the ticket stubs while she was sitting around last night. If her count is accurate, there were five-hundred-and-nineteen people over the age of twelve. Kids get in free, but Priscilla is estimating at least a hundred little kids. Not that we suspect the kids," Murph said.

"Did you tell Travis's family how he had been killed?" I asked.

"I did. The sister is the only one who changed her mind about who she thinks the killer might be. She's worried that the killer could be a current or former student in the archery club. She also thinks it's possible her brother angered the wrong person at a competition or while practicing at the range. Apparently, Travis could get really competitive and it annoyed a lot of people," Quaranta said.

"And it's not like Travis was hard to find considering the way Sterling advertises the shows. He has the website and the Facebook page. Plus, Twitter and Instagram. And I'm sure Travis does his own advertising on his social media pages," I said.

"And Sterling hangs up flyers all around the county," Quaranta said.

"I've seen SWAT flyers up in Tyler. Including ones for last night's show," Hardy said.

"Uncle Sterling will also go to other wrestling shows and hand out flyers. And I think some of the wrestlers will take flyers to other shows as well. Like I said, Travis wasn't hard to find last night," I said.

"Despite that, the stepfather, Mr. Thompson, is still convinced it was a crazy fan who was mad that Travis won the main event. Mrs. Thompson can't believe anyone would want to kill her son. She thinks he was mistaken for someone else," Murph said.

"That is a possibility," Quaranta said. "The parking lot was really dark. And one muscle-bound, Speedo-wearing wrestler could have easily been mistaken for another."

"Oh my God..." I whispered. "Red and Travis were parked next to each other. What if the killer mistook Travis and Marisol for me and Red? What if we were really the targets?"

"Have you provoked anyone lately?" Hardy asked.
"Seriously, Jerrod? I aggravate people every day. It's practically my job."

CHAPTER SEVEN

"**G**OD, I DO NOT want to move back here" Marisol whispered. "I can't deal with Mamá trying to control my life."

Marisol's family lived in the nicest, and richest, neighborhood within the Holler city limits. The neighborhood was less than a mile away from Wyatt County General Hospital and less than two miles from the center of town. An enclosed front porch ran along the entire front of the large, two-story yellow house. There was a two-car garage around back, and, perpendicular to the garage, was a metal carport with three cars parked under it.

As Hardy pulled up the circular drive to park in front of the house, the front door flew open. An older Latina woman, wearing a pale green pantsuit and three strands of pearls, rushed outside and barreled down the front walk. Hardy and I had already met Marisol's mother, Yesinia Santiago, at the hospital. When we went to see Marisol, we found Yesinia terrorizing the hospital staff and threatening to sue them if they didn't let her in the room to see her oldest daughter. Hardy had a deputy escort Yesinia home while he and I went in to see Marisol.

"Oh, Marisol, are you all right? How's your arm?" Yesinia asked as she wrenched open the rear passenger side door of Hardy's truck and hauled Marisol out of the backseat.

"My arm would feel much better if you stopped squeezing it, Mamá." Marisol peeled her mother's clutching hand off her injured bicep.

"I'm so sorry. How badly are you injured?" Mrs. Santiago asked as she transferred her vice-like grip to her daughter's wrist.

"Mamá, Travis is dead. Do you think I really care about my arm?"

"Oh, well, yes. Poor Travis. What a tragedy. You must be devastated. Mamá is going to put you right to bed. You need to rest," Yesinia said, sounding rather flippant considering her daughter's boyfriend had been murdered.

Pulling her by the arm, Yesinia guided Marisol up the front walk to the porch. Hardy and I followed Yesinia and Marisol up the porch steps to the front door. I was about to step through the doorway when Yesinia turned around, told us we weren't welcome at the moment, and tried to slam the door in my face. Hardy reached around me and braced his hand against the door, stopping it about an inch from my nose.

Stepping inside, I felt like I was walking on to the set of a photo shoot for an interior design magazine. Aside from the countless pictures of Marisol hanging on the walls or sitting in frames around the room, there weren't any personal touches in the Santiago's combined living and dining rooms. I spotted a few pictures of Marisol's sisters, as well as Mr. and Mrs. Santiago, but it seemed to me that the majority of the pictures on display were of Marisol. I noticed that Travis wasn't in any of the pictures with Marisol.

Seated throughout the spacious living room were a handful of people. Marisol quickly introduced them as her father, maternal grandmother, and two younger sisters. The sisters, Annalisa and Evita, had the same long, black hair as Marisol. Evita, with her brown eyes, high cheekbones, and pouty lips, was just as beautiful as Marisol. Annalisa was a shorter, chubbier version of her sisters. Her beauty was more natural, but she paled in comparison to her sisters.

"And that's Zachary. Travis's little brother," Marisol said as she pointed at the despondent looking teenager seated on the loveseat next to Evita. Marisol pushed past her family members to give her boyfriend's brother a hug. "I'm so sorry, Zachary. I'm so, so sorry. I know Travis was your hero."

When I first saw Zachary Yeager, I had to do a double take because I swore Travis had come back to life. On closer inspection, Zachary still had a baby face, and he wasn't quite as muscular as Travis. The brothers did have a similar shade of dark blue eyes and dirty blonde hair, though Zachary's was a little shaggier. I assumed that Travis and Zachary bore a close resemblance to their father.

"Zachary, can we have a word?" Hardy asked, rescuing the embarrassed teenager from Marisol's smothering hug. "We need to ask you some questions about Travis."

"Uh, yeah, sure." Zachary pulled away from Marisol, whispered something to Evita, and then followed me and Hardy onto the front porch. "I want to, you know, do whatever I can to help you guys find the guy who killed my brother. And attacked Marisol. Jesus, I'm glad she's going to be okay. She is going to be okay, right?"

"Marisol will be fine. Her wound is superficial," I said.

"Good. That's good. Travis loved her so much," Zachary said.

I waited until Zachary, Hardy, and I had a seat on the wicker furniture before asking, "Zachary, how did you wind up at the Santiago's house today?"

"Evie is my girlfriend," Travis said as he nervously drummed his fingers on this thighs. "And I really didn't have anywhere else to go. I mean, I could have gone home, I guess. But my parents aren't there. They've been in Corpus Christi for a wedding since Thursday. And I don't have any other family in the area. This was, like, the only place I could think of to go. Especially since I had to bring Evie home after Post Prom anyway."

"So you and Evita went to the prom?" I asked.

"Yep. We left a little early so we could go see Travis's match. Evie is a wrestling fan, too. We…we weren't going to go see the match, but Travis texted me and said he was going to win the title. I couldn't miss that…Your aunt Priscilla let me and Evie come in for free. She even let us stand on one of the merchandise tables so that we could see…" Scooting forward in his chair, Zachary leaned towards me and asked, "What happened last night, Detective Shatner? Because all the sheriff told me this morning was that Travis was fatally shot after the show."

"We're still trying to figure out what happened," I said. I then told Zachary about the last minute change in plans due to Red's retirement, and then gave him a rundown of the match and the following riot. "The majority of the fans were very upset that your brother beat Red. Right now, we don't know if a fan murdered your brother, but if you know of any fans who might have already had it out for Travis…"

"I assumed it was a nutcase fan as soon as the sheriff told me Travis was dead," Zachary said. "Travis loved playing the heel part. Probably 'cause he's such a nice guy in real life. Being the bad guy let him pretend to be someone totally different. And he thought it was hilarious that he was able to make the fans hate him so much. He loved getting booed and having the fans talk trash to him. And he got a kick out of all of the nasty letters and messages the fans sent him. But I don't know of anyone who seriously hated my brother enough to want to kill him."

"Zachary, were you and Travis close?" Hardy asked.

"Not really. He's ten yours older than me, so he was just the cool older brother that I looked up to and idolized. He didn't really have time for a tagalong little brother. And, growing up, I only ever saw him every other weekend. If that. Travis is my half-brother. Same dad. Different moms. Travis lived with his mom. That's why I didn't seen him much. It wasn't until the past couple years that we started bonding," Zachary said.

"Did Travis get you into pro wrestling and archery as well?" Hardy asked.

"Wrestling, yeah. I was never a fan until Travis started training. To be honest, I'm still not really a fan. I think it's kinda stupid. Grown men and women pretending to beat up each other…But I am a fan of my brother, so I would go to the shows to support him," Zachary said as he rubbed his hands up and down his thighs. "As for archery…years ago, Travis taught me how to do it. I liked it, but I couldn't really get into it. Not when I'm a baseball pitcher. I can't risk messing up my arm and ruining my baseball career. I think it's cool that he started the archery club at the high school though. I don't know too much about it, but Evie can probably tell you everything."

"How long have you and Evita been dating?" I asked.

"Since July. We were both volunteering as counselors at the summer camp they have at the high school. It's for the elementary age kids. Evita was doing arts and crafts classes, and I was teaching sports. All of us counselors started hanging out after camp ended each day."

"Were you two friends before you started dating?" I asked.

"No. There's, like, two groups of popular kids in our graduating class. The kids who are actually popular. And the kids who think they're popular but aren't exactly liked by the popular crowd. The two groups don't hang out together. I've been in the popular group since ninth grade. Evita was, you know, in the other group. She's also in all of the advanced classes. I'm not. So we never hung out until this past summer. Then, once we started hanging out, I realized that I liked her. So I asked her out."

"What did you and Evita do after you left the SWAT Zone?" I asked.

"We drove over to the high school and hung out in my car until it was almost midnight. Evie and I…we don't get a lot of alone time…So we took advantage of the time we had last night…" Zachary jumped to his feet when a Lexus turned into the Santiago's driveway. "That's my parents. I've got to go. I have to be with them. My dad is devastated. Can you tell the Santiagos that I said thank you. And that I'm going to leave my car here. I'll come get it, well, sometime. And let me know if you've got any more questions."

Zachary sprinted down the porch steps and jumped into the backseat of his parents' SUV. He didn't even have the back door shut before the SUV began to drive away.

"You'd think the Yeagers would have come in to check on Marisol," I said.

"They're probably too upset about Travis's death to think about anyone else right now," Hardy said as he stood up and headed towards the front door. "Come on, Carrie. I'll talk to Mr. and Mrs. Santiago while you talk to the sisters."

Inside, Hardy and I found Marisol's parents arguing in the living room. They stopped as soon as we walked in the room. Through the open doorway that led from the dining room to the spotless, roomy kitchen I saw that Marisol was seated at the island. Her grandmother bustled around the kitchen, helping herself to a glass of wine while she fried up sopaipillas. After snagging a plate of the fresh pastries, I headed upstairs in search of Evita and Annalisa.

As I walked up the steps, I could feel the immaculate, depersonalized first floor fade away. The girls, who each had their own bedroom upstairs, had turned the second floor of the house into their own personal domain, starting with the sky blue paint on the hallway walls.

At the top of the steps, I glanced around the landing at the five open doorways. I assumed that the empty bedroom at the top of the steps was Marisol's old bedroom. She'd just finished moving out of her parents' house, and now she would be moving back in.

Skipping the bathroom, I stuck my head into the other two bedrooms. The bedroom with the electric purple colored walls was a mess. Notebooks and textbooks were scattered all over the desk, and there were clothes all over the floor. The pictures of Zachary tacked to the walls informed me that this was Evita's room. Annalisa's room was orderly, and the only thing dressing up the sage walls were artistic pictures and paintings of flowers.

"Evita? Annalisa?" I called after finding both bedrooms empty.

"We're in here," one of the girls said.

Following the voice, I finished making my way down the hallway. I then pushed through a beaded curtain and walked into a large, open room that the Santiago sisters used as their personal living room. Annalisa lay curled up on the sectional with her face buried in a pillow as she cried. Evita sat beside Annalisa, rubbing her back and whispering to her. Evita's eyes were dry, and her heavily made up face was devoid of emotion. The fact that her makeup was perfect informed me that she hadn't done any crying. Or, at least, she hadn't cried since putting on the makeup.

"Sorry to disturb you, but…is she all right?" I asked.

Evita shook her head. "Annalisa has been having anxiety attacks ever since we found out that Marisol was attacked. She can't calm down."

Sitting up, Annalisa asked, "Are you going to find the person who tried to kill our sister?"

"Sergeant Hardy and I are going to do our best, but I can't promise you that we will," I said. Walking over to the other side of the room, I glanced out of one of the three windows and looked down at Hardy's truck parked in the driveway. "Would you two mind telling me about Marisol? Her depiction of herself was a bit biased."

"She's wonderful," Annalisa said. "Absolutely perfect."

Evita scrunched up her nose and snorted. "No, she's a perfectionist…"

"Evita!" Annalisa snapped as she shoved her sister and almost knocked her off the couch. "How can you talk badly about Marisol? She almost died last night!"

"I'm not talking badly about Marisol. I'm telling the truth," Evita said. Standing up, Evita put some distance between herself and Annalisa. "I can love her and still say bad things about her, right?"

"Sure you can," I said, thankful that Evita was willing to be candid. If everyone was going to tell us that Marisol and Travis were wonderful and perfect, it would be difficult to come up with a motive as to why someone wanted to kill either of them. "And I know what you mean, Evita. I have two older sisters, too. I love both of them, but there are still times when I want to jerk them both bald."

"Exactly!" Warming up to me, Evita sidled closer and whispered, "Marisol has a way of convincing everyone that she is this amazing person, but she isn't as perfect as she tries to make everyone believe. I'm not saying she isn't great, because she is. But she is a perfectionist and she gets all childish when things don't turn out the way she wants them to. Everything has to be her way. And she is super bossy. And that you can't deny, Annalisa."

"So what if she is bossy?" Annalisa asked. "Evita, our sister was almost killed last night. The least you can do is stop whining about how she bossed you around when we were kids."

"I'll stop whining if you stop worshipping the ground that Marisol walks on."

"Calm down, girls. This is not the time for fighting," I said stepping between the two angry young women. "Right now the most important thing is supporting Marisol. And helping me figure out who attacked her. Is there anyone you can come up with who might have wanted to kill your sister?"

"No. There is no one who could have wanted to kill Marisol. She is the nicest, sweetest person in the world," Annalisa said.

Evita rolled her eyes. "I can't come up with anyone off the top of my head, Detective Shatner. Other than Marisol's ex-boyfriend, Xavier. But he's been gone for years."

"What about Travis? Marisol said that both of you were his students," I said.

Calming down, Annalisa said, "I liked Travis way better as my future brother-in-law than I ever did as my teacher."

"That's because you hated gym class," Evita said.

"Well, that played a part. I'm really not that athletic," Annalisa admitted. "But I had Travis during his first semester as a gym teacher. He tried to make class fun, but then he would get super strict if we had too much fun. I thought he was annoying."

"Well, Travis was my favorite teacher. I thought he was awesome. But I'm athletic, so I love gym class," Evita said.

"You also had a major crush on Travis," Annalisa said.

"So did most of the other girls," Evita said as she lowered her head, allowing her long, black hair to fall in front of her face. "I just thought he was handsome."

"Was it awkward for you when Marisol and Travis started dating?" I asked.

"Maybe a little," Evita said. "But not because of my crush on Travis. That was nothing."

"Uh, yeah, it was definitely something," Annalisa said.

"Shut up, Annalisa!" Evita grabbed a sopaipilla and lobbed it at her sister. "I was over my crush by the time Travis and Marisol started dating. What made it awkward was that a bunch of my classmates were giving me crap about it. Actually, they're still giving me a hard time."

"You were at the prom and Post Prom last night?" I asked Evita.

"Yep. I went with Zachary. And a bunch of our friends. We had so much fun," Evita said.

"Zachary told me that you two left the prom a little early to go see Travis's match."

Evita nodded and said, "It was Travis's first time winning the SWAT Championship. Zachary and I had to see it. We just didn't expect the fans to start rioting. We ran outside as soon as the fans started throwing stuff. I wanted to go find Marisol and Travis afterwards, but Zachary was worried about getting over to the high school before midnight. Not that we didn't have plenty of time…"

"What time did you and Zachary go into the high school?" I asked.

"Right before midnight. We hung out in his car for a while and talked first," Evita said.

"I bet you two did more than talk," Annalisa snapped.

"You're just jealous because you don't have a boyfriend," Evita said.

"What were you up to last night, Annalisa?" I asked, hoping to diffuse the tension that was still mounting between the two sisters.

"I was hanging here with my parents," Annalisa said.

"God, Annalisa, you are so lame. Can't you, like, make some friends for once in your life?" Evita asked.

"Girls…Remember, now is not the time for you two to be fighting." Switching topics, I asked Evita, "How did you get into archery? Why join the club?"

"I joined when I was a freshman. Travis had just started the club." Evita gave me a small smile. "There was a senior boy in the club that I had a crush on. I joined, hoping that he would notice me. He didn't."

"Then why stay in the club?" I asked.

"She stayed because of her crush on Travis," Annalisa said.

"No. I stayed in the club because I really enjoy archery. I'm actually pretty good at it," Evita said.

"Yay, you're good at shooting arrows at targets. Yippee. How exciting," Annalisa said.

"I take it you're not into archery?" I asked Annalisa.

"Hardly. Evita showed me how to do it when she first started. And Travis gave me some lessons when he was teaching Marisol. But I just don't get the point of it," Annalisa said.

I was about to ask Evita about the kids in the archery club when Marisol wandered into the room. Knocking me aside, Evita launched herself into Marisol's arms. And then, for the first time since Hardy and I walked into the house, Evita began to cry. She literally clung to Marisol as she sobbed against her shoulder and bemoaned the loss of Travis.

Glancing over my shoulder, I made eye contact with Annalisa and raised my eyebrow in silent question. Annalisa rolled her eyes and stuck out her tongue in disgust.

A few minutes later, Hardy and I slipped out of the Santiago's house.

"I didn't get anything useful out of the parents. Mr. and Mrs. Santiago insist that their daughter is perfect, and that she has no enemies," Hardy said. "And, while they didn't come out and say it, I got the impression that they did not like Travis. At all."

"The youngest sister, Evita, had a major crush on Travis back when she was freshman. And I'm not quite sure that she's over it," I said.

"You don't suspect Evita killed Travis and attempted to kill her own sister, do you? Because that would be cold."

"Evita was with Zachary over at the high school when Travis was getting killed. I just think it's kind of weird that Evita started dating Travis's little brother a year or so after Marisol hooked up with Travis."

~*~*~

"How much longer do you think you can go, Jerrod?" I asked just after six o'clock.

"I'm exhausted. But I can go for a couple more hours, I guess. As long as it's for a good cause. Why? Is something going on?" Hardy asked.

"Uncle Sterling just texted me. He's down at Catfish's Cantina with a handful of the wrestlers and a bunch of fans. They're having some sort of impromptu vigil for Travis. And Sterling says he has something he needs to show us," I said.

"Then let's grab some deputies and get down there."

Catfish's Cantina was a dive bar at the southern edge of Holler. Red's father, Catfish, owned the bar. He also owned the liquor store next door. Red was the main bartender at the Cantina, and, now that he was retired from wrestling, he planned on taking over the bar fulltime.

It only took us a couple of minutes to drive from the sheriff's department to the bar. Pulling into the packed gravel parking lot, Hardy drove around the lot in search of an empty parking spot. Not finding one, Hardy was forced to park next door at Catfish's Beer and Fine Liquor Emporium.

Both the bar and the liquor store looked a bit rundown on the outside, and neither had an overly welcoming appearance. The inside of the bar used to be just as unsightly as the outside, but Red started remodeling it a few months ago. He was attempting to turn the dive bar into more of a sports bar.

Hardy was reaching for the handle of the heavy, wood front door of the bar when the door was suddenly flung open. Hardy and I instinctively jumped back from the door as Frank Smith and his wife, Oksana, stomped outside. Frank had on one of his Vladimir Khrushchev t-shirts and his ushanka hat. Oksana, who only came up to the middle of Frank's chest, had on a matching shirt and hat.

"You ain't still thinking I'm a suspect are you, Carrie?" Frank asked.

"Nice to see you, too, Frank," I said. "And, no, we don't consider you a suspect. We cleared you. Thank Sterling for putting up the security cameras inside the SWAT Zone. One of them caught you by the concession stands."

"Told you I didn't kill Travis," Frank said.

"You still threatened to kill him. I've got to take that kind of stuff seriously." Stepping closer to Oksana, I said, "But we haven't cleared you. Did you really take your daughter home last night? Or was that an excuse to lurk in the parking lot?"

"You think I waste my time on those useless fools? You think I shame my husband by killing them? No. Taking their lives is not worth sacrificing my own," Oksana said.

After calling me an unflattering name in Russian, Oksana stalked across the parking lot to Frank's car. Frank hurried along after her.

Hardy and I waited until after the Smiths tore out of the gravel parking lot on two wheels before we ventured inside. The compact barroom was nearly wall-to-wall with people. While I didn't frequent the Cantina, this was the most people I had seen in the place during one of my rare visits. I spotted a few wrestlers who had been at the SWAT event the night before, but the majority of the people in the crowd were wrestling fans.

Hardy and I were pushing our way through the crowd when someone grabbed me from behind and tightly wrapped her arms around me.

"Carrie! Oh, Carrie, honey, I've been so worried about you! Oh, sweetie, when I heard that one of the wrestlers had been killed I about had a heart attack. I knew it wasn't you since your Granddaddy was listening in on the police scanner and we heard you talking. But to think you were that close to danger just gives me the chills."

My grandma, Thelma Shatner, spun me around and then clutched me to her massive chest. She also planted a kiss on both of my cheeks. Grandma Thelma was shorter than me, and not much heavier. Her white hair was also currently dyed a remarkable shade of violet. I was scared to ask if the violet hair had been on purpose or an accident.

"I'm fine, Grandma. I was inside the building when Travis was murdered," I said. I extracted myself from her stranglehold of a hug only to be pulled into someone else's arms. "Hey, Granddaddy."

"You being careful out there, Carrie? You're not taking unnecessary risks, are you?" Granddaddy asked. David Crockett Shatner released me and then turned to Hardy. While enthusiastically shaking Hardy's hand, Granddaddy asked, "Are you taking care of my little girl? Making sure she stays out of trouble?"

"I'm not a little girl," I muttered.

"I'm not sure if anyone is up to the task of keeping Carrie out of trouble," Hardy said. "But I promise to make sure no harm comes to her during the investigation."

I rolled my eyes as Grandma tightly hugged Hardy and told him repeatedly that he was a nice young man.

My grandparents had been two of the only Shatners who had approved of my relationship with Hardy. I think Grandma might have been more upset over the breakup than I was. Then again, I had always been extremely close to my paternal grandparents. They had been better caretakers and role models than my own parents had been. I had missed them terribly during the years I had been away from home.

Grandma was the type of woman who didn't take crap from anyone, and she had raised me to be the same way. She hadn't been pleased when I followed in Granddaddy's and my dad's shoes and went to work for the sheriff's department. Like me, Granddaddy and Dad had been expected to clean up after the rest of the Shatners. And they had both been good at it. Granddaddy had also been an exemplary deputy, and later he was elected sheriff.

After talking to my grandparents for a few minutes, Hardy and I headed across the crowded barroom to join Red, Uncle Sterling, Naomi, and Deputy Timmy Grant at a table in the back corner.

"Why's Priscilla doing an impersonation of Scarlett O'Hara at the Twelve Oaks barbeque?" I asked Sterling as I pointed to where Aunt Priscilla held sway over half a dozen of the men who frequently wrestled for SWAT.

"The wrestlers are kissing her butt and bribing her to put in a good word for them. They all want to be the next SWAT Heavyweight Champion," Sterling said.

"Any idea who you're going to give the title to?" I asked, wondering who Uncle Sterling would choose to be the next SWAT Champion.

"I'll probably give it to Vladimir Khrushchev since that was the original plan. Or maybe I'll draw a name out of a hat. That's what I usually do when I can't decide who should win a match," Sterling said.

"And here I was convinced you put a lot of thought into deciding your storylines and who is going to win each match," I said as I adjusted Sterling's toupee so that it wasn't lopsided. "So what's so important that you wanted to show us?"

"Pull up a chair and I'll show you," Sterling said.

"You can have our chairs," Red said as he stood up. He then pulled Naomi's chair back from the table and gestured for her to get up. "I've got to get back behind the bar. And Naomi has been helping out by waitressing. We'll let you know if we overhear anything."

"Call when you decide who you're gonna wrestle at next month's show. I wanna start advertising the match as soon as possible," Sterling yelled after Red. He then grabbed the laptop that Timmy was looking at. "To answer your question, Carrie, the four of us were doing a little detective work to help y'all out."

"Sterling, please don't stick your nose in our investigation," Hardy said as he had a seat next to my uncle. "We're dealing with what appears to be a dangerous killer. Just let the professionals handle it. It's what we're trained to do."

"Y'all were busy earlier, so I called Deputy Grant. He's almost a professional. And one of my biggest fans," Sterling said.

"That doesn't explain why Naomi and Red are involved," I said.

"Yeah, well, deal with it. We're just trying to help," Sterling said as he brought up the Shatner Wrestling Association of Texas Facebook page and scrolled down to the most recent post. "It all started when I posted this… Murph said it was okay for me to put something on the SWAT page about Travis getting killed and Marisol being hurt. So I made an announcement and typed up something really nice about their contributions to SWAT. I also posted a bunch of pictures and started a donation fund. You know, to help pay for the funeral or for Marisol's hospital bills."

"You're a real saint, Uncle Sterling," I said.

"I'm just praying that Travis's family don't try to sue me. Or Marisol. That's why I made a hefty donation already," Sterling said. "Anywho, Priscilla checked the page about an hour later and found a bunch of idiots making ignorant comments. Pris wanted me to delete them, but I came to the conclusion that one of these idiots could be your killer…Let me read some of this crap to you."

As Sterling read some of the comments aloud, I scanned through the whole thread to see what people were saying about what happened last night. The majority of the people who commented on the post expressed grief and anger over what happened to Travis and Marisol. But there were also a handful of people who stated they were glad that Travis had been killed and lamented that Marisol hadn't been killed as well. A couple people wished that the killer had struck sooner and took out Travis before the match.

"This is disgusting. Travis was murdered, and these jerks are happy about it. There are some twisted people in this world," I said. Leaning around Sterling, I tapped Hardy on the shoulder. "Jerrod, did you see that Evita and Zachary have been trying to defend Travis and Marisol?"

"Yes. And it makes me sick that they have to see this stuff. I can't imagine how tough it must be for them." Turning to Timmy, Hardy asked, "Have you been jotting down a list of names, Deputy Grant? Every single one of these people needs to be questioned."

Timmy held up a notebook. "Mama and I know a few of the people who made comments. Some of them were at the show last night. And we recognized a couple more from their profile pictures. We've seen them around at events. I've already talked to the sheriff about tracking these people down."

"But it ain't just the SWAT page that people are commenting on. Travis's personal Facebook page is under a pseudonym and it's private, so I can't look at it without being his friend. Which I'm not since he never accepted my friend request. He does have a public Facebook fan page that we can look at." Sterling brought up a new internet tab and then opened up Travis's Beast from East Texas Facebook fan page. "People are making similar comments on here as well. And it's the same on Twitter."

"And we found the wrestler whose neck Travis broke," Timmy said. "His character's name is J-Dag. I've seen him a few times, but he mainly wrestles in West Texas and New Mexico. He's a very large black man. I don't know what Travis was thinking when he decided to go for the piledriver. J-Dag has to outweigh him by at least fifty pounds."

"J-Dag has been posting a lot of videos on Facebook over the past month. And he's been tagging Travis in them." Sterling clicked on a link that J-Dag had shared on Travis's page two days earlier. "This is the most recent one. You'll get to see the piledriver. And hear J-Dag threaten to kill Travis."

A black man wearing a neck brace popped up on screen and immediately went into a profanity-laced tirade about how much he hated Travis. After showing footage of the botched piledriver, J-Dag leaned closer to the camera and screamed, "I'm gonna git you, Travis! As soon as the doctors clear me, I'm gonna git your scrawny ass! I'm gonna beat you! I'm gonna make you wish you were dead! And then I'm gonna kill you!"

"Timmy, make a note that we need to talk to J-Dag. It's possible he decided that he couldn't wait until the doctors cleared him. He also appears to be the right kind of crazy to shoot someone with a bow and arrow," I said.

"Stay on this, Deputy Grant. Tracking these people is now your top priority," Hardy said as he pushed his chair back and stood up. "I'm going to get out of here, Carrie. Are you going to stick around? Or do you want a ride home?"

"I'm about to drop, so I'll take the ride," I said. "The deputies can stick around until Red shuts the bar down. They'll let us know if they find out anything."

Hardy and I were headed for the door when I heard someone shouting my name. Turning back towards the bar, I found Red pointing towards the other side of the room.

"Naomi found her next prey and is moving in for the kill. You might want to break it up," Red shouted.

I scanned the room and spotted Naomi perched on a man's lap. Considering that her tongue was down his throat, it looked like she'd already moved in for the kill and was in the process of devouring him.

"You may as well leave, Jerrod. I'll get a ride with Naomi."

Making my way over to the other side of the room, I tapped Naomi on the shoulder. When Naomi turned around, I realized she was making out with one of the wrestlers who had been at the SWAT Zone the night before. The man wasn't much taller than me, but he had massive muscles. He also had terrible 'roid rage thanks to his overuse of steroids.

"What do you want?" Naomi asked.

"I hate to interrupt. But I'm leaving," I said.

"Yeah, so what? You need a ride or something?" Naomi asked.

"I do. I also think it's time you went home," I said.

"Sorry, Carrie. Naomi is staying. Find someone else to take you home," the wrestler said. "Unless you want to come home with me, too."

"I don't think so," I said. For all I knew, Mr. 'Roid Rage would take Naomi back to his house, lock her up, and keep her as a sex slave. "You're going to have to find another chick."

I dragged Naomi off the guy's lap and hustled her out the door.

Out in the parking lot, Naomi pulled away from me and said, "I can't believe you just did that, Carrie. That guy was totally into me."

"The only thing he wanted to get into was your pants," I said as I grabbed Naomi's keys and gave her a shove in the direction of her car.

"That was the point!" Naomi shouted as she climbed into the passenger side of her convertible and slammed the door.

"You can do better than that guy. He isn't anywhere near your league," I said as I climbed in behind the wheel. "You have got to raise your standards."

"Well, duh. You think I don't know that? But what am I supposed to do? The good guys are either taken or prefer you."

"What are you talking about?" I asked.

"Oh, come on. Last night three wrestlers hit on you. And a bunch of fans. For every ten men that hit on you, one hit on me," Naomi said.

"Okay, I did notice that. But it's not like any of those men were prizes."

Hitting the gas, I pulled out of the parking lot and turned north towards Holler.

"Well, no…But Red has been in love with you for years."

"It's not like I encourage him."

"And the sexy Texas Ranger clearly wants to get back together with you."

"Oh, he does not," I said, wondering where Naomi came up with such a ridiculous idea. "Why do you say that?"

"Uh, hello. Have you noticed the way he was looking at you? It's pretty freaking obvious he regrets breaking up with you," Naomi said as she slumped over against the window. "Why should you have all the good men?"

"What are you talking about?" I asked, wondering if Naomi had lost her mind or if she had noticed something about Hardy that I hadn't. "I don't have anybody."

"Well, you're closer to having someone than I am! I'm never going to find anyone!" Naomi said. She then kicked the dashboard and screamed. "I'm going to turn into one of those crazy cat ladies who roams around town in her bathrobe."

"I won't let that happen. Besides, you're only twenty-six. You have plenty of time to find someone." I reached across the center console, grabbed Naomi's shoulder, and gave her a shake.

"If I'm not married by the time I'm your age, I think I'll kill myself."

"Don't be so dramatic. Thirty-one isn't that old," I said.

"Then why do you tell everyone that you're still twenty-nine?" Naomi asked.

"Because being over thirty sucks!" I said as I pulled in Naomi's driveway and turned off the engine. I then turned to her and said, "Naomi, you don't have a problem attracting men. You just need to focus your energies on finding a good one. Then maybe you will be married before you're as ancient as I am."

CHAPTER EIGHT

"Guns...and Stuff. An Outdoor Emporium," Hardy said, reading the billboard-sized sign hanging on the side of the building. The sides of the building were currently painted in a sloppy brown, green, and gray camouflage print. There was also a gigantic Texas flag painted on the roof. "I'm not sure I want to know what 'stuff' entails. Not when your family is involved."

My uncles' store, Guns n' Stuff, was housed in a renovated three-story wood and stone barn that my great-great-grandfather had built at the very southern edge of the original plot of land he purchased back in the late eighteen hundreds. Since then, my family had amassed roughly five thousand acres in the northern section of the county. A number of the Shatners lived on the land, and some had businesses – both legal and illegal – around the extensive property.

Mounting the porch steps, I walked between the two six-foot-tall cowboys carved from tree trunks that stood sentinel on either side of the front door. I then shoved aside the decorative wooden barn door to reveal the store's double glass doors.

"You know the saying 'don't mix business with pleasure'? Or how about 'don't shit where you eat'?" I asked Hardy. "A lot of my family members may be involved in various illegal activities, but all of them keep it separate from their one or two legal enterprises. Take Uncle Sterling for example...I'm betting I don't even know a fraction of what he's involved in. But I can guarantee he doesn't let anything illegal come near SWAT. So don't worry about what Leroy and Delmar are referring to as 'stuff,' because it's all legal."

Passing through the front doors, Hardy and I were greeted by a taxidermied black bear that my uncle Delmar shot while on a hunting trip in Canada. The bear, known as Doc Holliday, had an oversized foam cowboy hat perched on his head and he held a shotgun in his massive paws. Throughout the rest of the store were other taxidermied animals dressed in random outfits.

"Your uncles have some fascinating interior design ideas," Hardy said as he looked around the first floor of the store. "I particularly like the longhorn steer wearing the Elvis sunglasses and wig."

"Uncle Delmar kills them. Then Uncle Leroy stuffs and decorates them. My personal favorites are the six bucks dressed up as the Village People. They're on the wall above the gun counter," I said as I pointed towards the back wall of the store.

Hardy and I wandered around the cramped first floor, weaving our way through the racks and shelves full of ammunition, gun parts, and hunting paraphernalia, until we came across Uncle Leroy lounging in his usual position behind the firearms counter.

Leroy and Delmar were Uncle Houston's two sons. Leroy was also Naomi's dad, and, from him, she got her height. Luckily Naomi got her looks and body type from her mother. Leroy was a tall, gangly, unattractive man with a sweet disposition and a comb over that wasn't fooling anyone. When he wasn't selling firearms to people or dressing up dead animals, Leroy was more often than not at the family's still brewing moonshine.

"Hey, Uncle Leroy, thanks for opening up the store a couple of hours early for us," I said.

"Carrie. Mr. Ranger," Leroy said as he nodded at both of us. "Delmar and I don't mind losing a couple hours of sleep if it means helping y'all get to the bottom of who killed Travis. We both knew the boy, and we're real sorry he got himself killed. Now what is it you want me to look at?"

"We need some information on the murder weapon. But first we need you to promise not to tell anyone what the murder weapon is," I said.

"Must be real interesting if you ain't sharing it with the public yet."

"Interesting is one way to term it," Hardy said.

I had brought along the arrow that struck Marisol in the arm so that Leroy and Delmar could examine it. I laid the long evidence bag on the counter and pulled out the arrow, which was wrapped up in a thick layer of brown paper.

Once I had the arrow unwrapped save for a clear, plastic evidence bag, I pushed it closer to Leroy and asked, "What can you tell us about this?"

"Don't that take the cake?" Leroy asked as he leaned so far forward that his nose almost touched the blood-coated arrow. He remained that way for a few seconds before he looked up at me and said, "That there is an arrow."

"Oh, wow, Jerrod, did you hear that? Our murder weapon is an arrow. This is a major break in the case," I said before I smacked my hand down on the glass-topped gun display cabinet to get Leroy's attention. "Of course, we know it's an arrow."

"We were hoping you could tell us more about the arrow," Hardy said.

"Archery really ain't my specialty. I'm the gun guy," Leroy said.

"Yeah, I'm the archery specialist," Uncle Delmar said. Delmar, who was a slightly shorter, wider, and older version of Leroy, stepped through the metal door leading to the indoor gun range. They also had an indoor archery range, plus outdoor ranges. "Is that the murder weapon? Saddle my back and call me a horse."

"What can you tell us about the arrow?" Hardy asked.

"Well, the shaft is made out of aluminum. And it's got a small diameter, so it ain't too sturdy," Delmar said as he looked over the arrow from the broadhead to the vanes. "If it was me, I'd have used a carbon arrow with a bigger diameter."

"You want to explain all that to us, Uncle Delmar? Sergeant Hardy and I have no idea what you're talking about," I said.

"Be easier to show you. Come on upstairs to my archery department," Delmar said.

After wrapping up the arrow and putting it back in the evidence bag, Hardy and I followed my uncles upstairs. As we walked single-file up the narrow, wooden staircase, Delmar told us that Travis Yeager was a regular at Guns n' Stuff. He used the archery ranges on an almost weekly basis. According to Delmar, Travis was well liked around Guns n' Stuff and didn't have any problems with the other archers who used the ranges.

Upstairs, Delmar led us past the fishing and camping equipment and took us into the archery section. There were a few racks full of different brands of bows and arrows, along with piles of targets and shelves full of archery accessories.

"This here is an aluminum arrow. It's similar to your murder weapon," Delmar said as he pulled a long, thin arrow shaft out of a bucket. With his hands at either end of the shaft, Delmar slightly bent the arrow back and forth. "Notice how easily the spine bends? A carbon arrow ain't gonna bend like this. That's why I prefer carbon arrows. They're more durable. And I like durability when I'm hunting. I used to bend up a whole lot of aluminum arrows. You know, from hitting the prey's bones or a tree. Or because I dropped the arrow and accidently stepped on it." Delmar handed Hardy the aluminum arrow and then grabbed another arrow out of a different bucket. He tried to bend this arrow, but the spine wouldn't flex. "This arrow spine is one of the larger diameter carbon ones that I stock. You ain't gonna bend this one. That's not to say carbon arrows can't get damaged though. But this is the type of arrow spine I would have used if I was your killer."

"Is there anything significant about the arrow the killer used?" I asked.

"Nope. This is a common brand. We sell this kind in the store," Delmar said.

"Do you keep records of who you sell them to?" I asked.

"Of course, we keep records," Delmar said.

"We keep records of everything," Leroy added.

"We're going to need to see those records," Hardy said.

"Don't you need a warrant for that?" Delmar asked as he took a step backwards and crossed his arms over his chest. "It ain't like you can't get these shafts anywhere. You can even order 'em over the internet."

"Can't you just cooperate and give us the records?" I asked.

Leroy and Delmar both gave me withering looks that let me know they were ashamed I asked. Just because they didn't do anything wrong didn't mean they were going to go out of their way to help.

"Fine, we'll get a warrant," I said.

"See that you do," Leroy said.

Delmar rummaged around under the counter until he found a tape measure. While he measured the length of the murder weapon, he rambled on about things called draw length and weight – from what I could understand, draw length was how far back a bowstring could be pulled and draw weight was how much pressure it took to pull the bowstring back that far.

When Delmar started talking about arrow length, I interrupted and asked, "What does the length of the shaft have to do with anything?"

Leroy was the first to start laughing, but it didn't take long for Delmar to join in. Hardy was the only one not laughing, though his eyes were shining, his mouth kept twitching, and he snorted two or three times.

"Don't tell me you're one of those gals who says size don't matter," Delmar said.

"You guys are so mature," I said, glaring at all of them. "The reason I'm asking is because this arrow shaft is twenty-six inches long. The ones we collected from Travis's house are twenty-nine inches. I want to know why they're different lengths."

Delmar cleared his throat. "Uh, Carrie, to answer your question…arrow shafts can be cut down to different lengths. Like you said, this arrow you've got here is twenty-six inches long. Your killer would have used a bow with a draw length of twenty-six inches. Unless the killer was intentionally firing shorter arrows."

Hardy looked up from the notebook he was scribbling in and asked. "I'd like to know why someone would intentionally fire shorter arrows."

"It's simple, shorter arrows are lighter and they fly faster," Delmar said. "But it's dangerous to fire short arrows when you've got long arms. I've seen some men destroy their bows and their arms doing that. I've got some pictures if you want to see them."

"I think we'll pass," I said because I didn't think that looking at Delmar's grisly photo collection was necessary to our investigation. "What about the broadhead? I did a little research on the Bass Pro Shop's website and I figured out that it's a fixed-blade broadhead."

"Oh yeah, these suckers are meant to do some serious internal damage. In fact, if you're bowhunting in Texas, you gotta use one of these if you're going after turkeys and big game animals," Delmar said.

He then listed around two dozen animals he'd killed while bowhunting. These included a flock of turkeys, a cougar, two Rocky Mountain Elk, a handful of wild hogs and trophy bucks, and a massive bull moose whose head was now hanging above the cash register.

Flipping the arrow around so that we were looking at the back end of the shaft, Delmar said, "Problem is the weight of the broadheads can cause the arrows to fly a little wonky. These vanes are what's supposed to keep it on course by balancing out the weight and helping the arrow fly straighter. There are different ways to fletch, or place, the vanes on the shaft. There's straight, offset, and helical. The ones you got here are offset to the right. That causes the arrow to rotate in flight."

"Is there anything special about the colors?" I asked.

"No. Vanes come in all colors. And the colors don't mean nothing," Delmar said.

"I see you've got different kinds of bows. What kind of bows shoot this kind of arrow?" Hardy asked.

"There are four different kinds of bows," Delmar said. Sidestepping around me, Delmar picked up what looked like a mishmash of a bow and a long barrel gun. "This is a crossbow. Your killer didn't use this. It uses a different kind of arrow called a bolt. So if you've got a suspect and this is the only type of bow he's got, he ain't your man. Well, he could still be your man. But this ain't what fired your murder weapon."

"What did fire our murder weapon?" I asked.

"Could have been any of the three other types of bows," Delmar said.

Delmar showed us the traditional longbow, a recurve bow, and a compound bow. Each one was a little more elaborate looking than the last. Delmar went over each one, explaining the differences between the three. The ends of the longbow and recurve bow curved in different directions. And the compound bow looked intricate with all of the strings, wheels, and other accouterments.

"All of these can be used for hunting and for target shooting. But the recurve is the only one that's allowed if you're in the archery competitions in the Olympics," Delmar said.

"There's no way to narrow it down to just one of these bows?" I asked.

"Nope. You can use aluminum and carbon arrows on all three bows," Delmar said as he held up a compound bow. "But, if I was a betting man, I'd say your killer most likely used a compound bow. Once you get the hang of shooting a compound, it's easier and more accurate."

"You are a betting man, Delmar," I said.

"Like I said, you can use a longbow or a recurve for bowhunting. I don't. I use a compound. On the other hand, you ain't gonna use a broadhead if you're just target shooting. Those are for killing. I don't know much about the workings of a criminal mastermind – or at least the homicidal kind – but, considering the broadhead, your killer was hunting Travis. And if he was hunting, he was probably using a compound bow. At least that's what I would have done if I was your killer."

~*~*~

"It's about time the two of you got here," Uncle Murph said

"Delmar was giving us an archery demonstration. Jerrod and I got to shoot a longbow, a recurve, and a compound bow," I said as I walked into Murph's office a little after ten o'clock on Monday morning.

"Carrie's walking in high cotton because she hit the bullseye on her first try with the compound," Hardy said.

"I'm glad you kids learned a lot about the murder weapon, but you missed out on all the fun. We've got a suspect. Well, we have a long list of possible suspects. But this person is a legit suspect," Murph said.

"Who is it?" I asked.

"Marisol's ex-boyfriend, Xavier Ortega. Turns out he was released from the group home about six months ago. His grandma is confined to a wheelchair and she needed him to come home and help take care of her," Murph said.

"And the fact that he's no longer living in a group home puts him at the top of the suspect list?" Hardy asked.

"No. But his car being found near the crime scene does," Murph said.

"Back up, Uncle Murph. What's going on?" I asked.

"All right, all right. What happened is that about two hours ago, an old biddy came in to the department. Her name's Linda Barley. I think you've dealt with her before, Carrie."

Linda Barley was eighty-four years old and lived alone. She called us about everything from speeding cars to barking dogs. During the summer, she'd call us every single day to complain about the neighborhood kids because they were 'too loud.'

"Doesn't she live in that neighborhood on the other side of the street from the high school?" I asked.

"She does," Murph said. "So there was Old Lady Barley having a conniption out in the lobby because a car's been parked in front of her house since she got up on Sunday morning. She claims it wasn't there on Saturday night when she went to bed. Yesterday, when she got home from church, she called us to complain about the car. Obviously, we were a little busy with the homicide, so I didn't send anyone out to check on it. Old Lady Barley told me that because we wouldn't do anything, she had to do our job for us. Yesterday afternoon, she went door-to-door, asking her neighbors if they recognized the car. No one did. She called us last night. When we still didn't do anything, she decided to come on in to file a complaint. Against the car. And against us."

"Not the first time she's done that," I said.

"To shut her up, I sent Chief Deputy Quaranta out to have a look at the car. This is what he found," Murph said as he handed me a picture of the passenger seat of a car.

Scattered across the passenger side seat and the floor were at least ten flyers for last Saturday night's SWAT show. The flyers featured large, color pictures of me, Red, Travis, and Marisol. All four of our names were under the pictures. Also listed on the flyer were other wrestlers' names and their matches.

"I'm guessing Xavier saw Ms. Santiago's picture on the flyer and decided to come to the show," Hardy said.

"The collection of flyers is creepy, but how exactly does it make him a suspect?" I asked.

"The flyers don't quite make him a suspect, but this does," Murph said as he handed me another picture.

This picture was of the backseat of a car. Or at least I thought it was the backseat of a car. It was hard to tell because it was buried under a massive pile of clothes, pieces of cardboard, fast food bags and wrappers, a mannequin torso, and all sorts of other junk. Sticking out from under a wadded up, colorful Mexican blanket was a familiar looking item.

"Is that a compound bow?" I asked.

"Yes, it is," Murph said as he handed me another picture of the backseat. In this one, the blanket was gone and I could see the compound bow lying on top of the rest of the junk piled on the backseat. "Chief Deputy Quaranta and the deputies are going to have the car towed to the department once they're done processing the backseat."

"Do you know where Xavier is at? Did you bring him in yet?" Hardy asked.

"Not yet. I sent some deputies over to watch his grandma's house, but they don't think he's there. But I know where Xavier was on Saturday night," Murph said. "I can't put Xavier in the back parking lot. But I can put him at the SWAT Zone. With a compound bow in his car."

Murph held up one more picture. It was a slightly blurry picture of a section of the audience at Saturday night's show. Seated directly behind MeMaw Devereux was Xavier Ortega.

~*~*~

"You're too old to be selling Girl Scout cookies, missy. What do y'all want?"

Ida Ortega, Xavier's paternal grandmother, peered up at me through her ratty screen door. She was seated in a motorized wheelchair that had an oxygen tank strapped to the side. A thin, plastic tube traveled from the tank to her nose. The cigarette clenched between her crimson lips seemed like a bad idea.

"I want you to put that cigarette out before you blow us all up," I said.

"Ma'am, I'm Sergeant Hardy. I'm with the Texas Rangers," Hardy said as he tapped the badge pinned to his shirt. "And this is Chief Deputy Quaranta and Detective Shatner. They're with the Wyatt County Sheriff's Department."

"Y'all still ain't told me what you want," Ida said before she took one last, long drag on her cigarette. She then ground it out on the arm of the wheelchair. "Aside from the Girl Scout not wanting to get her pretty little face blown off. I've been smoking around this tank for almost a year now. Darn thing ain't blown up yet."

"There's always a first time for everything," I said.

"Ma'am, is you grandson, Xavier, home?" Hardy asked.

"Darn it, what's that boy done now?" Ida asked as she put her wheelchair in reverse and rolled away from the door. "Xavier! Git your scrawny butt out here!"

Nudging me aside, Hardy wrenched open the screen door and ran into the house with his gun drawn. Quaranta followed on his heels. I stayed outside to radio the deputies who were surrounding the house to let them know that the suspect might be inside.

"Suspect? What you calling my grandbaby a suspect for? And what are those men doing running around my house with their guns?" Ida asked as she pulled her wheelchair forward, blocking the doorway and preventing me from getting inside.

"Mrs. Ortega, is Xavier home? Or don't you know?" I asked.

Ida shrugged her boney shoulders. "The boy comes and goes when he wants to. I don't keep track of him. I know he wasn't here yesterday morning to take me to church like he's supposed to. I missed Mass because of him."

"If he's not here, do you have any idea where he might be?" I asked.

"I ain't got no clue. Like I already said, I don't keep track of his goings and comings." Ida spun the wheelchair around and started screaming, "Hey! Hey you! Just 'cause you a Texas Ranger don't mean you get to force your way into my bedroom."

Scooting between the doorframe and the wheelchair, I stepped inside. The front door opened directly into the combined living room and dining room. A path wide enough to accommodate Ida's wheelchair wound a serpentine path through the piles of newspapers, boxes, bags, and various detritus that were piled three and four feet high. The room off to the right of the living room was jam-packed to the ceiling with plastic containers, broken furniture, and a china cabinet full of cracked knick-knacks and decorative plates.

"Downstairs bedroom and bathroom are clear," Hardy announced as he walked out of what I guessed was Ida's bedroom.

"So is the kitchen," Quaranta said.

Hardy stepped over a cracked fish tank full of yarn bundles and handed a sheet of paper to Ida. "Ma'am, this is a warrant giving us permission to search your grandson's bedroom, along with the rest of your house for archery equipment."

"Oh no, y'all ain't searching my house for nothing," Ida said as her eyes skimmed over the warrant. "This is a violation against my rights as a United States citizen. Git out!"

"We're not going anywhere, ma'am," Hardy said. "Now, where are the stairs to get up to the second floor?"

"Find 'em yourself. I'm calling my lawyer." Ida crumpled up the warrant and threw it at Hardy's face.

"Stairs are in the kitchen," Quaranta said.

Ida's kitchen was no cleaner than the rest of the downstairs. Broken appliances and empty take-out containers took up nearly all of the counter space, and there was a small mountain of trash bags next to the French doors that led out onto the screened-in back porch.

"I'm hoping it's just rotting food, but it smells like something died in here," I said.

"It smells even worse on the porch. There are two deep freezers out there. One is broken, and there is meat rotting in it," Quaranta said.

"Come on, let's go upstairs and see if Xavier is hiding up there. We can address the hoarding situation later," Hardy said as he mounted the L-shaped staircase. Three steps up, the stairs made a ninety-degree turn. "It looks like the stairs open up directly into the bedroom. There's a half-wall on the right at the top of the steps. And there's a door on the left side of the landing up there. If Xavier is up there, he could be waiting to ambush us."

"Y'all get back here! You ain't got no right going up there!" Ida yelled as she rolled into the kitchen and crashed into a shopping cart sitting in the middle of the room. Unable to get around the cart, Ida heaved herself out of the wheelchair and lurched across the kitchen. Without her oxygen, Ida began to wheeze. Collapsing against Quaranta, Ida gasped, "Lord, I'm having a heart attack."

"You aren't having a heart attack. You just can't breathe." Quaranta picked up Ida around the waist and hauled her across the kitchen.

"Get your hands off me! Help! Help! Police brutality!" Ida screamed.

"Knock it off." Quaranta said as he sat Ida down in her wheelchair and then handed her the nasal cannula. Turning to me and Hardy, Quaranta waved us forward. "You two go ahead. I'll stay with her until I can get a deputy inside."

"You go in front of me, Carrie. I'll cover you and keep an eye on that doorway to the left. I'll be just one step behind you," Hardy said.

Stepping around Hardy, I crept up the rest of the stairs. With each step, I could see more of the ceiling and the wall that was directly in front of me. Both were covered in 8x10 sized pictures. The pictures were tacked up in perfect rows, with the pictures randomly alternating between horizontal and vertical. Forcing myself to ignore the pictures, I eyed up the sparsely furnished bedroom. Xavier's only furniture was a ratty recliner, a dresser, a card table, and a bare twin-size mattress on the floor. On the card table were a laptop and a printer.

"Bedroom is clear," I said.

"So is the walk-in closet," Hardy said. "There's another door in the closet. Looks like it's a bathroom. Cover me while I check it out."

Following behind Hardy, I walked through the walk-in closet. There weren't any clothes hanging on the racks – not that there would have been any room for clothes considering almost the entire closet was packed full of cardboard boxes.

"What is Ida storing in all of these boxes?" I asked.

"I'm afraid to find out. Good news is that the bathroom is clear. Bad news, Xavier isn't here," Hardy said.

After holstering my gun, I stepped into the dirty bathroom. Judging by the amount of loose hairs on the floor and the buildup of soap scum in the shower, the bathroom probably hadn't been cleaned since Xavier moved in six months earlier. I tugged open the vanity cabinet and found four orange prescription bottles lined up on the bottom shelf. All four of the bottles were full of pills.

"Uh oh, I don't think Xavier's currently medicated. And it doesn't look like he has been for the past four months," I said. I picked up one of the bottles, read the name of the medication on the label, and then Googled it. "Chlorpromazine…also known as Thorazine…It's to treat schizophrenia and other psychotic disorders."

"I am starting to get a really bad gut feeling about this guy." Hardy pointed to a bong and a baggie of marijuana sitting on the crowded sink counter. "Xavier might not be taking his prescriptions, but it looks like he is self-medicating. I'm going to call the sheriff and inform him of what we've just found."

"I'll be in the bedroom. I want to get a closer look at Xavier's homemade wallpaper," I said as I walked out of the bathroom and through the walk-in closet. In the bedroom, I spun around in a circle to take in all four walls. Every square inch of the walls and ceiling were covered in 8x10 sized pictures. I walked around the large room, scanning the pictures. "Oh my God…All of these pictures are of Marisol."

"Everything okay up there?" Quaranta called up the stairs.

"Xavier isn't here. But you need to get up here, Juan," I said. "And, Jerrod, you better get out here!"

Hardy ran out of the bathroom and into the bedroom. "Oh, now this is just creepy."

"What's going on? Did you find something?" Quaranta asked as he charged up the steps. Like me, he spun around to look at the hundreds of pictures. "What the…Creepy doesn't even begin to describe this room. This guy's obsessed. I'm going to set up a protective unit for Ms. Santiago. We need to keep her safe until we find Xavier."

"It looks like there are dates on all of these pictures," I said. Moving closer to the one wall, I scanned the small, colorful tags that Xavier had stuck to each of the photos. Following the dates written on the tags, I realized that the pictures had been hung up in chronological order. "It's like a photo documentary of Xavier's relationship with Marisol."

"No, it's a documentary of Marisol's life for the past few years. Some of these pictures are of Marisol and Travis. Xavier scribbled all over Travis's face. The most recent is apparently from last week," Quaranta said as he pointed at the pictures stuck to the ceiling.

"He's also Photoshopped pictures of himself over other people's heads," I said when I came across a picture of Marisol sitting at a picnic bench with another woman. Xavier had crudely Photoshopped a picture of his head over top of the woman's head.

"It doesn't look like these pictures over here were taken locally. I'm pretty sure those are the Rocky Mountains in the background," Hardy said as he looked at some of the pictures hanging on another wall. "It looks like Xavier has been stalking Marisol for years."

"Did Xavier's grandma give you any ideas on where he might be?" I asked.

"She hasn't said anything since you and Sergeant Hardy came upstairs. She is not going to help us find him," Quaranta said.

"Xavier has about a thirty-six hour head start. He could be anywhere by now," Hardy said.

Walking around the room, I looked behind the recliner and found an arrow leaning against the wall. It was the same brand as the murder weapon. The arrow had only one plastic vane – a neon orange one. Quaranta had found an orange vane and a lime green vane at the crime scene. Perhaps those two vanes had previously been attached to this specific arrow.

"It looks like Xavier's been here sometime since Saturday night," I said.

CHAPTER NINE

"Do you mind answering some questions about your grandson?" I asked.

"I'm guessing I don't have much of a choice, do I? Well, come on, missy, ask your questions. My show's about to start," Ida said.

Ida steered her wheelchair around a stack of plastic containers full of squashed Coke cans that acted as a half wall between the dining room and the living room. She then motored closer to the big screen mounted on the living room wall. If the house ever caught on fire – which was a good possibility considering the amount of junk making it a fire trap – the only thing worth saving would be the TV.

Hanging on the exposed parts of the living room and dining room walls were paintings of Jesus and pictures of Ida's late husband. As I wandered around, I noticed that in a few of the pictures Mr. Ortega held a compound bow as he knelt next to a dead animal. A younger Xavier was in some of the pictures with him. Seeing the pictures of Xavier with a compound bow in hand answered the question of whether or not he actually had any archery experience.

"Does Xavier still go bowhunting?" I casually asked.

"He ain't gone for years. Not since he was a teenager. Don't think the boy liked hunting all that much. He always cried and begged my husband not to make him go along. I told Hector that Xavier was too much like his daddy. They're both too sissy to be hunters," Ida said before she grabbed a can of SPAM off the cluttered coffee table and forked a glob of the canned meat into her mouth. "I can't remember the last time I had fresh deer meat…"

"Does Xavier still have his bow?" I asked.

"Now how should I know?" Ida asked around a piece of half-masticated meat. "He kept it as his parents' house. Stop bothering me and go ask them."

"What about your husband? Do you still have his bow and arrows?"

"They're probably around here somewhere. I haven't thrown anything out since Hector died nine months ago. He was a hoarder."

"You don't say."

Deciding that the recliner with the sunken seat was probably a safer option than the filthy couch, I sat down.

"Git off that chair!" Ida screamed as she flung a piece of SPAM in my direction. "My husband died in that recliner."

Springing off the recliner, I nearly tripped over a cat that came shooting out from behind an overturned, half-crushed dollhouse. The cat scarfed up the SPAM and then bolted out of the room. The poor thing looked like it had used up all of its nine lives and then spent a month or two in a shallow grave before it was dug up and brought back to life.

"You have any more cats?" I asked.

"Two or three. Though I ain't seen the gray one in a while. Either it got out or it crawled into something and died. I was smelling something funny a few weeks ago."

I sent a text to Quaranta, who was elsewhere in the house, and asked him to call Animal Control immediately. I wanted to get the cats out of the house and find them a new home.

"Mrs. Ortega, how long has Xavier been living with you?" I asked.

"The boy has been living with me off and on since he was a kid. Child Protective Services first gave me and Hector custody of Xavier when he was five or six. His parents couldn't take care of him properly. Wasn't nothing wrong with my son. But Xavier's mama was 'depressed'. I always thought that was just some fancy excuse she used to get away with being lazy. But every time his mama got 'depressed', CPS sent Xavier to live with me and his grandpa. Hector and I did our best to raise the boy right. I took him to church every Sunday. Hector did everything he could to turn him into a man. But his mama undid all our hard work every time he went back to live with her. She was weak, and it made him weak."

I took a deep breath and forced myself to withhold voicing my disgust with Ida's lack of empathy over her daughter-in-law's mental illness. "I understand that Xavier has been living with you since he was released from the group home six months ago."

"That's right. I can't get around without this chair so it was either find someone to help me or go to a nursing home," Ida said as she chucked the empty SPAM can into the corner and stuck the fork in her bra. The tines jabbed at her sagging neck as she talked. "Since Xavier was about to get released from that group home, I asked him to come live with me."

"Are you aware that Xavier hasn't been taking his medication?"

"I know. I'm the one that told him to stop taking it. The boy don't need pills. What he needs is the Lord." Ida pointed at one of the paintings of Jesus. "I've been taking Xavier to church every Sunday since he moved in with me. Except yesterday. And I've read the Bible to him almost every single night. It's the Good Lord that's going to save him from the devil, not some doctor's pills."

"Xavier needs saved from the devil?" I asked.

"The boy claims he hears voices. Who else would that be but the devil?" Ida asked. She yanked the fork out of her cleavage and stabbed in into the padded arm of her wheelchair. "If that handmaiden of the devil hadn't led Xavier into sin, the devil himself never would have gotten to my grandson."

"Handmaiden of the devil?" I asked, intrigued by where the conversation was going.

"That high school girlfriend of his," Ida said as she lit up a cigarette. "Mary something."

"Marisol Santiago?" I asked.

"Yeah, her. That stuck up little hussy. The first time I laid eyes on her I knew she was no good. I tried to tell Xavier, but it was too late. That little witch had put a spell on him back when he was in high school. Drove him half crazy. He followed her out to Colorado when she went to college. I don't know what she did to him out there, but he came back totally crazy. Not only did he say he was hearing voices, he was having conversations with them. She did that to him. Don't believe me? Go ask Xavier's doctor from the nuthouse. He even said that it was Marisol who drove Xavier crazy. Like I just said, had it not been for that handmaiden of the devil leading Xavier into sin, he never would have gone crazy."

Trying not to laugh at Ida's theory, I asked, "And what kinds of sins did Marisol lead Xavier into?"

"Drinking and drugs! Premarital fornication! My grandson could have been somebody. But she ruined his chances by driving him crazy."

"Well, uh…yeah. That's just terrible." I had a tentative seat on the edge of the couch and leaned closer to Ida. "Mrs. Ortega, are you aware that Marisol Santiago and her boyfriend were attacked on Saturday night? She was wounded. And her boyfriend was killed."

"Hard to miss since it's been all over the news. Didn't realize she was the same little witch. Now I'm sorry she didn't get killed, too. Someone needs to stop her before she ruins more lives than just my grandson's."

Ignoring Ida's nasty comments about Marisol, I asked, "Do you know where Xavier was on Saturday night?"

"I don't know." Ida ground out her cigarette on the edge of the coffee table.

She then lit up another one. "Why do you care?"

"Because I have proof that he was at the professional wrest–"

"Professional wrestling!" Ida yelled as she cut me off. "I done told that boy to stop going to that trash. Bad enough Marisol made him crazy, I don't need wrestling turning him into a homosexual!"

"Excuse me?" I asked.

"You heard me, missy. All them wrestlers are homosexuals. They'd have to be the way they roll around together in those little shorts."

Biting back a retort, I asked, "Has Xavier been going to a lot of pro wrestling events?"

"Every month since he moved in he's been going to the local one. I keep telling him to stay away. Boy just won't listen," Ida said.

Leaving Ida Ortega to her television show, I wandered through the house and found Quaranta taking pictures of the kitchen.

"How's it going?" I asked.

"It would take days to go through everything in here," Quaranta said. "Plus we found three attic crawl spaces upstairs. One on either side going up the steps, and another one that runs along the front of the house. They're packed full of junk. We're just lucky Xavier wasn't hiding in one of them."

"Oh, great," I said.

"I called the sheriff to get another warrant. We need to collect Xavier's photo collection as evidence," Quaranta said. "I also put in a call to the Department of Aging. They're sending someone out to assess the hoarding situation. We can't leave Mrs. Ortega in this squalor."

"I'm more concerned about her cats."

"Carrie! Quaranta!" Hardy shouted from the second floor. "I need you up here! Now!"

Quaranta and I took off running, racing each other up the narrow staircase.

"What's wrong?" Quaranta and I asked in unison.

Hardy stepped out of the doorway that led into one of the attic crawl spaces. None of us had noticed it earlier because the door was plastered over with pictures of Marisol.

Holding up a handful of arrow shafts, Hardy announced, "I didn't find a bow in here. But I found a box of arrows. The shafts are a little longer than the murder weapon, but they're the same brand. And the vane color and placement are the same."

~*~*~

"Have you found him? Have you found Xavier? Please tell me you have him in custody," Marisol said as she grabbed me by the upper arms and shook me.

Her mother and sisters crowded in around us. "I forgot that Xavier used to go bowhunting. He must be the killer."

"I'm sorry, Marisol. But we haven't been able to located Xavier yet," I said.

"Darn it! Detective Shatner, I'm counting on you!" Marisol stomped across the living room and threw herself down onto the couch.

"We're doing the best we can, Ms. Santiago," Hardy snapped. "Xavier has been living with his grandmother–"

"That gross old lady always hated me," Marisol said, sitting up and peering at us over the back of the couch. "Not that his parents liked me all that much. But at least they were nice to me. I only saw his abuela a few times, but each time she called me a witch and told me to go cast my spells elsewhere. Like, what was that supposed to mean?"

"We didn't exactly approve of Xavier either," Yesinia Santiago said as she ran her hands through Marisol's long, black hair. "If you recall, your padre and I asked you multiple times to break up with him. You were too young to be in a serious relationship. And Xavier just wasn't good enough for you."

"None of them were good enough for me, were they?" Marisol pulled away from her mother so that she could turn around and face her. "Not Xavier. Not Armando. Not Ian. Not Pablo or Miguel. And certainly not Travis!"

"At least the others were all Catholic. You know your padre and I would never have approved of a marriage between you and Travis. And we most certainly did not approve of you moving in with him. I'm sorry Travis is dead. It's truly horrific the way that he was murdered. But I'm not sorry that he's out of your life," Yesinia said.

Marisol screamed and charged off into the kitchen in tears. Annalisa ran after her.

"What about Zachary, Mamá? Or do you only care about Marisol's boyfriends?" Evita asked in a tiny, hollow voice.

"You're smarter than your sister when it comes to men," Yesinia said, absentmindedly patting her youngest daughter on the shoulder. "But no, I don't approve of Zachary. He's not a bad boy. And it seems he has a good baseball career ahead of him. But he's not Catholic. And I don't want him to get in the way of your future."

"Oh, Mamá…" Evita slowly headed towards the kitchen, dragging her feet. "Come on, Detective Shatner. I'll help you find Marisol. I'm sure you have questions."

Leaving Hardy alone with Yesinia Santiago, I followed Evita through her parents' kitchen and breakfast nook area. Four doors opened up off of the spacious kitchen – one led to the powder room under the stairs, another was to the small laundry room, and the third led into the master bedroom. We stuck our heads in each room to confirm that Marisol and Annalisa were not inside.

"Found them. They're in the sunroom," Evita said as she tried to open the sunroom door. It was locked. "Oh, now that's mature."

Pounding on the door, I motioned for Annalisa to come over and unlock the door.

"Marisol is too upset to talk to you," Annalisa said to me as she cracked open the door.

"I don't care how upset she is, Annalisa. I need to talk to her about Xavier. You know, so I can catch him and figure out if he killed Travis." I shoved past Annalisa and entered the sunroom. Pushing Marisol's legs off the wicker loveseat, I had a seat next to her. "Marisol, we have deputies at Xavier's grandmother's house. He's been living there the past six months. We also have deputies at his parents' house. But his parents claim they haven't seen or heard from him in weeks. Do you have any idea where Xavier might be?"

"No. If he's not at either of those two places, the only other place I think he would go would be here. Or to the house that Travis and I shared," Marisol said.

"And that's why we have deputies posted around your parents' house. I'll also get a team over to the house you were renting. If Xavier shows up at any of those places, the deputies will grab him," I said.

"Do you think Xavier is the killer?" Evita asked as she leaned over the back of the loveseat and stuck her head between mine and Marisol's.

"We don't know," I said. I handed Marisol my tablet so that she could see the picture of Xavier in the crowd at SWAT. "But we do know that Xavier was at the show on Saturday night."

"What?!? Are you kidding me? Oh my God, that little creep!" Marisol said.

"Ida told us that Xavier has gone to every SWAT show since he got out of the group home. It seems that he has also been stalking you," I said as I brought up the pictures I had taken of Xavier's bedroom. "The most recent pictures were taped to his ceiling."

"Oh…my…God…" Marisol whispered as she glanced over the pictures. "That was taken back at Christmas. Look, that's the green dress I wore for the Christmas Eve Mass. It's the only time I wore it."

"And that's from when we went shopping for my prom dress," Evita said.

"There's pictures of me at the stables. And of me and Travis when we moved into the house together back in February. And that's from when we drove over to Shreveport for a long weekend last month. I can't believe Xavier followed us," Marisol said.

"Marisol, I need you to tell me about your relationship with Xavier," I said as I pulled the tablet out of her hands. "I need to understand why he's obsessed with you."

"He's obsessed with me because he's crazy," Marisol said.

"Xavier is schizophrenic," I said.

"Put whatever fancy name you want on it, he's still crazy," Marisol said as she stood up and then paced the length of the sunroom. "I didn't meet Xavier until high school. We went to different junior highs. Not that I noticed him in ninth grade. He was a quiet, shy kid. But he was really smart. And kinda cute. At least back then he was cute. Once I got him cleaned up."

"When did you start dating?" I asked.

"End of tenth grade. We had a class together. The office screwed up my schedule for that semester so I somehow wound up in Honors Chemistry. None of my friends had the class, so I got stuck with Xavier as my lab partner. He was weird at first. You know how teenage boys are…He wouldn't look at me and he mumbled a lot. By the end of the semester, we'd become really good friends. I was the one who asked him out. My friends thought I was nuts."

"Your friends didn't like Xavier?" I asked.

"Never did. He was always awkward around them. Xavier is one of those guys that you had to get to know to really like," Marisol said.

"Doesn't hurt he did all your homework for you," Evita said.

"Shut up, Evie," Marisol snapped. "We were together for a year when Xavier started acting weird. We were going into senior year, so we were trying to figure out what we wanted to do for the rest of our lives. Xavier wanted to get married right away, but I wanted to go to college. My dream job has always been to work around horses, so I started applying to all of the colleges that have equine studies. I also applied to ones with Zoology degrees. Xavier applied to all of the same colleges because he wanted to go to the same school as me, regardless of what other majors that college offered."

"Did he get accepted to Colorado State University?" I asked.

"No. He didn't. He begged me not to go. He was also getting really clingy. And he was freaking out all of the time. He also started failing all of his classes. I finally said something to him that maybe we should break up. He threatened to kill himself," Marisol said.

"Xavier also kept begging me to talk to you," Annalisa said. "He thought maybe I could talk you out of going away to college."

"But I went to CSU," Marisol said. "Xavier got accepted to McKinley College. It's also in Fort Collins. He must have never gone to class because he was always hanging around CSU. I'd come out of class and he'd be waiting for me. Every single class. I couldn't do anything without him being there. By the time we came home for summer break, I couldn't take it anymore. So I told Xavier that it was over between us. Xavier flipped out and threatened to kill himself again, but I…well, I cared. But I didn't care. You know what I mean?"

"I understand." Standing up, I moved closer to Marisol and said, "I don't know if Xavier did this. But we have some compelling evidence. I want you – all three of you and your parents – to be careful. Xavier is currently not medicated. If you see him or hear from him, you scream. The deputies won't be going anywhere until we have Xavier in custody."

~*~*~

"Thanks for letting me stay here tonight, Carrie. I really appreciate it," Hardy said as he padded into my living room in his bare feet. He'd just taken a shower and the occasional bead of water dripped from his wet hair down onto his faded t-shirt. "I just hope it won't be too weird for you considering... you know."

"I know. And it's not weird. Now awkward at all," I said.

Okay, it was really weird. Like, insanely weird. I had no idea what I was thinking when I told Hardy he could stay at my place that night. He had only just mentioned his plan to check into a local hotel for the night – he didn't want to go home to Tyler when there were deputies still out looking for Xavier – when I offered him my currently unoccupied guest room. The words were out of my mouth before I realized what I was saying. And once I'd made the offer, it was too late to take it back. All I could do was hope that Hardy declined. Which he didn't. So there he was, walking around my house in his Deadpool pajama pants.

"So what's on TV?" Hardy asked as he had a seat next to me on the cowhide couch.

"I'm catching up on WWE Monday Night Raw from earlier tonight. What else is on TV on Monday nights other than pro wrestling?"

"Probably nothing worth watching," Hardy said as he turned up the volume and settled back against the cushions.

I scooted towards my end of the couch to put a couple more inches between me and Hardy. I debated moving over to one of the two recliners that Hardy could have also sat on, but I didn't want it to look like I was making a big deal about the invasion of my personal space. Sitting that close to him now that we were no longer in a relationship shouldn't have been that big of a deal. Except it was. Especially since I couldn't stop thinking about how Naomi was convinced Hardy wanted to get back together with me. I hadn't noticed anything different about him – he still looked at me and talked to me in the same way that he had been since we met. Because he wasn't treating me any differently, I had no idea what to think. So I was overthinking it.

Drawing my legs up to my chest, I massaged my aching feet. I had been on them way too much since Saturday night, and they'd been complaining most of today.

At least I didn't have a bullet wound in one of them like Dustin Thompson. I was going to have to find the time to pay him a visit and make sure that he was keeping his mouth shut. Protecting Naomi was just as important as finding Travis Yeager's killer. Maybe even more important. I might still be mad at Naomi for her poor decision making, but I didn't want her to wind up in jail for shooting Dustin in the foot. Not when he kind of deserved it considering he was cheating on his wife. Maybe I'd have Uncle Murph or Uncle Houston stop by Dustin's house when Belinda wasn't around. A visit from them should scare him into keeping his mouth shut. And Uncle Houston had the spare cash to bribe Dustin into keeping quiet. And pay Dustin's medical bills, if he had any. I couldn't imagine it was cheap to get that bullet wound patched up.

Hardy put his hand on my left thigh, startling me and breaking up my train of thought.

"You all right there, darling? You're just holding on to your foot and staring at the floor."

"Huh? Oh, I'm fine. Just thinking."

"Well how about I rub your feet while you keep on thinking?" Hardy asked, motioning for me to swing my legs over and put my feet on his lap. "You know I'm better at rubbing your feet than you are."

"Um, well…that's okay. They're fine now. I'll just wear different shoes tomorrow. That should alleviate the problem," I said. My feet still really hurt, but I wasn't comfortable with Hardy touching them. He'd given me numerous foot massages when we were dating, but it seemed a little too personal now that we were broken up.

"Then how about your shoulders? You've been rubbing at the left one all day. Is that big knot back?" Hardy asked.

"It's fine. Just really tense. You know, from working on the case. I'm due for a professional massage. I'll get one soon," I said even though the large muscle knot that kept forming where my neck met my left shoulder had been throbbing all day.

"Come here." Hardy shifted closer and reached for my left shoulder. "Let me work that knot out for you. You know you'll feel better."

Hardy's hand had just brushed my shoulder when I slid off the couch and stood up. Putting some distance between us, I said, "I'm getting tired. I think I'll just go to bed now."

"You okay, Carrie?" Hardy asked.

"Yes…Well, to be honest, no. This is really weird, okay. I know we weren't together very long, but I'm not quite over it. Working with you on the case is one thing because we're, you know, working. But hanging out…this is really awkward. I don't know how to act. And you offering me a foot and shoulder massage is just…I don't know, it's kind of making me uncomfortable. And if

I've learned anything from all the times that I've watched Pulp Fiction, it's that foot massages definitely mean something."

"I'm sorry, darling. I don't want to make you feel uncomfortable. I'll just grab my stuff and get out of here. It's not too late to check into a hotel."

Hardy stood up and then brushed past me on the way back the hall to the bedrooms.

"No, you don't have to leave. Seriously, Jerrod, it's just for one night. And we'll both probably go to bed soon anyway."

I followed Hardy back the hall to the spare bedroom. It used to be my sister's bedroom when we were kids. I had the room next door, which was now my home office. My sisters always resented me for getting my own room. I spent most of my childhood feeling like they wished I had never been born because my birth forced them to bunk together. Holly spent years campaigning that she should have her own room because she was the oldest. Luckily for me, no one ever gave in to her demands.

"It's not a big deal, Carrie," Hardy said as he tugged his jeans on over his pajama pants. "And I'm not going to lie. This is awkward for me, too. It has been ever since I showed up at the crime scene yesterday morning. I don't know how to act around you. Not when I've spent the past month driving myself nuts second guessing if breaking up was the right thing to do. I miss you. I miss hanging out with you. I miss having you in my life."

"You miss me?" I asked, feeling partially shocked but mostly thrilled. "I miss you, too, Jerrod. But what chance did we have? If you weren't a Texas Ranger or if I wasn't related to a bunch of criminals…But that's who we are. And it's just not compatible. I wanted this to work. I really did. But it wasn't going to. We're both smart enough to see that."

"Then I must be really dumb…"

Hardy pulled me against his chest, buried his hands in my hair, and tilted my head back. His mouth moved over mine, gentle but demanding, as he thoroughly kissed me. Before I had a chance to react, Hardy let go of me and stepped back.

"Now I need to go, darling. Before I lose my self-control."

His self-control? What about my quickly deteriorating self-control? Just because I knew we were wrong for each other didn't stop me from wanting him.

"Jerrod, you can stay." Blocking the doorway, I pried the duffle bag out of Hardy's hand and then tossed it onto the bed. I grabbed him by the shirt and pulled him closer as I said, "I want you to stay."

CHAPTER TEN

"Thanks for tuning in this morning," said the super animated, overly caffeinated morning newscaster. "Our top story this Tuesday morning concerns the weekend homicide in Wyatt County. As we've previously reported, gym teacher and professional wrestler Travis Yeager was killed after leaving the SWAT Zone just before midnight on Saturday night. Mr. Yeager's girlfriend was also wounded in the attack."

"Oh, Uncle Sterling is going to love this," I said when a slow pan of the SWAT Zone replaced a promotional photo of Travis and Marisol on the screen.

"The Wyatt County Sheriff's Department is now asking for your help in locating a person who they wish to question in relation to the homicide," said the newscaster as a picture of Xavier popped up on the screen. "If you know the whereabouts of Xavier Ortega – or if you have any information regarding the homicide of Travis Yeager and the attack on Marisol Santiago– please contact the Wyatt County Sheriff's Department's tip line."

"Seriously, Uncle Murph…You couldn't have given me a heads up that you were planning to ask the public for help?" I mumbled as I grabbed my phone and sent a scathing text message to Murph. "Are you hearing this, Jerrod?"

"Yes, and I'm not any happier than you are. But there's nothing we can do about it now," Hardy said. He was out in the kitchen, cleaning up his cereal bowl while I watched the news in the living room. "I think Manny missed me. He keeps rubbing up against my legs."

"If his food bowl is still full it just means he doesn't like the wet cat food I gave him and is trying to sucker you into giving him something else."

"And here I thought you might finally like me," Hardy said to the orange cat who was loudly meowing at him. "Oh no, don't complain to me about your breakfast. Go talk to your person. Miss Carrie is the one who feeds you. Probably overfeeds you. You weren't this chubby when you were my cat."

"He's not fat. He's fluffy." I leaned over to pick up my cereal bowl off the coffee table only to find that someone else was devouring my breakfast. Molly, my mutt who resembled a golden retriever, had her snout submerged in my bowl and was scarfing up my Frosted Flakes. "Molly, you ate all of it. And that was the last of the cereal, too."

Hardy walked into the room, laughing as he carried Manny. After depositing the cat on one of the recliners, Hardy leaned over and gave me a quick kiss on the lips.

"I'm going to head over to the sheriff's department. I need to make some calls to follow up on my other cases. I've been neglecting them the past few days and I don't want to fall any farther behind."

"Okay, I'll see you there. Oh, and Jerrod, about last night…And this morning…"

"Let's get through the next couple days and then we'll sit down and talk about it," Hardy said. He blew me a kiss before he grabbed his duffle bag and headed for the front door. "I really want to figure things out and find a way to make this work, Carrie. I think we both know that it won't be easy. But we're too good together."

"I hope you've got a plan, because I don't," I mumbled after Hardy slammed the front door shut.

Grabbing my empty cereal bowl, I headed into my recently remodeled kitchen. Last month I had the cabinets, counters, and floor replaced. I also had the walls painted a bright blue color and had a backsplash installed.

I rummaged around the kitchen in search of something else to eat. I was running dangerously low on human food, but I had plenty of dog food. Just because Molly ate my breakfast did not mean that I was going to snack on hers. I also had a plethora of cat food cans, but I wasn't that desperate.

Glancing at the clock, I realized that I was running late. "I've got to get a move on."

I ran back the hall to my bedroom. Ignoring the unmade king-sized bed, I flung open my closet doors and grabbed some clothes. After quickly changing, I ran back to the kitchen to make sure that my pets had plenty of food and water. I then grabbed my keys and rushed into the one-car garage.

Backing out of my garage, I almost ran over Naomi and my best friend, Veda Houser. They were standing at the end of my driveway, and neither of them looked happy. Veda had been my best friend for as long as either of us could remember. We met back in preschool and had been friends ever since.

"Are you two insane?" I yelled as I climbed out of my Jeep and stomped down the driveway to confront them. "I could have run you two over."

"Don't be questioning my sanity!" Veda said, giving me a smack on the arm. "I've always been the sane one in this friendship!"

"You? Sane? That's funny! Everyone knows that I'm the sane one." I jabbed Veda in the chest with my index finger. At the end of last year, Veda had a boob job that jumped her from an A-cup to a Double D. I'm still not used to her having breasts as big as mine. The change wasn't quite as jarring as the time Veda cut off her long locks and then dyed her naturally blonde hair a dark purplish-red.

"You're both sane!" Naomi screamed. "And you're both crazy! And you're both making me want to scream."

"You're screaming right now," I said.

"And who asked for your opinion on my sanity?" Veda asked.

"Now what is going on? Who's giving you a problem with the wedding now? And do I have to threaten them so you can have your way? And don't even tell me it's Aunt Loretta. I'm done putting up with her. Tell Bubba that his mother is his problem."

When we were in high school, Veda started dating my cousin, Bubba. After thirteen years of breaking up and making up, Bubba finally proposed a few months ago. The reason it took him so long was because his mother couldn't stand Veda. And because Veda refused to live in Nashville, which was where Bubba had been living off-and-on for the past ten years. Veda couldn't stand the instability or the long periods of being home alone while Bubba was off touring with the band he was part of. One of Veda's stipulations was that Bubba quit the band and move home. After helping finish up the new album, Bubba planned to obey Veda's command. In the meantime, I was helping Veda plan the wedding for later in the summer. As Veda's Maid of Honor, it was my sacred duty to calm her down and help take care of the latest problem. While I loved Veda, and would do just about anything for her, the wedding planning was driving me homicidal. Or maybe it was Veda's recent bridezilla behavior that was causing me to seriously consider driving a stake through her heart.

"This has nothing to do with the wedding. Or Loretta. She's actually been leaving me alone. This has to do with your overnight guest!" Veda shouted.

"And how do you know about that? Are you driving around to spy on me?" I asked.

Veda's apartment, which was on the southern side of Holler, was fifteen minutes from my house. And she had no reason to drive past my place to get to work at the beauty salon where she was a hair stylist. The only way Veda would know that Hardy had spent the night would be if someone told her.

Looking at Naomi, who was inching backwards with downcast eyes and a guilty look on her face, I asked, "Or do you have someone spying on me for you? Like maybe Naomi?"

"Who? Me?" Naomi asked.

"No. The other person named Naomi. Of course, I'm talking about you. Can't you just mind your own business?" I asked, feeling a surge of anger towards my cousin.

"Don't yell at her!" Veda clucked her tongue and waved her finger around under my nose. "You're the one who doesn't have the sense that God gave an armadillo. I wasn't too concerned when Naomi texted me last night to say that Jerrod was at your house. I figured you two were working on the case. By the way, I get that you're busy trying to find a killer, but could you return my calls? I just got the invitations and I want you to see them before I send them out. Anyway, I about lost my mind this morning when Naomi called and told me that Jerrod's truck was still parked in your driveway. What were you thinking hooking back up with him?"

"First of all, Veda, I've seen your wedding invitations so many times that I'll never be able to unsee them. I'm the one who designed them. Second, how do you know Jerrod didn't spend the night on the couch?" Turning to Naomi, I asked, "Or were you sneaking around and peeking in the windows?"

"You willing to swear on everything you deem holy that you and Jerrod didn't have sex last night?" Veda asked.

No," I said.

"Ah ha! I knew it!" Veda shouted.

"Look, Jerrod and I talked. We miss each other and we both regret breaking up. We want to give it another go," I said.

"So that means you just jump into bed together? Are you two that dumb that you can't realize your relationship is clearly doomed? Which is what I've been telling you from the start," Veda said.

"No. At the beginning of the relationship you were really supportive. It wasn't until Jerrod and I broke up that you suddenly decided it was a bad idea and claimed that you knew it was doomed from the start."

Veda wasn't the only one who didn't exactly approve of my relationship with Hardy. My family members were torn over how they felt. Some of them were worried that Hardy was dating me to get to them, and they kept begging me to end the relationship before Hardy was able to gather too much evidence against them. Others were excited, thinking that my relationship with Hardy would somehow benefit them. They were under the impression that he would help cover up their crimes, and nothing I said to the contrary could convince them otherwise. And then there were my grandparents, who didn't really care one way or the other about how the relationship would affect the family. They were just happy that I had found a good man, and that he was treating me right.

"For the record, I always thought it was a bad idea," Naomi said.

"Yeah, I know. You only told me a hundred times between asking for details of my sex life," I said. Even though Naomi had been part of the group who was worried that Hardy might be using me to get to the family, she still wanted all of the details.

"I'm still trying to figure out what it is that Jerrod likes about you," Veda said.

"Excuse me? What is that supposed to mean?" I asked.

"The physical attraction I can understand. You're gorgeous," Veda said.

Since childhood, Veda and I had said countless unpleasant yet straightforward things to each other. This was turning out to be one of the more offensive conversations we'd had in recent years, but, considering our history, Veda had a free pass to speak her mind. After all, Veda knew me better than anyone else.

"Are you saying Jerrod wouldn't be attracted to me if I was ugly? How do you know he doesn't like me for me? I have a lot of good qualities."

"Yes, you do. You're smart, funny, and confident," Veda said.

"You're not high-maintenance. And you have huge boobs," Naomi added.

"What do my boobs have to do with anything?" I asked.

"Carrie, you are my best friend and I love you, but, let's face it, you also have a lot of bad qualities." One by one, Veda held up her fingers as she said, "You're reckless. You're stubborn. You're unconventional. You break almost all the rules. I'm pretty sure there hasn't been a line drawn that you haven't crossed. And, let's face it, you do not hide the crazy."

"I never said I was an angel," I said, though I'd been told by multiple people that I looked like one. "Or perfect."

"No, you're just you. You're one of a kind. And, hey, for all we know, Jerrod's into crazy chicks. But I doubt he's going to put up with your questionable police tactics. At least not for long. Wasn't that one of the reasons you two broke up the first time?" Veda asked.

"I'm done covering up my family's indiscretions," I said.

"When did that start?" Naomi asked. "Just the other day I shot a guy, and you helped me cover that up."

"You shot a guy?" Veda asked. Her loud voice attracted the attention of a young man walking his dog down the street. "Did you kill him?"

"No. I barely nicked him," Naomi said, sounding disappointed.

Despite my insistence that she keep her mouth shut, Naomi told Veda about what happened on Saturday night. Veda thought the story was wildly entertaining.

"See what I mean, Carrie?" Veda asked. "Questionable police tactics."

"That doesn't count," I said, knowing that it did. "It was an extenuating circumstance."

"No, it was you covering Naomi's butt because you didn't want her to get in trouble," Veda said. "Your family is like the mob, Carrie. Once you're in, there's no getting out. And you better do what they say."

"Remember, Veda, you're about to marry into that family. Besides Jerrod knows that the majority of the Shatners are criminals," I said.

But Veda's analogy was on point. A few months earlier, I tried to tell my family that I was done covering up their various crimes, but most of them didn't take me seriously. And those that did take me seriously made it clear that I had no choice but to keep cleaning up after the family.

"But I'm sure Jerrod doesn't approve," Veda said. "And how do you know he isn't hooking back up with you just to get closer to your family? For years, the law has been after y'all, but no one has ever been able to get enough evidence to bring y'all down. Dating you will certainly get Jerrod closer to your family. Which is what I've been telling you for months."

"Jerrod is not using me to get to my family," I said.

"Admit it, Carrie, it's a possibility," Veda said. "Naomi, how would you feel if Jerrod accidently came across some evidence against your daddy and arrested him?"

"I'd be mad," Naomi said.

"But who would you be mad at? Your daddy for doing illegal stuff? Jerrod for catching your daddy doing illegal stuff? Or Carrie for bringing Jerrod into our lives and exposing the Shatners' dirty little secrets to him?" Veda asked.

"Uh…I guess I'd be mad at Carrie." Naomi grabbed my shoulder. "I don't want my daddy to go to jail because you're dating a Texas Ranger!"

"That's not going to happen, Naomi," I said, hoping I was right.

But Veda was also right, when she said Hardy wasn't going to be able to put up with my family's indiscretions for long. It was a large part of the reason we broke up the first time. And I doubted my family was going to stop breaking the law anytime soon. As far as I knew, my family members didn't commit any really serious crimes – we didn't kill people, rape women, or molest children. But we did brew illegal moonshine, grow and sell marijuana, and engage in all sorts of other general lawlessness. And then there were all the physical altercations that the Shatners got involved in. If Hardy found evidence concerning any of my family's illegal activities or criminal acts, he'd be compelled to do something about it. But I didn't think Hardy was trying to get back together with me just to get evidence against my family. Dating me to get incriminating evidence against my family seemed too devious for an honorable man like him.

"I'm sorry, Carrie. I know I'm telling you things you don't want to hear, but you have a tendency to jump head-first into things. Just promise me that you'll think about all this before you get back together with Jerrod. I'm not saying there's no chance this will work out, but I just don't want to see it blow up in your face either." Veda gave me a hug and then walked over to her car. "I need to go, ladies. I've got appointments at the salon this morning. Can't keep the old ladies waiting. Oh, and Carrie, call me. You really need a trim."

"I've got to get to work, too. Thanks to you two, I'm going to be late," I said.

"I saw on the news that y'all are looking for someone. Is he a suspect?" Naomi asked.

"He's a person of interest," I said.

"Is that a fancy way of saying 'suspect'?"

"Yes it is. And I heard you're going to be doing Travis's hair and makeup for the memorial service," I said. Naomi was the makeup artist at the End of the Line Funeral Home. "Remind everyone at work not to go blabbing about Travis's cause of death."

"I know, I know. We already got a lecture at work," Naomi said as she rolled her eyes. "We have to get started on Travis today. The viewing is going to be Thursday night at the funeral home. And the funeral service will be Friday morning at the Grace Methodist Church."

"I'll probably be attending both. Now I really have to go," I said.

"Good luck finding that guy," Naomi said. "Oh, and Carrie, I know I'm not the best person to give advice…But think about what you're doing, okay? I know you like the Ranger, but do you really think everything will work out for you two?"

~*~*~

When I got to work, I found a council of war taking place in the conference room. Hardy, Uncle Murph, Quaranta, and a few deputies were sitting around the table while they read through police reports and looked at pictures of Xavier's bedroom. On the one wall, Quaranta had hung up crime scene and autopsy pictures. He'd also dragged a dry erase board into the room and wrote out a detailed timeline of Saturday night's events on it.

"Thanks for finally joining us, Carrie," Murph said.

"Yeah, yeah, yeah, I know I'm late," I said as I slipped into a chair next to Quaranta. There was an empty chair next to Hardy at the other end of the table, but, thanks to Veda's lecture, I spent the fifteen minute drive to work questioning everything. For the time being, I needed to put some distance between us so that I could focus on the case. "Fill me in."

"I've still got a team of deputies posted at Ida Ortega's house. And other teams are at Marisol's parents' house, the house she and Travis were renting, and Xavier's parents' house. So far Xavier hasn't made an appearance at any of those places. By the way, I sent a couple deputies over to Xavier's parent's house last night. They haven't seen him in weeks. And his old archery equipment is still in the garage," Murph said as he paced around the conference room table. "This morning I sent out a team of deputies to sit on the SWAT Zone, and I've got another at Big Pine High School. School was cancelled yesterday in respect for Travis, but the kids are back today and they're starting a memorial for Travis around the flagpole. I want to keep an eye on it just in case Xavier hears about the memorial and decides to pay a visit."

"Marisol called me as I was pulling into the parking lot," I said. "She saw the news report and wanted to talk to me. She's completely freaked out by all this and is terrified to leave her parents' house until Xavier is in custody."

"She's got plenty of people looking out for her. She'll be all right," Quaranta said.

"Did we get any calls about Xavier yet?" I asked.

Murph nodded. "Ida Ortega was the first to call. She threatened to sue the department."

"She then called us two more times," Quaranta said. "The second time was to scream obscenities, tell us that we're all going to Hell, and complain about the deputies parked in front of her house. And the third was to warn us that she has a lawyer."

"We also got seventeen calls from people asking if there's a reward for finding Xavier. I had to explain to some idiot that there is no 'dead or alive' stipulation," Murph said.

"Excuse me, Sher– AHH!" One of the receptionists walked in the conference room and caught sight of the crime scene and autopsy pictures taped to the wall. Using her hand to cover her eyes, she took a deep breath and said, "We just got a call from a woman claiming she saw the suspect at the Veterans' Memorial Park. She was taking her baby on a morning walk when she spotted a young man resembling Xavier. She said he's just sitting on top of the jungle gym, talking to himself."

"How far away is the park from here?" Hardy asked.

"About a mile or so west," I said. "It's a small, neighborhood park."

"Then let's get over there," Hardy said.

We were scrambling around, grabbing our car keys and arguing over who was going to check out the park and who was going to stay behind, when another one of our receptionists walked in the room and announced that we'd gotten a second call about an Xavier sighting. The manager at Walmart claimed Xavier had just walked in the store.

"Carrie and I will take a few deputies to Walmart," Hardy said to Quaranta. "The rest of y'all head out to the park."

The only Walmart in Wyatt County was in the Lone Star Strip Mall on the southwestern edge of Holler. It was across the street from Wyatt County General Hospital. Also in the strip mall was a furniture store, a bank, a fast food restaurant, a gas station, and a couple other small stores. With the sirens wailing and emergency lights flashing, it took us a matter of minutes to drive from the sheriff's department to the strip mall.

Hardy and I, along with two of the deputies, had just passed through the second set of automatic doors when we were accosted by a man claiming he was the Walmart manager. He barely looked old enough to shave.

"Boy, am I glad you're here, man." The manager grabbed Hardy's hand and shook it vigorously. "I was up front making sure that our Memorial Day displays are stocked when that guy y'all are looking for strolled in the front door."

Extracting his hand from the manager's, Hardy asked, "Do you know where he's at?"

"Not at the moment, but I have one of my clerks trailing the guy around the store. He's been all over the place. Last I heard, he was in the toy department. Let me radio my clerk for an update," the manager said before he stepped to the side and radioed the person he had following Xavier throughout the store. "My clerk says the suspect just left the toy department and is heading towards sporting goods."

"Lead the way," Hardy said.

The manager took off at a trot, dodging around customers, shopping carts, and displays exhibiting everything from cat food to feminine products. Hardy and I went after the manager while the two deputies looped around to approach the sporting goods department from another direction.

"Where's the suspect at now?" the manager asked a blue-vested clerk who was straightening a display of fishing rods.

"Over in the archery section. He's looking at the arrows," replied the clerk.

Taking up an interest in a display of fishing lures, the manager, Hardy, and I covertly checked out the person at the far end of the aisle. The man, who was standing with his left profile facing us, was of medium height and weight. He had close-cut, dark hair.

"What do you think, Carrie? Is that Xavier?" Hardy asked.

"I'm not sure. It kind of looks like him. But it's been years since I last saw him. And, remember, I only saw him that one time. We need to get a closer look."

Hardy and I were about to walk down the aisle when Xavier accidently knocked an archery sight off of the shelf. Bending over to pick it up, his oversized t-shirt gaped open and revealed that he was most definitely a she. Xavier didn't have breasts a few years ago, and I doubt he'd acquired any since then.

"I guess that's not your guy…Jeez, she even had facial hair…" the manager said as the grin faded from his face. "I'm sorry. I really did think it was your guy."

"You might want to direct her over to the women's clothing section and show her where the bras are," I said.

After thanking the manager for being alert and trying to help, Hardy and I headed towards the front of the store.

"This is what the rest of the day is going to be like, isn't it?" I asked Hardy.

"Most likely," Hardy said. "I just hope Xavier is still in the area and that one of the tips pays off. If he's fled the county, or the state, this is going to get very tedious."

Out in the parking lot, I called Murph. "Well that was a bust. Turns out that it was a woman who looks like Xavier. How'd things go at Veteran's Park? Was that Xavier?"

"It might have been. But whoever it was hightailed it out of there before Quaranta and the deputies arrived."

"So we've got nothing," I said.

"We don't have Xavier. But we finally got his medical records," Murph said. "The group home sent over a copy of their record. But you and Hardy will have to go pick up the record from the hospital's psych ward. Xavier's former doctor won't release them until after he's talked to you."

CHAPTER ELEVEN

"I saw on the news that you're looking for one of my former patients. Was it necessary to start a witch hunt for Xavier Ortega?" asked Dr. Vaughn.

I peered across the massive oak desk at Dr. Vaughn. It was hard to tell exactly what he looked like because of the vast distance between us. The desk was so large that it took up the majority of his office. There was just enough room for the two guest chairs that Hardy and I occupied. On the wall behind Vaughn, hanging above his bookcase, were his medical school diplomas. The rest of the walls were covered in Dallas Cowboys' memorabilia.

"Are you aware that the man who was murdered on Saturday night is Xavier's ex-girlfriend's new man? If Xavier was your patient both times that he was committed here, you must know who Marisol Santiago is," I said.

"Yes. Yes, of course, I know who Marisol is," Dr. Vaughn snapped. "Could you tell me what happened? What exactly makes you suspect Xavier had anything to do with this tragedy?"

"Travis Yeager was killed instantly when an arrow struck him in the back. Ms. Santiago was hit in the arm with a second arrow. She didn't see the shooter, but we've come to learn that Xavier has bowhunting experience," Hardy said, giving Dr. Vaughn the bare minimum of facts. "And, on Monday, Xavier's car was found parked not too far away from the crime scene. There was a compound bow in the backseat. And Detective Shatner found an arrow matching the murder weapon in Xavier's bedroom. We also have proof that Xavier was in the SWAT Zone not long before the attack."

"Also, in the six or so months that Xavier has been living with his grandmother, he's turned his bedroom into a shrine to Marisol," I said as I handed Vaughn my tablet so that he could see some of the pictures I had taken of Xavier's room. "The oldest pictures are from around the time that Marisol and Xavier started dating when they were in high school. The most recent are from just a few days before the shooting. As you can see, Xavier mutilated the faces of some of the people in the most recent pictures. That includes the victim."

"Oh, dear. That is not good. Not good at all." Vaughn said as he looked through the pictures and a fine sheen of sweat appeared on his wrinkled forehead. "After Xavier was transferred to the group home, he was no longer in my care. I was unaware until this morning that he had been released from the group home, and that he was back to living with his grandmother. Had I still been involved with Xavier's care, I would not have allowed him to return to her home. His grandmother is…"

"We've had the pleasure of meeting Ida. She told me that she doesn't think Xavier has a mental illness. She thinks it's the devil and that the church will cure him," I said.

"Yes, she told me the same thing both times Xavier was committed," Vaughn said.

"But now do you understand why we are looking for Xavier? And why we're concerned about his current mental state?" I asked.

"What can you tell us about him?" Hardy asked.

"These should give you a better understanding of Xavier's diagnoses," Vaughn said as spun around in his office chair and grabbed a couple pamphlets off of the bookcase behind him. He then tossed the pamphlets across the desk to us. One was about paranoid schizophrenia and the other was about depression. "I'm bound by the HIPAA Privacy Rule. I cannot discuss my former patient with you. All I can do is give you his medical record. And that is only because of the warrant forcing me to give it to you."

"As far as we can tell, Xavier is not currently medicated. And, if the four full bottles of Chlorpromazine that we found are any indication…Xavier has not been medicated in a few months," Hardy said.

"If Xavier is a danger to himself or to others, you are required to pass along relevant information to us. HIPAA allows for that," I said, pointing out that the Healthy Insurance Portability and Accountability Act Privacy Rule allows for health care professional to pass along information to law enforcement, as well as the patient's family, if the patient poses a threat to himself or others.

"I cannot speak for Xavier's current medical state. But when he was my patient, he suffered from delusions. And the main one was that Marisol was in danger and only he could protect her. Once we had him medicated, the delusions faded. It is possible, now that he is no longer medicated, that he is suffering from those same delusions. And, if he is, that could make him a danger to Marisol and anyone associated with her," Vaughn said, speaking with obvious reluctance.

"Do you think Xavier could have done this?" I asked.

"People with schizophrenia are rarely violent towards other people. Now, obviously, Xavier has proven that he is capable of violence. But, so far, he has only become violent when he's under the impression that Marisol might be in danger," Vaughn said before he pressed his palms against his forehead and groaned. "Do I think he could have killed Marisol's current boyfriend? Yes. Yes, I do. But to also hurt Marisol? To attempt to kill her as well? No, I cannot believe Xavier would do that. But it's hard for me to say what is going on in Xavier's head. Not until he is back in my care. But he hears voices. If one of them told him to kill Travis and Marisol, he might have tried to do it."

~*~*~

"What'cha doing?" I asked.

Back at the sheriff's department, Hardy and I found Uncle Murph hanging out in the front office with the receptionists. He had a map of Wyatt County tacked to a corkboard and was stabbing colored pins into it.

"I'm keeping track of all the Xavier sightings. We got three more while you were talking to Xavier's doctor," Murph said as he pointed at each of the push pins on the map. "So far all have been false alarms."

One of the receptionists slammed down the phone and announced, "Got another sighting. One of the librarians at the Mooresville Library swore Xavier came in to drop off a copy of Gone With the Wind. The book. Not the movie."

Murph picked up another pin and, after accidently jabbing it into his palm, he stuck it almost dead-center in small town of Mooresville. Mooresville is a small town located in the southwestern part of Wyatt County.

I gathered up my hair and pulled it back in a ponytail. I was afraid that if I left it hanging down, I'd start pulling it out in frustration.

"If Xavier's smart, he's either fled the area or is holed up somewhere. Unfortunately, Dr. Vaughn didn't give us a very good idea of how Xavier's brain works," I said.

"That's because he's not sure how it works," Hardy said.

During the next two and a half hours, we received five more calls from people claiming to have seen Xavier. All five were mistaken identities. Uncle Murph was beginning to regret his decision to ask for the public's help when a call came over the radio from the deputies watching the high school.

"Suspect spotted at Big Pine. Attempting to apprehend."

Hardy, Murph, and I sat up straighter. The receptionists spun around in their chairs and stared at the scanner. We were anxiously waiting for the announcement that the deputies had Xavier in custody when one of the deputies came back on the radio.

"We have a 411 in progress. Suspect took off in a late model van. Dark purple in color. License plate starts with 'Romeo-Lima-Bravo.' Suspect headed west on Cameron Street. We are not in pursuit. I repeat, we are not in pursuit."

"Damn it!" Hardy shouted. He slammed his coffee mug down on the table, shattering it. "Why aren't they pursuing him? What kind of department are you running around here, Sheriff Shatner?"

"I'm doing the best that I can with what I've got, Sergeant Hardy," Murph said, his voice rising with each word. "If you think you can do a better job, why don't you get out there and find Xavier?"

"That's exactly what I'm going to do," Hardy said as he used a handful of tissues to soak up the coffee. "Come on, Carrie. Let's go find Xavier."

"How exactly do you plan to find him?" I asked.

"By heading east on Cameron Street and looking for a purple late model van."

The sheriff's department is on the corner of Main Street and Holler Avenue near the center of the town of Holler. The Wyatt County Sheriff's Department was housed in an old general store. After the store closed, the county renovated the large building and put up additional interior walls to create various smaller rooms.

My alma mater, Big Pine High School, was a couple miles east of Holler. The high school, which had been built to replace the old high school building around the same time that I was born, wasn't too far from my house. It was also right next door to the SWAT Zone.

After pulling out of the sheriff's department's parking lot, I headed east on Holler Avenue before cutting south to Cameron Street. Along the way, Hardy and I spotted eleven vans – none of them were purple.

Quaranta, who had been responding to a call at Abbott Equestrian Center, was already at Big Pine High School when Hardy and I got there. We found him talking to the two deputies posted at the school while another deputy questioned a teenager.

Piled up around the school's flag pole that was in front of the school's main entrance was a mound of stuffed animals and flowers. Candles, religious statuettes, and all sorts of other little mementoes were lined up along the edge of the sidewalk. There were also pictures, cards, and signs clipped to the clothesline that someone had used to rope off the sidewalk that led to the front doors.

"Y'all want to explain to me how you let the suspect steal a car and get away?" Hardy asked the deputies.

"They didn't let Xavier do anything, Hardy," Quaranta said in an attempt to defend his deputies. "He just did it."

Deputy Richards glared at Hardy and said, "Deputy Mathews and I have been here all day, keeping an eye on the people coming to the memorial. Some guy wearing a baseball cap walked up –"

"Deputy Richards and I thought it was a student walking over from the parking lot. School had just gotten out for the day when this happened. We didn't know it was the suspect until he took off the hat," Deputy Mathews said as he nervously wrung his hands.

"I radioed that the suspect was here and we went after him. He spotted us and started running towards the street," Deputy Richards said.

"That's when this purple van drove past," Deputy Mathews said, pointing at the blonde teenager who was crying on the third deputy's shoulder. "The suspect jumped in front of the van. When the driver stopped, he pulled that nice young lady out of her van, jumped in, and took off. He sideswiped another car and he almost hit two other kids on his way out of the parking lot."

"Deputy Mathews and I ran back to our car and were about to go in pursuit when another student stopped his truck right in front of us and got out to put flowers on the memorial. All we could do was watch the suspect drive off," Deputy Richards said.

Hardy sighed, earning himself another vile look from Deputy Richards.

Nudging Deputy Richards and Deputy Mathews away from Hardy, Quaranta commended them for doing what they could. He told them it wasn't their fault Xavier got away.

"Let's get out of here, Carrie," Hardy said. "We may as well drive around and join in the search for the purple van."

"May as well," I said as I turned and headed back to my Jeep.

Pulling out onto Cameron Street, I turned west and headed back towards town. Quaranta followed me in his cruiser. Just down the street from the high school, we came to a four-way stop. To our left was the high school football field and to our right was a gas station. On the other side of the road was a Baptist Church and a small neighborhood. It was in the small neighborhood that nosy Linda Barley found Xavier's grandmother's car abandoned in front of her house.

Honking his horn to get my attention, Quaranta pulled up next to me.

"Any guesses on which way Xavier went?" Quaranta asked.

"When Hardy and I drove out this way, we didn't see any purple minivans," I said. "But that doesn't mean Xavier didn't go straight and then turn off before we would have passed him."

"I'm sure the Holler Police are already searching the town for the van," Quaranta said. "If Xavier's driving it through Holler, or ditched it somewhere in town, they'll find it."

"You want to head south on East End?" I asked. "Hardy and I can go north."

"Radio me if you see anything," Quaranta said.

A mile down the road, I hung a right and then headed north on East End Road. The road edged along the eastern side of Holler. I took East End on a frequent basis to get to my grandparents' house. They, along with a number of other Shatners, lived on a five thousand acre section of land in the northern part of the county. Also on the Shatner homestead was the moonshine still, a few Cold War era bomb shelters housing the marijuana plants, and probably a few dead bodies that were disposed of long before I was born. A few of my family members' legitimate businesses were scattered throughout the vast acreage, including Guns n' Stuff, a no-kill animal shelter, and the Alpaca Farm and Wild West Town that served as Wyatt County's most popular tourist trap.

Hardy and I had only driven about a half mile or so north when we came across a purple minivan in a ditch by the side of the road. If a pine tree with a thick trunk hadn't been in the van's path, the van would have crashed into the front porch of a small home.

Three people – two men and a woman – wandered around the van, peering in the windows and checking out the damage to the crumpled front end of the van. At the back of the van, a mangy looking dog lifted his leg and watered the right rear tire.

Pulling to the side of the road, Hardy and I jumped out of my Jeep and ran over to assess the situation. I made sure to take my keys with me. I didn't want to leave them in the ignition only to have Xavier dart out from behind a tree and steal my car.

"Y'all sure got here quick," the woman said. "I ain't even done calling the po-po yet."

"Did you witness the accident?" Hardy asked.

"Naw, but we sure did hear it. Squealing tires and then BAM! We looked out the front window and this is what we saw," the younger man said. He dropped down to his knees and shoved his head under the van. "Radiator is busted. Better git a tow truck."

Hardy edged closer to the van and leaned in the driver's side door that was hanging open.

"Xavier's not here. But the airbag did deploy, and there's blood all over it," Hardy said.

"The airbag probably broke Xavier's nose when it hit him in the face," I said. I then turned to the witnesses and asked, "Did any of you see what happened to the driver?"

"Uh huh," the woman said. "He got out of the van and stumbled around. I came out onto the front porch and asked if he was okay. I guess he was, since he took off running."

"Which way did he go?" Hardy and I asked at the same time.

"Thataway," the woman pointed north. "Last I saw, he was running up the middle of the road like he was Forrest Gump himself."

"Thanks for your help." Hardy tipped his white Stetson towards the woman. "We'll need to get witness statements from y'all. But, right now, Detective Shatner and I need to go find the driver. Someone will be by to talk to you and take care of the van."

Hardy and I went back to my Jeep, where I grabbed my radio and let everyone know that we found the stolen minivan and that Xavier had fled the scene.

"Xavier can't have gotten far on foot. Especially if he was injured in the crash," Hardy said. "What else is along this road?"

"Not much. There's a lot of trees and some houses. There's also an antiques store and a really crappy restaurant. And, about two mile from here, East End merges with Main Street and heads north out of the county," I said.

"Maybe Xavier was planning to flee the county when he crashed. He knows we're looking for him now."

"Maybe…There's also a bunch of roads that branch off East End. Some are main roads that head back into Holler, or to other parts of the county. There are also some backroads that branch off as well. Xavier could have taken any one of those."

"Are any of the places we have deputies stationed at in the northern part of the county?" Hardy asked.

"Xavier's parents' house is northwest of Holler. He could be headed there. Or…oh crap! I know where Xavier's going. Get in the car! Hurry!" I shouted. I jumped in the front seat and jammed the key in the ignition. "The End of the Line is on Chestnut Avenue. It's right up the road from here."

"What's the End of the Line?" Hardy asked as he dove in the passenger seat.

"It's a funeral home. It's where the medical examiner sent Travis's body."

CHAPTER TWELVE

Chestnut Avenue was only a couple hundred yards up the road from where Xavier crashed the van, and then the End of the Line was about a half a mile down Chestnut Avenue towards the center of town. Despite the short distance, I got up to almost ninety miles an hour before I slammed on the brakes and whipped into the funeral home's parking lot.

I parked my car next to the circular fountain in front of the funeral home and then charged towards the side entrance of the one-story, orange brick building. I was reaching for the door handle when Hardy, who was a step behind me, grabbed my arm and pulled me back.

"Careful. There's fresh blood on that handle," Hardy said as he pointed towards the drying blood that was smeared all over one of the antique-looking, bronze handles.

"That's gotta mean Xavier was here," I said, spotting a bloody handprint on the white wood door.

Pulling away from Hardy, I drew my gun. I then grabbed the door handle that wasn't covered in blood and swung open the door.

Stepping into the funeral home's subdued but stylishly decorated lobby, I spotted another bloody handprint streaked across the ivory and gold striped wallpaper next to the door leading into the chapel. Poking my head into the room, I found a group of funeral home employees neatening up Xavier's path of destruction. Chairs lay on their sides, and there were broken vases and scattered flowers along the back of the room. Before being knocked or thrown to the ground, the vases had been setting on wooden pedestals that were lined up behind the last row of chairs. There were more flowers and pedestals at the front of the room – most of which had also been knocked over.

"Looks like Xavier made a mess." Hardy handed me a funeral program featuring a picture of an elderly woman with blue hair. "This poor woman's viewing starts in two hours."

"Someone is bound to be upset about this," I said.

"Especially since Xavier made it to the casket. It looks like those two people are working on the body," Hardy said, pointing at the two funeral home employees who were hunched over the open casket. "I'm not sure I want to know what Xavier did to the deceased. But I've got to tell them to stop cleaning up. This is now a crime scene."

"While you do that, I'll go find Naomi or the owner, Oswald Line. We need to know what happened here. And if Xavier is still in the building."

As I hurried across the lobby to the manager's office, I spotted a fresh hole in the drywall near the hallway that led back to the workroom. I was about to swerve over to take a look at the damage when I heard raised voices coming from the manager's office.

"This is an absolute disgrace! And an insult to my wife," shouted an elderly man as he waved his cane under the End of the Line owner's snub nose. "I should sue you!"

"Now, Papa, what happened isn't Mr. Line's fault," said a middle-aged woman.

"He still could have done something to stop that madman from barging in here! There is no fixing what that monster destroyed!"

Knocking on the door to get their attention, I held up my badge and asked, "Can I have a word, Oswald?"

Oswald Line, who was impeccable in a three-piece suit, tramped out into the lobby.

"Goldarnit, Detective Shatner, you couldn't have gotten here fifteen minutes ago when that nutcase was tearing up my funeral home and destroying everything we've got set up for tonight's viewing? The son of a gun was dripping blood everywhere. Including on the body. Darn near ruined her makeup. Thank God he came in now and not in a few hours when the viewing is taking place. Only the husband and daughter witnessed the debacle," Oswald said.

"Where's the nutcase at now?" I asked.

"How should I know? He ran off down the hallway towards the workrooms. I would have followed, but I've got the irate old man to deal with. I did hear someone yelling that the nutcase ran out the back."

"Twice now we've just missed him," Hardy said as walked up and then grabbed the radio off my belt so he could request that everyone who was available head over towards the funeral home and start combing the area for Xavier.

"Is this the nutcase, Oswald?" I asked, holding up a picture of Xavier.

"It might be. Like I said, he was covered in blood and going bananas. I never really got that good of a look at him," Oswald said.

"Did he knock over the chairs and the flowers? And did he make that hole in the wall?" Hardy asked.

"He caused most of the damage, yes. Though I can't put all of the blame on him. Some of my employees knocked over chairs and flowers as they attempted to stop him. As for the hole… the nut shoved Naomi when she tried to stop him from going back the hall to our workrooms. Naomi fell against the wall and her shoulder punched through the drywall," Oswald said.

"What? Is Naomi all right?" I asked.

Oswald shrugged. "I guess. She took off after the nutcase when he headed for the workroom."

Leaving Hardy and Oswald in the lobby, I went in search of Naomi. To the right of the chapel was a corridor that led to the back part of the funeral home. I was almost to the door marked 'employee's only' when the door flew open and Naomi stomped out of the room.

"Oh, hey. I was just about to call you," Naomi said as she crashed into me. Her skimpy, see-through, pale pink camisole and short skirt hardly seemed appropriate for work.

"Are you all right?" I asked.

"No, I'm not all right. Look at what Xavier did to me," Naomi said. She turned so that I could see the bruise forming on her right shoulder. "And I think I'm going to have another bruise on my butt."

"You think you need to go to the hospital?" I asked.

"I'll live. But that crazy guy tore my new shirt." Naomi waved a dark pink, frilly blouse in my face.

Hardy walked up behind me and asked, "You want to tell us what happened, Naomi?"

"So, I was, like, standing in the lobby when this guy comes barging in," Naomi said, beginning her story. "He's covered in blood, and I'm like 'Oh my God, what happened to you?' I didn't realize it was the guy y'all are looking for until he started screaming. I have no idea what he was saying, but I definitely heard him say 'Marisol.' He ran into the chapel, looked in the casket, and flipped out. Then he came back into the lobby and demanded to know where Travis was. I was, like, 'calm down, buddy.' That's when he shoved me into the wall and ran towards the back. I yelled for my coworkers to call the cops and then I went after him."

"You shouldn't have tried to interfere," Hardy said. "You could have gotten hurt worse than you did."

Naomi started to shrug but wound up wincing when she moved her bruised shoulder. She said, "Someone had to stop him and it didn't look like anyone else was going to. So I chased him into the back and found him standing over Travis's body."

"Travis is just lying out in the open?" I asked.

"At the moment, yeah. We had just finished embalming Travis's body and were planning to get him dressed and made up once we finished getting set up for tonight's viewing. I was trying to get Xavier away from the body. That's when he knocked me down and took off out the back door. You know, my butt really hurts," Naomi said. She then turned around, pulled up the back of her short, black skirt, and revealed a bright blue thong. "Do I have a bruise on my butt?"

"Not yet." I grabbed Naomi's skirt and yanked it back down over her butt. "But you will when I'm done kicking it."

Hardy cleared his throat. "Naomi, there is a pink spot on your…uh…"

"On my right butt cheek?" Naomi asked. "Yeah, that's a tattoo. It's a pair of lips. It's just like Carrie's aside from the color."

"I see that." Turning to me, Hardy said, "Carrie, you never would tell me the story behind that sexy little tattoo. Nor did you tell me that you and Naomi have matching tattoos."

"A bunch of us Shatner girls have them. Though Carrie was the first to get one. You were, what, eighteen when you got it?" Naomi asked.

"Nineteen. I was going through a stage where I wanted the world to kiss my butt. Now it's just an embarrassing reminder of my immaturity," I said. Unfortunately, my getting the pair of red lips tattooed on my butt cheek started a bad trend among the women in my family. At last count, a dozen of us now have the matching tattoos in various shades of red and pink. Changing the subject, I asked, "Did Xavier do any damage to Travis's body?"

"Xavier almost knocked Travis's body off the embalming table. And he got blood all over it. He also stabbed Travis through the stomach with a pair of scissors. Come on, I'll show you," Naomi said.

Naomi led the way into the small, sterile preparation room. Travis was lying on one of the steel embalming tables with a pair of scissors buried up to the handles in his stomach.

"The fortunate thing is that Xavier stabbed Travis right through the autopsy incision. Except for severing a few of the stitches, he didn't do too much additional damage," Naomi said.

"No, but he could have," Hardy said.

"Xavier went out this way," Naomi said, opening a door that led into a small storage area. A door on the other side of that room opened up into the garage. "The mortician heard all the shouting and came in from the garage. He was supervising a delivery. Xavier shoved him out of the way, ran out through the garage, and drove off in our hearse."

"Hold on a second…did you just say that Xavier carjacked your hearse?" I asked.

"Yes. Or would it be considered hearse-jacking?" Naomi paused for a few seconds to think about it. "And is it possible to kidnap a corpse? Because Xavier did that, too."

"Oh my God," I mumbled.

"You want to back up and explain all this, Naomi?" Hardy asked as he walked out into the funeral home's garage. The garage had two bays – one for the hearse and another for the limo. The white limo was parked in the far garage bay. The one closest to us was empty, and the garage door was open to reveal the wooded area behind the funeral home.

"There was a viewing and memorial service over at the Presbyterian church earlier today. The deceased is being cremated so we had to bring the body back here after the service. Oswald's son had just gotten back with the body when Xavier came tearing through here and took off in the hearse," Naomi said.

"The good news is that there can't be too many hearses driving around Wyatt County. I'll put it out on the police scanner that everyone needs to be on the lookout for a hearse. Then I'll get a couple deputies started on photographing Xavier's path of destruction through here," Hardy said as he headed back into the workroom and then set off at a jog towards the lobby.

I followed after Hardy, and Naomi limped along at my heels.

"You sure you're okay?" I asked Naomi.

"Yeah, I'll be fine. Just need some ice. See ya later, Carrie," Naomi said as she veered off into the employee breakroom.

When I walked into the lobby, I found Hardy talking to Granddaddy, Uncle Houston, and Uncle Bowie. Granddaddy and his brothers were squeezed together on a gold brocade chaise lounge next to a half-dead potted pink calla lily. The overhead florescent lights reflected off all three of their bald heads. While the three brothers all looked similar, Houston and Bowie were edging towards overweight, while Granddaddy appeared not to have had a solid meal in months.

Uncle Houston was the patriarch of the Shatner family. A few months earlier, I tried to knock him off his lofty perch by reminding him that he was a criminal, not God. I only managed to bring Houston down a rung or two. I comforted myself in the knowledge that Houston was in his late-eighties and one of these days would either give up his criminal activities or die.

Uncle Bowie was, and always had been, Houston's lackey. Aside from going to the bathroom, Bowie didn't do anything without Houston's approval.

As for Granddaddy, he was the Yin to his brothers combined Yang. They were opposite forces that were interdependent of each other.

Granddaddy, Houston, and Bowie had also had a sister and younger brother, both of whom had already passed away. Benjamin Milam Shatner died when he was nineteen. I don't know the details, but I've heard that Uncle Ben died in some sort of criminal endeavor. Prior to Aunt Emily Morgan's death two years ago, she had been the matriarch of the Shatner family. And she had done a much better job at running the criminal operation, and keeping it on the down low, than Uncle Houston managed to.

"What are y'all doing here?" I asked, directing the question to Granddaddy.

"We were across the street playing checkers with the boys at the VFW when we saw your Jeep and the sheriff's department cruisers over here. I figured I'd come over and see what was going on. Tweedledee and Tweedledum insisted on tagging along," Granddaddy said. Even though he retired from the sheriff's position thirteen years ago, Granddaddy couldn't help but stick his nose into the department's business. Retirement didn't suit him well.

"Did y'all happen to witness anything? Like a blood-covered man running up the street? Or a hearse peeling out of here?" I asked.

"Houston and me saw the hearse take off when we were smoking cigars out by the old World War Two tank that's in front of the VFW," Bowie said.

"Figured something weird was goin' on considerin' the hearse took the turn on two wheels," Houston added.

Houston and Bowie then talked over each other as they told me and Hardy about what they witnessed. Listening to them, you'd think it was the most exciting thing they'd ever seen in their long lives.

"It sure is comforting to know that you're investigating this latest killing, Mr. Ranger," Houston said, failing to recognize that it was actually the sheriff's department's case and that Hardy was only helping us out.

"I'm happier than a hog in slop that a lawman of your quality is looking out for our little county," Bowie added, laying on the flattery a little too thick.

"I just don't know what Wyatt County is coming to with all these criminals," Houston said. "It's making law abiding citizens like us shake in our boots."

Granddaddy snorted in amusement.

"I'm sure it is," Hardy said. "Have you two been staying out of trouble?"

"Trouble? Son, I'll have you know that we Shatners have never been in trouble. As I'm sure my brother Crockett can tell you," Houston said. "Hell, the Shatners wouldn't even know what trouble was if it came up and bit us on the butt."

"I'm sure you wouldn't," Hardy said as he took me by the elbow and began to pull me away from Granddaddy and my uncles. "Now, if you'll excuse us, Carrie and I need to get back to work. We've got a hearse to find."

"Hold up there, son. My brothers and I got some questions for you."

Houston stood up and took a couple steps towards where Hardy and I stood. Houston then stuck his liver spotted face as close to Hardy's as he could get. "You got a lot of friends, Mr. Ranger?"

"You best button your lips before you say something stupid, brother," Granddaddy said.

"I've got some friends," Hardy said, sounding confused as he looked back and forth between Granddaddy and Houston.

"Is Carrie one of your friends?" Houston asked.

"I'd like to think that Carrie and I are more than just friends," Hardy said.

"I hope so, too, son," Houston said. "I heard about your little slumber party last night. And, let me tell you, it does my heart good knowing you two kids are back to rolling in the hay."

"For God's sake, who didn't Naomi call this morning? Or did she send out a group text to everyone," I asked, hoping Houston would shut up and stop sticking his nose into my sex life. "How many times do I have to tell you people that my love life is none of your business?"

"I've been trying to explain that to Houston all morning," Granddaddy said. "But you know my brother was born with a thick skull."

Not long after Hardy showed up in town a few months ago to start investigating the body in the fairgrounds' dumpster, Houston pulled me aside and told me that I needed to keep Hardy 'distracted' so that he wouldn't look too closely at the Shatners. What he really wanted me to do was sleep with Hardy. When I didn't do that, Houston chastised me for not getting Hardy into my bed. He also said that if I didn't sleep with Hardy, he'd get one of my female cousins to do it. Once I did hook up with Hardy, Houston congratulated me for following his instructions. I had to explain to Houston that I wasn't dating Hardy because he told me to.

"Everything regarding the Shatners is my business, Carrie," Houston said. He then reached over and thumped Hardy on the shoulder. "Carrie always was a wild girl. What she needs is a strong man to reel her in and make her behave. I'm thinking you're the right man for the job."

"I'd like to think I am, too." Hardy squeezed my elbow that he was still gripping.

"Good. That's real good, son." Houston rewarded Hardy with a lascivious grin. "Now, while we're on the topic of friendship...There are a lot of Shatners, Mr. Ranger, and we all want to be friends with you, too. Not the rolling-in-the-hay type of friends. Just the hanging out, having a good time kind of friends."

"I got no problem being friendly with y'all." Hardy gave my elbow another squeeze.

"Jesus, Houston, would you just shut up?" Granddaddy asked. He tried to steer Houston towards the door, but Houston was having none of it. "Carrie and Jerrod have to get back to work. They don't have time to listen to you ramble."

I had a good idea where the conversation was headed and I planned to get Hardy out of there before Houston said something offensive – or anything more offensive than he already had said. I could only hope Houston would listen to Granddaddy and stop talking.

"You know, Jerrod, we really should be getting out of here." I tried to pull Hardy towards the door, but he was twice my size and I could barely budge him. "We've got to get back out there and help look for Xavier."

"Hush, Carrie. Us men are talking," Houston said.

"Did you really just tell me to hush?" I asked.

"You could talk a man's ear clear off, Carrie. Give it a rest for a while. I'm sure the Ranger gets sick of all your yapping." Houston looked over at Hardy and gave him a conspiratorial smile. "Women talk too much, don't they, son? And there's much better things Carrie could be doing with her pretty little mouth."

"I don't mind her talking, Houston. I kinda like it," Hardy said.

"You better like it," I said. "Now, can we please get out of here?"

"Not yet. I want to hear what Houston has to say," Hardy said.

"What I'm saying, Mr. Ranger, is that the Shatners are good friends to have," Houston said. "We're real loyal and we look out for our friends."

"We're also the kind of people that help our friends hide the bodies," Bowie added.

"The thing is, we expect the same from our friends in return," Houston said.

"Do y'all have a body that you need help hiding?" Hardy asked.

"Oh, no, not at all. We ain't the kind of people that have bodies to hide. But, if we did, we need to know which of our friends have shovels," Houston said. He tried to look innocent, but, the more he tried, the guiltier he looked. Of course, despite what he was doing, Houston always looked like he was up to no good.

"Hold on a second." Hardy held up his hands and gestured for Houston and Bowie to stop talking. "Are y'all asking me to look the other way and help cover up your crimes?"

"We'll make it worthwhile." Houston gave Hardy an exaggerated wink. "You'll get even more perks than the ones that Carrie should be giving you."

"Houston! Do you seriously think of me as nothing more than a perk?" I asked.

"Ain't you dating the Ranger 'cause I told you to?" Houston asked.

"You told Carrie to date me?" Hardy turned to me and asked, "Were you dating me because your uncle told you to?"

"No! Absolutely not!" I said.

"My grandbaby ain't the kind of woman who would do that," Granddaddy said.

"Your grandbaby will do what I tell her to," Houston said to Granddaddy.

"Can we please get out of here, Jerrod?" I asked.

"Yes." Hardy leaned forward Houston so that his nose was almost touching my great-uncle's nose. "Let me make something clear, Houston. I am a Texas Ranger. I didn't get to where I am by looking the other way or taking bribes. I've never done that and I'm certainly not going to start now. Whatever goes on between me and Carrie is not going to affect how I treat the rest of y'all. If one of you commits a crime, there is nothing you or Carrie can do to stop me from doing my job. If I have to lock y'all up in jail, I'll do it."

Hardy then spun around on the heel of his black cowboy boot and marched across the funeral home's lobby.

"Nice job, Houston," I said. "If dumb was money, you'd be a billionaire."

"Who pissed in your Coke?" Houston, who always had to get the last word, yelled, "Hey, Mr. Ranger, us Shatners make great friends. But we make even worse enemies."

"Give it a rest, will you?" Granddaddy said to Houston.

I ran across the lobby to catch up to Hardy. "Wait up, Jerrod!"

Hardy and I were barely out the door and in the parking lot when he took me by both arms and pushed me up against the building. He then planted a hand on either side of my head, trapping me between his arms.

"Is what Houston said true? Did he tell you to date me?" Hardy asked.

"No. Houston told me to screw you to keep you distracted during the investigation. He didn't want you looking too closely at the Shatners," I said.

"Is that what this is? Are you trying to get back together with me because you want to be with me? Or is it because someone is telling you to? And are you doing it because you hope I'll help you cover up your family's crimes? Was last night supposed to be some sort of trap?"

"Are you kidding me, Jerrod? What kind of woman do you think I am?"

"I think you're a woman who loves her family and will do anything you can to keep them out of trouble."

"But there are certain things I won't do for them." I put my hands on Hardy's chest and shoved him backwards. "At the top of that list is sleeping with a man just to protect them."

"How am I supposed to be in a relationship with you when I can't even trust you?" Hardy whipped off his Stetson and ran his hand through his hair. "I really did want to get back together with you. Now I'm not so sure that it's a good idea. I don't want your uncles to get the wrong idea. Or anyone else, for that matter."

"Hey, how do I know you weren't dating me just so you can get closer to my family? Maybe you thought I'd confess everything during a little pillow talk and then you could use it to bring us all down. You'd be pulling off the one thing that no other lawman has been able to do – putting a stop to the Shatners' illegal activities."

"Do you really think that?" Hardy slammed his fist into the wall just to the left of my head. "You're the most gorgeous woman I've ever seen –"

"I know, I know. I'm also the funniest, sexiest, and smartest. We've been over this before," I said. "I guess this is just a sexual attraction for you, isn't it? I can't fathom why a man like you would possibly want to be with a woman like me."

Hardy and I had a big fight even before we started dating. It was during our first criminal investigation together. Despite the fact that Hardy asked me to help him with the case, he accused me of manipulating him into accepting my help – which was at least partially true. Hardy also accused me of using him as a pawn and making him look like a fool.

"That's not it at all, Carrie." Hardy stepped closer and put his hands on my hips. "There are things about me…If you knew, you'd head for the hills and never come back."

"And there are things about my family…" I didn't realize I was crying until a tear dripped off my chin and splashed onto the front of Hardy's shirt. I used my sleeve to wipe away the rest of the tears. "I'm part of a package deal, Jerrod. You can't have me without getting the rest of my family. They're going to keep committing crimes. And, as long as we're dating, they're going to be bugging you to help cover it up."

"I know they're going to ask me, darling. I'm telling you right now that I can't help them." Hardy pulled me away from the wall and into his arms. "Just promise me that you'll never ask me to look the other way or cover something up."

I opened my mouth to reassure Hardy that I would never ask him to get involved in covering up a crime, but, before I could say anything, I thought about Naomi shooting Dustin in the foot. What would I have done if Hardy had been at my house when Naomi called and begged me to come over? Hardy would have insisted on going over to Naomi's house with me and he wouldn't have thought twice before arresting Naomi. And I would have tried to talk him out of that.

When I didn't say anything, Hardy pushed me away and said, "Don't do this to me."

CHAPTER THIRTEEN

"It's probably for the best that this happened before you and Sergeant Hardy really got back together. Makes it easier for both of you," Murph said. "He's a good guy, but he's a Texas Ranger. I'm uneasy enough about the boys my daughter dates. I don't need to worry about how your love life might affect me. I doubt Sergeant Hardy would ever arrest you, but there's nothing to stop him from sending me to the big house."

"Thanks, Uncle Murph. Your little pep talks are always so inspiring," I said, laying on the sarcasm. "And Hardy and I aren't officially over. Not as far as I know."

"Face it, Carrie. Y'all's relationship is deader than every armadillo dumb enough to cross the road. Why else have you been hiding out in my office ever since you and Sergeant Hardy got back from getting yelled at by the Santiagos? You're avoiding him because you know things are over between y'all."

Murph had moved the map of Wyatt County, which was now stuck full of colored pins, into his office. We'd gotten almost thirty reported sightings since the morning – including some that were from surrounding counties. After so many sightings, I was beginning to think that people were calling in and making up false reports just to mess with us.

"I'm not hiding in here, Uncle Murph. I'm helping you monitor the latest calls about Xavier sightings. Someone needs to help you keep track of them. Especially since we haven't had a confirmed sighting since the one at Marisol's parents' house."

Hardy and I were still arguing in the funeral home parking lot when one of the deputies interrupted. The deputy told us that Xavier had just been spotted near the Santiago's house. The deputies and Mr. Santiago, who was home at the time, gave chase, but Xavier managed to get away. The hearse that Xavier stole was found half-submerged in a koi pond one street over from where the Santiagos lived. Postponing our argument for a later time, Hardy and I headed over to the Santiago's house. We were too late to help look for Xavier, but we were just in time to get yelled at by the entire Santiago family. The only one of them who didn't scream at us was Evita.

There was a knock on Murph's office door and then Hardy walked in.

"We just got a call from one of the guys working at the Dancing Cowgirl. He says that a young man looking a lot like Xavier just came in," Hardy said.

"That's one of the few places in the county where Xavier hasn't been spotted yet," I said.

The Dancing Cowgirl had the dubious honor of being the only strip club in Wyatt County. It was owned by the Palmer family, who my family had been feuding with since the end of the Civil War.

"Deputies are already on their way to the club. Quaranta and I are heading out there to join them," Hardy said.

"Hey, Carrie, you should tag along," Murph said.

"No thanks," I said. "I've been to the Dancing Cowgirl twice. And that's two times too many for me. But try not to get molested, Jerrod."

During my first visit, a stripper coated in glitter tried to feel up Hardy. The next time I was at the club, an older man groped me.

Hardy cringed. "It's after seven. You may as well go home, Carrie. Quaranta will let you know what happens."

Hardy turned around and walked out of the room. Even though I had no desire to step foot in the Dancing Cowgirl again, I was a little disappointed because Hardy didn't want me to come along. Given he had previously stated that it was no place for a lady.

Murph stood up, and said, "Come on, Carrie, you're going with them."

"They've got all those deputies with them, Jerrod and Juan don't need me," I said.

"Regardless, you need to be there."

"Uncle Murph, what is the big deal about the Dancing Cowgirl?"

Murph sat back down and whispered, "I didn't want you to know about this, but the Shatners are currently selling moonshine and drugs out of the strip club."

"Are you kidding me?" I asked as I sprung out of my chair. I walked over to the crash test dummy that was still lying on the floor and kicked it as hard as I could in the crotch. "Are you telling me that the Shatners and Palmers are now working together? You're right, I need to get over there and shut the operation down."

~*~*~

The gravel parking lot at the Dancing Cowgirl was almost full when I got there. The only parking spaces left were those that the various protest groups had taken over at the far end of the parking lot. The protesters were marching around, waving signs, and chanting.

Across the street, the Den of Depravity was dealing with their own horde of protesters. The Den was the most recent of Uncle Houston's legal, but questionable, undertakings. He'd purchased the dilapidated one-story building late last year, and then spent the past six months completely renovating and adding on to it. Wyatt County's first adult store had its grand opening this past Saturday, but the festivities were continuing through the week before the store's official hours kicked in on this upcoming Saturday. From what I'd heard, the various groups of protestors planned to be at the adult store and the strip club for the entire week. One of the groups vowed to stick around and protest every night until the store and club were shut down.

As I drove through the mass of people protesting in the Dancing Cowgirl's parking lot, I spotted a few familiar faces among the people who jumped in front of my car to shout at me and wave their signs around. Most of the people I recognized went to the same church as my family. I also saw some of my former teachers.

Driving around the side of the long, low building, I parked in the larger lot out back. Keeping my distance from the two deputies standing guard at the back door, I crept around to the front of the building. There were two more deputies watching the front door. Sticking to the shadows – and as far away from the protestors as possible – I anxiously waited for Hardy, Quaranta, and the deputies to come back outside.

After ten nerve-racking minutes spent hiding in the shadows while I visualized Hardy stumbling upon one or more Shatners committing crimes, I was able to breathe a sigh of relief when Hardy strode outside with Quaranta and the deputies on his heels. I was both thankful and disappointed to see that they were empty handed. I'd hoped they would find Xavier in the strip club, finally putting an end to our search. But I had also dreaded seeing them drag a Shatner out in handcuffs.

"Are you shutting down this wicked establishment?" shouted a protestor who had ventured away from his group and approached Hardy and Quaranta. "You've been inside. You've seen the sins of the flesh that are being committed in there."

"We're here looking for a suspect in a murder investigation. I do appreciate what you're doing, but I have no legal cause to shut this place down," Hardy said.

"Women are being paid to take their clothing off in there!" Pointing to the Den of Depravity across the street, the man said, "And that atrocious place sells objects of a sexual nature. Just the fact that they are corrupting the county's youth and providing perverts, sinners, and sodomites a house of refuge should be cause enough to shut them both down. My flock has prayed for God to smite both of these hellholes to the ground, but so far he has not answered our prayers. When we saw you pull up, we thought you had been sent by God to help us."

"All I can say is to keep praying. Or file some complaints. Because until one or both places breaks the law, there is nothing anyone can really do to shut them down," Hardy said. Stepping around the man, Hardy climbed into his truck. "I'll be at the Roadhouse Motel if y'all need me, Quaranta. Otherwise, I'll see you in the morning."

Quaranta saluted Hardy, and then he, along with the deputies, got in their cruisers and drove off.

Ignoring the nasty comments being hurled my way by the protestors, I sucked in a deep breath and then marched through the front door of the Dancing Cowgirl. After passing through a little foyer, I shoved aside the faded velvet curtains and entered the main room of the strip club. On the left side of the crowded, dimly lit room, a curvy brunette dressed as a naughty schoolgirl strutted her stuff on stage.

I took a minute to survey the crowd, and, while I recognized a few of the people who were sitting on the edges of the mismatched lawn furniture, I quickly surmised that none of the people in the main room were Shatners.

"Ugh, I hate this place," I muttered as I hustled through the crowd towards the doorway that led to the back rooms. Along the way, I had to dodge a topless woman giving a lap dance to an octogenarian, two bikini-clad women carrying drink trays, and three inebriated, handsy men who offered me various amounts of money to take my clothes off. Shoving my badge into the one man's face, I said, "This is real. Not a prop. Want to offer me money again? Because I'll arrest you for solicitation."

"Carrie? What are you doing here?" my younger cousin, Festus Devereux, asked. "I thought the po-po already left. Why are you still here?"

Festus grabbed me by the arm and pulled me down the short hallway towards the strip club's office. Festus was another one of Uncle Bowie's grandchildren. His parents are my aunt Margaret and Red's older half-brother, Kinky.

"I heard there's some activities going on here tonight that I wouldn't approve of," I said.

"But women are getting paid to take their clothes off every night. Nothing new about that," Festus said as swung open the office door and set free a dense cloud of marijuana smoke. "Or is this what you're talking about?"

"This. Definitely this," I said as I tugged the collar of my shirt up over my nose and tried to breathe in as little of the smoke as possible. Despite the easy access I'd always had to marijuana, I'd never once smoked it. And I had no desire to. "Since when have you gotten involved in selling drugs, Festus? And why are you? You've got a baby at home."

"And that's why I've gotten in to selling…stuff. You have any idea how expensive diapers are?" Festus asked. "And Jolene told me I had to get a second job so she can stay home with the baby."

I stepped into the office and glared at the Shatner and the Palmer who were passing a pipe back and forth. On one hand, it was good to see members of the two families getting along. On the other, why did the Shatners and Palmers have to meld together their criminal enterprises? Especially since the Palmers were into more evil stuff than we were.

"And you two! Do you idiots have any idea how close you just came to getting caught?" I asked.

"It was fine, Carrie. Dad called and told me the Ranger and the deputies were on their way. We had plenty of time to hide everything," said the younger of Murph's two sons.

"Richard Petty Shatner…and here I thought your brother was the dumb one. But at least he's kept his nose clean," I said.

"You think Dale isn't involved in the family business? Ha! He's running a chop shop out of that garage he works at. You Wreck 'Em, We Fix 'Em? More like 'You Steal 'Em, I'll Get Rid of the Parts'," Dickie said.

"What?!? Dickie, don't even tell me if your sister is involved in something illegal. I don't think I could handle it if Luanne was breaking the law." Leaning across the old, metal desk I stuck my face close to Levi Palmer's and said, "I really don't give a crap about what you and your family are up to. But dragging my family into your business has made it my business. I want it all on the table. Now!"

Levi Palmer, who closely resembled a Neanderthal, leaned back in his metal lawn chair and then slammed the heels of his boots down onto the desk. He said, "I don't think so, Carrie. My patrons have come to expect a, shall we say, certain kind of atmosphere. For the past few years I've provide them with the finest entertainment to be found in this county. Now I'm supplying them with…well…Anyway, my business has tripled since your Uncle Houston set up shop in here. If I stop selling his stuff, my profit drops."

"Cry me a river," I said as I grabbed Levi by the ankles and then dumped him over backwards. As Levi rolled around on the grimy floor, I turned to Dickie and shouted, "I want all of it! Now!"

"Hold your horses," Dickie said as he tossed a shoebox on the desk. "The moonshine is in them water bottles next to the door. Uncle Houston figured it'd be best to disguise them in the plastic bottles instead of handing out mason jars."

"Festus, grab the bottles and dump them out back," I said.

"Yes, ma'am," Festus said.

I waited until Festus picked up the case of water bottles and left the room before I knocked the lid off the shoebox. Nestled in the bottom of the box were baggies of marijuana. Alongside them were baggies of white powder and others of pills in every size, shape, and color.

"You've got to be kidding me. Cocaine! You are selling cocaine?" I asked.

Dickie and Levi both shrugged.

"Makes good money," Levi said.

"And the pills? Where did they come from?" I asked.

"Aunt Priscilla gave us some of the prescription pads she steals from different doctors. How do you think she gets all those anxiety meds? No doctor is writing her that many prescriptions," Dickie said.

"What else?" I asked. "What else is going on that I don't know about?"

"Probably a lot. I don't know what all you know about. And I ain't going to be the one to tell you," Dickie said.

"Get rid of this. All of it. And not by selling it to people. You need to destroy it," I said. I slammed the lid on the shoebox and then tossed it to Dickie. "You're done here. I find out you're selling this stuff here, or anywhere else, I'll arrest you. This is the last time I'm saving you. Do you understand what I'm saying? This! Is! It! No more. Never again. I'm done!"

Leaving Dickie and Levi in the office, I ran through the strip club and burst through the front door. Holding my badge above my head so that the protestors would see it and leave me alone, I headed towards the Den of Depravity. I was about to cross the road when a pink convertible slammed on its brakes and narrowly missed running me over.

"Watch what you're doing, Carrie!" Naomi shouted at me.

Running around to the driver's side of the car, I asked, "Where are you headed?"

"The Den. I haven't had a chance to check it out yet."

"That's where I'm headed," I said.

Since Naomi had the top down, I didn't bother to go around to the passenger side of the car. Instead, I jumped over the side of the car and landed in the tiny backseat. I then scrambled into the passenger seat.

"Did you bring your coupon? Ten percent off your first purchase. And that's on top of the twenty-five percent family discount," Naomi said as she pulled into the Den's parking lot and almost ran over a woman holding up a sign that read 'Think of the children'. "Crazy old broad."

"I'm not shopping, Naomi. I need to talk to Uncle Houston, and I've heard he's been here every night this week."

"Well I'm definitely shopping."

As Naomi drove around the crowded parking lot in search of an empty space, I spotted Belinda Thompson among the protestors who were accosting the Den's customers. Belinda's frilly white shirt and floor-length purple skirt would have been considered fashionable in a previous century.

"There's your ex-boyfriend's wife," I said.

"Which boyfriend? And which woman?" Naomi asked.

"Dustin. And the woman who's dressed like Miss Beadle from Little House on the Prairie," I said, gesturing towards where Belinda was standing with a group of women.

"What? Her? I don't get it. Why do men want to sleep with me, but then marry women like that?" Naomi asked as she squirmed around in the driver's seat to get a better look. I had to grab the wheel and turn it to avoid running over some protesters and plowing into a parked car.

"Remember, he married her before he met you. And, besides, if I understood why men do what they do, I'd be a genius."

"Ain't that the truth?" Naomi said.

After forcing a group of protesters out of one of the few remaining parking spots, Naomi and I ran the gauntlet to get to the store. By the time we made it to the shabby strip of red carpet that led to the front door, we'd collected fifteen religious pamphlets and three miniature-sized Bibles. We were also called every name in the book, and accused of participating in all sorts of deviant sexual acts.

Rotating spotlights lit up the front of the Den of Depravity, revealing that the "CUMMING SOON" sign that had hung on the front of the store for the past few months had been replaced with one that said "NOW OPEN."

"Detective Shatner, can I have a word with you?" shouted one of the protestors.

"Oh, great…" I mumbled. Turning around, I found Belinda Thompson headed in my direction. "What can I help you with Belinda?"

"I was just wondering if you have any updates on my brother-in-law's case. The family is just so distraught. I was hoping you might have some good news," Belinda said.

"Nothing yet. But once we have something, we will let you know," I said.

"What a horrific tragedy." Belinda pulled a handkerchief out of her pocket and used it to dab at her eyes. "It is always heartbreaking when a young person dies long before their time. It is so much worse when the person dies as a result of violence. But it is the Good Lord's will and Travis is in His hands now. Though that does not ease the heartache of my in-laws. Father Thompson is prostrate with grief over his stepson's death. He blames himself for not waiting around after the event ended so that he could speak with Travis. He has gone so far as to blame Mother Thompson and both of their daughters for forcing him to leave early due to them wanting to change out of their wet clothes. Mother Thompson is distraught over losing her only son, and the last thing she needs is her husband blaming her for it. And my poor husband has buried his emotions in an attempt to be the rock on which the rest of his family can lean on. He loved his stepbrother so much."

"Yes, such a tragedy," Naomi said. "Speaking of tragedies, how's Dustin's foot?"

"How do you know my husband?" Belinda asked, acknowledging Naomi for the first time.

Digging my elbow in Naomi's ribs to shut her up, I said, "Belinda, this is my cousin, Naomi. Dustin is a friend of another one of our cousins. Naomi met Dustin once or twice."

"Oh. Of course. Dustin's foot is healing up just fine, thank God. I'm just so thankful he didn't hurt himself any worse than he did," Belinda said.

"So are we." Nudging Naomi towards the front door of the Den, I said, "Excuse us, Belinda. We have to get inside."

"Turn back from sin, Detective Shatner. It's not too late to turn back," Belinda shouted.

"I think it's a little too late for me," I mumbled.

Stepping through the front door, Naomi and I almost tripped over Houston.

"Welcome to the Den of Depravity, girls!" Houston said.

Uncle Houston was perched on a lawn chair just inside the door. There were two life-sized blow up dolls on either side of the chair. Houston and the inflatables took up the majority of the foyer. There was just enough room to squeeze around the chair to get to the main door into the store.

"Hi, Grandpa." Naomi kissed Houston on the cheek.

"Hi, honey," Houston said as he patted Naomi on the head. Houston then turned to me and gave me the stink eye. "Wasn't figuring I'd see you here, Carrie. You ain't looking to shut us down, is you? 'Cause we ain't doing nothing illegal."

"Don't shit where you eat, right?" I asked. I gave Houston a stiff nod and fought the urge to scream at him. "But I found out about what you have going on over at the Cowgirl. Including the cocaine. I had Dickie and Festus destroy the products, and then I shut the operation down."

"Why can't you mind your own business, Carrie?" Houston asked.

"Because it's against the law!" Leaning closer to Houston, I asked, "What is wrong with you? Have you lost your mind or are you getting senile? Or do you want your family members to wind up in jail? Because that's where they're headed."

"No. That's where you come in. You and Murph are supposed to make it go away."

"How are we supposed to make it go away when you've got your family selling drugs within the Holler city limits? Because that's where the Dancing Cowgirl is. It's in the city limits. That means it's not within Uncle Murph's and my jurisdiction."

"You think I don't know that?" Houston asked. "And that's why I paid off Holler's new Chief of Police. He named his price to look the other way, and I paid it."

"This is insane!" I said, punching one of the blow up dolls in the face in frustration. "Well, you know what, I'm done. You hear me? I'm done! I'm not covering anything else up. I'm not turning a blind eye. If I catch a Shatner breaking the law, I'm going to arrest him or her. Spread the word, Houston. Let everyone know that I'm washing my hands of y'all"

"What about me?" Naomi asked.

"Until a few days ago, you weren't a problem, Naomi. Let's just get back to that, okay? Because I would hate to arrest you. The others…not so much."

"You listen up, Carrie," Houston said. He pushed himself out of his chair so that he could look me in the eye. "It's your job to take care of your family. To keep them out of jail. You and that Ranger you're screwing. I know he ain't on board yet. But I expect you to change his mind."

"You really have lost your mind! Jerrod and I had a huge fight because of you. He isn't really talking to me. And he certainly doesn't want to date me anymore."

"That boy only has one oar in the water, but he'll come around," Houston said. "Might be you can find something here that'll make him come around quicker. We got some nice unmentionables in the back room."

"Uncle Houston, are you telling me I should buy lingerie to wear for Jerrod?" I asked.

"Oh, no, I ain't telling you nothing. I'm just suggesting it. I've seen the way the Ranger looks at you. I bet he'd like seeing you in some of them knickers that don't cover your butt."

"He's probably right, Carrie," Naomi said. "And a thong would show off your tattoo."

"I'm aware of that, Naomi. But that doesn't mean I'm going to do it. I'm not going to seduce Hardy again because Uncle Houston wants me to. Not that I seduced him in the first place."

"I just don't see what's so hard about lying on your back," Houston said. "Naomi does it all the time, don't you, honey?"

"You really need to knock it off, Houston," I said. "You're on your own tonight, Naomi. If I don't get out of here, and away from Uncle Houston, I'm going to be sick."

CHAPTER FOURTEEN

It was just after three in the morning when my cell phone rang. Normally, I put my phone on silent when I went to bed. The way I saw it, if anyone was that desperate to get ahold of me during the night, they could call my home phone. The only reason I left my cell phone on tonight was because the sheriff's department was still getting the occasional call about Xavier sightings, and, just because none of the calls had panned out, I didn't want to miss anything.

I snatched my phone off of the nightstand and checked the caller ID. It was Festus's younger brother, Cletus. We might be family, but Cletus and I were not close. He wouldn't be calling me in the middle of the night to chat. The only reason he would be calling me at all would be if he was in trouble and wanted my help to get out of it.

"What do you want, Cletus?"

"I want you to stop messing with my business. First it was the pizza parlor. Then it was the flower shop, and then the gas station. Now it's the strip club. You're depriving me and Festus and everyone else of our income."

"Y'all are aware that what you're doing is illegal, right?"

"Aw, come on, Carrie, you know it's only illegal if you get caught. Plus, weed is practically legal."

"Just because weed is practically legal doesn't make the weed y'all are growing in old bomb shelters legal," I said. "Plus, the Ranger was at the Dancing Cowgirl just before I got there. You're lucky he didn't figure out what was going on because he'd have thrown your brother's scrawny butt in jail."

"Ain't that why you're sleeping with the Ranger? So he don't arrest us."

"No! Thanks to your grandpa and Houston, my chances of getting back together with Hardy are about slim to none," I said. I rolled over and punched my pillow. "Now, is there a reason you're calling me at three in the morning or did you just want to yell at me?"

"I got my reasons," Cletus said. "Though I'm tempted not to help you out because of the way you've been treating the family lately."

"What could you possibly help me out with?"

"Well, if y'all are still looking for Xavier, I can tell you right where to find him."

I sat up and turned on my bedside lamp. Molly, who lay curled up next to me, woke up with a start. She then rolled over and went back to sleep. Manny, who was making himself at home on the other pillow, hissed at me before he jumped off the bed and dashed out of the room.

"What are you talking about?" I asked. "How do you know where to find Xavier?"

"First you gotta promise you ain't gonna be mad at me."

"Cletus, I can't promise that I won't be mad. But I swear to you that I will overlook any illegal activities you might currently be engaged in," I said. I couldn't promise that anyone else would overlook it, but I didn't tell Cletus that.

"I guess that's good enough," Cletus said after thinking about it for about thirty seconds. "I went to school with Xavier. And Marisol, too. Marisol didn't have nothing to do with me unless she…well, I ain't calling about her. I'm calling about Xavier. He and I were kinda friends for a while. I, uh, I helped him out with some things."

I remembered the baggie of marijuana and the bong we found in Xavier's room. At the time, I'd suspected that the marijuana came from my family's supply. It seemed I was right.

"Cletus, are you planning on selling pot to Xavier?"

"Naw, I already sold him the pot. The guy is in serious need. He's talking to himself and it looks like he got kicked in the face by a horse. To be honest, he's kinda freaking me out."

"Are you with Xavier right now?

"Uh, yeah. That's what I've been trying to tell you, Carrie. Xavier is at my apartment. He's sitting on the couch smoking a bowl. You wanna come get him or not?"

"Why didn't you just say that? I'll be over in a few minutes. Do not let Xavier leave your place. Sit on him if you have to. And text me if anything happens."

Hanging up on Cletus, I called Hardy.

"Jerrod…we've got him. We've got Xavier."

~*~*~

Fifteen minutes after getting off the phone with Cletus, I met up with Hardy and four deputies at the apartment complex where Cletus lived. The sprawling, two-story structure was on the northern outskirts of Holler.

"You never did say why Xavier showed up at your cousin's place," Hardy said.

"Cletus and Xavier were friends in high school," I said as I pulled my phone out of my jeans pocket. Cletus had sent me five texts since I hung up on him. All of the texts were about how much marijuana Xavier had smoked and how high he was getting. I texted Cletus, telling him that we were outside his door and asking him for a more useful update. "Jerrod, there might be some illegal activities taking place in Cletus's apartment. I'm not asking you to overlook it –"

"Don't piss on my leg and tell me it's raining Carrie," Hardy said. "I knew this would happen sooner or later."

"Jerrod, I'm just asking you to go easy on Cletus. I mean, he's helping us apprehend Xavier...Oh, I got a text," I said before reading the message. "Cletus says that the door is unlocked. Xavier is on the couch."

The deputies waited a minute to give Cletus a chance to go into another room. They then shoved open the door and rushed inside. As the deputies went in, a cloud of marijuana smoke billowed out. Hardy and I both started coughing.

"Second time tonight," I mumbled to myself.

"I see what you mean about illegal activities," Hardy said.

Hardy and I got inside just in time to see the deputies pull Xavier off the couch and shove him face-first onto the filthy, stained carpet. They were having a hard time getting the squirming and keening Xavier handcuffed, and Hardy had to step in and help.

While the men handcuffed Xavier, I looked around the living room and noticed a large, green bong sitting on the wooden wire spool that Cletus used for a coffee table. Also in the living room was a hideous, plaid couch and a matching, broken down armchair. A large screen TV was mounted on the wall across from the couch.

Once the handcuffs were on, the deputies pulled Xavier up into a sitting position and leaned him against the couch. Both of Xavier's eyes had dark purple bruises surrounding them and one of them was partially swollen shut. A fresh trickle of blood dribbled from his crooked and puffy nose.

"Can I come out now?" Cletus yelled from somewhere in the apartment.

"Yes, you can come out," I said.

Cletus came bounding out of either the bedroom or the bathroom. After taking a deep drag off of the joint that was sticking out of the corner of his mouth, he asked, "Hey, is there some sort of reward for catching Xavier? I'm a little low on funds at the moment."

"Son, your reward is not going to jail for being in possession of an illegal substance," Hardy said. "I'm only overlooking what you're doing because you helped us apprehend Xavier. Next time I catch you, I'll arrest you."

"Aw, come on, man. I did your job for you. I deserve a medal or something."

"Cletus, shut up. And give me that," I said as I grabbed the joint out of Cletus's mouth and dropped it into a bottle of water that was sitting next to the bong.

"I thought you promised not to be pissed, Carrie," Cletus said. He then went over to Hardy and jabbed him in the ribs. "You're a bad influence on my cousin. Ever since you showed up, she's been trying to shut down all of our 'illegal operations.' In less than two months, she's chased us out of four fine establishments. We was making a killing at the strip club."

"What exactly were you doing at the strip club?" Hardy asked.

"Don't worry about it, Jerrod. I shut it down," I said.

"When did this happen?" Hardy asked.

"Right after you and Quaranta left the club. I had no idea my family was… doing what they were doing at the strip club until today."

"Don't be telling the Ranger our business, Carrie." Cletus turned back to Hardy and leaned closer. "You know what, Mr. Ranger, Carrie ain't sleeping with you for anyone's benefit but her own. She ain't doing it to protect none of us, which is totally unfair because you're a Texas Ranger and you could really help us out."

"Is that so?" Hardy asked.

"Cletus, you need to stop running your mouth. Now go to your room," I said.

I waited until Cletus disappeared, and then I went over to sit on the floor near Xavier. He hadn't said a word since he was handcuffed, but he was still making soft keening sounds.

"Xavier, I'm Detective Shatner and this is Sergeant Hardy with the Texas Rangers. We've been looking for you all day."

"We've got some questions for you," Hardy said. "Do you mind talking to us?"

"Talk. I can talk. Yeah, yeah, let's talk. You have to talk loud so I can hear you over the devil. He's been talking to me for days now."

I glanced over my shoulder at Hardy, who motioned for me to back away from Xavier.

I scooted back a couple feet and then asked, "Xavier, do you know where you are right now?"

Xavier's glassy eyes shifted to take in the room and he asked, "Where's Cletus? Cletus gives me medicine. I need medicine."

"Xavier, marijuana is not medicine. Or, at least, it's not the medicine you were prescribed," I said. I picked up the bong and put it on the floor where Xavier couldn't see it. "The pills Dr. Vaughn gave you are medicine."

"No! Pills make Xavier feel funny. Tata says pills are the work of the devil. Tata won't let me take doctor's pills."

"Of course she doesn't," Hardy whispered. He knelt on the floor next to me and waved to get Xavier's attention. "Xavier, what can you tell us about Marisol Santiago and Travis Yeager?"

"Mi novia. Mi princesa. Marisol is my love," Xavier said. The smile faded from his face and he started screaming. "Arrows! Flying arrows. Hitting. Killing. Travis dead. Marisol hit. Marisol hurt. Need help. Xavier needs help."

"We'll get you help, Xavier," Hardy said. "Someone call the hospital and tell them to get an ambulance over here. We can't take him back to the department and question him when he's in this condition."

"No! Not hospital. No more hospitals. Need Marisol. Marisol helps," Xavier screamed as he bashed his head into the edge of the wooden wire spool.

Xavier smashed his forehead into the edge of the wooden wire spool two more times before the deputies were able to grab him and haul him into the middle of the room. By then, Xavier had split open his forehead and had blood running down his face.

"Arrows. Need to stop the arrows. Xavier needs help!"

~*~*~

"The kid just started whacking his head into the coffee table? Sounds like he's lost a few too many balls out in the high weeds," Murph said as leaned back in his chair and propped his feet up on the conference room table on Wednesday morning. "When can you talk to him?"

"Probably not till tomorrow. I talked to Dr. Vaughn a little while ago. Xavier's in bad shape and is refusing medication. He just keeps asking for Marisol," Hardy said.

"You think he's the shooter?" Quaranta asked.

Hardy shrugged. "He could be, but the way his hands were shaking… I'm not sure if he could even hold the bow and arrow, much less be able to accurately aim it."

"Xavier could have gotten lucky when he fired the arrow at Travis. His physical state could also explain why he only hit Marisol in the arm," I said.

"Either way, we're going to have to be careful going about this. Xavier's mental illness is going to make things difficult," Hardy said.

"Was there anything interesting on Xavier's laptop?" I asked as I thought back over the evidence we'd collected over the past few days. "And were we able to match the fingerprints I lifted off of the murder weapon?"

"Fingerprints were no good. Not enough ridge details to make a match," Quaranta said.

I smacked my hand down on top of the table in frustration.

"As for Xavier's laptop…There wasn't much on it aside from thousands of pictures of Marisol. And the only sites in his internet history were for porn, schizophrenia, and the SWAT website. As far as we can tell, Xavier didn't have any social media accounts," Murph said.

"Deputy Grant…what about Travis's and Marisol's electronics? You find anything interesting on them?" I asked.

"Oh, I found lots on their electronics," Timmy said. He looked up from where he was scribbling in a notebook at the other end of the conference table. "Their text messages were pretty boring. Travis's were all with wrestlers or archery people or his family. And aside from Travis, Marisol really only texted her sisters, her mom, and some friends. And her coworkers at the stables."

"I sent a couple deputies down to the Abbott Equestrian Center yesterday. You know, just in case Xavier showed up," Murph said, cutting Timmy off. "While the deputies were there, they talked to Marisol's boss and her coworkers. Turns out she isn't as well liked as she seems to think. They said she's stuck up and can get on their nerves."

"Has she had any problems with people who stable their horses there? Or with the people she gives horseback riding lessons to?" Hardy asked.

"If Marisol did, none of her coworkers heard about it. I've got a list of people that she interacted with on a frequent basis. Now that Xavier is in custody, and I don't have my deputies running around like a bunch of chickens with their heads cut off, maybe I can finally send them out to interview some more people," Murph said.

"Who still needs interviewed?" I asked.

"A lot of people," Murph said as he flipped open his notebook. "So far we've only been able to interview Travis's immediate family members, as well as Marisol's. We've still got to interview friends and extended family members. Plus Travis's coworkers at the high school and the kids in the archery club. We should probably talk to his current students as well. And we definitely need to track down all of Travis's archery friends since they probably all own at least one bow. At least one of them must have hated Travis enough to have wanted to kill him. And then there's whoever else Deputy Grant has come up with."

"How many people have you come up with, Deputy Grant?" Hardy asked.

"A whole bunch," Timmy said, holding up a sheet of paper with a lengthy list of names written on it. "And this is a narrowed down list. You guys have no idea how many people hated Travis. Well, Travis's wrestling persona. His sister gave us the binders he kept the hate mail in, and I got access to his email and social media accounts. Some of the people sending Travis nasty messages were intense. He even got some death threats. But the majority of the hate mail was from over-the-top wrestling fans who just wanted to tell Travis that he sucks."

"What about the stuff people have been posting on social media?" I asked.

"That's died down for the most part, and a lot of the people who were posting on Sunday night have deleted their nasty comments. But don't worry, I've got a record of everything that's been posted on the SWAT page and Travis's fan page. And I'm still watching them for new comments because some jerks won't let up. They're the ones who keep posting that they're glad Travis is dead and wish that Marisol got killed too," Timmy said. "And remember that J-Dag guy? The wrestler who's neck Travis broke? Well, I talked to him, and there's no way he's the killer. He had surgery on Friday and was only released from the hospital on Saturday afternoon."

"Good job, Timmy. Keep an eye on the rest of these people. And see if you can narrow down your list of fans some more," Murph said. He stood up and headed for the conference room door. "I think it's time the rest of us head over to the high school to chat with Travis's coworkers and the archery kids. We need to find some more suspects in case Xavier isn't the killer."

~*~

"You spend a lot of time in the principal's office when you were a kid?" Hardy asked.

"It was basically my second home. I'm pretty sure these are the same chairs from when I was in high school." Aside from the receptionists, the electronics, and the Student of the Month pictures hanging on the wall, it didn't look like much had changed in the Big Pine Administrative Offices since I had graduated. "Every time something bad happened, all of the Shatner kids got called down to the principal's office."

Hardy laughed. "Same here. Josh and I spent more time in the principal's office than we did in class. Since we were identical, everyone had a hard time telling us apart. So when one of us was accused or suspected of doing something, and no one was positive about which one of us did it, we both would get called down to the principal's office. During eleventh grade we set the record for most detentions ever served in a single school year."

I was about to ask Hardy which one of them was the evil twin when the door next to me swung open and Phyllis Edelman, the principal of Big Pine, stepped out of her office and glared at me. Phyllis passed retirement age years ago, but refused to step down because she believed that the high school would fall apart without her there to hold things together. Phyllis glared at me as she tugged on the bottom of her hideous blue and orange floral jacket. For as long as I'd known her, Phyllis had worn unflattering pantsuits made out of the ugliest patterned fabrics that I'd ever seen.

"Hello Phyllis," I said, greeting the woman whose office I spent a chunk of time in while in high school. "Long time, no see."

"Caroline Shatner…I will see you in my office now."

"It's been a while since you've said that to me," I said as Hardy and I followed Phyllis into the small, undecorated office. After eighteen years, you'd think she'd hang up some pictures or set some knickknacks out on the desk. "And I keep telling you that it's Carrie. Mom is the only person who calls me Caroline."

"It feels just like yesterday to me, Caroline," Phyllis said, stressing my first name. "Though I guess I should be calling you Detective Shatner."

Ever since first grade, when Phyllis was my teacher, she had insisted on calling me Caroline. I'd say she did it just to annoy me, but she refused to call anyone by their nickname.

"Were you Detective Shatner's principal?" Hardy asked.

Phyllis nodded. "I've been the principal here for almost twenty years now. Before that, I taught first grade at Olson Elementary. That's when I first encountered Caroline. She was one of the most adorable children I have ever seen."

"In case you haven't noticed, I'm still adorable," I said.

"And you're still a holy terror," Phyllis snapped. She tilted her head to the side and gave me a reproachful look over her tortoise shell glasses. She then turned to Hardy and said, "I had Caroline's older sisters as students, and they were two of the most well-behaved and ladylike little girls I've ever had the pleasure of teaching. I had hoped Caroline would be more like her sisters and less like her rowdy, older cousins. But while I might have initially been fooled by her cute face, it didn't take me long to discover that she was a wild, impertinent, and devious child."

"Why don't you just call me the antichrist and be done with it?" I asked.

Ignoring me, Phyllis explained to Hardy what it was that changed her original opinion of me. During the second week of first grade, Phyllis handed out a questionnaire we were to fill out about our mothers. The simple questions were along the line of 'what is your mom's favorite color?' and 'where was your mom born?' For 'what is your mom's favorite drink?', I wrote down margaritas. Phyllis was absolutely horrified. Mom, who still had years to go before she admitted to having a drinking problem, blamed my overactive imagination.

"Of course, it wasn't just Caroline. I also had two of her cousins and her best friend, Veda, that year. The four of them were responsible for my first gray hair," Phyllis said.

"Are you going to blame us for the rest of your gray hairs, too?"

"I'd put the blame on all of you Shatners collectively." Phyllis patted her salt and pepper hair. She had the same helmet-like hairstyle now that she had back when I was in first grade. "But I don't believe it's a coincidence that the rest of my hair turned gray not long after I started here as the principal. I went from having the occasional Shatner child in my class to having a plethora of them in my school."

"I wouldn't say there was a plethora of us," I said. "Maybe just a small horde."

"What did Detective Shatner and the others do that was so bad?" Hardy asked.

"They were disruptive in class," Phyllis said, making it sound like interrupting class was on par in severity with murdering someone. "And they were constantly playing pranks. During the years Caroline attended Olson, we were frequently finding fake feces in the toilets."

"That doesn't sound so bad. My brother and I were doing far worse when we were in elementary school. One time we almost had the school shut down because we hid plastic cockroaches in the cafeteria," Hardy said.

Phyllis snorted. "When I was hired as principal and moved over to Big Pine, I had more Shatners to deal with. And, the older they got, the worse the pranks were."

"Do you have any proof that Detective Shatner was involved in these pranks?" Hardy asked.

"No, I could never prove Caroline was involved," Phyllis said. "I have no evidence that any of the Shatners were involved."

"Exactly. You just assume that we were behind all the pranks," I said. "But that's just how it's always been. Whenever something bad happens, or a crime is committed, everyone just blames the Shatners. I bet we haven't committed a fraction of the crimes that we've been accused of."

"Oh, I have no doubt that the boys were involved," Phyllis said. "They were crafty enough to come up with the pranks, but they weren't smart enough to pull it off without getting caught. That's where you came in. You always were a sneaky child."

"What else did the Shatners allegedly do?" Hardy asked.

"Oh, the pranks those Shatner kids played while in high school are countless," Phyllis said. Not that it stopped her from recounting the most memorable. "Every year they let various animals loose in the school. There were pigs, goats, and armadillos. And one time there was a cow wandering around the gymnasium –"

"Didn't Animal Control determine that the armadillos got into the school on their own?" I asked.

"One time the Shatners managed to cause all of the toilets in Big Pine to overflow –"

"That was a legitimate plumbing problem," I said

"They filled my office full of those Styrofoam packing peanuts. They glued all of the classroom doors shut. They ran naked through almost every sporting event, dance, graduation, and school function –"

"In case you failed to notice, all of those streakers were definitely male."

"I didn't say that you were one of the streakers, Caroline," Phyllis said, finally acknowledging me in the peanut gallery. "The Shatners vandalized the front lawn of the school with hundreds of those tacky, plastic lawn flamingos. They broke into Big Pine over Christmas break and removed all of the stalls in every single bathroom. They snuck into the high school teachers' lounge and, don't ask me how they did it, but they somehow managed to put goldfish in the water cooler."

"I have no idea how we did it either," I said before snapping my fingers. "Oh, wait, that's because we didn't do it."

Ignoring me, Phyllis said, "But the worst thing Caroline did was when she was in ninth grade. She and her friends, Veda and Paige, choose the foods and nutrition class as one of their electives. At the end of the semester, the class makes a special lunch for the administrators. The girls ruined it by putting laxatives in the chocolate cake."

"How could we have done that, Phyllis? We didn't make the cake!" My friends and I were stuck preparing the vegetables for the meal. Our teacher barely trusted us enough to do that. Veda, Paige, and I were not culinary masters.

"No, but you were in the same room as the students who made the cake," Phyllis said. "I'm positive the three of you slipped the laxatives in to the batter."

"Sounds like the Shatners were some serious troublemakers," Hardy said.

"They were hooligans as children. And they're still hooligans as adults," Phyllis said.

Tiring of Phyllis's storytelling, I said, "Excuse me, we're here to talk about Travis Yeager. You know, the Big Pine teacher who was brutally murdered on Saturday night. We're not here to trash my good name."

"Very true. Dr. Edelman, what can you tell us about Travis?" Hardy asked.

"Travis was one of the most popular teachers at Big Pine. I've never heard any of the students complain about him," Phyllis said.

"There's just over five hundred children who attend Big Pine. Statistically, it's impossible for every single student to have adored Travis. Some of the students must not like him. Some of them might even hate him," Hardy said.

"Teenagers can be overly emotional. And they make bad decisions," I added.

"I don't understand. I heard on the news this morning that you have Xavier Ortega in custody," Phyllis said.

"Just because we have a suspect in custody doesn't mean we stop investigating other possibilities," Hardy said.

"Then the answer is no! I refuse to entertain the possibility that one of my students could have done this," Phyllis said, her voice rising a couple octaves as her anger built. "Not even the worst of the troublemakers."

"Not even a Shatner?" I asked.

"No, not even a Shatner," Phyllis said.

"What about the other faculty members?" Hardy asked.

"There is some professional jealousy, of course. But you can't really blame the other faculty members for being a little miffed because the students like Travis more than them."

"We can blame them if professional jealousy drove one of them to kill Travis. A lot of people have killed over jealousy," I said.

"No, absolutely not. I know all of the faculty and staff members, and they're all good people. At Big Pine we're not just coworkers, we're family," Phyllis said.

"That doesn't mean anything. Plenty of people kill their family members," I said.

In the past four years, I've frequently thought about bumping off a few of the Shatners. It would certainly make my job, and my life, a whole lot easier. But I would never actually do it.

"Tell us about the archery club. And the kids in it," Hardy said.

"Travis came to me towards the end of his first year and pitched the idea of the archery club. He realized that there are a number of students who go bowhunting and he wanted to provide them with another avenue in which to use their skills. I thought it was a good idea and allowed him to proceed," Phyllis said, handing me a picture of Travis surrounded by twelve teenagers. "This is a picture of the current club members. I've never had to call any of them down to my office for disciplinary reasons. And, as far as I know, Travis never had a problem with any of them. He wouldn't have allowed them to stay in the club had there been a problem. That was one of my stipulations. I was supportive of the archery club, but I did not want any student who had a behavioral issue in it. Not when the kids are handling deadly weapons."

Hardy and I talked to Phyllis for a while longer, getting more information about Travis as well as his younger brother, the Santiago sisters, and Xavier Ortega. Unfortunately, she wasn't able to provide us with anything that seemed relevant to our case. Phyllis had too many students to be able to keep track of all of them – especially ones who had already graduated.

As Hardy and I headed out of the office to meet up with Murph and Quaranta before we started interviewing the archery kids, Phyllis called me back. "I'll admit you turned out a lot better than I ever thought you would, Caroline."

"Let me guess, you figured I'd be in jail by now."

"That or dead," Phyllis.

Grumbling, I followed Hardy out into the administrative office.

"I've got a question for you," Hardy said. "Did you girls put the laxatives in the cake?"

"Of course we did."

CHAPTER FIFTEEN

"Carrie Shatner! No way! This is so awesome!" said RJ, the first of the four archery club kids who I would be interviewing. He was a short, squat kid with a head roughly the same size, shape, and color of a basketball. "What are you doing here?"

Hardy, Quaranta, and I had divided up the twelve archery kids. I lucked out and got the four seniors. Since all of them were over eighteen, I didn't have to wait around until their parents got there before I could start asking questions.

"I'm here to ask you some questions about Mr. Yeager," I said. "I see you've got on a Beast from East Texas shirt. Were you a fan?"

"Yeah, I'm a huge fan. But, like, wow! This is freaking awesome! My friends are never gonna believe this. Is the Ravishing Redneck here, too? And what about Naomi?" RJ asked.

"No. Why would they be here?" I asked.

"RJ, Detective Shatner works for the Wyatt County Sheriff's Department. She's investigating what happened to Mr. Yeager on Saturday night," Phyllis said.

Despite the fact that I didn't have to put up with the students' parents, I still had to put up with Phyllis. Since I was using her office to conduct the interviews, she insisted on being present. Personally, I didn't think it was a bad idea having another adult in the room as a witness.

"Oh…Gotcha. I just figured that you and the Ravishing Redneck…I don't know, I guess I never gave it much thought about what you and Red do outside of SWAT. But it's pretty cool you're a detective," RJ said. He pulled his cell phone out of his back pocket and held it up. "Can I, like, get a picture with you? Like I said, my friends are never gonna believe this."

"RJ! That is extremely inappropriate!" Phyllis said.

"Oh, yeah, I guess it is." RJ plopped down into the chair next to mine.

"You're the kid who asked me and Naomi for pictures before the show started on Saturday, aren't you?" I asked, finally remembering where I had seen the basketball-shaped head before. RJ, along with a group of his friends, had hung around Red's merchandise table for about fifteen minutes before one of them had built up the nerve to ask me and Naomi for pictures. "Did you really skip your prom to go to SWAT?"

"Well, duh. A bunch of us did. Pro wrestling is way more important to us than a stupid school dance. Thanks to the riot, we almost didn't make it over to the high school in time to get in for Post Prom. We were hanging out in the parking lot talking to people about Red's last match when I realized we were running out of time to get checked in for Post Prom. So the seven of us walked over to the high school. We're, like, pretty freaked out over walking through the back parking lot right before Mr. Yeager got killed."

"Did you just say that you walked through the back parking lot? What time was that? Where exactly did you walk?" I asked, crossing my fingers that RJ might have seen something.

"It was probably right after eleven-thirty when we walked over to the high school. We had parked there instead of at the SWAT Zone since it can be, like, total chaos trying to get out of the Zone's parking lot after an event. So we, well, after the riot, we went out through the front doors along with everyone else. After a couple minutes in the front parking lot, we walked along the side of the building to the back parking lot. Then we cut through the woods and over the soccer field," RJ said.

"Was there anyone else in the back parking lot when you walked through?" I asked.

"Not that I saw. But I was busy talking to my friends. And it's kinda dark back there."

"I'm going to need your friends' names." I handed RJ a notebook. "You might not have seen anything, but one of them could have."

~*~*~

"I'm a bowhunter. And so is, like, everyone in my family. Except my mom," said Stephanie, the second archery club kid that I questioned. She had unnaturally red hair that clashed horribly with her magenta tank top. "My older brother was in the archery club, and now my younger brother is in it, too. It's pretty cool that Mr. Yeager started it for kids like us. Gives us a chance to keep up our skills between bowhunting seasons."

"What did you think of Mr. Yeager?" I asked.

"He was all right," Stephanie glanced towards Phyllis and gave a little jump. "I mean, he was awesome. It's terrible what happened to him. I was crying all day Monday over it."

"It's okay if you didn't exactly like him, Steph," I said.

"It's not that I didn't like Mr. Yeager. I really did. He knew his stuff when it came to archery. And he didn't talk down to us like a lot of teachers. You know, he didn't treat us like we're still in elementary school and only capable of using those crappy safety scissors." Stephanie leaned closer to me and whispered, "I just don't have a crush on him like some of the people in the club. Or in the school, for that matter. A lot of my classmates are half in love with Mr. Yeager. And I don't just mean the girls. Some of the boys have creepy man crushes on him. Like RJ. Total man crush."

"Could you explain these man crushes? And regular crushes?" I asked.

"Well, like with RJ…Always talking pro wrestling with Mr. Yeager and treating him like he's a celebrity. A lot of the other guys in the school do, too. But RJ and his weird friends are the worst. Almost as bad as some of the girls. But Evita Santiago has the biggest crush of anyone that I know about. I'm talking full-blown, writing 'Mrs. Travis Yeager' all over her notebooks kind of crush. It's even creepier considering Mr. Yeager was dating Evita's older sister. And Evita has been dating Mr. Yeager's half-brother since this past summer. A bunch of us think she's only dating Zachary because she couldn't have Mr. Yeager."

"Why do you think that?" I asked to keep Stephanie talking.

"Uh, hello…since she met Zachary in seventh grade, she had nothing to do with him. Well, he didn't exactly have anything to do with her either. Then, after three years of having a crush on his big brother, she suddenly starts dating Zachary? Yeah, no. She hooked up with little brother because she can't have big brother. And she only started dating Zachary after her sister started dating Mr. Yeager. It probably drives her insane thinking about her sister and Mr. Yeager…well, you know. I don't know how or why Zachary puts up with her."

"You and Evita aren't friends, are you?" I asked.

"Uh, not really. I've known her since kindergarten, so we were kinda friends back in elementary school. But that's only because I was stuck with her. Come on, Detective Shatner, you went to one of the elementary schools in BPSD, right? You know what it's like. Once we got to junior high, Evita and I, like, pretty much had nothing to do with each other. These days, if it wasn't for archery club, I wouldn't even talk to her. She's annoying. And totally cray-cray."

~*~*~

"I don't know nothing 'bout what happened to Mr. Yeager." Vladimir Khrushchev Smith, the other senior boy on the archery team, leaned against the wall and crossed his arms over his slender chest. Khrush was Frank's and Oksana's only son. Like his father, Khrush was over six feet tall, but he was willowy like his mother. I'd known him since he was a little, rambunctious child who cried at every wrestling event because he couldn't be ringside with his parents. Talking to him, it hit me that I hadn't seen him at an event in at least a year. "And my pops said I shouldn't be talking to you unless I've got a lawyer present. Not after you already accused both of my parents of killing Mr. Yeager."

I bit back my sigh of frustration and said, "I didn't accuse either of your parents of killing Mr. Yeager. I nicely asked them what they were doing during the fifteen or so minutes during which Mr. Yeager was getting killed."

"Same thing," Khrush said. "I don't know what my pops was doing. But I know Mom was home with Sonya. She's got some nasty stomach bug. And now Tatyana has it. Mom is at her wits end taking care of my sisters. It's not like Pops is much help when it comes to that sort of thing. Or anything else, really."

"Your parents have already been cleared," I said as I looked down at the Post Prom sign in sheets that I had spread out over Phyllis's desk. I found Khrush's name halfway down the second page. "Khrush, according to the Post Prom sign in sheet, you and your girlfriend were already inside the high school before Mr. Yeager was killed."

"Exactly. That means I ain't your killer. And I didn't see nothing. So there ain't no point for you to be talking to me. Or my girlfriend. So what if we're both in Mr. Yeager's archery club? Why's that make us so special? Just about everyone in this school had Mr. Yeager for at least one gym unit. You gonna talk to every single one of them?"

"Don't you want the sheriff's department to figure out who killed Mr. Yeager?" I asked. "What if you hold the one crucial bit of information that would help us find the killer?"

"Yeah, well, I don't. I don't know nothing. And as for y'all finding the killer…Look, I like Mr. Yeager. And the archery club was one of the few things I've enjoyed about high school. I want y'all to find his killer so you can fry him. But I ain't got any useful information. And, like I said, my pops said not to talk to you without a lawyer present. So I, uh, I'm going back to class," Khrush said. He then swung open the office door and bolted.

"Khrush clearly got his stubborn streak from his father," I said to Phyllis. "Not that I really expected him to break the case."

~*~*~

"How's your sister holding up?" I asked.

"She isn't. Marisol is a wreck. She can't stop crying, and she won't eat. But she's calmed down some since Xavier was caught. Our mamá won't leave her alone because she's afraid Marisol will kill herself or something," Evita said. She glanced up at me, making eye contact for the first time since she had walked into Phyllis's office. There was a flash of anger in her bloodshot eyes, but it was quickly drowned by a rush of tears. "And I have no idea how Zachary is doing. He's only texted me a couple times since Sunday morning. I tried calling him, but he won't answer. I want to go over to his parents' house to see him, but Papá yelled at me and told me to leave them alone. He says the Yeagers aren't going to want me hanging around their house when they're grieving. And Papá doesn't want me moping around our house along with Marisol, so he made me come to school today. He said I can't let Mr. Yeager's murder interfere with finishing up these last couple weeks of school. God, I freaking hate him so much!"

"Your father is right, Evita. You are our valedictorian for this year. It would be a shame if you ruin your record of straight-A's now," Phyllis said.

"Are you kidding me? Mr. Yeager is dead, and you're worried about my grades? You sound just like my Papá," Evita said.

"Evita…take a couple deep breaths and try to calm down. You have every right to grieve for Mr. Yeager. Your father and Dr. Edelman aren't telling you that you can't mourn for him. They're just reminding you that your life is still going on despite what happened," I said.

"I know, I know. I just feel like I'm totally alone in my grief. Zachary has his parents. And Marisol has Mamá, Papá, and Annalisa. I tried to talk to Marisol last night, and, I don't know, comfort her. But I only upset her more. Then my parents yelled at me for bothering her. This really sucks."

"I know, Evita. Right now is a really weird time for everyone affected, and people are reacting differently." I reached over and grasped one of Evita's clenched fists. "The reason I called you down here is because you were very emotional on Sunday when we talked. And I haven't had a chance to sit down with just you yet. I need to know if you've thought of any new information regarding your sister and Mr. Yeager. Or Saturday night in general."

"Well…there is one thing. I was too upset on Sunday to even think about it. And then on Monday…well, I forgot about it once you brought up Xavier. You have no idea how much that guy scared me. Still scares me now that I know he was stalking Marisol. Anyway, it wasn't until yesterday that I realized this could be evidence. But then I wasn't sure if I wanted to share it because it's going to hurt my sister and Mr. Yeager's family and probably the school. And it's going to make Mr. Yeager look really bad."

"Oh dear," Phyllis mumbled.

"Evita, there is nothing you can say or do that will hurt Mr. Yeager now. If you think that whatever you know could possibly help my case, then you need to share it with me, regardless of who or what it might damage," I said.

"Okay...You're right, Detective Shatner. Helping your case is more important than anything else. But this really sucks." Evita ran her hands over her face and through her hair. "Last Friday, I stuck around after school because Zachary had a baseball game."

"We're all very proud of Zachary. The Big Pine baseball team made it to the regional quarterfinals thanks to that young man's arm. It also got him a full ride to Texas Tech," Phyllis said, interrupting Evita. "And don't sell yourself short, young lady. Evita has a full scholarship to Arizona State University."

"Good for you," I said.

"Thanks. It's pretty cool. Anyway, on Friday, I wanted to talk to Mr. Yeager before I headed over to Zachary's game. Archery is pretty much over for the year. We were supposed to have one last practice next Tuesday, and then a party on Thursday. I wanted to talk to Mr. Yeager about the party, so I headed over to the gym because he hangs out there after school on days we don't have archery practice or competitions. He likes to encourage whatever athletes happen to be practicing in the gym that day. I ran into a couple friends on my way to the gym, and wound up talking to them about prom for a few minutes. By the time I got to the gym, it was empty. So I stuck my head in the office that the gym teachers share to see if Mr. Yeager was there," Evita said as her hands began to shake and tears flowed down her cheeks. "I...I walked up to the office and...and...Mr. Yeager was there. But he wasn't alone."

Concerned about how upset Evita was getting, I said, "Take your time, Evita. Walk me through what happened. Who was with Mr. Yeager?"

"I'm not sure. I just know it was a woman."

"What were they doing?" I asked.

"They were kissing," Evita said. "And touching each other."

"Oh, Good Lord," Phyllis said. She picked up a slim, paperback book and used it to fan herself. "I can't believe it. I won't believe it. Evita, are you sure that's what you saw? Perhaps you saw something else and got confused."

"I know what I saw. They had their arms around each other and were making kissing sounds. And Mr. Yeager had his hand under the woman's skirt and she was telling him to –"

"Evita! That's enough!" I said.

I would have let Evita go on, but Phyllis appeared to be on the verge of fainting. The color had drained from Phyllis's face except for two bright red spots staining her cheeks. Beads of sweat rolled down her forehead.

"But don't you want to know about everything I saw?" Evita asked.

"I do. But this isn't gossip. This could be evidence and I'm going to need to take it down as a statement," I said as I turned to a fresh page in my notebook and jotted down some general notes about the interview. I then had Evita go back to the beginning and start her story over. "Evita, is it possible the woman was your sister?"

"No way. I couldn't see much of the woman besides her hands. Travis's body completely blocked hers. But I know for sure that those hands weren't Marisol's. My sister has acrylic nails, and this woman definitely didn't. And her hands were way too pale to be Marisol's."

"What about rings? Was the woman wearing any rings?" I asked.

"I don't know. Maybe. I wasn't really looking at her hands. But I think her fingernails were painted light purple. Does that help?"

"It might," I said even though it probably wouldn't. Nail polish was easily changeable and usually pretty indistinctive. A gaudy or unique ring would be easier to track down.

I walked Evita through the encounter, starting with when she left her last class and headed to the gym to find Travis. Despite Phyllis's obvious discomfort and disgust, I had Evita describe every little detail of what she saw.

"Did Mr. Yeager or the woman see you? Did they realize they'd been caught?" I asked.

"I don't think so. The office door was only open a little bit. And I heard… well, I heard them before I knocked. So it's not like I drew attention to myself. I just peeked through the crack in the doorway and…and I saw Travis cheating on my sister."

"Then what did you do?" I asked, hoping that Evita didn't stick around to watch. Though part of me wished she had lingered long enough to figure out the identity of the woman.

"I…I was so confused and angry. I wanted to barge in and ask Travis what he was doing. What he was thinking. How could he cheat on my sister like that?"

"Evita, what did you do?" I asked.

"I know it was totally wrong to do, but I took a picture."

"Picture? Whoa, you took a picture of Mr. Yeager and the woman?" I asked, feeling both mortified and proud at the same time.

Evita nodded. "I had my cell phone in my hand, so I just took a picture."

"This is exactly why I want to ban cell phones from the school," Phyllis muttered.

"Please tell me you still have the picture on your phone," I said.

"I do," Evita said. She unzipped her backpack and pulled out her cell phone. After bringing up the picture, she handed me her phone. "It's a little blurry."

"That's okay," I said.

On the phone was a slightly blurry picture of a man standing with his back to the camera. I couldn't be sure it was Travis just from the back of his head, but I had to assume that's who it was. The blonde hair and fake tan matched Travis's. All I could really see of the woman were her hands and a sliver of her shoulder. Long, black or brown hair lay across part of the shoulder. I zoomed in on the woman's left hand that was clenching Travis's butt. I could just make out a ring on the woman's third finger.

"I didn't show it to anyone. I was still trying to figure out what to do when I found out Mr. Yeager had been killed," Evita said, wiping away her tears. "After I took the picture, I left. I went outside, got in my car, and drove over to watch Zachary's game. Marisol wasn't home on Friday night. I didn't see her until Saturday afternoon when she helped me get ready for the prom. I wanted to tell her then, but I…I just couldn't bring myself to do it. And I was still debating on whether I should say something to Mr. Yeager first."

"So, as far as you know, no one knows that you saw Mr. Yeager and this mystery woman in his office? And no one knows that you took a picture of them?" I asked.

"Nope. I didn't tell anyone. And it was really hard not to."

"I'm going to need to borrow your phone for a while, Evita. This picture is evidence. I'll make sure you get it back sometime today," I said. By the time Evita got her phone back, the picture would have been downloaded onto one of the department's computers. "For now you can head back to class. I'll let you know if we need any additional information from you."

"Okay. I guess I'll see you later, Detective Shatner." Evita picked up her backpack and left the room, shutting the door behind her.

"This is an embarrassment to all of Big Pine. I can't believe Travis would desecrate his workplace with such an act. I refuse to believe he was using his office to conduct an affair." Phyllis said. The color was returning to her face and she'd wiped away the sweat. "The woman must have been Marisol. Evita must have been mistaken about the skin tone. After all, she only saw the woman's hands."

"No, it's not Marisol. Evita is right. The skin is way too pale," I said, handing the phone to Phyllis so that she could see the picture.

Phyllis glanced at the phone, gasped, and then handed it back to me. "Disgusting."

"It's that and a whole lot of other things," I said, pressing my palms to my pounding forehead. The headache developed after Evita told me she'd caught Yeager and the mystery woman making out in the high school's gym teachers' office. "This woman could be any white woman with pale skin who paints her fingernails light purple. I just hope it's another teacher."

"Why do you want her to be a faculty member?"

"Because I don't want her to be a student."

"Oh! No! Not a student." Phyllis grabbed her book and fanned herself again.

"Relax, Phyllis, it looks like the woman is wearing a wedding ring."

"Or it could be a promise ring. I know of a few girls whose boyfriends gave them a promise ring. And I think the girls wear promise rings on their left hands."

"Oh, please, no," I whispered. I then snatched Phyllis's book away and slammed it down on the desk. "Phyllis, I'm going to need a copy of this year's yearbook so I can look at the faculty pictures. Do you have a yearbook I can borrow?"

Phyllis shook her head. "The yearbooks won't be handed out until Friday. But I can have the yearbook advisor bring one down for you. I'm sure she can spare one for your investigation."

While we waited for the yearbook advisor, I had Phyllis print out a list of the current seventy-seven faculty and staff members, as well as a list of which of them were at school the previous Friday.

"How many of the faculty and staff are female?" I asked.

"Around fifty. I'd have to double check to get the exact number."

"That's a lot." Whistling, I tossed the stack of papers onto the empty chair beside me. "Though I'm guessing not all of them have long, dark hair."

There was a knock on Phyllis's office door and then a tall, paint spattered woman stuck her head in the office. Her short, dirty blonde hair immediately allowed me to remove her from my suspect list before I even knew her name.

"Dr. Edelman, I've got the yearbook you asked for. Since you said it was for the detectives investigating the murder, I brought down the proofs for all of the faculty and student photos. I thought that the loose pages might make it easier for them to...well, I'm not sure what you need it for, ma'am."

"I appreciate it. The proofs will help out a lot," I said as I snagged the yearbook and folder full of loose pages out of the yearbook advisor's hands. I then gently closed the door in her face.

After spreading the proofs for the faculty and staff pages out on Phyllis's desk, I grabbed a stack of her sticky notes and cut them in half. I then went through the five pages and used the sticky notes to cover up all of the males. I also put sticky notes over any woman who didn't have fair-colored skin. I was left with thirty-eight white females.

"This is where you come in, Phyllis. You know all of these women. I need your input."

"Oh, dear. I can't imagine any of these women committing such a vile act in the workplace. A lot of them are married or engaged. They have children."

"Phyllis, part of my job is to suspend my moral judgments. We know a white woman with shoulder-length or longer dark hair was caught making out with Travis Yeager. Don't think of whether or not you believe these thirty-eight women could have done it. Think of who matches the description," I said as I handed the sticky notes to Phyllis. "Cover up any woman who doesn't fit the physical description."

"Well it was most certainly not me, Caroline," Phyllis said as she slapped a sticky note over her school picture. "I cannot believe you wouldn't give me the benefit of the doubt. I'm old enough to be Travis's mother! And I have short hair."

"My bad," I said, ducking my head so Phyllis wouldn't see my smirk. "Let's start from the beginning…Gail Ackerman."

"The head lunch lady? I hardly think it would be her. Or any of the other cafeteria workers. They are gone by the end of the school day. And, I don't mean to be rude, but I have my doubts that Travis would have been interested in any of these women. None of them are under forty."

Once I got Phyllis started, she got into narrowing down the list of Travis's potential partners. She eliminated some of the female faculty and staff members because their hands were either too large, too tan, too fat, too muscular, too wrinkled and liver-spotted, or the fingers were either too long, stubby, or plump. The female gym teacher broke her left wrist earlier in the month and was still wearing a cast, giving me a good reason to eliminate her from my list. Another teacher was missing part of her left pinkie finger thanks to a childhood farming accident. And at least a dozen of the women had acrylic nails.

"What about the head librarian?" I asked. "She's cute."

"I don't know. She wears a purity ring. And it's on her left ring finger," Phyllis said.

"How do you know it's a purity ring?" I asked.

"Because she told me that it's a purity ring. She's had it since she was sixteen," Phyllis said. "She's now in her mid-thirties."

"Well, whether it's a purity ring or not doesn't matter. It's still a ring." I put a question mark next to the librarian's name. "Next up is Belinda Thompson."

"Travis's sister-in-law? I hardly think so," Phyllis said. "I don't believe Belinda is Travis's type. She's…well, she's a bit on the frumpy side. And very old fashioned. She's not a thing like Marisol."

"And I can't imagine her making out with anybody. Including her husband. But she's white, has long, dark hair, and wears a ring. I guess I'll have to leave her on my suspect list."

The two of us went over the remaining faculty members and I crossed off a few more names. In the end, Phyllis helped me narrow it down to eight female faculty and staff members. I jotted all of their names down in my notebook, and then had Phyllis answer some simple questions about each women.

"Thanks for all your help, Phyllis. I'll let you know if I need anything else," I said.

"You're welcome, Caroline. I wish I could have done more." Phyllis got up and walked me out of the office. "If the woman Evita saw with Travis is one of my faculty or staff members, will you let me know? I will have to take action."

"As long as it doesn't compromise my case, I'll let you know."

~*~*~

"Learn anything interesting, boys?" I asked as I walked into the high school's conference room and joined Hardy, Murph, and Quaranta. After tossing my pile of notes and the yearbook onto the table, I had a seat next to Hardy. "Because I did."

"Then you're the only one of us. Aside from alibiing all but two of the archery club kids, we got next to nothing. And we highly doubt that either of the two kids without an alibi is the killer," Quaranta said as he shoved a notebook across the table towards me. On it he had written down the names of all twelve of the kids in the archery club. Notes had been written down next to eight of the names. "The deputies are still talking to some teachers, but so far none of them have learned anything that seems pertinent to the investigation."

"Come on, Chief Deputy Quaranta, we did get some good gossip out of the teenagers who came forward. We now have a whole list of female students who had crushes on Travis. We also learned that he's, like, totally the coolest gym teacher, like, ever," Hardy said, slipping into a Valley Girl voice as he mocked the way the teenagers talked.

"As for the teachers, some of them barely ever interacted with Yeager. But even the ones who didn't know him very well seemed to like him," Murph said.

"What about the group of boys who walked through the back parking lot of the SWAT Zone while on their way to the high school? Did any of them see anything?" I asked.

"According to the deputies who interviewed RJ's six friends, five of them wouldn't have noticed anything short of the zombie apocalypse. And they might not have even noticed that. The boys were too busy talking about wrestling, and freaking out over what had happened to pay attention to anything else that might be going on around them. One of them saw someone walking around the cars, but he didn't pay attention. The deputy showed him one of our photo lineups that included a picture of Xavier, but the kid didn't pick him out. He said he only got a glimpse of the person and assumed it was a wrestler," Quaranta said.

"Well that sucks. I had hoped one of those kids saw something," I said.

"You going to tell us about what you learned?" Hardy asked.

"I can do better than that. I can show you," I said. I brought up the picture of Travis Yeager and the mystery woman on Evita's phone and then handed it to Hardy. "Last Friday, Evita Santiago stayed after school to talk to Travis. She almost walked in on this."

"Wow…That is Travis, right?" Hardy said.

"Yes, it is. And that is definitely not Marisol," I said.

"Then who is she?" Quaranta asked.

"That I don't know. But we're going to find out. I've got a copy of this year's yearbook, and Phyllis helped me narrow down the thirty-eight female faculty and staff members down to eight possibilities," I said.

"That's still too many," Hardy said. "It's not like you can go up to each of those women, show them the picture, and ask 'Is this you?' Though, we can try interviewing all of them again. Maybe one of them will admit something."

"And that'll only work if the mystery woman is a faculty member," Murph said.

"I know, I know. It would make our jobs a lot easier if this woman came forward and confessed to the affair," I said.

~*~*~

"You people again? Now what do you want?" asked Annalisa.

"To figure out who killed Travis and attempted to kill your sister," I said. "I also need to give Evita her phone. She, uh, left it behind when I talked to her at the high school."

After finishing up at the high school, Hardy and I returned to the sheriff's department long enough for me to download the picture of Travis off of Evita's cell phone. In the process, I accidently downloaded the hundreds of other pictures saved on her phone – the majority of which were selfies or of Zachary. Hardy and I then headed over to the Santiagos' house so that we could talk to Marisol.

Opening the front door a little wider, Annalisa stuck her arm out and tried to grab the cell phone out of my hand. "I can give Evita her phone."

"I'd prefer to give it to her myself." I held the phone out of Annalisa's reach. "We also need to talk to Marisol. Is she around?"

"Not right now. My parents took her over to the church for grief counseling. Come back in, like, an hour. They should be home then."

Annalisa went to shut the door, but Hardy stuck his foot in the door to stop her. He was shoving the door open when we heard someone shouting inside the house. Ducking under Hardy's arm, I pushed past Annalisa and forced my way inside.

Glancing around the formal-looking living room and dining room, I spotted around twenty floral arrangements scattered throughout the two rooms. There had to be at least ten of them on the dining room table alone. And there were more on the sideboard, as well as lining the fireplace mantle. The Santiago family would need to have a yard sale to get rid of all of the vases.

"You're such a fibber, Evie! I can't believe you're making up lies about my brother!" shouted Zachary Yeager.

Following the voices, Hardy and I found Zachary and Evita in the kitchen. Evita sat slumped over at the kitchen table while Zachary paced in circles around the room.

"I'm not making it up," Evita sobbed. "I saw Travis and another woman."

"What's going on in here?" Hardy asked.

"Evita just told us that she caught my half-brother cheating on Marisol last Friday. Travis never would have done that. Ever! He loved Marisol. Travis's and my dad is going to flip out when he hears about this," Zachary said.

"I'm sorry, Detective Shatner. I know I shouldn't have said anything," Evita said before loudly blowing her nose. "Either I don't say enough or I can't shut up."

"It's okay, Evita. As long you didn't tell anyone else," I said. I wasn't pleased with her for telling Zachary and Annalisa about what she saw, but I wasn't going to chastise her when she was an emotional mess. There was no point in making her feel worse than she already did.

"I didn't. I swear that I didn't," Evita said.

"You better not! I won't have you slandering my brother with your lies," Zachary said.

"Why do you have to be such a selfish brat, Evita? Marisol is hurting bad enough as it is. Why do you have to make up stories about Travis cheating on her? Do you have any idea what this will do to her? It'll destroy her!" Annalisa said.

"I'm not making anything up. I know what I saw," Evita said.

"You're a pathological liar!" Annalisa stalked across the kitchen until she was practically on top of Evita. "You were always jealous of Marisol. Ever since you were born, your goal has been to make Marisol look bad and get her in trouble. You always wanted to be better than her, but you're not. You're just a greedy, bratty child!"

"At least I didn't spend twenty-one years of my life with my head shoved up Marisol's butt. She isn't perfect, Annalisa. You need to stop worshipping her and start living your own life instead of letting Marisol dictate it for you," Evita said.

"I wish you had never been born!" Annalisa screamed.

"I know you're upset, Annalisa, but that is no way to speak to your sister," I said.

"I don't care." Annalisa turned her back to Evita and said, "Evita has always been horrible to Marisol. But it got worse when Marisol and Travis hooked up. Evita may claim she was over her crush, but she wasn't. She still isn't. Up until the day he was killed, she flirted with Travis. She practically threw herself at him. It was disgusting. I really don't know why you want anything to do with her, Zachary."

"Because I love her. I'm just…I'm just mad right now," Zachary said. Despite the anger twisting his handsome features into a snarl, Zachary managed to give Evita a kind look.

"Sergeant Hardy! Detective Shatner!" screeched Marisol as she ran in through the back door. Her parents were right behind her. "Did he confess? Did Xavier kill Travis?"

"We're not sure yet, Ms. Santiago. We haven't been able to speak with Xavier yet since he is currently hospitalized," Hardy said.

"Ugh! Then what are you doing here?" Marisol asked.

"They're here because Evita is making up stories about Travis cheating on you," Annalisa said before Hardy or I could stop her.

"What? You little brat!" Marisol shrieked. "How could you? How could you say something so horrible about Travis? He never would have cheated on me! He loved me! But that's what all this is about, isn't it? You're jealous because Travis loved me!"

Marisol charged towards the table and struck Evita across the face. As Evita toppled out of her chair, I saw that Marisol's acrylic nails left four bloody slashes across her little sister's left cheek.

"That's enough, Ms. Santiago. Hit her again, and I'll arrest you for assault," Hardy said as he pulled Marisol away from where Evita lay curled up on the floor. During Marisol's tirade, no one else had stepped forward to stop her or to defend Evita. Instead, Mr. and Mrs. Santiago joined in on yelling at their youngest daughter.

"Arrest me? You should arrest her for making up lies about Travis," Marisol screamed.

"I'm not lying!" Evita used the chair to pull herself up off the floor. "Show her, Detective Shatner. Show Marisol the picture."

"All right, Evita," I said. I didn't really want to show everyone the picture of Travis and the other woman, but it looked like I didn't have much of a choice. Bringing the picture up on my tablet, I handed it to Marisol. "That picture was taken last Friday in Travis's office at the high school. We know that the woman isn't you."

"Oh…my…God…Qué chingados! Hijo de puta!" As Marisol slipped into cussing Travis out in Spanish, she shoved the tablet back into my hands. "You little puta! You've known about this since Friday and you didn't tell me? What kind of sister are you?"

"I'm sorry, Marisol. I didn't know what to do!" Evita said.

"You could have told me! But, no, you had to protect Travis!" Marisol said.

Stepping between Marisol and Evita, I asked, "Marisol, do you have any idea who this woman could be? We need to figure out who this woman is so that we can question her."

"No. I have no idea. I can't believe Travis would cheat on me." Marisol screamed and then pulled away from Hardy. "Find her! Find that puta and ask her what she was doing with my man! And figure out if Xavier killed him or not!"

CHAPTER SIXTEEN

"I strongly advise you not to agitate Xavier," Dr. Vaughn said to Hardy. "Speak calmly to him and ask simple questions. And do not push him for answers."

"Except what I need are some damn answers," Hardy said, letting his frustration show.

Vaughn, Hardy, and I were in the sheriff's department's cramped observation room watching Xavier through the one-way glass. Xavier's eyes were still ringed in dark purple circles, but the swelling around his eyes and nose had gone down. His hands were also trembling almost nonstop, and, every once in a while, his body spasmed violently and almost caused him to fall off his chair. Had Xavier been in the same physical state on Saturday night, there was no way he could have held the bow and accurately aimed the arrows.

Seated next to Xavier was the lawyer that Ida Ortega hired. Mike Gottfried's cheap, rumpled suit jacket was at least two sizes too big, and he had to turn up the cuffs of the matching pants to avoid tripping over them. Gottfried had his own law firm called Gottfried & Associates. There were no associates. His office was above a discount tattoo parlor, and he advertised on the back of take-out menus. As far as I knew, he'd never successfully defended a client in his thirteen years as a lawyer.

"Has Xavier said anything about the shooting?" I asked Dr. Vaughn, hoping he would be a little more forthcoming than he had been the other day. Dr. Vaughn hadn't been at the hospital on the night that we apprehended Xavier and then sent him over to the Emergency Room to be checked out. But one of the deputies had been with Xavier up until he had been admitted into the psychiatric ward. The deputy had informed me that Xavier had been carrying on about Marisol and his mission to help her up until he had been sedated.

"Not that I'm aware of," Vaughn said. "My main goal is getting Xavier properly medicated. Determining what happened the night of the homicide is your job."

"Well now's Xavier's chance to talk about what happened that night," Hardy said.

Leaving me and Vaughn in the observation room, Hardy went into the interrogation room. Due to Xavier's mental state, Vaughn thought it would be best if only one person were to question him. Hardy decided he was going to be that person.

As soon as Hardy walked into the interrogation room, Gottfried stood up and said, "Sergeant Hardy, I want you to know that I will be pursuing an insanity defense for my client. The kid is off his rocker."

"Is this an admission of guilt?" Hardy asked. "Is Xavier confessing to shooting and killing Travis Yeager? And for attempting to kill Marisol Santiago?"

"I have no idea if the kid did it or not. I'm just telling you that the kid's got a big hole in his screen door and that I'm going for the insanity defense."

"Gottfried, your client hasn't been charged with anything yet. I'm intrigued that you already have your defense lined up," Hardy said. He then leaned across the table and waved his hand around in front of Xavier's glazed, unblinking eyes. "Xavier? Xavier, I'm Sergeant Jerrod Hardy with the Texas Rangers. I have a few questions to ask you. Do you mind talking to me?"

Xavier didn't respond. And, aside from his trembling hands, he didn't even move.

"Is Xavier okay?" I asked Vaughn.

"It's a side effect of the medication," Vaughn said. "It makes him a little foggy at first. In another day or two, Xavier will be in much better shape. I believe I made it clear to you over the phone that Xavier is still very agitated. Yes, he might appear calm –"

"He's heading towards comatose. How many medications do you have him on?" I asked, holding up a warrant that required Dr. Vaughn to share Xavier's current medical record with me.

"Xavier is currently taking two medications. An antipsychotic and a mood-stabilizer. The antipsychotic is already beginning to work. That is why Xavier appears calmer and is exhibiting less symptoms than he was when you apprehended him. It is the mood-stabilizer that will take longer to make a difference. Mentally and emotionally, Xavier is very unstable.

In a week or so – when Xavier is better medicated – he'll behave like a completely different person. The delusions he is currently having will fade away. That's why I'm not sure how useful this conversation will be. Whatever Xavier tells you today might not match up with what he'll tell you a week from now."

"We can't wait a week. We've got a homicide to solve. And your patient either committed it or witnessed it. And it could be detrimental to our investigation if we don't find out everything that he knows," I said

"I know," Dr. Vaughn sighed.

Earlier, when Dr. Vaughn and two orderlies brought Xavier into the sheriff's department, Xavier just shuffled along and recited Bible passages from memory. Both Vaughn and Gottfried had tried to engage Xavier in conversation, but he didn't respond or acknowledge either of them. If Xavier wasn't still quoting the Bible, I'd think he had fallen asleep.

~*~*~

In the interrogation room, Hardy was trying to question Xavier about what happened to Marisol and Travis. He was having a hard time because Xavier wasn't paying attention and kept interrupting with random tangents. No matter what Hardy said or asked, all Xavier wanted to talk about was either Marisol or the devil. At one point, Xavier got up and tried to leave the room. He claimed that Marisol was in grave danger and that he needed to protect her. Hardy and Gottfried had to forcefully return Xavier to his seat.

When Hardy began questioning Xavier about the compound bow and the arrow, Gottfried protested. "I don't really feel comfortable with you asking these questions, Sergeant Hardy. For all I know, you planted the compound bow in his grandmother's car and the arrow in his bedroom to frame my client."

"Is this your other defense?" Hardy asked. "If the insanity defense doesn't work, you'll accuse me and the sheriff's department of planting evidence to make Xavier look guilty."

"Hey, it might work," Gottfried said. He flipped open his notebook and scribbled something on a page. "I mean, it hasn't in the past. But it doesn't hurt to try."

"It's not going to work, Gottfried," Hardy said. He then got up and went to stand beside Xavier's chair. "Son, I need to know exactly what happened on Saturday night. Why did you have a compound bow in your car? Did you use it to kill Travis and wound Marisol? And what about the arrow in your room? It's an exact match to the murder weapon. Where did that come from? Is it yours?"

As Hardy spouted out the consecutive questions, Xavier slid down in the chair until he fell out of it. He then lay on the floor beneath the table, banging his heels on the tiles.

"That's enough of this." Vaughn moved towards the door.

"You can't go in there, Dr. Vaughn," I said, taking up a stance in front of the door to prevent Dr. Vaughn from leaving the observation room. "Sergeant Hardy needs to question Xavier. We need to know what happened on Saturday night."

"And I need to protect my patient!" Vaughn snapped as he shoved me aside. He then ran out of the observation room and burst into the interrogation room. He pushed Hardy away from Xavier, heaved the table to the side of the room, and knelt beside Xavier. "That's enough, Sergeant Hardy. I told you not to agitate Xavier."

"And I told you that I need answers," Hardy said before he stomped out of the interrogation room and joined me in the hallway. "I didn't expect that to go well, but it was actually worse than I anticipated."

"Sorry about Dr. Vaughn. I tried to stop him but he shoved me out of the way," I said.

"The doctor put his hands on you?" Hardy stopped pacing and spun around to face me. His eyebrows were drawn into a sharp V and his eyes flashed with rage.

"It's okay, Jerrod. Dr. Vaughn didn't hurt me. He was just desperate to get to his patient and I was in his way. You were pushing Xavier a little too hard."

"That's because we need answers. Am I the only one who can comprehend that?" Hardy asked as he paced up the hallway and back. "Either Xavier witnessed the shooting, or he committed it and has himself convinced that he only witnessed it. I need to know which it is. Between the bow in his car, the arrow in his room, and all of his stalker pictures of Ms. Santiago, I could charge Xavier with homicide and attempted homicide. But I don't want to do that yet. I'm just not convinced Xavier did it. What do you think?"

"On the night of the murder, I said that it took a special kind of crazy to kill Marisol. I don't think Xavier's the right kind of crazy."

"Me either." Hardy kicked the wall and growled.

"Sergeant Hardy, may I have a word with you and Detective Shatner?" Dr. Vaughn asked as he walked out of the interrogation room and shut the door behind him. He then gestured for me and Hardy to follow him into the observation room. "I've managed to get Xavier calmed down. Out of respect for your investigation…because I do understand the importance of questioning Xavier…I will allow the interview to continue. But only if someone else questions Xavier. You make him uncomfortable, Sergeant Hardy. Xavier is afraid of you."

"I'll talk to him," I said. "I can be, uh, less forceful than Sergeant Hardy."

"Hello? Is anyone in there?" Mike Gottfried knocked on the one-way glass, and then shielded his eyes as if that could somehow help him look through the mirror. At the table behind him, Xavier Ortega flinched every time his attorney's hand connected with the glass. "Are you planning to come back? Or are you going to leave us sitting in here all day?"

"Cool it, Mike, it hasn't even been five minutes," I mumbled, rolling my eyes as Gottfried tapped on the glass again.

"Go on, Carrie. See what you can get out of him," Hardy said.

Xavier didn't react, or even look up, when I walked into the stuffy interrogation room, but Gottfried said, "It's about time, Detective Shatner."

"You got a lot of appointments lined up for today that this is keeping you from?" I asked.

"Well, no. But I had been planning on knocking off early today. I, uh, I'm all caught up on my paperwork."

"Paperwork. Sure…For all the clients you don't have," I said as I had a seat at the interrogation table.

Xavier briefly made eye contact with me before he tucked his chin down and transferred his focus to where his trembling hands were clenched together on top of the table. I waited until Xavier finished reciting the Lord's Prayer before I addressed him.

"Xavier, my name is Detective Carrie Shatner. We met the other night at my cousin Cletus's apartment."

"Don't want to talk to you," Xavier mumbled. "Want to talk to Marisol."

"You love Marisol, don't you?" I asked, starting off with a simple question.

Xavier nodded. "Is Marisol here? Can I see her?"

"No, Xavier, Marisol is not here right now."

"Does her arm still hurt?"

"Yes. It hurts very badly. And her friend, Travis, is dead. I'm trying to figure out who is responsible. And I could use your help."

"Help. Marisol needs help."

"And so do I," I said. Shifting forward in my chair, I propped my elbows on the edge of the table and leaned closer to Xavier. "Were you in the parking lot when Marisol was hurt?"

Xavier nodded. "Waiting for Marisol. Wanted to talk. Travis there."

"Where were you?" I asked, hoping Xavier could give me an idea of where he had been standing when the killer struck.

"Trees. Behind tree. Next to car."

I didn't bother to ask which car. Maybe, once he was feeling better and the medication was working, we could take Xavier to the SWAT Zone and see if he could show us where he was standing.

Moving on, I asked, "What did you see?"

"Arrow!" Xavier rocked back in his chair and almost caused it to topple over backwards. Gottfried got his hand on the back of the chair and pushed it forward just in time. "Travis hurt! Travis dead! Must help Marisol!"

"Xavier, who hurt Marisol? Who killed Travis?" I asked.

"Dark. Too dark. Tried to stop. I ran…the woods. Found arrow. Nobody there," Xavier gasped as sweat poured down his face, soaking the bandage on his forehead. "Marisol hurt! Travis dead! Need my help. Marisol needs my help."

"Marisol is safe. She's hurt, but she's safe," I said, speaking calmly. "If you want to help Marisol, you need to help me figure out who hurt her. Did you see the person who hurt Marisol and killed Travis?"

"She did! She did! She did it!" Shoving back his chair, Xavier launched himself across the interrogation table and grabbed the front of my uniform. Pulling me out of my chair, Xavier pressed his sweaty forehead against mine and screamed, "You have to stop her!"

Before I could ask who 'she' was, Hardy, Dr. Vaughn, and both orderlies rushed into the room and grabbed the nearly hysterical Xavier. While Vaughn tried to calm his patient down, the orderlies and Gottfried pried Xavier's hands off my disheveled, torn shirt.

"I believe we're done here," Dr. Vaughn said as the orderlies hustled Xavier out of the interrogation room. "I will let you know when Xavier is feeling better and is up for another interview. I'm sorry you didn't get all of the answers you want, but I need to get Xavier back to the hospital."

"You all right, Carrie?" Hardy asked as he flicked the collar that Xavier had partially torn off my shirt. "Did he hurt you?"

"I might have had a small heart attack, but I'm fine." I went over to the mirror and examined the damage to my uniform top. Aside from partially ripping off the collar, Xavier's fingernails had also pierced the fabric, leaving behind four holes. It looked like this shirt was headed for the trash. "I didn't expect Xavier to come across the table at me."

"What do you think? Is he the killer or a witness?"

"Definitely a witness. Had Travis and Marisol been attacked by someone wielding a knife or another handheld weapon, then I might think Xavier is the killer. But I can't believe he shot Travis almost dead center in the back. Not with the way his hands are shaking. And, even at his worst, I don't believe he would hurt Marisol," I said before I pulled my shirt over my head and then adjusted my tank top so that my bra wasn't showing. "I can't wait until the medications kick in. I need to know what Xavier saw that night. And I need to know it yesterday. Especially now that he's spouting off that 'she' did it. Who is 'she'?"

"The woman Travis was having an affair with?" Hardy asked.

"I repeat, who is she?" I asked.

Stomping out of the interrogation room, I walked two doors down the hallway to my tiny office. After tossing my ruined shirt into the trash, I rummaged around my office in search of a spare. All I could find was an old jersey from when I played on the department's kickball team. It would have to do until I could get home and grab something else.

"I know we have to leave all possibilities open, but I can't believe that Travis and Marisol weren't targeted. The killer was lying in wait," Hardy said. He then pulled his phone out of his pocket and groaned. "Now why is she calling me?"

"Who's she?" I asked, feeling irrationally jealous because some woman called Hardy.

"My...well, technically she's my stepmother. Vanessa," Hardy said.

Even if I hadn't been able to hear the voicemail recording, I would have known what the call was about just by the irritated look on Hardy's face. His father had passed away.

"I'm sorry, Jerrod."

"Don't be."

"Despite how you feel about him, he's still your father."

"Knocking up a woman doesn't make a man a father. It makes him a sperm donor," Hardy said.

Hardy called his stepmother and I eavesdropped on his side of the conversation.

"Hi Vanessa. I just got your message...I was interviewing a suspect...I can't just drop everything I'm doing and drive up there. I'm in the middle of a couple investigations, but I'll try to make it for the funeral if you and Jake want me there that badly...I know he's my father, Vanessa. But I had no relationship with him...All right, all right, I'll get there as soon as I can."

"I guess this means you're going back to Kansas City," I said.

"Unfortunately. This is the last thing I wanted to do." Hardy looked over at me. "Think you can handle the investigation without my help?"

"I'll try not to screw up too badly."

~*~*~

"Detective Shatner, have you talked to Xavier yet? Did he confess to killing Travis?" Marisol asked. She grabbed me by the arm and yanked me out of the receiving line that wound its way past Travis's casket, passing first his father's family who stood at the foot of the casket and then his mother's family at the head. "And what about that other woman? Did you figure out who she is? Esa perra puta...What if she's here tonight and is laughing at me?"

"Marisol, I can't share all of the details of my investigation. But, no, Xavier has not confessed and I don't know who the other woman is," I said.

"You're totally letting me down. Do you have any idea how terrified I am? At least Xavier is back in the nuthouse where he belongs. So I don't have to worry about him anymore. But what if he's not the killer? The real killer could still be coming for me!" Marisol snapped.

"We're doing everything we can. Murder investigations aren't as easy as television makes it seem." I pulled my arm away from Marisol's clutching hands and headed back to the receiving line to join Uncle Murph and Quaranta. Mumbling under my breath, I said, "And it's not my fault Travis has a lot of people who apparently hated him and are glad that he's dead."

"Ms. Santiago is starting to get on my nerves," Murph whispered to me. "I didn't tell you this earlier, but she called the department three times this afternoon to demand answers. She kept asking to talk to you, but I had the receptionists tell her that you were out of the office."

"I appreciate it. I can't blame Marisol for wanting answers, but she's getting a little too pushy," I said.

"They all want answers, but Travis's family members aren't pushing nearly as hard as Ms. Santiago," Quaranta said.

After Hardy left to head up to Kansas City to be with his newfound family, I sat down with Travis's cell phone and read through all of his text messages to see if there was anything that Deputy Timmy Grant missed. I was looking for threats from any of the people who he exchanged texts with, as well as intimate texts with a woman who wasn't Marisol. After hours of reading through the texts – apparently Travis never deleted any of his texts messages – I never did find what I was looking for. I then started going through Travis's personal emails, but I didn't get through too many before I had to head home so I could change my clothes for Travis's viewing at the End of the Line Funeral Home.

After expressing our condolences to the Yeagers, Murph, Quaranta, and I walked by the open casket. I gave Travis's corpse an obligatory glance as I hurried past. Dead people didn't really bother me – not after the years I'd spent working as a crime scene technician – but ogling dead people in their caskets gave me the creeps. From what I could tell, Naomi did a spectacular job with his hair and makeup. Sure, Travis still looked dead. But he was one of the more attractive corpses I'd seen.

Following the line of people, the three of us then stopped to say a few words to Travis's mother's family. It was also my first time meeting Travis's mother, step-father, older sister, and both of his younger half-sisters. Out of all of them, the step-father seemed the most upset. He was crying so hard that he could barely speak, and he looked like he might collapse at any moment.

Sidling up to Dustin Thompson, who was lurking behind his distraught father, I whispered, "How's your foot?"

"Healing," Dustin whispered back. He didn't seem overly emotional considering he was at his stepbrother's viewing. "I even managed to get my foot into a dress shoe for tonight. But that's only 'cause Belinda said flip flops ain't appropriate."

"They're not." I glanced around the chapel for Belinda and spotted her speaking to Naomi at the back of the room. I could only imagine what that conversation might be about. "How's your mouth?"

"Shut."

"Let's keep it that way." Leaving Dustin with his family, I made my way to the back of the room to join Naomi and Belinda. "How's it going, ladies?"

"Dreadful." Belinda sniffled into a tissue. "This is just so sad. Travis's mother and stepfather are barely speaking to each other today. Father Thompson made another accusation where he blamed Mother Thompson and the girls for making him leave the event early because they wanted to change out of their wet clothes. Father Thompson still believes that had he still been at the arena, he would have somehow prevented Travis's murder. Dustin is trying to help his half-sisters keep the peace, but his father is angry at him for not attending the show."

"Does Dustin normally attended the SWAT shows?" I asked.

"Dustin always attends. The only reason he did not go on Saturday night was because he injured his foot," Belinda said.

"I'm glad Dustin's foot is healing. That was a nasty looking wound," I said as I used my elbow to give Naomi a sharp jab in the side.

"Thank you, Detective Shatner. If you and Naomi will excuse me, I need to get back to Dustin and my in-laws," Belinda said before she hurried back to the front of the chapel.

"What was that about?" I asked Naomi.

"No clue. I stuck my head in the room to see if you were here yet or not, and Belinda accosted me. I have no idea what Dustin sees in that woman."

"And I have no idea what you saw in him."

"Temporary insanity." Turning to face me, Naomi said, "Hey, something is wrong with my car and I had to take it to the garage. Can you stick around for a little bit after the viewing and then give me a ride home?"

"Only if you don't mind swinging by the Cantina on the way home. I'm meeting Veda there for an emergency wedding planning session."

"That's fine. Someone needs to stop you from losing your cool on her for being a bridezilla." Naomi leaned closer and whispered, "There's some teenage girl who keeps turning around and giving you a desperate look. I think she might want to talk to you."

Glancing over my shoulder, I spotted Evita Santiago sitting by herself in one of the middle rows of chairs. I waved her over. I then turned back around to say something to Naomi, but she had already slipped out of the chapel.

"Hi, Detective Shatner," Evita said as she materialized at my side.

"How's everything going at home?" I asked.

"Not good. Everyone is mad at me. My parents and sisters won't talk to me unless they have to. And Marisol has yelled at me a bunch of times since yesterday evening. At least Zachary isn't mad at me anymore. I mean, he's upset I didn't say anything to you sooner. But he gets why I didn't."

"That's good," I said. "And your family will come around. You did the right thing by coming forward. Don't feel bad about upsetting Marisol."

"You don't know Marisol like I do, Detective Shatner. I know you've heard that old cliché about beauty only being skin deep…Well, that perfectly describes Marisol. She's so beautiful on the outside, but she's ugly on the inside. You know those people who are just completely fake? Everything is an act with them. That's Marisol. There's nothing genuine about her. But she's so good at faking it, that it seems real. She has this talent for manipulating people into seeing her as this great person."

"I thought you and Marisol are super close," I said, wondering how much I could believe. Evita was mad at Marisol because Marisol was mad at her. It was possible Evita just wanted to run down her sister and make her look bad. If Marisol and Annalisa could be believed, Evita had been doing it since she was a little girl.

"Well, we are. But we aren't. Growing up, Annalisa was practically Marisol's slave. She worshiped Marisol. And she still does. And Marisol loves the adoration. But it's like she got sick of it while she was away at college. She's been pushing Annalisa away ever since she moved home. And for some reason she's been hanging out with me."

"Maybe Marisol is finally seeing you as a contemporary. Five years can be a big age difference when you're kids. It's not that big of a deal when you're adults," I said.

Having two older sisters myself, I understood what Evita was saying. My older sisters, Holly and Rosie, always left me out when we were growing up. To this day, Holly and I still haven't really bonded. And it wasn't until Holly went away to college that Rosie and I started hanging out and formed a connection.

"No, Detective Shatner. Marisol hated me when we were kids. So did Annalisa." Tears overflowed from Evita's eyes and ran down her cheeks. "They practically tortured me. I'm talking legitimate abuse. Physical, mental, and emotional."

"Did you tell your parents what was going on?" I asked.

"It was no use. They didn't want to hear anything bad about Marisol," Evita said as she used her sleeve to wipe away the tears. "Besides Marisol would just deny everything and Annalisa would back her up. Then my parents would accuse me of lying and punish me."

"What about Annalisa? How did Marisol treat her?"

"Marisol treated Annalisa better than she treated me, but not by much. From the day she was born, Annalisa has worshipped the ground that Marisol walked on. She would do anything for Marisol. And that includes helping Marisol torment me."

"How long did this abuse go on?" I asked.

"It never really stopped. They just gave up on the physical abuse when I went through a growth spurt. It was harder for them to beat up on me when I was the same size as them."

Evita listed off some examples of the verbal abuse that Marisol had dished out over the years. While cruel, it wasn't anything I hadn't heard from my own sisters. And I'm sure plenty of other kids received the same abuse from their older siblings. According to Evita, Marisol was constantly telling her that she was adopted, ugly, stupid, a failure, and that she would never amount to anything. Marisol also went around purposely breaking or destroying things, and then blaming it on her youngest sister. Marisol's path of destruction included Evita's toys and personal belongings, along with Annalisa's and her own. Marisol even destroyed some of their parents' things just so she could blame it on Evita. Evita tried to tell her parents that it was Marisol who was responsible, but they never believed her.

"Give me some examples of what Marisol has done to you recently," I said.

"Well…All right, I lied the other day when I said I was over my crush when Marisol and Travis hooked up. Marisol knew about my crush. I swear the only reason she started dating Travis was because she knew it would hurt me. After the first date, she told me Travis wasn't really her type, but that she was going to go out with him again because she knew it hurt me."

"Okay, I can see how Marisol was being cruel, but I wouldn't call it abuse," I said.

"Would you say it was abuse when Marisol told me every detail about their sex life?"

"Okay, that definitely counts as abuse," I said.

"Look, Detective Shatner, I love my sister. I just don't like her. You know what I mean?"

"I completely understand," I said. I felt the same way about the majority of the Shatners. "Remember, Evita, in two weeks you're going to graduate from high school. And a few months after that you'll be in Arizona for college. You'll get to escape all this. And you don't need to come back."

~*~*~

"Oh yeah, I've got all three of the hottest women in Wyatt County gracing my bar with their sexiness. I don't think my usual customers can handle this," Red said as set three drinks down on the bar – a Coke for me and margaritas for Naomi and Veda. He then stepped back and flexed his muscles. The pinup girl's breasts swelled to gigantic proportions. "But, Carrie and Naomi, you two just can't seem stay away from me, can you? Are you girls gonna draw straws to decide who comes home with me tonight? Or do you both wanna come over?"

"Stop being a pervert and turn on some wrestling." I grabbed a handful of pretzels out of a bowl and then chucked them at Red's smiling face.

"You know I'll do anything for you, Carrie, And I do mean anything." Red reached under the bar and grabbed a remote. He then flipped through the channels on one of the TVs mounted above the bar until he found some pro wrestling. "Speaking of wrestling…Carrie, I've got to tell you about my idea for my last match."

"Later, Red," Veda snapped. "I've got wedding stuff to go over first."

Instead of watching wrestling, I spent the next hour going over wedding plans with Veda. There was a lot that we still had to do, and less than three months to do it. Because there was no way Veda could handle it all by herself, she handed out tasks to me and Naomi. Even Red, who made the mistake of refilling our drinks at the wrong moment, wound up getting roped into helping.

After having a third wedding-related task forced upon her, Naomi slid off her barstool and stretched.

"I'll be back. I'm going to the bathroom," Naomi said.

Veda waited until Naomi walked away and then she asked, "So how are things going with Jerrod? Naomi told me that you guys had some sort of fight the other day."

"Don't you and Naomi have anything better to talk about than my love life?" I asked.

"Prior to your current love life, Naomi and I never talked at all. Aren't you happy that I'm bonding with your family members? I need to win over more of them before my wedding. I can't count on you being the only one on my side should my future mother-in-law decide to protest. You've got more important things to do at my wedding than strangle Loretta."

"I told you, Veda, I'll hogtie Aunt Loretta and stuff her in a car trunk until after the ceremony if she causes too much of a commotion on your wedding day. No one is going to ruin it," I said.

"Well, if you have to hogtie Loretta, just make sure you do it before you get your makeup and hair done. I need my Maid of Honor looking gorgeous. Just not as gorgeous as me," Veda said. She flicked her long, blonde hair over her shoulder and then leaned closer to me. "Now, tell me everything about Jerrod. I know Naomi didn't tell me the whole story."

"She doesn't know the whole story."

I was debating over how many details I wanted to share with Veda when Red walked over and slammed his fists down on the bar in front of me.

"What is Naomi doing?" Red asked.

"She went to the bathroom," I said.

Red put his hand on my shoulder and pushed, forcing the barstool to spin me around so that I faced the barroom.

"Does it look like Naomi is going to the bathroom to you?" Red asked.

Scanning the room, I spotted Naomi. She was in the same position she was in on Sunday night – perched on a man's lap with her tongue down his throat. When they came up for air, I could see that Naomi was making out with a man who was missing more teeth than most professional hockey players.

"Oh, not again," I said as I stood up on the stool's footrest so that I could see over the barflies who were blocking my view. "She told me she was raising her standards."

"I think Naomi needs to get her vision checked," Veda said.

"What she needs is to have more respect for herself," Red said as threw down the dripping rag that he held. "Are you gonna do something about this, Carrie?"

"What do you want me to do, Red? I've tried talking to her. She doesn't listen."

The toothless man put his hand on Naomi's butt and hauled her closer.

"Well, if you ain't gonna do something, I am," Red said as he popped his knuckles.

"What are you going to do?" I asked, noticing that Red was breathing heavier than usual and that his overdeveloped muscles were tensing up.

"Something you ain't gonna approve of. But I'm doing it with the best of intentions." Red stomped out from behind the bar and headed towards Naomi and the toothless man.

"What do you think he's gonna do?" Veda asked.

"He's probably going to knock out the rest of that man's teeth," I said.

"Aren't you going to stop him?"

"I'm a little scared to get in his way."

Knowing I couldn't physically stop Red, I began scrambling for excuses. If he did assault the man, I certainly didn't want him to get charged for it. I knew I could come up with something, but the problem was all of the witnesses. I doubted I could convince all of them to back my story. The toothless man was bound to have some friends who would take his side.

Red walked up behind Naomi and roughly pulled her off the toothless man's lap. He said something to her, but Veda and I were too far away to hear it. Red then pulled Naomi tightly against him before guiding her head towards his and kissing her.

"He's right," I said. "I definitely do not approve."

"Aw, they're kinda cute together," Veda said.

I could have sworn Naomi was kissing Red back until she squirmed out of his arms. I couldn't tell if she was aroused, shocked, or angry until she pulled her arm back and slapped Red across the face. She then screamed something at him and took off running towards the bathroom. She blindly bumped into people, tables, and chairs during her flight.

Red watched her until she disappeared. He then hauled back and punched the toothless man in the mouth before bolting into the back room. The toothless man leaned over and spit a tooth onto the floor. He then went back to sipping his beer.

"I'll talk to Red. You talk to Naomi," I said. On my way to find Red, I strolled by the toothless man's table and used a napkin to pick up his tooth. It looked like a molar. I plunked it down on the table in front of him. "Sorry about your tooth."

"Ain't nothing." The toothless man leered at me, showing off the bloody hole in the back of his mouth. "That one was already loose. Red just saved me a trip to the dentist."

"Uh huh," I mumbled, backing away from the toothless man. "Well, you might want to take care of the few teeth you have left."

In the back room, I found Red sitting on a lawn chair next to a tower of beer kegs. He had a can of Shiner Bock pressed to his cheek. I pulled the can away and inspected the damage. The mark Naomi left covered Red's entire cheek, and there was a half-moon shaped crease by his eye that must have been caused by one of Naomi's rings.

"That's not quite how I expected it would go," Red said.

"What were you thinking?" I asked, feeling a combination of pity and anger.

"I don't know. But I'm thinking it was a mistake."

I sat down on the floor in front of Red, propped my chin on my knees, and asked, "What did you say to Naomi?"

"I told her that if she wants to make out with a scumbag, she should make out with one who cares about her."

"That's romantic. What did she say to you?"

"That she doesn't want to be another notch on my bedpost."

"Do you have any bedposts left to make notches in?" I asked.

Even in high school, Red had a reputation. It had only gotten worse since then.

"First of all, I don't make notches in my bedpost. Or anywhere else." Red opened up the can and took a swig. "Second, the rumors about me ain't exactly true. I don't have a woman in every town I wrestle in."

"The rumors are that you have five to ten women in every town," I said, giving Red a whack on his muscular thigh. "But I know the rumors aren't true. At least not all of them. But I know you've had countless women of all ages throwing themselves at you ever since you started wrestling. You telling me you've never taken any of them up on it."

"That's exactly what I'm telling you. Look, Carrie, just because I have more women than I can count trying to get me into their beds doesn't mean I go home with all of them. To be honest, I don't go home with any of them."

Red chugged the rest of the beer and smashed the can against his forehead. He then grabbed another one. Instead of opening it, he held it to his cheek.

"You being serious right now?" I asked.

"Of course I'm being serious. You think this is a joke?"

"Sometimes it's hard to tell with you, Red." I leaned back on my arms and studied the pipes crisscrossing the ceiling. "Now, tell me why you kissed Naomi."

"Because I like her, all right."

"You like her? Or do you just want to sleep with her?"

"Damn it, Carrie." Red chucked the unopened can into the wall. It exploded on impact, showering both of us with suds. "I more than like Naomi. I think I might be in love with her."

My hands slid on the smooth concrete and I fell back on the floor with a thud. Red grabbed me by the front of my shirt and pulled me up.

"You want to repeat that?" I asked. "I'm not sure I heard you right."

"I just said that I think I'm in love with Naomi." Red picked up a third beer can, but didn't open it. "No, I've gotten beyond the thinking stage. I'm in the knowing stage."

My jaw dropped and smacked into my kneecap. Of all the crazy things Red had said to me over the years, this was the most fascinating. He was in love with Naomi? When did this happen? And when had he fallen out of love with me? Not that it really mattered since I was never going to return his feelings. But I kind of liked knowing that Red was longing for me.

"If you're in love with her, then why have you been hitting on me in front of her?"

"Because I'm an idiot. And we've been talking to each other like that since we were teenagers, Carrie. Of course, back when we were teenagers, I'd have given anything to get you into bed." Red nudged my leg with his boot and asked, "You ain't jealous, are you?"

"No. Well, maybe a little. But not really," I said.

"So, you gonna help me or not?"

I laid back on the floor and covered my face with my arms. The more that I thought about it, the more it dawned on me that Naomi and Red might actually be good for each other.

"I'll help you on two conditions." I held up my arm, sticking my index finger in the air. "One, you gotta stop hitting on me. And that includes even when Naomi isn't around."

"I think I can manage that."

"Two." I held up another finger. "You do something about that tattoo."

"All right, all right. I'll figure something out." Red twisted his arm so that he could talk to the tattoo. "I guess it'll soon be goodbye, old friend."

"I can't make any promises, but I'll talk to Naomi."

"I appreciate it, Carrie," Red said as he helped me to my feet. "If you can't get Naomi to come around right away, can you at least try to keep her from hooking up with another scumbag? I see her with another one and I'm bound to get violent."

"I'll do my best. Just don't call me if you have a body to dispose of."

"Ain't it your job to dispose of dead bodies?" Red joked.

Exiting the back room, Red and I found Veda by the bar. Naomi was not with her.

"I couldn't get much out of Naomi," Veda said. "But she's upset. She grabbed your keys off the bar and ran outside."

I cursed myself for leaving my keys lying on the bar. "You think she took my car and went home?"

Veda shrugged. "If she did, I'll give you a ride."

After once again promising Red that I'd do my best, Veda and I went out into the parking lot. My Jeep was gone.

"Seriously, Naomi? You crash my car and I'll kill you." I gave Veda a push towards her car. "Come on, let's get going."

It took about fifteen minutes to get to my house, and I spent the entire ride convinced that we were going to come across my Jeep crashed along the side of the road. I was pleased to find it haphazardly parked on Naomi's front lawn.

"You want me to come in and help you deal with her?" Veda asked when she pulled up to the curb in front of Naomi's house.

"Naw, I got it covered," I said.

"I still think I should come in and make sure you don't kill her for stealing your car."

"I'm not going to kill her," I said.

I climbed out of Veda's car and headed towards my Jeep. After making sure there wasn't any damage, I went inside the house and I found Naomi sprawled out on her pink leather sofa. She was sobbing into a throw pillow while one of her cats chewed on her hair. After shooing the cat away, I collapsed on the couch beside Naomi.

"I'm going to be blunt about this, Naomi. Red's in love with you."

"No, he's not. He just wants to get me naked. That's all any man wants me for."

"Then stop taking your clothes off." I smacked her on the butt. "Sit up and look at me."

"Why can't you just leave me alone?" Naomi refused to sit up, but she did turn her head so that she was peeking at me over her arm.

"Tell me what it is you don't like about Red," I said. "And forget about the rumors because they aren't true."

Naomi laughed. "Let me see, what don't I like about Red? Hmmm… well, you're the one the jerk clearly wants. I mean, he's been after you for, what, fifteen years. He's just, like, settling for second best by picking me. And, besides, Red's my friend. I don't have sex with my friends."

"No, you have sex with nasty men that you meet at bars. Come on, Naomi, you've done a lot worse than Red."

"Yeah, well…You know, I had a huge crush on Red when I was a kid. I thought he was so hot and cool. But you two were always together. And then he got that tattoo that looks like you. I always figured you two would wind up getting married."

"Me and Red? Oh, jeez. No, it was never like that between us. Ever. I can see why you would think that though," I said.

Red and I hung out all the time when we were teenagers. Most people were under the impression that we were dating.

"So you and Red never…" Naomi said, trailing off.

"No! He wanted to. And he tried to talk me into it. But, no, we never did more than make out a few times." And go skinny dipping at the public pool, but that was ancient history. I pulled Naomi up into a sitting position and hugged her. "You've been running around with these gross men, and then running away from them, ever since your fiancé called off the wedding. I think it's about time you stop running."

"You're right, maybe it is. I'm going to need some time to get my head straight, but I think I will give it a chance with Red," Naomi said. She leaned her head against mine and sighed. "And, Carrie, if it's time for me to stop running, then maybe it's time you stopped chasing."

"What are you talking about?" I asked.

"Sergeant Hardy. I know you like him, but…well, I just don't want to see you stuck in another dead-end relationship that you're trying to revive long after it's dead."

CHAPTER SEVENTEEN

"I hate funerals."

"We know, Uncle Murph. You've only told us ten times already," I said.

"I'm just saying…Where were all of these people when Travis was alive? Who was sending him flowers then? And what are all these people doing here? They're ghouls. I bet Travis wouldn't have had this much of a turnout had he been killed in a car accident. This is why I hate funerals." Murph said as he waved his arms around and gestured at the hundred or so people gathered around Travis's cemetery plot on Friday morning. Travis's family, as well as Marisol and the Santiagos, were under a small tent along with the casket. Everyone else was crowded around the tent, including me, Murph, and Quaranta.

"You've made your point, Uncle Murph," I said.

"And if you don't knock it off, the next funeral you'll be attending will be your own," Quaranta hissed.

Glancing around at the growing crowd, I spotted Red standing with a group of wrestlers. Vladimir Khrushchev was there, as was Mr. 'Roid Rage, and my cousins, Keaton and Kermit. They, along with Uncle Sterling, had served as the pallbearers. I waved to get Red's attention, and then motioned him over.

"How'd you guys get roped into being the pallbearers?" I asked as I led Red away from Travis's gravesite.

"We carried him in the ring since he was a horrible wrestler and needed his opponent to make the match go over smoothly. Figured we may as well carry him one last time. Plus, Travis's archery buddies refused to do it because they were afraid they would hurt their arms," Red said as he wandered into the Shatner family plot and had a seat on my great-grandparents' elaborate headstone. "Since you couldn't be bothered to call me back last night or this morning…How's Naomi? I tried to talk to her at the church, but she blew me off."

"She's a hot mess." I had a seat on another Shatner headstone. "I was up half the night with her. She's in a better place than she was when we started talking, but she's emotionally drained right now."

"What does that mean?"

"It means Naomi needs to find herself and heal."

"Does that mean she likes me or not?" Red buried his head in his hands and groaned. "I sound like a freaking teenager…"

"She likes you, Red. She like likes you," I said, replying like a teenager would.

"Sweet!" Red pumped his fists in the air, and then said, "So, hey, tomorrow night I'm heading up to Tyler for a show. The promoter called me this morning and asked if I want to make a retirement speech. You wanna go with me?"

"As your valet? Or as a detective?" I asked.

"Both. I'm only going to be in the ring for a few minutes. The rest of the time you can snoop around and talk to the wrestlers. A lot of the guys who are gonna be at the show were at SWAT last Saturday."

"And a lot of the same fans will be there as well. I'll take some of my deputies along. If they're in street clothes, they can wander around and eavesdrop on the fans," I said. Travis was bound to be the main topic of conversation among the fans and the wrestlers. Maybe we would get lucky and learn some new information. "Travis the person seemed well liked, but the Beast from East Texas had a lot of enemies."

~*~*~

"I know you can't tell us anything, but are you any closer to finding the person who killed Travis?" Frank Smith asked. "A few of the boys are worried that the killer might come after one of them next. You know, like, tonight."

Frank dropped a stack of 8x10 photos of himself dressed up in his Vladimir Khrushchev outfit on the table next to where I was helping Red set up his merchandise. Oksana, Khrush, Tatyana, and Sonya were setting out piles of Vladimir Khrushchev t-shirts and sweatshirts. Neither of the girls looked quite well enough to be there. The wrestling event was being held in an elementary school's gymnasium, and the merchandise tables were lined up right inside the double doors that led out into the parking lot.

"You mean the other wrestlers think the person who killed Travis is a serial killer that is targeting wrestlers on the independent scene? We've already considered that possibility. But until another wrestler is murdered…" I said.

"Don't even joke about that," Red said as he turned to me with a horrified look. "I've spent the past week wondering if maybe the killer mistook Travis and Marisol for you and me. Travis and I were parked next to each other."

"You and I have certainly ticked off a lot of people over the years," I said.

"Yeah, well, neither of us are saints…I mean, the only reason you still have a halo is because it's caught on your horns," Red said, giving me a nudge in the side.

"Oh my God, you'll never guess who's backstage! Marisol Santiago is here! And she looks like a freaking car crash. Her makeup looks terrible, and it doesn't look like she's slept in a week," Naomi said as she rushed up to the table. Instead of helping me and Red get set up, Naomi had disappeared into the bathroom to fix her hair and makeup for the third time in an hour.

"She probably hasn't considering what all she's been through during the past seven days," Red said.

Stepping up onto the table, I had the dozen deputies who I had brought along to the show gather around me. Before bringing my deputies to the show, I had to get permission from the Smith County Sheriff's Department and the Tyler Police Department for us to come into their territory to question people. Half of my deputies were in their uniforms, and would be made available to fans who wanted to come forward with any information about Travis Yeager. The other deputies were in plain clothes and would mingle with the fans, and, hopefully, overhear something interesting.

"Y'all know what you're supposed to do tonight," I said. "Keep your eyes and ears open, ask questions, and take notes. Aside from the five or so minutes when I'll be in the ring with the Ravishing Redneck, I'll be right here. If you need me, come get me."

A few minutes later, the doors opened and the fans poured in. The majority of the fans made a beeline for Red's table. After buying up his remaining merchandise, the fans thanked Red for the years of entertainment he provided. A number of fans also gave Red all sorts of artwork they had made or mementos they had collected over the years. And they all had stories and memories they wanted to share.

The fans who weren't fighting for a moment with Red, crowded around me – asking questions and providing their theories on who killed the Beast from East Texas and why. The theories I was forced to listen to ranged from the plausible to the downright insane. The majority of the fans believed Travis was killed for defeating Red in the Loser Leaves Town match – they either didn't realize or didn't want to accept that the outcome had been planned out in advance and that Red was supposed to lose the match to Travis. Other fans provided me with names of people who Travis had altercations with in the past. A lot of the people named were ones that we had already looked into and cleared. But I got a few new promising suspects to look into. I was also told by four separate fans to look for possible mob connections. A couple fans shuffled the blame to Marisol, though none of them really had a reason why. And then there was one really dumb fan who made the mistake of blaming the Shatners simply because my family was a known criminal element in Wyatt County. I made sure that person knew who he was talking to.

I was in the middle of being subjected to a fifth theory involving the mob when the house lights dimmed and the event's promotor walked out to the ring along with Marisol. I hadn't had a chance to talk to Marisol before the event. I hadn't even seen her. But, according to Naomi, Marisol looked even more disheveled than she had when she arrived at the event.

"Ladies and gentleman, welcome to tonight's show," the promoter said after he climbed into the ring. "As many of you know, the Beast from East Texas, Travis Yeager, was killed after last Saturday's SWAT Show down near Holler, Texas. Yeager has wrestled here for us many times, and, while his matches weren't always the best, and he wasn't the most likable wrestler on the card, I want to take a moment to honor the man. We're going to sound the ring bell ten times, and then we'll take a moment of silence."

Ding…Ding…Ding…

"Travis Yeager sucked!" yelled a male fan, interrupting the moment of silence and prompting other fans to join in on the taunts. Marisol's head snapped up and her eyes slowly scanned the jeering crowd.

"What a jerk," I mumbled.

"That's the beauty of professional wrestling. Most of us are just here to have fun. Then there are the morons who take it way too seriously," Red said.

"Now there's no reason to be saying nasty stuff about Yeager," the promoter said. "I didn't like him either, but y'all shouldn't be cheering because he's dead. This ain't part of the storyline people. This is real life!"

After yanking the microphone out of the promoter's hand, Marisol screamed, "What is wrong with all of you people? My boyfriend was murdered! Shot down by some lunatic with a bow and arrow!"

"No, Marisol! You weren't supposed to tell anyone that!" I shouted even though Marisol was too far away to hear me. Not that anyone could really hear me over the fans' thunderous reaction to Marisol's announcement. Turning to Naomi, I said, "Marisol's single car wreck is turning into a multi-car pileup."

"Did she just say a bow and arrow?" Oksana asked me before mumbling something in Russian. "I was part of Russia's Olympic archery team years ago. I met Frank when I traveled to the States for competition."

"Oksana, unless you killed Travis, I don't care. I've got more important things to worry about. Like shutting Marisol up before she shares anything else about Travis's murder."

I scrambled around the merchandise table and then shoved my way through the crowd to the ringside barricade. After leaping over the barricade, I climbed into the ring and approached the hysterical Marisol. The fans began to cheer when they saw me in the ring.

"Marisol…you need to take a deep breath and calm down. Stop letting these people get to you," I said.

"Stop letting them get to me? One of them might be the person who killed Travis! But instead of doing your job, you're over there selling t-shirts! What kind of detective are you?"

Marisol drew back her arm to either slap me or punch me. Before she could follow through, I grabbed her arm and stopped her. I then spun her around, twisting her arm behind her back as I pushed her into the ropes that surrounded the ring.

"It might look like I'm just over there selling t-shirts, but I'm really trying to solve Travis's case. You coming out here and going crazy on the fans is not helping matters. So just shut up, calm down, and go backstage. And let me get back to my job!" I said.

CHAPTER EIGHTEEN

"Hey, Jerrod. You're back already?" I asked, when I found Hardy in the sheriff's department's conference room on Sunday morning. Our investigation into who had killed Travis Yeager had been going on for a week now. "How did it go in Kansas City?"

"It was awkward, and I felt like I was in over my head. I spent all day Friday and most of Saturday with my father's wife and my nephew. As well as my dad's mother and his two younger sisters. I like all of them, but they were driving me nuts with all their stories about what a great guy my father was. They kept crying and talking about how much they're going to miss him. Meanwhile, I'm sitting there feeling nothing but annoyance and indifference towards my father."

"I'm sorry, Jerrod."

"Don't be, darling."

"I guess you'll also have to go back to Kansas City for the funeral," I said as I pulled up a chair and had a seat next to Hardy at the conference table.

"I'm skipping it. My stepmother wants me there, but I can't see it being anything other than uncomfortable. What am I supposed to say when someone asks who I am? 'I'm Stephen's son. He abandoned me and my twin brother before we were born. Until the other week I hadn't seen him since I was seven. I also had no idea that he and his wife had adopted my dead brother's son and raised him as their own'…That's just going to lead to lot of questions that I don't want to answer."

"I see what you mean," I said, reaching over to squeeze Hardy's hand. "But you didn't miss much here. I'm no closer to finding Travis's killer than I was when you left."

"Then let's go back to the beginning. I want to go back to last Saturday night and go over everything that happened in the hours before Travis was killed. Starting with Travis's match against Red," Hardy said as he pulled his laptop closer and brought up the footage of the wrestling match. "Talk me through the match. You know far more about it than this video shows us."

Hardy and I watched the match from every camera angle available – the ringside camera, the stationary camera at the top of the stands, and all four security cameras. We also watched the footage of the riot, but there was too much going on and too many people involved for us to be able to make any sense of it. Giving up on the footage, we moved on to the crime scene photos and the notes that Quaranta and I had taken while processing the scene.

Hardy and I had been at it for almost three hours when Quaranta wandered into the conference room. He would have been helping us, but there had been a break-in down in the southern end of the county last night, and it had fallen to him to get the investigation started.

"Figuring anything out?" Quaranta asked.

"Nope. We just keep going in circles," I said.

"Take a break for a while. Belinda Thompson's here asking to talk to you, Carrie. She said it's important. She's waiting for you up in the reception area," Quaranta said.

"Oh, great." I crossed my fingers, hoping that Belinda wasn't there about Dustin. If he let it slip that he was cheating and that my cousin shot him in the foot, things would get ugly. "Can't wait to find out what this is about."

"I'll clean up in here and then meet you in your office," Hardy said.

The conference room was located in the right front corner of the sheriff's department. The main office and reception area were front and center in the building. In the short time it took me to walk down the hallway, passing the breakroom and the bathrooms, I broke out into a sweat and could feel an anxiety attack building. Cutting through the copier room, I peeked around the doorway to see what was going on in the reception area.

Aside from the weekend receptionist, who sat at her desk knitting a baby blanket, Belinda was the only person in the reception area. She paced back and forth across the small room, swishing her floor-length green and white checkered sundress around her ankles. She didn't look angry. If anything, she looked more anxious than I felt.

"Hello, Belinda," I said, leaving the safety of my hiding spot and entering the reception area. "The Chief Deputy said you wanted to talk to me about something."

"Yes, Detective Shatner, there is something very important that I need to speak with you about. It concerns my husband," Belinda said.

"Let's go back to my office."

I used my key card to unlock the main door into the rest of the department. I then led Belinda back the hallway to my office. Hardy was already in the small office waiting for us.

"How's Dustin's foot?" I asked.

"Healing. He has been able to get around considerably better the past day or two."

"That's good," I said as I gestured for Belinda to have a seat in one of my guest chairs. "I hope Dustin learned a lesson and is more careful in the future."

"That's what I came in to speak to you about. I do not believe that Dustin injured his foot in the way that he claims," Belinda said, leaning back in the chair. Her perfect posture slipped into a slouch. "I spent the past week praying over it, and, after speaking to my pastor this morning, I've come to the conclusion that I must come forward with what I suspect."

"And this is about how Dustin injured his foot? And it's somehow a police matter?" Hardy asked, sounding annoyed.

"Last week, on Friday, at the end of the day, I was outside helping supervise the children as they boarded the buses. I overheard a couple of the students speaking about how there is a rumor going around that Evita Santiago walked in on Travis engaging in sexual relations with a female while in the physical education teachers' office," Belinda said.

I opened my mouth to say something, but Belinda held up her hand to stop me.

"I do not need you to confirm the rumor, Detective Shatner. I know it is true because I am the woman who was with Travis."

I had to clench my jaw to keep my mouth from falling open in shock. Prim, proper, and frumpy Belinda Thompson was cheating on her husband with his stepbrother? Yes, Belinda was on the narrowed down list of female faculty and staff members, but, out of all of them, she was the one I suspected the least. I just couldn't imagine Belinda doing such a thing. I reminded myself that looks can be deceiving. Just because Belinda dressed like a nineteenth century schoolmarm didn't mean that she wasn't a professional dominatrix behind closed doors.

"You're the other woman? Why didn't you say something before this?" I asked.

"I am so ashamed of my actions." Belinda dabbed at her eyes with a cloth handkerchief. "We disgraced the sanctity of my marriage, Travis's relationship, and our workplace. It is horrible enough knowing that I committed such a shameful act, but finding out that another person witnessed it is mortifying."

"Why didn't you come forward on Friday after you heard the rumor," Hardy asked.

"I was too embarrassed! I also did not know that Evita had...had documented what she witnessed!" Belinda said as she wadded up the damp handkerchief and shoved it into her purse. "Marisol called me this morning. She is upset that you have yet to locate the other woman, and she wanted to know if I was aware of any rumors concerning Travis. I denied knowing anything. Marisol then asked me to snoop around the school to see if I can determine the identity of the other woman."

"How long have you been having an affair with Travis?" Hardy asked.

"There was no affair. What happened that day was a mistake. A mistake that was only made one time," Belinda said.

"How exactly did this one time mistake come about?" I asked.

"Because Dustin resents his father for leaving his mother to start a new family, we do not see his father's side of the family very often. Last month, at the family's Easter dinner, Dustin had a little too much to drink at dinner, and he criticized me in front of his family. He…he told them that we have not had marital relations in nearly two years, and then cast blame on me because he says he is no longer attracted to me. It was humiliating, especially when Marisol and Dustin's stepmother and younger half-sisters laughed at me. They…they confronted me later and offered to help me with a makeover so that I would be more desirable to Dustin. The only one who showed me any sympathy was Travis. He sought me out at school a few days later to see if I was all right."

"You and Travis didn't talk much before this?" I asked.

"Hardly ever. We are in different departments and rarely encounter each other at work. But for the past month, Travis and I have been speaking regularly. He claimed he was concerned for me and was encouraging me to leave Dustin. He also confessed to me that he was having issues with Marisol."

"Oh, really?" Hardy and I said at the same time. This was the first time we'd heard of them having any sort of problems. Marisol claimed that the relationship had been perfect, and no one else has said otherwise.

"What kinds of issues?" Hardy asked.

"Marisol was pushing for Travis to marry her. From what Travis mentioned, it seems Marisol was being very demanding and needy. She insisted that she always get her way. Travis was feeling overwhelmed by the relationship. He was speaking of breaking it off, but he was not sure how. Not when they had just moved in together."

"What happened that day in Travis's office?" I asked.

"Since Easter, Dustin has become very critical of me. He has continuously put me down and made me feel badly about myself. He also has been disappearing and not providing me with information on his whereabouts. I finally decided I can no longer bear living with him, so I told Travis that I was going to leave Dustin. Travis was very happy for me. And then he said that he was planning on breaking things off with Marisol in the next week or two. I thought…I was mistaken…I believed Travis was leaving Marisol to be with me. I kissed him. And I initiated the…It was my fault."

"Did you and Travis do anything aside from kiss?" I asked.

Belinda nodded. "Although Travis and I agreed to never speak about what had transpired, I was compelled to confess my transgression to Dustin. I did so last Saturday afternoon. Dustin was so very angry with me. I think my husband might have been so outraged that he went to the SWAT Zone later that night and killed Travis."

"What makes you think that?" Hardy asked.

"I know that Travis was killed when the assailant shot an arrow into his back," Belinda said. "And my husband is an accomplished bowhunter. That's the other reason I suspect my husband might be the killer. I'm sorry I didn't come forward about this sooner, but I did not want to wrongfully accuse Dustin."

"Did you ask Dustin about what he was doing while you were at Post Prom? Or did he give you any indication that he might be the killer?" I asked. I had seen Dustin mere hours before Travis was killed. He hadn't said anything about his wife cheating on him. His main concern was that Belinda not find out that he had cheated on her.

Belinda slowly shook her head. "No, Dustin did not say anything. But, when I returned home on Sunday morning, I found Dustin in our bathroom. He was crying and cleaning up a bloody wound on his foot. He told me that he'd sustained the injury when he was walking around the garage in his bare feet. He claims he tripped and then mangled his foot on a tool. At the time, I was more concerned about getting him medical attention than anything else. It was not until I found out how Travis had been killed that I began to suspect my husband."

"What do you think really happened to your husband's foot?" Hardy asked.

"I believe he cut it on one of the broadheads that he uses on his arrows," Belinda said.

I leaned closer to Hardy and whispered, "I need to have a word with you. In private."

"Sure." Hardy stood up and then gave me a hand up. "Excuse us for a minute, Mrs. Thompson. Detective Shatner and I will be right back."

Hardy and I walked out of my office and headed down the hall towards the breakroom.

"We completely overlooked the fact that Dustin is a bowhunter. And that he didn't have an alibi. He said he was home alone watching NASCAR and taking care of his foot when Travis was killed," Hardy said.

"Yeah, well…I'm not buying her story, Jerrod. I think Belinda's going out on a limb accusing Dustin of being the killer. I don't think he did it," I said.

"Why not? Finding out his wife was carrying on with another man is a pretty good motive," Hardy said, holding open the breakroom door for me. "Is it possible you're taking Dustin's side because he's your friend?"

"No. Dustin is not my friend. I've only talked to the guy three times. And you were there the second time."

"Then how do you know that he isn't the killer? I already suspected that his story about cutting his foot while chopping up that tree was a lie. And the story about mangling it when he tripped in the garage is only slightly more believable," Hardy said as he swung open the refrigerator door and grabbed two water bottles. He tossed one of the bottles to me.

"You're right. Both stories are lies. I know what happened to Dustin's foot. But he didn't hurt it with an arrow. Or by hitting it with an axe. Or by injuring it on a tool."

"I knew you two were hiding something that day we ran into Dustin at the hospital. You were so anxious and shifty." Hardy drained the water bottle and then threw it into the recycle bin. "Were you there when Dustin hurt his foot?"

"Yes, I was."

Having a seat at the breakroom table, I mentally prepared myself to tell Hardy about what happened at Naomi's house when she shot Dustin in the foot. Telling Hardy about it was going to be the figurative bullet into the foot of our relationship. Not that we had much of a relationship left anymore.

As I made my way through retelling the events that took place in Naomi's house last Saturday night, I slightly altered certain facts and left other details completely out. Hardy let me tell the story without interruption, but his body language began to show signs of anger and disappointment.

"Why didn't you tell me about this?" Hardy asked.

"I didn't think you'd be too happy with me if you knew what happened."

"You're right. I'm not happy. I'm livid! Good God, Carrie, I can't believe you did that. Except I can, because it's what you do. Considering how sketchy you and Dustin were acting at the hospital, I should have known you were covering for one of your family members. You practically admitted that's what you were doing. I don't have time to deal with this now. But, when we're done with this homicide investigation, you and I are going to have a long chat about your inappropriate actions," Hardy said. He spun my chair around, leaned towards me, and braced an arm on either side of me. It reminded me of our encounter in the funeral home's parking lot. "Regardless of your gut feeling that Dustin isn't the killer, we're going to need to investigate him. He had a motive, and he has a familiarity with the murder weapon."

"What's his motive?" I asked.

"Seriously, Carrie? His wife was cheating on him. That's more than enough to drive a man to kill." Hardy pushed away from me and backed up a couple steps. "Have you ever been cheated on by someone you were in a serious relationship with?"

"Not that I know of," I said.

"Yeah, I didn't think any man would be dumb enough to screw around behind your back. If you didn't kill him, I'm sure one of your family members would. And then you would have helped cover it up." Hardy moved away from me and leaned against the wall. "But I have been cheated on and it's –"

"Are you kidding me? What kind of woman would do that to you?" I asked. Jumping out of the chair, I rushed across the room to where Hardy was standing. "Who is she and why would she cheat on you?"

"Well, it wasn't entirely her fault. I'm really not the best boyfriend. I, uh, it's a long story," Hardy said. He briefly made eye contact with me and then looked away. "It was a couple years ago. The woman was my last serious girlfriend. I walked in on her having sex with one of my close friends. Now they're getting married. They even invited me to the wedding."

"That's just cold," I said.

"Yeah…Anyway, I was pretty upset when I caught them. I wasn't upset enough to kill either of them, but just because I didn't turn homicidal doesn't mean that Dustin didn't."

~*~*~

After finishing up the conversation with Belinda, we followed her to her house on the south side of Holler. The exterior of the one-story brick house was edging towards run-down, and the grass needed mowed a week ago. On the other hand, the interior was spotless. The couch and loveseat were both covered in plastic, there wasn't a speck of dirt to be seen, and nothing appeared to be out of place.

"Since Dustin and I were not blessed with children, he converted our spare bedroom into his 'man cave.' He stores his archery equipment in there," Belinda said. She swung open the door at the end of the hallway, and then gestured for me and Hardy to go inside. "I never go in this room. Dustin wouldn't like it if I did."

Flipping the light switch, Belinda lit up the small room. The gun case, recliner, and small bar took up the majority of the room. There was a big screen TV mounted on the one wall, and his archery equipment hung on another. Belinda walked into the room and glanced around. She hissed when she saw a nudity magazine lying on the floor next to the recliner.

"Are these all of Dustin's bows?" Hardy pointed at the compound bow and two longbows that were hanging from the wall. "And where are his arrows?"

"The smaller longbow is mine. Dustin purchased it for me early on in our relationship. I have not used it in years. I'm not sure where he stores the arrows. I just know that he keeps them in here. I've seen him take the arrows in and out of this room," Belinda said.

"We'll find them," I said.

While Hardy took the bows down from the walls, I looked around the room for Dustin's arrows. I found them in a wooden box on top of the gun cabinet.

"Dustin's arrows are longer than the murder weapon. And a different brand." I held up an arrow that was shorter than the rest. "I'm guessing this is Belinda's. Right length. Wrong brand."

"Maybe we should stop focusing on the brand. If I was going to kill someone using a bow, I would probably go out and purchase different arrows. Why use the ones that I always use and risk having them get traced back to me?"

"Now you think of that," I said.

Hardy rolled his eyes. "Let's get these out to my truck. Then we can decide the next step. We don't exactly have a warrant for anything. And Belinda can only give us so much."

After loading Dustin's archery equipment into the backseat of Hardy's truck, we stood around in the street discussing what to do next. We were about to go inside to ask Belinda a few more questions when a beat-up truck drove down the street and parked behind us. Dustin climbed out of the truck and limped over to us.

"What are you two doing here?" Dustin asked.

"I could say the same to you. Your wife said you would be gone all day watching the races. The Indy 500 only just started. What are you doing home already?" I asked.

It was the Sunday of Memorial Day weekend. IndyCar's Indianapolis 500 was on in the afternoon, and NASCAR's Coca-Cola 600 would be on during the evening. My relatives were gathered together at someone's house to watch the races, and I longed to be with them.

"I was down at Catfish's Cantina. They're having an all-day party for the races. But the douchebag bartender kicked me out. He threatened to beat me up if I ever come back. I'm thinking I should press charges against him," Dustin said.

"I wouldn't do that if I were you. That bartender is Naomi's new boyfriend. If you know what's good for you, you should avoid Catfish's for the rest of your life," I said.

Dustin shrugged. "Neither of you answered my question. What'cha doing at my house? This about Travis? I ain't got no idea who killed him. I wasn't close to my stepbrother."

"Belinda came in to the sheriff's department with some new information," I said.

"Don't know what she would know unless she heard something at work. Not like she ever talked to Travis," Dustin said. He moved closer to Hardy's truck and peered in the windows. "Hey! That's my archery equipment. Why are you taking it?"

"Dustin!" Belinda shouted as she burst out the front door of the Thompsons' house. She then ran down the front walk. After throwing her arms around her husband, she said, "I'm sorry. I am so, so sorry."

"What you got to apologize for, Belinda? What could you do if they had a warrant? Though I still don't understand why you're taking my stuff," Dustin said.

"It's my fault," Belinda wailed. "I told them that I think you killed Travis."

"What?" Dustin pushed Belinda away so that he could look at her face. "What makes you think I killed anybody?"

"Oh, Dustin, you know why I think you did it. I confessed to you about what I did."

"You did? What did you do?" Dustin asked.

Dustin looked genuinely confused. He kept looking back and forth between me, Hardy, and Belinda with a dumbfounded look on his face.

Belinda used a handkerchief to wipe away her tears. "Last Saturday afternoon, I confessed to you that I…that I cheated on you with Travis."

"You did?" Dustin started to laugh. "Shoot, honey, I wasn't paying any attention to what you were saying."

"You weren't paying attention?" Belinda snapped as she smacked Dustin on the arm. "I was confessing my transgression and you could not even bother to pay attention to me? But you were so angry at me at the time."

"Of course, I was angry. I was trying to watch the game and you wouldn't shut up," Dustin said. He looked over his wife's head at me and Hardy. If he was looking for sympathy or understanding, he wasn't going to get it from either of us. Dustin then looked back at Belinda. "But, Belinda, what business do you have messing around with my stepbrother?"

"Perhaps you two could discuss your martial problems later," Hardy said. "Right now, we need to talk about the homicide. Mrs. Thompson, could you please go back inside your house?"

Dustin waited until Belinda had gone inside and shut the door before he turned to me and Hardy and said, "Ain't nothing to talk about. I didn't kill Travis. And, if I had, why would I have tried to kill Marisol? She wasn't the one my wife was doing me wrong with."

"What were you doing on the night of the homicide?" Hardy asked.

"I, uh, I was…" Dustin glanced over at me and gave me a pleading look.

"Dustin, I already told Sergeant Hardy about what really happened to your foot. You can tell him the truth about what happened that night," I said.

"Thank God. So you know that Detective Shatner's crazy cousin shot me in the foot? Then why ain't you arrested either of them?" Dustin asked Hardy.

"I've got more important things to deal with at the moment," Hardy said. "Besides, I'm thinking you're fortunate Carrie and Naomi didn't do worse to you."

"Don't I know it? Luckily, Naomi's got no skills or aim."

Dustin told us that his plan for last Saturday night was to hang out with Naomi and have some fun. Feeling guilty because he was cheating on his wife, and afraid that Naomi might start talking about their relationship, Dustin decided to tell her that he was married. His hope was that they could continue the affair without anyone finding out. Naomi was nowhere near as receptive to the plan as he had hoped.

"After I left Naomi's house, I went home and took care of my foot. I was bleeding all over the place. It was still bleeding when Belinda got home in the morning. She was chaperoning the Post Prom at the high school all night. As soon as she saw my foot, she started pestering me about what happened."

"After taking care of your foot, what did you do for the rest of the night?" Hardy asked.

"I told you already. While I was taking care of my foot, I watched the NASCAR race."

"Are you sure you didn't go over to the SWAT Zone for the event. We heard you like to go to them," Hardy said.

"I could barely walk after getting shot. How was I supposed to go to 'rassling? Or kill somebody? Which I didn't do!" Dustin said.

"Dustin, go inside while Detective Shatner and I figure out how we want to handle this."

Dustin limped up to the house and then slammed the front door behind him.

"You think Dustin will admit he was cheating?" I asked as I paced up and down the Thompsons' driveway.

"He should," Hardy said. "So, what do you think?"

"Like I said earlier, Dustin is not the killer. I can understand why Belinda accused him, but I can't believe he did it. For all we know, Belinda might be pointing the finger at Dustin because she's the killer," I said.

"I'm thinking the same thing. Belinda was only a few hundred yards away from the SWAT Zone. All she would have had to do was sneak out of the high school, grab her bow and arrows out of her car, and run down to the SWAT Zone. And she had motive. She might have wanted to kill Marisol so she could have Travis for herself. Or she might have wanted to kill Travis so that there was no one else who knew about what they did in the gym teachers' office."

"But how would she have known Travis and Marisol would come out of the SWAT Zone when they did?" I asked.

"How did anyone know that they'd come out of the SWAT Zone when they did? For all we know, Belinda wasn't really at Post Prom. Have we actually confirmed that she was there?" Hardy asked. He then marched up the front walk to the Thompsons' front door. "Come on, let's go talk to them some more."

Hardy was reaching up to knock on the front door when my cell phone rang. I pulled the phone out of my pocket and saw that it was Uncle Murph who was calling.

"Hey, Uncle Murph, what's going on?" I asked.

"Evita and Marisol Santiago are at Wyatt County General. They both just overdosed," Murph said.

CHAPTER NINETEEN

"What do you mean they overdosed?" I asked.

"What's going on, Carrie?" Hardy asked.

Hardy grabbed the phone out of my shaking hand. He then steered me over to the porch swing that hung at the far end of the Thompsons' front porch. I collapsed onto the swing, my head reeling from Murph's announcement.

Hardy put Murph on speakerphone and asked, "Hey, Sheriff, what's this about an overdose?"

"Evita and Marisol Santiago," Murph said. "I don't have all of the details yet. What I do know is that the Santiagos called us a little while ago and told us that they found Evita and Marisol passed out. When they couldn't revive them, they called nine-one-one. Then they called us and asked for someone from our department to come out to the house. Juan and a couple deputies headed over. They got there as the girls were being taken out."

"Are they going to be okay?" I asked.

"Juan said they were unconscious but alive when the paramedics loaded them into the ambulance. He also said that it looks like one of them threw up a lot. He wasn't sure which one it was when he called," Murph said.

"Does the Chief Deputy have any idea what they overdosed on?" Hardy asked.

"He said the Santiagos found an empty bottle of vodka in the trash, and Mrs. Santiago said her sleeping pills are missing," Murph said. He then noisily cleared his throat. "Carrie, you're not going to like this. But Juan found a note."

"What do you mean he found a note? What kind of note?" I asked.

"Evita left a suicide note," Murph said. "Though it was more of a confession..."

"I don't understand? A suicide note? And what did Evita have to confess to?" I asked.

"Killing Travis Yeager. And attempting to kill Marisol," Murph said. "Though Evita might have accomplished it today if this turns out to be a successful murder-suicide."

"What?!? No! No, I don't believe it," I said.

Hardy squeezed my hand. "Did Evita say why she killed Travis and attempted to kill her sister?"

"Combination of hatred for Marisol and love for Travis," Murph said. "Apparently, Evita wasn't over her crush, and she finally decided to do something about it."

~*~*~

Because Quaranta and the deputies, along with two Holler police officers, had things under control at the Santiagos' house, Hardy and I immediately headed over to Wyatt County General to meet up with Mr. and Mrs. Santiago, as well as Annalisa.

"Carrie, stop! Don't go charging in there," Hardy said. He grabbed my arm and prevented me from jumping out of the truck and rushing into the Emergency Room. "You're going to have to keep it together, or I'm not going to let you go in there. Remember we are the professionals. We can't let our emotions or personal feelings get in the way of doing our job."

"I don't need a lecture, Jerrod. I know what my job is," I said.

"But that doesn't stop you from letting your emotions take control of your actions." Hardy let go of my arm and allowed me to climb out of the truck. "I know you like Evita. You've got the baby sister connection going. But the fact of the matter is that Evita might have killed Travis and attempted to kill her sister last week. And today she might have tried to kill Marisol and herself with an overdose. For all we know, she might have succeeded."

"Might have," I said. "I'll believe it when we have all of the evidence."

"Detective Shatner! Sergeant Hardy!" Zachary Yeager shouted our names as he sprinted across the hospital's parking lot. The teenager had sweat rolling down his pale face, and his hands were shaking. "Annalisa called me and told me about what happened. Is Evie okay? Have you seen her?"

"We haven't been inside yet," Hardy said.

"We have to get in there. I have to tell them that Evie is pregnant!" Zachary shouted as he pushed past us and burst through the Emergency Room doors.

"Evita's pregnant!" Hardy and I shouted at each other.

I took off running after Zachary, catching up to him at the check-in station. After shushing the hysterical Zachary, I held up my badge so that the nurses could see it.

"I'm Detective Shatner with the Wyatt County Sheriff's Department. The younger of the two overdoses…Evita Santiago…she's pregnant!"

"About nine weeks," Zachary added.

"I'll let the doctors know. Both of the patients are currently getting their stomachs pumped." The nurse grabbed the phone and jammed her finger into one of the buttons.

"Come on, Zachary. There's nothing more you can do." I drew Zachary away from the check-in station and then guided him towards a quiet corner of the Emergency Room. "How long has Evita known she was pregnant?"

"Like four or five weeks. She didn't want to tell anyone. Not until we decided what to do about it. I've got…we've both got scholarships. Me for baseball and Evie for chemistry," Zachary said. "Evie has been super depressed since she took the pregnancy test. She hasn't been acting right. I should have done something. Told someone. But she begged me not to."

"Zachary, you can't blame yourself for what happened," I said.

"Yes, I can! I knew something wasn't right with her. But I didn't think she'd try to kill herself. Or Marisol. And Travis…she killed Travis didn't she, Detective Shatner?"

"Zachary, last Sunday you told me and Sergeant Hardy that you and Evita were together from when you left the SWAT Zone until you went into the high school just before midnight. Which is it, Zachary? Was Evita with you? Or was she murdering your brother?" I said. Exactly a week ago, Zachary had provided Evita with an alibi. Today he was accusing Evita of killing his brother during the exact time in which he'd said she was with him.

"I don't…I don't know, Detective Shatner," Zachary said as he glanced around the waiting room with wild, dilated eyes. "Evie and I left the SWAT Zone when the riot started. I wanted to stick around to make sure everything was okay, but Evie demanded we leave to head over to the high school. But we didn't hang out in my car like I'd told you. We both got out of the car and started hanging out with some of our friends. Evie disappeared for a while. I figured she had gone off to talk to some of the girls or something. It wasn't until later that Evie asked me to lie and say we were in my car the whole time. I was too upset over my brother to ask why she wanted me to lie."

"If that's the case, where did Evita get the bow and arrows?" I asked.

"Evie had them in my car. I took her to the archery range a few days before the prom. I didn't think anything of it before now. I'm sorry, Detective Shatner."

"It's not your fault, Zachary."

I patted Zachary on the shoulder as I pretended to comfort him. Something about his story didn't quite make sense. But it would be easy to check into his new alibi. Had Zachary and Evita really been hanging out in the high school's parking lot during the time that Travis was killed, surely someone must have seen Evita sneaking around with her bow and arrows.

"How about you have a seat over here while I go talk to the Santiagos. You understand that this is a police investigation, correct?" I asked.

"I understand." Zachary sucked in a deep breath and then exhaled. "What happens now?"

"I figure out what really happened last Saturday night," I said. Leaving Zachary by himself, I walked across the waiting room to join Hardy and the Santiagos. "What happened this morning?"

"That's what I've been trying to find out," Hardy said.

"Then fill me in," I snapped.

"My husband, daughters, and I went to church like we do every Sunday morning," Yesinia Santiago said as she dabbed at her eyes with a tissue, taking care not to smudge her makeup. "Afterwards, my husband and I took my mother out to dinner. We always have an early Sunday dinner with her. Normally the girls go with us, but they've been so stressed this week that my husband and I excused them."

"Had your mother not felt poorly, we would still be visiting with her at the nursing home. We wouldn't have found the girls in time. If we found them in time," Mr. Santiago said.

"Yes, dear, I know," Yesinia said as she absentmindedly patted her husband's arm. "When my husband and I got home, I went upstairs to check on Evita and Marisol. I found them in their living room area. Evita was slumped over the side of the armchair, and Marisol was lying on the floor. I thought…I don't know what I thought. I saw that Evita had vomited on the floor and I knew something was wrong. I called nine-one-one while my husband tried to revive the girls. We were waiting for the EMTs to arrive when Annalisa found the empty vodka bottle and Evita's note."

"If only I'd gone upstairs to check on them, I might have been able to stop Evita." Annalisa, who'd been quietly crying, suddenly began to sob. "Oh, Marisol, please don't die."

"Detective Shatner, why don't you talk to Annalisa while I talk to Mr. and Mrs. Santiago?" Hardy asked.

I gave Annalisa a minute or two to calm down before I asked, "What happened when you got home? How long were you girls there before your parents got home?"

"I don't know. Maybe an hour. We didn't go straight home after church. We stopped and had a quick lunch," Annalisa said. "When we got home, we went upstairs to change out of our church clothes. Then Marisol and Evita sat down and started talking about Travis. They were crying and carrying on, so I left them to it. I went downstairs and started going through the floral arrangements that people sent to Marisol. I wanted to see if any of the flowers needed more water. I also started pulling out the dead flowers."

"Were you aware of anything going on upstairs?" I asked.

"No. I mean, I could hear Marisol and Evita talking. But I couldn't hear what they were saying. I wasn't really paying attention either, so I didn't notice when they stopped talking. I was still downstairs, cleaning up around the kitchen when my parents got home. Mamá went upstairs to see what Evita and Marisol were up to. Papá and I ran upstairs when we heard Mamá screaming for help."

"What happened upstairs?" I asked.

"Marisol and Evita were passed out. Papá tried to wake them up while Mamá called nine-one-one. I freaked out, you know. Seeing my sisters like that. I wanted to help, so I ran into Evita's bedroom. She has her own bathroom. Me and Marisol share the one in the hallway. It always sucked having to share. We have a double sink, but Marisol hogged the whole counter. Evita was so lucky to get her own bathroom."

Confused by Annalisa's random tangent, I asked, "Why did you go in Evita's bedroom?"

"I wanted to get water from the bathroom. I thought maybe that would help," Annalisa snapped. "When I ran in Evita's bathroom, I found the empty vodka bottle. I don't know where she got it. Or how she got it. I also found the prescription bottle for Mamá's sleeping pills."

"They were just sitting out in the counter?" I asked.

"No, they were in the trash. But I knew something was wrong when I saw them. Not that I thought everything was normal. But I didn't have time to think about it. I was running back through the bedroom with the water when I saw there were some arrows on Evita's bed. And a piece of paper. It was a suicide note."

"Detective Shatner," Hardy shouted across the Emergency Room. "Could you and Annalisa come over here?"

Annalisa and I jumped up and then rushed over to the check-in station where a doctor was waiting.

"Marisol and Evita are being moved to the ICU," the female doctor announced. "We pumped their stomachs to get out the alcohol and sleeping pills. If that is what they overdosed on. Both of your daughters are in stable condition though Evita is still unconscious. Marisol is awake and alert."

"Can I see Marisol?" Yesinia asked. "Can I see my baby girl?"

"You may see both of your daughters once we are done running tests on them," the doctor said. "Right now it's still too early to tell if either of them suffered any organ damage. Kidney and liver damage is a possibility.

And so is brain damage. Mixing alcohol and sleeping pills is very dangerous. The combination causes the body to relax more than it should. The extreme relaxation can cause a person to stop breathing."

"When will you know if they've suffered any…damage?" Mr. Santiago asked.

"We are currently running multiple tests on Evita. Right now, she is in stable condition. But we are concerned about her because she suffered a miscarriage."

"My baby!" Zachary gasped as he sank to the floor. "My baby…"

"Evita was pregnant?" Annalisa grabbed Zachary by the shoulder and shook him. "You got my sister pregnant? I didn't…I had no idea."

"We will give you an update as soon as we have one," the doctor said.

"Maybe it would be for the best if Evita didn't wake up," Yesinia said. "I don't know how I could bear sitting through a trial knowing my youngest daughter tried to kill my oldest."

"Then you believe Evita killed Travis and attempted to kill Marisol?" I asked.

"No, I don't want to believe it," Yesinia said. "But Evita confessed! Or at least that's what Annalisa said. She's the only one of us who saw the note."

"Evita was always jealous of Marisol," Annalisa said.

"That is true," Mr. Santiago said, as he helped his wife over to a chair. "Ever since she was a little girl, Evita has been making up these absurd stories about how Marisol was teasing and torturing her. Her habit was very distressing to us. We tried to talk to Evita about her lies, but she kept insisting that it was all true. Then we tried punishing her, but still she wouldn't stop making up lies. It really upset Marisol, and she begged us to send Evita away to live with relatives."

"There were times I seriously considered it, but I didn't want to pass along the burden to someone else. Now I wish I had," Yesinia said.

"Did it ever cross your minds that maybe Evita was telling the truth?" I asked. "Maybe it was Marisol who was lying to you."

"How dare you accuse Marisol?" Yesinia hissed. "She was the kindest, sweetest girl. She loves Evita dearly and would have done nothing to hurt her."

"Detective Shatner," the doctor said as she placed her hand on my arm. "One of the nurses just told me that Marisol is asking to see you. She refuses to allow us to run any more tests on her until after she's spoken to you."

"Then I guess I better go talk to her," I said as I followed the doctor.

Hardy tagged along, following me and doctor up to the ICU on the second floor. The doctor led us into the room where Marisol was recovering. She was propped up against the pillows, finger combing her disheveled hair. Hardy remained in the hallway with the doctor while I went inside the room.

"How are you feeling Marisol?" I asked.

"Awful," Marisol whispered. Her throat was raspy from having the tube snaked down her esophagus to pump her stomach. "You heard about what Evita did, right? That she killed Travis and tried to kill me?"

"I heard about the suicide note," I said.

"Yeah, well, I heard it straight from Evita's mouth!" Marisol slapped her hands down onto the hospital bed. "I knew there was vodka in the fruit punch she made. That's how we've been making it for years. With fruit punch flavored vodka. I didn't know she'd put sleeping pills in it until I started drinking it. Then she confessed. The little puta told me everything! About how she'd been planning this for weeks. About how she had Zachary lie for her so that she had an alibi. God, I hope she dies!"

"Marisol, you need to calm down. You can tell me all this later. Right now, you need to get some tests done to make sure you're okay."

Behind me, the door into the room opened. I expected it to be the doctor telling me that my time with Marisol was up. Instead it was two orderlies wheeling in a gurney on which Evita was lying. She was still unconscious, and was hooked up to multiple machines.

"You little bitch!" Marisol screamed when she saw her sister. A primal scream full of rage and grief. She scrambled off the hospital bed and charged at Evita. "Why didn't you die?"

"Marisol, stop!" I shouted.

Not caring about whether I hurt her or not, I tackled Marisol. We both crashed to the ground, taking one of the orderlies down with us. Standing up, I yanked Marisol to her feet and shoved her into the other orderly's arms. Hardy rushed into the room as soon as the orderlies wrestled the hysterical Marisol out into the hallway. The doctor went along with the orderlies as they escorted Marisol out of the ICU.

"Everything okay, Carrie?" Hardy asked.

"Not at all, Jerrod. I need to get out of here. I don't think I can stomach sitting with the Santiagos. And I also have a gut feeling that something isn't right. Something isn't adding up. Can you handle this without me?" I asked.

"I've got it covered." Hardy pulled his truck keys out of his pocket and handed them to me. "Drive around for a while and clear your head. I'll call you when I'm ready to leave."

Before leaving, I went over to Evita and whispered, "I need you to wake up, Evita. I need you to wake up and tell me what really happened. Because I don't think you did any of this."

~*~*~

Because there were two sheriff's department cruisers and a Holler police department cruiser parked along the road in front of the Santiagos' house, I pulled Hardy's truck to a stop in front of the next door neighbor's house.

I was halfway up the Santiagos' driveway when Quaranta, three deputies, and two police officers walked out the front door and gathered on the porch. The Holler police were there because the Santiagos lived within the Holler City limits, making this their crime scene. They were nice enough to allow us to take over because of our investigation into who injured Marisol and killed Travis.

Two of the deputies were carrying a rolled up rug, Deputy Timmy Grant held a large box, and Quaranta had a crime scene kit.

"What are you doing here?" Quaranta asked. "And where's Sergeant Hardy?"

"He's still at the hospital with the Santiagos. He's going to need a ride."

"I'm about to head over there to collect Evita's and Marisol's clothing. I'll get him," Quaranta said.

"Tell me about what you've found," I said.

After instructing the deputies to take the evidence back to the sheriff's department and store it in the evidence locker, Quaranta opened up his crime scene kit and pulled out his digital camera. He handed me the camera.

The first few pictures were of the Evita's bathroom. Like Annalisa said, there was an empty vodka bottle and prescription pill bottle in the trash can. The next set of pictures were of Evita's messy bedroom. Lying in the middle of the unmade bed was a piece of paper and a handful of arrows.

"Don't tell me…the arrows are an exact match to the murder weapon."

"Yes, they are," Quaranta said. "Well, none of these have a broadhead on them. But, yes, they are the same length and brand as the murder weapon. And the vanes are orange and green."

"We never looked at Evita's equipment. We thought she had an alibi," I said.

"Zachary backed her up." Quaranta clicked through a few more photos and then showed me a close up of Evita's suicide note. "Here's a picture of the note."

"It's typed," I said, finding that odd. Why would Evita type up her confession and suicide note instead of handwriting it? "And it's not addressed to anyone."

"No, it's very impersonal. Evita just generally apologizes and then explains that she killed Travis and attempted to kill Marisol."

"And nowhere does she say that she was pregnant. I spoke with Zachary at the hospital, and he told me that Evita has been despondent ever since she found out that she was pregnant. You'd think she'd at least mention the baby. All she talks about is hating Marisol and loving Travis. Really loving Travis."

I said.

"Maybe the baby didn't matter."

"I guess Evita wasn't over that crush," I said. I turned the camera off and handed it back to Quaranta. Leaving him on the front porch, I headed inside. "I'm going inside to look around for a little bit. See you back at the department."

"Sure you'll be okay by yourself? I can stick around if you want."

"No, I'll be fine. I just need a couple minutes to look around and accept things." And to look for evidence that you might have missed, I thought.

I walked inside the Santiagos' house and headed upstairs. The girls' living room area still reeked of vomit. The chair Evita had passed out in was turned over on its side, and the coffee table had been shoved up against the wall. That could have happened when the Santiagos tried to help their daughters, or when the EMTs tried to revive the girls, or when Quaranta and the deputies collected the rug as evidence. Backing out of the room, I retreated into Evita's room and had a seat on the bed. I then buried my face in my hands and tried to get my jumbled thoughts in order.

"I still can't believe she did it," I whispered. Despite the evidence, and Evita's combination of motives, I still couldn't bring myself to accept that she killed Travis and attempted to kill Marisol. Sure, it seemed like Evita had issues with Marisol since childhood. Whether those issues were legitimate or lies Evita concocted had yet to be determined. I suspected that it was a combination of both – Marisol probably hadn't been very nice to her little sister, and Evita had embellished on the stories to make them sound worse than they were.

Evita also had a crush on Travis for some time before he met Marisol. When her sister hooked up with Travis, Evita felt betrayed by both of them. Perhaps that betrayal had then simmered for two years before Evita finally snapped.

Then there was the fact that Evita was an accomplished archer.

Everything fit so nicely together.

But it still wasn't adding up.

"I need to get back to the hospital."

Jumping up from the bed, I rushed out of Evita's bedroom and headed for the stairs. I was almost at the bottom step when I heard a female's voice. The sound was coming from the first floor.

"She was pregnant! How could you not tell me she was pregnant?" the woman shouted. "Did Marisol know Evita was pregnant? Or did you keep that all to yourself? But that's what all this was about for you, right? Getting rid of Evita and the baby? You couldn't exactly break up with her and go on your merry way when she was having your kid!"

"Zachary? And Annalisa and Marisol? They all worked together?" I mouthed.

I knew it. I knew Evita wasn't the killer. But I hadn't expected that Zachary, Annalisa, and Marisol had all worked together to kill Travis and attempt to kill Evita. I'd never suspected that Marisol was involved. Creeping down the last step, I peeked around the wall into the kitchen and spotted Annalisa pacing back and forth. I waited until she hung up on her accomplice before I stepped into the room.

"Hello, Annalisa."

"Detective Shatner! What are you doing here?" Annalisa tossed her phone on the counter and then spun to face me. "You scared me. I had no idea you were here."

"I assumed as much. I'm not sure how smart you are, but you don't seem dumb enough to call your accomplice to talk about your crime while there is an officer of the law in the house."

"What are you talking about? What crime? You're nuts."

"You have no idea how crazy I am," I said.

Annalisa tried to push past me, but I stuck out my arm and held her back.

"Were you the one lurking behind the SWAT Zone with the bow and arrows? Or was it Zachary? Or did Marisol do it?" I asked. "And who mixed up the vodka and pills? I'm assuming it was you. Or was it Marisol?"

"Are you serious? I didn't kill Travis. Evita killed him. And she tried to kill Marisol. And herself."

"No. She didn't do anything. You did. And Zachary and Marisol. Y'all made a nice little team. I wonder which one of you will turn on the others first."

Annalisa dropped into a crouch, covered her head with her arms, and screamed. I clamped my hand down on her shoulder and tried to push Annalisa to her knees. Knocking my arm away, Annalisa made a frantic dash for the front door. I managed to grab her by the arm and, using her own momentum against her, spun her away from the door and back into the foyer.

"Get your hands off me! I didn't do anything!"

Annalisa ran into the dining room and headed around the table towards the kitchen.

"Whose idea was it?" I asked as I ran around the other side of the table hoping to either catch up to Annalisa or cut her off before she got into the kitchen. "I'm betting it was Marisol's idea and she dragged you into it since you've always worshiped the ground she walked on. But how did Zachary get involved?"

"It was Marisol and Zachary! Marisol knew her relationship with Travis was almost over. That he was never going to marry her. So she decided he had to die. I don't know whose idea it was to frame Evita! All I know is that Zachary and Marisol wanted her gone. And so did I!" Annalisa shouted. Anticipating what I was doing, Annalisa stopped moving towards the kitchen. "You know, Detective Shatner, sometimes it's better to be the right hand of the devil than in its path. I'm not saying that Marisol is the devil, but she is pretty close. So when she asked me to kill Travis and help her kill Evita, I agreed. I didn't want to wind up being the third person on her hit list."

"Chances are Marisol would have come after you next. She would have had to make sure you'd never talk," I said, causing Annalisa to scream.

Not only was Annalisa crazy, she was downright scary. I didn't feel safe being alone with her and I just wanted to get her out of the house and back to the sheriff's department. I reached down to grab my gun only to realize that I didn't have it. The seatbelt in Hardy's truck had kept getting caught on the holster, so I took it off and stuck the gun in the glove compartment. I also hadn't brought along my stun gun or mace. All I had were my handcuffs.

"Annalisa, I need you to get down on your knees and put your hands behind your head."

Annalisa picked up one of the smaller floral arrangement and lobbed it across the table at me. The blue glass vase was stuffed full of roses, daisies, and other flowers. And it was coming right towards my head. I ducked and the vase smashed into the wall behind me, spraying me with pieces of glass, flowers, and water.

"Big mistake, Annalisa," I said.

I scrambled around the table and caught up to Annalisa as she headed for the front door. I grabbed her arm and spun her around, momentarily knocking her off balance. While Annalisa tried to regain her footing, I bent down and rammed my shoulder into her midsection, driving her backward and dropping her to the floor.

"What amazes me is that you thought you'd get away with it," I said.

I pulled my handcuffs off my belt and tried to put them around Annalisa's wrists. She kept flopping around and yanking her arms away. As I leaned over Annalisa, she brought her legs up between us. She then drove her feet into my stomach and sent me careening backwards into the table. When I hit the table, most of the vases toppled over and a few rolled over the edge and onto the floor. The vases shattered, coating the wooden floor with pieces of broken glass, flowers, and water. As I moved away from the table, my feet slipped in the water and I sat down hard. When I hit the floor, something sharp jabbed me in the butt.

I crawled over to where Annalisa lay on the floor. As I got closer, she kicked out at me again. I rolled to the side to avoid her feet. I then jumped on top of her, slamming my body down onto her midsection. Annalisa yelped in pain when my elbows connected with her ribs. I knocked the wind out of her, but not the fight.

I attempted to roll Annalisa over onto her stomach, but she grabbed a handful of my hair and yanked. With her other hand, she slashed out at my face, just narrowly missing me with her nails. Annalisa and I rolled around the dining room scuffling with each other. As we did so, we rolled through the debris field of broken glass, ruined flowers, and water. I could feel the glass shards jabbing and scratching my body.

Annalisa picked up a large glass shard and was trying to cut my face with it when Hardy and Quaranta ran into the house and broke us up.

"That's enough!" Hardy shouted. He squeezed Annalisa's wrist until she dropped the glass. "Annalisa Santiago, you are under arrest for the murder of Travis Yeager, the attempted murder of Evita Santiago, and assault on Detective Shatner. I'm sure we'll find a few more offenses to charge you with later."

Quaranta stepped up behind Annalisa, roughly pulled her hands behind her back, and handcuffed her.

"You were right, Carrie. It did take a special kind of crazy," Quaranta said.

"I told you Evita wasn't the killer."

Annalisa started to scream, cursing Evita, Marisol, her parents, Travis, and Zachary.

"Get Annalisa out of here, Chief Deputy Quaranta," Hardy said.

"I'll take her back to the department." Quaranta hauled Annalisa outside and stuck her in the back of his cruiser.

"How did you know to come here?" I asked.

"Evita woke up. She started screaming that Marisol and Annalisa tried to kill her. Apparently, they held her down and forced her to drink the spiked fruit punch. Quaranta just happened to be walking into the ICU as she woke up. We ran downstairs to the ER to talk to Annalisa, but Mr. and Mrs. Santiago told us that she had gone home to get some clothes for her sisters," Hardy said as he walked around the Santiagos' dining room to take in the damage caused by me and Annalisa. "You all right?"

"I think so." I plucked a shard of glass out of my sleeve and tossed it onto the floor. I noticed that there were countless tears all over the shirt. I also had numerous small cuts and scratches on my arms and hands. "Most of these cuts look superficial."

"Your shirt is full of glass. Let's get this off you and shake it out." Hardy helped me carefully extract myself from my ruined shirt.

While Hardy knocked the various bits of glass out of the fabric, I looked over my upper arms and stomach. I found a long scratch on my left side, but it wasn't deep and had already stopped bleeding.

"Anything on my back?" I asked.

"A couple scratches. And you've got a bloodstain on your butt."

I craned my neck to see my backside. The entire right side of my butt was red with blood, but the fact that my pants were soaking wet made it look worse than it was.

"I slipped and fell onto a bunch of broken glass. I felt something jab me."

"You better let me take a look." Hardy winked at me.

"You just want to get me out of my pants."

I undid the button and zipper, and then eased my pants and underwear down over my butt. I felt really self-conscious baring my butt for Hardy's examination. It made me even more self-conscious when Hardy started to laugh.

"Well, darling, the good news is that the glass just missed your tattoo." Hardy gave me a soft but solid pat on the butt. "The bad news is that you're probably going to need stitches."

CHAPTER TWENTY

"I heard you're getting discharged later today. How are you feeling?"
I pulled a chair closer to Evita's hospital bed and had a seat. It had been three days since Annalisa and Marisol tried to kill Evita by forcing her to overdose on alcohol and sleeping pills. Aside from the miscarriage and some minor liver damage, she hadn't been too adversely affected by the overdose.

"Physically I'm okay. Or at least that's what the doctor's say. Otherwise..." Evita said. She used the bedsheet to wipe away her tears. "I don't know how to feel about losing the baby. Zachary had wanted me to get rid of the baby, but I couldn't have an abortion. I just couldn't do that. But that's why he did this, isn't it? He was that desperate for me to get rid of the baby. He wasn't about to let anything get between him and his baseball career. I kinda figured we would break up before we started college. I...I loved him, but I...I had a full ride out in Arizona. I wasn't going to give that up. It was my ticket out. Zachary was...he was just my high school sweetheart. Until I realized I was pregnant."

"It's part of the reason. Remember, Marisol and Annalisa also wanted you gone," I said before giving Evita a summary of what Annalisa, Marisol, and Zachary had told me and Hardy.

After getting the puncture wound on my butt stitched up, Hardy and I had headed over to the sheriff's department to question Annalisa and Zachary. Because Marisol had consumed a small amount of the spiked fruit punch, we weren't able to question her until she was released from the hospital the next day. Annalisa and Zachary quickly confessed to what they had done. And both of them pointed the finger at Marisol as their ringleader. Zachary had been very active in planning out how to kill Travis and frame Evita. Annalisa might have been the one to shoot Travis, but she was mainly Marisol's pawn in the whole thing. Marisol was still denying her involvement and claiming that Annalisa and Zachary were lying.

If Annalisa and Zachary could be believed, Marisol came up with the plan to kill Travis. According to Annalisa, Marisol's and Travis's relationship was falling apart. Marisol decided to kill him before he could break up with her. According to Annalisa, Marisol was of the belief that if she couldn't have Travis, then no woman could have him. It was Zachary who proposed framing Evita and then killing her off in a botched murder-suicide. Zachary had just found out that Evita was pregnant, and he was convinced that his life would be ruined if Evita didn't have an abortion or give up the baby for adoption. When Evita told him she wanted to keep the baby, Zachary decided she had to die. Because Marisol and Annalisa had always hated their younger sister, they were more than willing to help kill Evita.

After coming up with and then discarding multiple plans, the three finally settled on shooting Travis with a bow and arrow. All Annalisa had to do was improve her limited archery skills using Evita's old compound bow and arrows. On the night of the murder, Annalisa told her parents that she was going upstairs to watch a movie. Knowing they would leave her alone, Annalisa was easily able to sneak out of the house and drive over to the SWAT Zone. She then waited in the back parking lot until Marisol dragged Travis outside almost immediately after his match. Annalisa shot Travis in the back, and then she stabbed Marisol in the arm.

"Evita, you're lucky that Xavier Ortega was released from the group home a few months ago. When Marisol found out that he was stalking her, she put off staging the murder-suicide. Part of her hoped we'd decide Xavier was the killer and put him in jail. Had Marisol and Annalisa tried to kill you a few days earlier, you might not have been so lucky. Between you throwing up and getting most of the alcohol and sleeping pills out of your system, and your parents coming home when they did, you might not be here."

"What about Travis? I understand why Marisol wanted to kill him. Though it does seem way over the top. And Annalisa will do anything that Marisol tells her to. But what about Zachary?" Evita asked.

"I'm not sure how much of Zachary's story I believe, but he claims Travis beat him up and molested him as a kid. I think it's just a story, but we're looking into it. Personally, I think Zachary just hated his half-brother and wanted him gone."

"I just can't believe all this happened," Evita said.

"Evita, can you tell me about what exactly happened the other day?"

"I don't remember all the details," Evita said. "I know I went to church with my family in the morning. Then my sisters and I went back to the house while our parents went to see my abuela. Marisol and I were hanging out when Annalisa came upstairs with the pitcher of fruit punch. I didn't think anything was wrong. Annalisa makes the fruit punch all the time. I started drinking it, and I realized there was alcohol in it. Obviously, I couldn't drink it because of the baby. But I didn't tell my sisters that. When I refused to drink any more, they held me down and dumped it into my mouth. I remember feeling really sick and throwing up. I don't remember anything after that."

"Annalisa spiked the punch with a fruit punch flavored vodka. She also ground up a handful of your mother's sleeping pills and mixed the powder up into the punch. Both of your sisters claim that's how you've been making the punch for years. Just without the pills."

"No, it definitely is not…" Evita sighed. "Like I said, I don't remember anything after I threw up. But it couldn't have been too much later that my parents came home. The next thing I know, I woke up here."

"The good thing is that you woke up." I patted Evita on the knee and then stood up. "And that your grandmother wasn't feeling well. Otherwise, your parents wouldn't have come home early. You probably would have died. And Marisol, Annalisa, and Zachary might have gotten away with it."

"Detective Shatner…what am I supposed to do now? I mean, how do I get past all this and move on with my life?"

"I think you need to take it one day at time." I handed Evita a business card with my cell phone number written on the back. "And, if you need someone to talk to, I'm here for you."

"Thanks, Detective Shatner. I think I'll be calling you a lot."

~*~*~

"We need to talk," Hardy said.

"Hello to you, too." I stepped away from the door so that Hardy could come inside.

"Are you finally going to lecture me about Naomi?"

"No, I'm not going to lecture you. I don't think it would do any good. You did the wrong thing for what you thought were the right reasons." Hardy walked into my living room and had a seat on the couch. "Besides, I talked to Dustin Thompson and he's decided not to press charges against Naomi. And he said that if I arrest Naomi, he will deny that she shot him."

"Well, considering what he put Naomi through, I should hope he wouldn't press charges." I'd also talked to Dustin. I was the one who convinced him not to press charges. I did appreciate Dustin saying that he would deny that Naomi shot him. It was a nice touch. "And I didn't exactly see her shoot him. So I can't really testify that she did."

"I just don't get you, Carrie. You complain about how your family members are out there breaking the law, but you don't do anything to stop them."

"Yes, I do. I've chased them out of multiple places where they were selling drugs and moonshine."

"So what? You didn't really accomplish anything by chasing them out of any of those places. It's like you're playing a game of whack-a-mole with your family. You beat them down in one place, but they just pop back up somewhere else. The only way you're ever going to stop them is if you start arresting some of them for their crimes."

"Jerrod, I just can't –"

"Yes, you can. And you should. How much longer do you think your family can get away with this? All it will take is one slip-up, and they'll all go down. You included. Is that what you want? To go to jail for your family's crimes?"

"No! Of course not!" I sat down on the couch and leaned against Hardy.

"Then do something about it before it's too late!"

"What do you want me to do, Jerrod? Turn over evidence against them? You know I can't do that. I won't do that. You think I'm playing whack-a-mole? I see it as Jenga. And I don't know which block is the one that's going to bring the whole family crashing down. I'm not doing…what I do to protect the guilty ones. I'm trying to protect the innocent!"

"But are any of them really innocent?" Hardy asked. He scooted further down the couch, putting some distance between us. "If you can't do something about the criminals in your family, then I can't do this. I can't be involved with you knowing that you're out there covering up your family members' various crimes. And while I know you're not trying to seduce me into helping you clean up after your family, I certainly can't be around your family when they're trying to bribe me into looking the other way."

"So this is it then, isn't it?" I asked. I'd been dreading this moment since the day we fought in the funeral home's parking lot. I'd hoped we could work it out, but I suspected it would end with us breaking up for good.

"I think it would be for the best. I like you, Carrie. I really like you. And if it was just you, it wouldn't be a problem. But you're right, you are a package deal. And your family isn't something I can get involved with. If I wasn't a Texas Ranger, or in any type of law enforcement, it wouldn't matter so much."

"Don't give me that crap, Jerrod. You're too ethical and straight-laced of a person to want anything to do with my family regardless of your job."

"Darling, if you knew what kind of person I really am –"

"You keep saying that, but you never explain why!" I shouted in frustration. This was not the first time that Hardy had tried to convince me that if I knew what kind of person he really was I wouldn't want anything to do with him. "I know you don't have any ex-wives or kids that you haven't told me about. So what is it? What kind of skeletons do you have hanging in your closet? And how could they be any worse than mine? Do you have bad credit? Or what about another girlfriend? Is that it? Or are you really Josh and it was actually Jerrod who got killed in the car accident?"

"No, Carrie, it's not any of that."

"Then what is it?"

"I'm a fraud!" Hardy yelled as he spun to face me. "I'm not this perfect knight in shining armor that you want to believe that I am. I don't see things only in black-and-white. And I've done plenty of bad things in my life aside from play some harmless pranks while in high school, The real reason why I can't be with you…be part of your criminally inclined family…well, it's because I used to be just like them!"

"What are you talking about?" I asked.

"You want my dirty little secret? Well, here it is…Had it not been for a lucky twist of fate – and a man who gave me a second chance when I didn't deserve one – I probably would have wound up going down a very different path than the one I'm on now. A path that would have led straight to prison," Hardy said.

"I don't believe you," I said, laughing a little because I really didn't believe him.

"You only know the man, Carrie. You never met the confused and scared teenage boy." Hardy stood up so that he could pace back-and-forth across my living room. Manny scampered along at his heels. "You know how I told you my stepfather worked out in the oil fields around Odessa for the first few years that Josh and I lived with him and my mom?"

"I remember," I said.

Hardy and his brother had gone to live with their mom when they were seven or eight years old. She had just gotten married, and her husband physically abused the boys on a regular basis. Luckily for Jerrod and Josh, their stepfather was away for long periods of time due to his job. Then, when the boys were eleven or twelve, their stepfather was injured and could no longer work on the rigs. That's when the abuse really picked up, and the boys suffered until they were thirteen and the school finally found out what was going on and intervened. Their stepfather was then arrested and jailed for child abuse. Their mom then moved the boys to Waco to start over.

"Well…during that year-and-a-half to two years that my step-father was home, he got into selling drugs. And he made me and Josh help him," Hardy said.

"But that's not your fault." I seized Hardy's hand and forced him to stop pacing. "You and Josh were just kids. And I'm sure your stepfather didn't give you a choice."

"He didn't. But Josh and I had a choice later." Hardy pulled his hand way from mine and resumed pacing. "After Mom moved us to Waco, Josh and I fell in with a crowd of bad kids. They were all in high school, though most of them had dropped out. They were into drinking and smoking and doing drugs, and they got me and Josh into all of that shit as well. We also started stealing and committing other small crimes. We were on a downward spiral, and neither of us cared. Maybe if Mom had gotten us some therapy like she was supposed to…"

"Who is the man who gave you a second chance?" I asked, hoping to draw Hardy out of his bleak trip down memory lane.

"My high school football coach. Turns out that the boys we were friends with had all gotten kicked off of the football team because the coach found out they were smoking pot. They wanted revenge against him, and they decided to use me and Josh to get it. A few weeks before Josh and I were to start high school, our friends dared us to steal the football coach's brand new car and drive it somewhere so that they could destroy it. Though to this day I don't know why they asked two fourteen year old kids to steal a car. It's not like we could drive…" Hardy looked over at me and smiled. "Either way, Josh and I failed at stealing the car. Coach caught us trying to break into his car, and he and his neighbor grabbed us. Coach could have called the police. He probably should have. Instead, he sat me and Josh down and gave us a choice. We could either turn our lives around, or we could ruin them. He then let us go. A week later, Josh and I tried out for our high school's football team. Coach helped us get our lives back together, and Josh and I grabbed our second chance and held on for dear life. If it hadn't been for Coach…who knows what could have happened."

"I'm sorry, Jerrod. I had no idea. But I'm glad you didn't go any farther down that wrong road," I said.

"Me too. But I'm ashamed of my past and the person I was back then. And that's why I'm afraid to be with…well, not you. I'm afraid to be around your family. I'm worried I'll get caught up in their crimes and wind up back on that wrong road. Because I'd go down it if I had to. I'd do it for you. And that's why I need to walk away now. While I can still recognize the man in the mirror and before I start questioning myself."

"I understand, Jerrod. I don't want you to compromise yourself over me." I shifted around so that Hardy could no longer see my face. I didn't want him to see how much I was struggling not to cry.

"I'm sorry, Carrie. I really thought we had a chance and I didn't want it to end like this." Hardy put his arms around me and turned me so that I was facing him. He then brushed his lips against mine. "I'll see you around the next time there's a big crime."

"I guess you were just crazy, right?" I asked, referring to a statement Hardy made a few months earlier. Initially, when Hardy asked me out, I turned him down. When I had asked Hardy why he wanted to date me, he said something about how he was either crazy about me or just plain crazy.

"Yeah, I'm crazy, darling." Hardy stood up and walked into the foyer. Before going out the door, Hardy turned around and gave me one last, long look. "I'd have to be crazy to do this."

I got up and walked over to the front window in time to see Hardy back his truck out of my driveway and then drive out of my life. Or, at least, he would be out of my life until the next major crime in Wyatt County.

Once Hardy turned off my street and passed out of my sight, I leaned my head against the glass and sighed. I didn't want to admit it out loud, but Hardy was right when he told me that I needed to do something about my family. Something more than I had been doing. Chasing them around the county from one selling spot to the next wasn't accomplishing anything. I might be shutting them down for a few days, but what I needed to do was shut them down permanently. Otherwise, the wrong person might stumble across them and bring the entire Jenga tower tumbling down around us. I loved my family, and I wanted to protect them. But I also had to think about myself, and how I wasn't willing to go down in a blaze of glory with the rest of the Shatners. The question was what could I do to stop them?

CHAPTER TWENTY-ONE

Three weeks later…

"This is it…My final match…Last one ever…" Red whispered as he bounced around on the balls of his feet in anticipation. "I'm still not ready for this to be over."

Red and I were backstage at the SWAT Zone, anxiously waiting to be called to the ring for the final match of the night. For the final match of Red's career as the Ravishing Redneck.

He was dressed in his typical Ravishing Redneck attire of beat-up jeans and a sleeveless t-shirt. His long, blonde locks brushed his brawny shoulders. I had on a Ravishing Redneck t-shirt and a pair of jean shorts. And my brown curls had been teased out and then hair sprayed into submission by Aunt Priscilla. She had been raised on the belief that 'the higher the hair, the closer to God,' and that was the look she had gone for when she styled my hair.

"I just hope tonight's match ends better than last month's. You know, without the riot. And then your opponent getting murdered in the parking lot afterwards," I said.

"That's why I gave my retirement speech earlier tonight. After that, I don't think there's going to be a doubt in anyone's mind that this is my last match," Red said, referring to the ten minute-long, emotional speech that he had given at the beginning of the show. By the time he was done, there hadn't been a dry eye in the SWAT Zone. "That's also why I'm winning the match tonight."

"The fans still won't be happy that you're retiring. But they should, at least, be satisfied that you won your last match," I said.

I peeked through a crack in the black velvet curtain to see what was taking so long out in the arena. In the ring, Uncle Sterling was making a big deal out of announcing that Vladimir Khrushchev was the new SWAT Heavyweight Champion. Since he had a vacant title belt thanks to Travis Yeager's unfortunate demise less than an hour after defeating Red for the SWAT Heavyweight Championship last month, Uncle Sterling had decided the best way to crown a new champion would be to have a Four Way Match. In the match, four of the veteran SWAT wrestlers battled against each other to see who could make the first pinfall. It had been decided beforehand that Vladimir Khrushchev would win the match and the title. Uncle Sterling had decided to stick with his original plan to have a heel wrestler as the champion throughout the summer SWAT events.

The SWAT Zone was packed to capacity with fans – most of whom didn't appear to be overly thrilled that Vladimir Khrushchev was the new champion. The fans were loudly booing Vladimir and Oksana as they strutted around the ring and showed off the title belt.

Uncle Sterling had been afraid that Travis getting killed in the parking lot after last month's show would negatively affect the attendance of future SWAT shows. Instead, Travis's death seemed to draw in more fans. It probably didn't hurt that Travis's killer and her accomplices were all behind bars and were no longer a physical threat to anyone aside from other inmates. The June SWAT show had sold out over a week beforehand, and the fans were packed like sardines in the sweltering room.

Suddenly Red's honky tonk entrance music began to play, signaling his entrance in the arena. The fans began to scream, almost drowning out the sound of the guitars blasting out of the speakers. In the end, Uncle Sterling had decided not to promote Red's final match. He hadn't made any mention of it at all except to a select handful of people. All Sterling had promised the fans was a special appearance of the Ravishing Redneck at the show. Most of the fans had probably assumed that Red's special appearance was when he had made his retirement speech at the beginning of the show. They probably hadn't counted on Red making a second in-ring appearance.

Flinging the curtains back, I sauntered out on stage, waving and blowing kisses at the boisterous fans. Red followed me a couple seconds later, and we Texas Two-Stepped back-and-forth across the stage.

"Well, well, well, if it isn't Mr. Ravishing Redneck and his little female companion," Vladimir Khrushchev said in a passable Russian accent. Frank Smith might play the role of a stereotypical evil Russian, but he certainly was good at it. "Come out to rain on my parade as the new SWAT champion. I thought you retire last month, Red. Or am I confused? In Russia, getting beat in a Loser Leaves Town Match means…well, it used to mean you got shipped off to middle of nowhere Siberia. Now it just means that you leave town and don't come back. But, like hemorrhoids, you seem to just keep coming back and annoying me. Why can't you just ride off into sunset with your little friend?"

Red pulled a microphone out of his back pocket and said, "Oh, I'll leave. I'm a man of my word. But before I ride off into the sunset, like you suggested, there's one thing I need to do. I need to prove to you, and to everyone else in this arena, that I am, and will forever be, the King of SWAT! You might have won the SWAT Heavyweight Championship earlier. But you need to beat me to earn the title of King."

I grabbed the microphone from Red and said, "And Oksana you've got to beat me to be able to call yourself the Queen."

Uncle Sterling grabbed the microphone out of Vladimir's hand, cutting off any response that Vladimir had been about to make.

"I don't see why we can't have us a good ol' fashioned Mixed Tag Team Match," Sterling announced. "If Red and Carrie win, they get to retire as the King and Queen of SWAT. If Vladimir and Oksana win, they can now call themselves the King and Queen."

Red's honky tonk entrance began to play again, and he and I strolled to the ring while Vladimir turned to the fuming Oksana and tried to reassure her that everything was going to be okay. Oksana wasn't a trained professional wrestler, but she had agreed to get into the ring this one time to wrestle against me. We only had a couple moves planned, and we had spent the afternoon practicing them.

"Making their way to the ring for their final match…Hailing from Holler, Texas…They are the King and Queen of SWAT…the Dixie Diva, Carrie Shatner, and the Ravishing Redneck, Red Devereux!" Aunt Priscilla announced.

"I can't believe I let you talk me into this, Red."

"I didn't talk you into nothing, Carrie. You practically jumped at the chance to get back in the ring for another match. My opponent for my very last match isn't what's important. It's who I've got by my side. You were in my corner at my first match. What better way for me to end my career than to have you as my tag partner?" Red asked. He spun me around and dipped me one more time when we reached the bottom of the short ramp. "Come on, Carrie, let's go have one more match and prove to everyone that we really are the King and Queen."

Before getting in the ring, Red and I took a lap around the ringside area. All of the front row seats were filled by Shatners and Devereuxs, and they were all cheering and carrying on. We found Naomi among my unruly relatives. She was one of the few people who had known about the Mixed Tag Team Match. Red and I had kept the rest of our relatives in the dark about it.

Red and I had both asked Naomi to act as our valet for the match, but

Naomi had declined. She said this was Red's and my moment, and she was content to sit in the audience. Things between Red and Naomi were going slowly, but anyone who saw them together could tell that they were meant to be with each other.

"Fuck Vladimir up, Red!" MeMaw Devereux screamed as Red and I went by her. As usual, MeMaw was cursing like a drunk sailor and beating her cane onto the barricade that separated the fans from the ring. "Bash Oksana's face in, Carrie!"

"I hope MeMaw doesn't lose the will to live after I'm officially retired. You know how she looks forward to my matches," Red whispered to me as he climbed into the ring.

"I doubt it, Red. MeMaw is going to outlive us all," I said.

We had decided prior to the show that Red and Vladimir would start out the match. We planned to keep things short and sweet, finishing up the match in less than five minutes. While Red and Vladimir faced each other in the center of the ring, Oksana and I took up a position outside the ring. We stood at opposite corners, and glared at each other.

After Aunt Priscilla rang the ring bell to start the match, Red and Vladimir shook hands in a demonstration of respect for each other. Instead of releasing Red's hand, Vladimir used it to yank Red closer to him. Vladimir then wrapped his arms around Red's waist before he threw himself backwards, drastically bridging his body as he flipped Red over him. Red landed on his back, and then rolled around as he held onto his back and pretended to squirm in pain.

Vladimir dominated the first minute or two of the match, hitting various moves and locking on a couple of submission holds. The majority of Vladimir's attack on Red focused on Red's back. Targeting Red's injured back was a way for Vladimir to wear his opponent down. It also earned Vladimir a lot of heat, or negative reactions, from the crowd.

At about the two-minute mark of the match, Red grabbed Vladimir around the neck and pulled him downward so that Vladimir's jaw slammed into Red's knee. This allowed Red a few moments to fight back before stumbling over towards the corner of the ring where I stood.

Climbing up onto the bottom ring rope, I leaned over the top rope and smacked Red on the shoulder to tag myself into the match. Across the ring from me, Oksana screamed and begged the referee not to force her to get into the ring. In a Mixed Tag Team Match, the competitors have to wrestle against the person who is of the same gender. With me the legal competitor for my team, Oksana had no choice but to reluctantly get into the ring and face off against me.

"Come on, Oksana! I'll even give you first shot!" I yelled, tapping myself on the chin as I leaned closer to her.

Oksana drew her arm back and then took a wild swing at me. I ducked down, avoiding the blow. I then grabbed Oksana around the knees and yanked her off her feet so that she fell onto her back. I then began to throw punches at her, making it appear that I was hitting her when I was barely touching her at all. Oksana put on a good show by screaming and thrashing about. She then grabbed me by the hair, causing our wrestling match to break down into a cat fight.

"Break it up, ladies. Break it up!" the referee shouted as he waded into the cat fight and pulled us apart.

Once Oksana was free from me, she scurried over to where Vladimir stood and whacked him across the chest to tag him into the match.

Red vaulted over the top ring rope and then raced across the ring to grab Vladimir as he climbed into the ring. I followed behind Red, grabbing Oksana as she tried to escape the ring. Instead of battling any farther – and dragging the match out any longer – Red and I immediately set up for our simultaneous finishing moves.

I picked Oksana up in a fireman's carry, and then settled her so that she was lying across my shoulders. Luckily she weighed about the same as I did, so I wasn't struggling too much under her weight. Across the ring from me, Red did the same thing with Vladimir. Red and I then began to spin, counting our rotations out loud as we spun around the ring. As we both yelled "five," we threw our opponents over our heads and caused them to crash down onto the mat.

Red and I staggered around the ring for a couple seconds, pretending we were dizzy. Bumping into each other, we immediately gained our equilibrium. We then pointed at the two corners of the ring closest to where Oksana and Vladimir lay.

"Let's do this!" Red shouted at me, giving me a push towards Oksana.

I climbed to the top rope at the corner of the ring that Oksana lay closest to. Across the ring from me, Red was doing the same thing. Once I was balancing on the top rope, I glanced over my shoulder at Red and saw that he was also in position. We then signaled to each other that it was time to go.

Throwing myself backwards, I forced my body into a backflip. As I spun through the air, I caught a quick glimpse of the terrified look on Oksana's face just before I splashed down on top of her. We had practiced the move multiple times earlier, but Oksana had still been afraid that I would inadvertently injure her. But we had pulled off the move perfectly.

Hooking my arm under Oksana's leg, I leaned over and pressed her shoulders onto the mat. Even though I couldn't see him, I knew Red was doing the same thing to Vladimir.

"One! Two! Three!" the referee shouted as he slammed his hand down on the mat as he counted the pinfall. "Ring the bell!"

Aunt Priscilla rang the bell and then announced, "Your winners...and forever the King and Queen of SWAT...the Dixie Diva, Carrie Shatner...and the Ravishing Redneck, Red Devereux!"

An avalanche of confetti began to fall from the ceiling as Red and I jumped around the ring in celebration. Uncle Sterling handed us a crown and tiara that he had picked up at the local costume store earlier that day. The fans went wild, throwing streamers and whatever else they had at hand into the ring. A cupcake went whizzing by my head, and a bra landed on Red's shoulder.

"Thank you, Red! Thank you, Carrie! Thank you, Red!" chanted the fans.

Acknowledgments

Many thanks to my agent, Jessica Alvarez, for believing in both me and Carrie Shatner. And for finding both of us a home at Camel Press.

And, of course, to Jennifer McCord, and everyone else at Camel Press, thank you so much for all of your hard work and support.

Thanks to Nick 'Sicend' Taylor and Matt Wylde of Riot City's Most Wanted for answering my questions about professional wrestling.

Also thanks to Officer Jeffrey Margevich for answering my questions about archery, and Liz Humphries at Lancaster Archery Academy for the archery lessons.

Finally, thanks to Molly and Snookums for the love and support that only pets can provide. Thank you to my mom for (mostly) not complaining every time that I've handed you a new manuscript with the expectation that you find and correct all of my grammatical and punctuation errors. And thank you to my dad for subjecting me to professional wrestling, NASCAR, The Doors, Neil Diamond, and Star Trek: The Original Series at such a young age.

Randee Green is the author of the Carrie Shatner Mystery series. Her passion for reading began in grade school with LITTLE HOUSE IN THE BIG WOODS by Laura Ingalls Wilder. She has a bachelor's degree in English Literature, as well as a master's and an MFA in Creative Writing. When not writing, she's usually reading, indulging in her passion for Texas country music, traveling, or hanging out with her favorite feline friend, Mr. Snookums G. Cat.

Website: www.randeegreen.com